Praise for the novels of Chandra Blumberg

"Replete with instantly likable characters and relatable pop-culture references, Blumberg's debut is warm, engaging, and emotionally honest. Alisha and Quentin's gradual movement toward companionship hits all the right notes, and their interactions are both meaningful and fun." —*Kirkus Reviews* on *Digging Up Love*

"The headline-making dinosaur dig offers a unique spin on the classic small-town contemporary romance, and readers will be craving treats after reading the descriptions of Alisha's baked goods. Blumberg's sweet romance offers a perfect recipe for a delectable read, combining diversity, smart characters, and a delicious love story." —*Booklist*, starred review, on *Digging Up Love*

"Rival chefs are forced into a business partnership that sparks unlikely love in Blumberg's sweet second Taste of Love romance… Readers will root for this couple in both business and love." —*Publishers Weekly* on *Stirring Up Love*

"A moving story imbued with thoughtfulness and generosity of spirit." —*Kirkus Reviews* on *Stirring Up Love*

"Like a good barbecue sauce, *Stirring Up Love* is sweet, tangy, and has the perfect amount of heat. Small-town romance fans will adore watching Simone and Finn fall in love." —Jennifer Bardsley, author of *Sweet Bliss*

Also available from Chandra Blumberg

Digging Up Love
Stirring Up Love

And look out for Chandra Blumberg's next novel
available from Canary Street Press.

CHANDRA BLUMBERG

Second Tide's the Charm

CANARY STREET PRESS

CANARY
STREET
PRESS™

Recycling programs
for this product may
not exist in your area.

ISBN-13: 978-1-335-47699-9

Second Tide's the Charm

Canary Street Press
22 Adelaide St. West, 41st Floor
Toronto, Ontario M5H 4E3, Canada
CanaryStPress.com

Printed in U.S.A.

To anyone who's ever wished for a second chance.
Life is full of fresh starts, and it's never too late to go after your dreams.

one

hope

There's a mother barreling toward me with rage-eyes and a kayak paddle, but it's not my fault her kid interrupted the lesson to spout fishy inaccuracies. She must catch sight of me eyeing the paddle because she jabs it into the sand—not a whole lot less terrifying—before advancing toward me empty-handed but still radiating anger.

"Did you tell my son there are sharks out there?" She gestures behind her at the sparkling, sharkless blue water of Lake Michigan.

I should probably close my eyes and count to three or something, but instead I ignore her, grab the paddle out of an abundance of caution, and carry it back toward the rack. The squeak of sand lets me know I'm being followed, and the woman calls out, "Is this a joke to you?"

Am I laughing? I am not. Not on the outside at least. Besides, her kid isn't scared in the slightest, just embarrassed I didn't let him get away with shaming the younger teen who asked about freshwater sharks. Could I have let it go? Probably. Possibly. Not really.

Misconceptions about sharks abound, and it's my job to correct that. Well, not in my current job description. But it's a strain to take off my marine biologist hat for the sake of good customer service.

"The website listed paddleboarding as a family-friendly activity. I am this close to giving your company a one-star review."

That threat brings me up short. My best friend, Zuri, worked incredibly hard to launch her own business, and I can't be responsible for her losing it. Not when she's already lost so much.

I suck in a deep breath, then exhale and turn to face the woman. "Like I told your son—" after a circuitous explanation involving salinity and shark adaptations "—there are no sharks in the Great Lakes."

To illustrate that fact, I swallow down the humiliation and dip my chin toward the T-shirt Zuri insists I wear while on the clock, identical to the ones she sells in the gift shop. The lettering says: LAKE MICHIGAN, UNSALTED AND SHARK-FREE. She thinks it's cute, and despite my grumbling, I think it's a great conversation starter. Case in point, this one.

"I can read, thank you," the woman says through her teeth. "What I want to know is why you told my son some sharks can survive in fresh water?"

"Because they can?" I scrunch my face up. Not the right response, but I can't bring myself to be sorry. "Bull sharks have been found miles upriver. Their kidneys are uniquely adapted to handle varying salinity levels. However, that's the exception—"

"To summarize—" my best friend's voice cuts through the humid air "—there are no sharks here. Right, Hope?"

I clamp my mouth shut as Zuri strides over, her braids twisted into a bun on top of her head, secured with a Surf to Shore visor. She's right of course. This discussion is a moot point since river sharks don't live on this continent and regardless, no shark could make its way to Lake Michigan via the waterways.

"Correct." I turn a closed-lip smile on the woman, making

sure to block her access to the canoe paddles with my body, just in case. "There are zero sharks in the Great Lakes."

"Not even bull sharks?"

"Definitely not bull sharks," I tell her. "Also, most shark species are harmless to humans, and there're far scarier things in the Great Lakes than sharks. Take toxic algae—"

Zuri steps between me and the woman. "Did I mention we offer our customers a half-off coupon for shaved ice?" She digs into her belt bag and pulls one out. "And if you stop in at Surf to Shore, you and your son are welcome to pick out a T-shirt for your troubles." Holding out the coupon, she lifts her chin toward town. "Head up Pine Street and it'll be on your right after you cross the bridge. Impossible to miss."

The woman shoots me one last glare before telling her kid it's time to go. They're the last of the 12:30 slot of paddleboarders, and I've got two hours before the next group arrives, but Zuri's scowl lets me know I won't be taking it easy during my break.

"Toxic algae?"

I grimace. "Okay, not exactly tourism website worthy. But—"

"That's a new low, even for you."

Harsh, especially since I took this job as a favor when she had trouble finding seasonal help. Though the line's become blurred as to who's helping whom at this point, three years after a holiday visit to my hometown became a permanent move in the wake of her husband's death.

"If you would've let me finish, I would've told her toxic algae blooms aren't affecting our area. Yet," I finish under my breath, and she points a finger at me.

"See, this is why I didn't want to hire you. You've never been able to resist saying scary shit."

"Sharks are fascinating, not scary." Not to mention vital and misunderstood. "As for the algae, what's scary is how uninformed the general public is about the issue."

She sighs, head tipping to the side.

"Hear me out." I gather my curls into a high ponytail and use my teeth to pull the hair tie off my wrist. "That woman might go home, fire up her internet browser, read up on harmful algae blooms and decide to—"

"Write a blank check for freshwater conservation?" Zuri's dark brows disappear in the shadow of her visor.

Doubtful, but I double down. "Maybe she lives in one of the beachfront mansions and is on the lookout for a worthy environmental cause to support." The multimillion-dollar homes that line the bluff bring an influx of residents to our tourist town every summer, and their spending cash keeps the town afloat.

"Or maybe she's not going to wait till she gets home." Zuri gestures toward the crowded beach parking lot, where the woman in question is handing over her credit card to placate her son with a shaved ice from the food truck. "Maybe she's going to find a shady spot, fire up her cell phone, and leave me yet another scathing review."

Darn. That is the more plausible scenario.

"I could go say sorry."

"Oh my gosh no." She grabs my arm before I can head toward the sandy boardwalk, her palm clammy against my sun-warmed skin. "Do not chase that woman down. That's a guaranteed one-star. Maybe even a complaint to the Better Business Bureau." A shudder goes through her, then she lets go and looks me in the face.

Uh-oh. I know that look.

"Hope, I love you."

"Back at you." I bare my teeth in my most charming smile.

Her lips flatten into a line, the same exasperated expression I often receive from friends and family. "I love you, but that would be the third one-star rating I've had since I hired you."

"Technically, the first one came when I was still training, so..."

"Hope." She repeats my name with the warning tone of a mom threatening to turn the car around. "You're fired."

I've never been fired before, and it's a unique sensation. Like bungee jumping at a discounted rate. A thrill mixed with a reasonable amount of panic. Freeing, but also mildly horrifying.

"*Fired*, fired?" My voice sounds stunned, even to my own ears. The fact that I didn't want this job in the first place doesn't mean I want it snatched out from under me. Shepherding tourists on paddleboards and kayaks isn't where I saw myself at thirty, but helping out Zuri has given me an excuse to put off coming to grips with the embarrassing truth that I've let heartbreak derail my career. "Or more of a temporary suspension?"

"You really think I can pay you to sit the bench?"

"Fair point." Surf to Shore is not exactly a corporation. "But I promise I can do better. Especially if you stop making me wear these shirts." I pluck the fabric away from my chest, damp in the muggy June heat. "They're an open invitation to—"

"Deliver unsolicited lectures about sharks?"

My mouth drops open, then I shrug. "I mean, yes."

"Everything is an open invitation for you to educate people about sharks." She sighs. "Which isn't a bad thing, necessarily. That's why I'm kicking you out of the nest."

I squint against the sun reflecting off the brilliant turquoise of the lake behind her, my sunglasses forgotten in my beach bag as usual. "Are you the mama bird in this scenario?"

"When am I not?" she asks, and I chuckle, thinking of how she rounded up the employees this morning and checked to make sure everyone had a water bottle and snacks. Her smile fades, though. "I honestly don't know what I would've done without your help after Eric's accident." She sniffs, but her eyes are dry, holding my gaze. "But I've found my way. And I refuse to be your excuse to keep hiding."

I'm used to being called impulsive and single-minded, but I am not timid. I'm not hiding from anything. Except my old colleagues, career, and a certain shark researcher with midnight-dark eyes and a lopsided grin who broke my heart by letting go.

"I've only been here for a month." My previous job, working on an invasive species study in northern Michigan, wrapped up in the spring. Knowing the project was coming to an end, I should've had something lined up, but returning to shark research also means facing my ex-boyfriend. The possibility of running into him has kept me stalled, procrastinating my job hunt as if delaying the inevitable will make a difference.

"Long enough to make it clear to everyone, including my *customers*—" I flinch at the emphasis "—that you don't want to be here."

Shoreline Dunes is one of my favorite places. But while the lack of sharks in the Great Lakes is a huge draw for some people, for me, it's a drawback. I can't reboot my career if I refuse to leave the safety net of my hometown.

"It's embarrassing, how much time I let pass." The words scrape their way past a throat gone dry. I drop my head, catching sight of the turquoise nail polish on my toes, chipped from navigating the rocks at the water's edge.

What began as a few months away to help Zuri care for her young children after the sudden loss of her husband somehow turned into three years. Somewhere along the way, shark research became entangled with my feelings for Adrian, and if I can't manage to separate the two, I'll remain stranded.

A moment later, an arm comes around my shoulders. Zuri, pulling me in for a hug. "Life happens. But we keep going, right?" Her words are born of experience, picking up the pieces after unimaginable loss, and my heart lurches for her.

The truth is, I have no qualms about defending my employment history. My work in the lab gave me worthwhile experience. But applying for jobs or going back for a PhD means coming to grips with the fact that not only am I starting over but that my worst fears about love were absolutely founded.

"I was thinking of applying to the Shedd," I tell her, and she pulls away, frowning.

"You'd work at an aquarium in Chicago? With tourists?" Her skepticism tells me she's fully aware of how I view tourists. One star. Would not recommend.

"Not like I plan to work the ticket counter." Besides, I worked at an aquarium for a time, while earning my master's degree, and unlike my current—former, I guess—gig working for Zuri, there were no complaints on my job performance back then.

A warm breeze shifts off the lake, bringing with it the crisp, earthy scent of fresh water, so different from the briny tang of the Atlantic. Here, at least, memories of the man I used to love with my whole heart aren't everywhere I look, but the call of gulls is enough to transport me back to a dock at sunrise. Adrian's calloused palm against mine, our fingers laced together.

The first time he'd told me caught me by surprise. *I love you.* I'd looked up at him, backlit by pink and violet and tangerine hues of dawn, all broad-shouldered vulnerability, and when he spoke those three words, my whole world changed.

Before that, I loved how effortless it felt to be near him. I loved how we fit together, even when we were apart. But that morning, I realized I loved *him.* Loved Adrian with a fierceness that defied comprehension.

Even now, my lips part in memory of the kiss that followed those words, threaded through with want and promise, my fingers flexing at the phantom touch of his tight curls beneath my fingertips, his touch remembered by every cell of my body.

But all I want is to forget.

A volleyball lands nearby, splattering my shins with grains of sand, and the wisps of memory dissolve. I toss it back to the group of swimsuit-clad beachgoers by the net. "I just thought I'd be over him by now."

"You're really going to let a guy keep you away from sharks?"

She grabs one end of a kayak and I stoop to lift the other. It sounds irrational because it is, even though she knows full well Adrian isn't just any guy. He's *the* guy, the one I never expected to find, never went looking for. The one who showed me a kind of love I didn't think existed.

My feelings for him defy logic. No person should have that strong an effect on another. Love isn't quantifiable, and yet here I am, still trying to fall out of love with a man I haven't spoken to in years.

We hoist the kayak onto the rack, the fiberglass hull a reminder of the moments I spent with Adrian at sea, rushing to catch a glimpse of my first shark, pointing overboard at the dark shape below, his presence warm and solid against my shoulder, both of us breathless with excitement. Memories I can't seem to leave in the past. "It just feels so daunting to start over."

"Why don't you reach out to some of your old contacts?" Zuri suggests, like I haven't thought about that. But thinking is all I seem to do lately. The lack of action is unlike me. "They might have leads you're not seeing online."

Nothing I haven't already considered and discarded. "I barely speak to anyone in the shark community." Too painful without taking part. I don't even have social media anymore to keep tabs on people. "Marissa is the only one who keeps in touch, and the last time we talked was her birthday."

"Reach out. It's worth a try."

"Why, so she can tell Adrian I'm desperate?" She's Adrian's cousin, and while our friendship outlasted my relationship with him, I have no doubts of her ultimate loyalty.

"Aren't you?" At my glare, she relents. "Is she that kind of person?"

"No." Marissa's not vindictive, or else she wouldn't have spoken to me after I stopped dating Adrian. But family comes first, and distance has weakened our once strong friendship. "At least, I don't think so, but—"

"Text her," Zuri insists. "What have you got to lose?"

Good question. I've already lost the love of my life, my career, and as of five minutes ago, my day job. And I know Zuri won't let up until I follow her advice. It's impossible to bluff with a friend who's known me since we both staged a walk-out—or maybe it was a crawl-out?—of tiny tot ballet class.

I squat by my backpack and dig out my phone, scrolling down to the thread with Marissa. Our last conversation was months ago, and I wince at the idea of breaking the silence with a request. But one thing that's kept my friendship with Marissa intact is we always pick up right where we left off. Except this time, I'm going to raise the subject I haven't broached in years.

> Hope: Long story, but say I was looking to get back into shark research...

> Marissa: I don't care how long the story is, I need details! But first: are you really thinking of coming back??

> Hope: Not just thinking about it.

> Marissa: Please tell me you're serious, because if so, your timing is perfection.

A thrill of anticipation runs through me. Another text appears, but the wind whips streaks of sand across my screen, obscuring the words. Hands unsteady, I swipe away the grains to reveal what might be my way back into shark research.

> Marissa: Don't get too excited. There's a catch.

My mind instantly floods with potential issues. An unpaid position? Not ideal at this stage in my career, but I've got savings. Something that starts immediately? I could pack my bags and be gone tomorrow. A job outside the country? Logistical hurdles, but an exciting opportunity. I can only think of one deal-breaker. Working with Adrian.

two

adrian

The distinctive dorsal fin of a shark protrudes above the waves, but unlike the sinister narration of the shark documentaries I used to binge as a kid, the only blood here is a carefully collected sample in a syringe. We've got a sandbar shark secured alongside the boat and I'm bent double over the railing, arms submerged up to the elbow in the warm water of the bay, holding the animal steady.

Acoustic tag placed and scientific work-up complete, I maneuver a pair of pliers toward the glint of metal beneath the surface. Our specially designed hook is already out, but before we release the shark, I'd like to remove the old fishhook we discovered embedded in the shark's jaw. Just when I'm at the right angle to grasp it, the boat lurches upward on a wave, knocking against my arm, and my grip slips.

"Shit." I lunge farther over the edge and grab the pliers before they sink out of reach.

"There goes that footage," Gabe says from over my shoulder, but I know he's messing with me. He's been filming with us long enough to know that a few choice words come with the territory of working with wild animals. Nothing that can't be fixed in editing.

The shark's tail thrashes and droplets splash across my face. I swipe away the saltwater and glance over to find my cousin Marissa's gloved fists clenched tight on the tail rope, intent on her task. A dramatic shark work-up would put a spike in our viewership, but that's not the kind of clickbait we want. Our aim is to teach people about sharks, not create sensationalized content.

"Done?" Marissa's question comes out as a grunt.

I shake my head. "Almost." I take a firm grip on the pliers and return to my task. Time is of the essence, but taking out this steel hook could forestall potential complications for the shark.

My forearms flex with the effort of working quickly and carefully. Up until a few years ago, I'd never seen the inside of a gym, but the physicality of long days on the boat is less of a strain since I started lifting weights. What began as a hobby to distract myself from my absent girlfriend became a permanent routine when our six-year relationship fizzled out like a doused match.

Hope is never far from my mind, but with an effort, I push aside thoughts of the woman I lost my heart to, and this time I'm ready when an errant wave rocks the boat. For a moment, the sun slides behind a shifting cloud, and with the glare gone, I'm able to see what's below the surface clearly.

The shark's eye has the wide, curious look of a cat, the white of her underbelly fading into a sandy brown. I latch onto the hook in the corner of the shark's mouth and tug the piece of metal free. Winded by adrenaline more than exertion, I drop the hook and pliers on the deck with a clatter. Releasing the shark will be tricky without another assistant. "Can I get a hand?" I ask Gabe, and when he doesn't answer right away, I turn to find him frowning from behind the camcorder. "Leave it." My words come out curt, but while filming is important, the animals are our top priority.

Gabe isn't a shark researcher, but he has a background in

wildlife biology and has grown more comfortable working with sharks since we hired him. Setting down the camera, he comes to lend a hand.

Despite a brisk breeze, the early morning air is already warm, and I'm sweating under my long-sleeved tee. A wide headband holds back my locs. One hand on the sleek dorsal fin, I check in with Marissa, her expression serious but calm. "Ready?"

She gives a brief nod. Working in the field isn't her favorite. Not like Hope, who lit up every time we brought in a shark. Three years since she left, yet her absence still stings like saltwater in a wound. But the dull thump of the shark's caudal fin against the hull reminds me now is not the time to dwell on what's lost. Hope's not coming back, and I need to learn to live without her.

Feet planted wide, my knees flex with the boat's motion, the shark's sandpaper skin rough against my palms as I slip off the rope. Marissa does the same and we guide the animal away from the boat and let go. My heart pounds for a breathless moment, and next to me, Gabe is tense.

"C'mon, lady," Marissa says. We're all focused on the shark, willing her to swim away. "You got this."

After a dazed beat, the shark propels herself forward, churning the surface into a white froth, then arrows downward, no doubt eager to put as much distance between herself and humanity as possible. My eyes remain fixed on the water until the shark disappears, the brownish gray of her back an excellent match for the water of the bay.

Gabe heads over to check on his camera, and Marissa rises to her feet, grinning. "Another successful tag."

I nod but can't muster a smile. Despite the result, I'd feel more comfortable with another marine biologist onboard, but all my colleagues are busy with their own research. We've had some luck getting grad students to help out, but we made the decision to spend the summer filming too late in the year and haven't found anyone available long-term.

"Would be nice if Gabe didn't need to keep stepping in." I turn toward him, realizing how that might've sounded. "Not that we're not grateful."

"No arguments here. I'd rather be filming." He hoists the camcorder. "Just wait till you see the footage I got of that Carolina hammerhead earlier. The internet is going to eat it up."

I hate when he anthropomorphizes the internet like it's a sentient being, but when he tips the screen toward me, replaying the footage, I can't help but agree. Viewers will devour this like sharks in a feeding frenzy. Gabe's been instrumental in taking the quality of our videos to the next level. He reached out to us last fall after stumbling upon our socials, and helped me grasp the far-reaching potential of our platform.

An accidental viral moment sparked our decision to start the channel. Footage of me maneuvering a blacktip shark back into the water after a novice fisherman pulled it onto a crowded beach went viral with the hashtag #SharkSavior. A matter of right place, right time, and I'm just thankful my years of education and experience kept a tricky situation from getting worse.

My instinct was to hunker down and wait for the unsolicited publicity to pass, but Marissa is a conservation biologist, and she convinced me to leverage my momentary internet stardom into an opportunity to make a lasting impact on the public's perception of sharks.

Stepping in front of the camera was a big change from teaching classes, and even further from working in the quiet confines of a lab, but I've adjusted to life as one of the prominent faces of shark research. Learned to tune out the trolls and stay focused on our mission. Haven't quite broken the habit of scrolling through comments searching for one from Hope, though. Impossible not to wonder if she's watching. If she misses this kind of work. If she misses *me*.

Ten years ago, I never would've guessed the serious girl with the quiet sense of humor I met on the first day of our internship would become the most important person in my life. She was stoic as we loaded the equipment on the boat, but didn't bother to conceal her excitement as we set off, her eyes gleaming with enthusiasm. I noticed they were the bright copper of a new penny, and when she smiled at me, it felt like a gift.

Our first day tagging sharks had ended with us exhausted and giddy, sharing a melted protein bar on the dock, instant friends but nothing more. My heart was bruised from a recent breakup, and she was being pursued by a lanky grad student who thought "Hopeless" was a cute pet name. I hated him.

She confessed one night that she thought romance was a sham and love was a distraction, right before she kissed me. Ignoring the voice that told me I was headed for heartbreak, I fell hard and fast and expected her to dump me at summer's end when we left to start graduate studies—she to the University of Miami and me to Duke—but instead she held me tight and said, "I never expected to feel this way." Her lips pressed against mine, soft and bittersweet, then she pulled away and told me, "You'd better be able to go the distance, Hollis-Parker."

Our relationship flourished on long weekends and during sun-drenched summers, the sporadic, inseparable moments together carrying us through long months apart. We'd save up for plane tickets and spend the holidays with each other's families, meshing our lives even as we lived apart. Our love story felt inevitable in the most unexpected way. We were meant to be. Until the day came that we weren't anything to one another, besides gone.

Sharks and Hope were the two constants in my life. I thought she felt the same. Turns out I was wrong about a lot of things.

But I need to keep pressing forward. Not dwell on what might've been. I lean toward Marissa, raising my voice to be heard over the wind. "Any leads on finding someone to join our team this summer?"

"Actually, yeah." She's hauling the buoy in, hand over hand, the line dripping with water tinged with the faint scent of fish and seaweed. "And she has immediate availability."

Her voice is pitched suspiciously high, and I tilt my head, on alert. "Is she qualified?"

"Very. Master's degree in marine science and she's been working in a related field."

"Sounds like you're ready to offer her the job." Even though we've discussed hiring someone, I'm still wary about expanding our tight-knit group. This work is so far outside the scope of the academic realm I'm used to, but Marissa doesn't share my reservations.

Her brown eyes flash with indignation. "I already did." Chin high, she says, "We've been doing things your way, vetting every candidate within an inch of their life—"

"This isn't typical fieldwork. It's not just technical skills that matter." I cross my arms, rumpling the screen-printed logo that represents everything we've worked to accomplish over the past year and a half. "We need to make sure whoever comes to work with us is a good fit for such a public-facing position."

"You think I don't know that?" She's short of breath and pauses to push back the headband wrapped around her braids, the line going slack on the water. "I'm the one who's worked in policy jobs. I know what's at stake. Are you going to trust my hiring decision, or would you like to call her yourself and let her know we no longer need her assistance?"

I grit my teeth. Working with family has definite upsides. I do trust Marissa, with my life, as well as my career. But I grew up spending every summer visiting her family on the coast, our relationship close as siblings, and it's hard to successfully stare down someone who's seen you cry your eyes out during *Finding Nemo*.

The fact is, we need another researcher, and all that really matters is the scientist can do the job competently, and knows what they're getting into. Maybe I've been too cautious. Every video we share is a calculated risk, and I've already lost the most important person in my life because I was scared to take chances.

"I trust your judgment." I grind out the words, and Marissa grins, gloating already. "When can she start?"

three

hope

Adrian's contact is on my screen. Ever since I accepted Marissa's offer to join her on a research team with him this summer, I've been debating whether to reach out. We haven't spoken in almost three years, and every text I've drafted feels inadequate as an umbrella in a hurricane.

Eyes bleary from lack of sleep, I lean against the kitchen counter and reread my latest attempt to ask if he's sure he wants to work with me, then hit backspace and delete the whole thing. Marissa says he okayed it, and summer field research in South Carolina is too good an opportunity to miss. Plus, what better way to get over Adrian than by confronting him and proving to myself there's nothing left between us?

Steam hisses out of the teakettle and I lift it off the burner so the whistle won't wake the kids. I opt for herbal tea over coffee most days. Zuri brews jet fuel, and with my nerves on edge this morning, I don't need to add caffeine to the mix. My car is prepped for the fifteen-hour drive with a fresh oil change and full tank of gas thanks to Zuri's pestering. All that's left to do is pack, but packing means I'm one step closer to seeing Adrian again.

"Is this reckless, working with Adrian of all people?"

Zuri glances up from the pot she's stirring. "Nothing you can't handle." She points the wooden spoon in my direction, and a glop of oatmeal falls off the end. "You need closure."

My stomach sours at the finality of the word. *Closure*. My relationship with Adrian never had an end date. We were a couple and then slowly, gradually—suddenly—we weren't. He came for Zuri's husband's funeral—he wasn't close with Eric, though they got along well—mostly to be there for me. Even though we'd been arguing. Even though he'd moved into a one-bedroom apartment instead of the condos we'd been looking at. He told me to take my time. That he'd be waiting, however long it took.

We'd been long-distance for our entire relationship and made it work with frequent visits and late-night phone calls and the certainty of a future with each other in it. But with Zuri's loss and my subsequent move out of the southeast, the distance felt heavier than before. Insurmountable.

And once I shut down my social media accounts, I didn't hear from him again. I should've reached out and told him why social media no longer felt like a safe space. Explained why I felt the need to stay and keep working on the freshwater study I'd originally joined for just the summer. But instead of opening up, I let time and space dismantle our relationship. Now the success of my foray back into shark research will hinge on our ability to work as a team.

I take a sip of tea to settle myself, but it tastes off. I peer into the cup and find stray leaves floating in the lukewarm water. The tea bag must've torn when I ripped open the packet. *Hasty.* That's what he said about my decision to get a job in Michigan when our future was waiting. And now here I am, moving south for the summer on a moment's notice, proving him right.

Good thing I don't care what he thinks anymore.

Hands clenched around the mug, I lean toward Zuri and whisper, "I'll keep paying rent while I'm gone."

Zuri glances up, brown eyes invisible behind the fogged lenses of her glasses. "You will not." The whispered retort manages to invoke the stern tone she uses on misbehaving kids and shirking employees, but the dancing penguins on her robe undermine the effect.

"I will." I moved in with Zuri even though my parents offered to clear out my old bedroom when I moved back, long since converted to a quilting room for Mom, but staying with Zuri meant I could help out with the kids.

I said my goodbyes to my parents last night. It didn't cross my mind to hold back the truth about working with Adrian. They've always trusted me, and supported me the best they could, even when I left our lakeside town to study sharks or moved back to Michigan instead of starting a new chapter with the boyfriend who'd become like a son to them.

They told me they were happy I'd be working with sharks again, and though a brief look passed between them—my mom's gray-blue eyes meeting my dad's dark brown ones behind his bifocals—they didn't question my decision to do so alongside Adrian.

On the way out the door, Mom hugged me so tight that the fine strands of her wavy bob, slightly stiff with hair spray, pressed tight against my cheek, and whispered she knows I'll keep finding my way. She trusts me to figure life out in my own time, confident I know my own mind, which is wonderful, except it's my heart that I'm unsure of.

My decision is made, though, and I'm committed to making sure leaving so suddenly doesn't put a burden on Zuri. She's a single mom responsible for three human beings and I'm a single woman with zero interest in things like clothes or the latest technology, unless it relates to shark research.

"I'll be staying with Marissa all summer. My rent budget is

yours. Consider it one less thing for me to worry about when I'm juggling sharks and my ex-boyfriend."

To show this isn't up for debate, I set down my tea and get started on the kids' lunches. I wrestle open the busted crisper drawer and fish out a bag of baby carrots. Half the appliances are run-down in this rental, but in a beach town, housing comes at a steep cost. Zuri lines up lunchboxes on the counter and fetches bread. We've reached a symbiosis on busy weekday mornings, but my presence is no replacement for her late husband.

A car accident left Zuri widowed in an instant. I received the news while Adrian and I were at an impasse about the next step in our relationship. The clarity I lacked about my own future morphed into an urgent need to be present for Zuri. Widowed, with a baby and two young kids, she needed support, and I needed time. Time to assess. Time away. Time to sort out my heart and my head and the chasm between.

Time that stretched into distance, pulling Adrian and I apart. Time he could spare. Uncertainty was what stretched our bond to the breaking point. I'd begun to question us, and before I found my answer, it was too late.

"I looked him up." Zuri's too-casual words tighten my shoulder blades. I should've known she wouldn't let me ship off without due diligence.

My eyelids pinch shut. Yearning rises in my chest, and a question escapes on an errant exhale. "Married?"

"No." The word is firm and solid. A paramedic's tone to a patient in crisis. "At least, not from what I could tell. Doesn't look like he's got a girlfriend, either."

My heart begins to beat again. Married would've made things simpler.

Married would've torn me in two.

A moment to breathe through the averted panic, then I open my eyes. "In that case, don't tell me." I'm on a need-to-know basis with all things Adrian. And right now all I need to know is he and Marissa are giving me a chance to work with sharks again.

"What if he's a murderer?" Zuri isn't letting it go.

"Then he'd be in jail." I pause. "Or really sneaky."

"Hope!"

I shrug. Adrian's most definitely not a murderer.

"What if he owns a Michelin-starred restaurant?" she asks.

"They're giving out stars for microwaved PB&J?"

"Who does that?"

"Adrian." Or at least he did. Now maybe he eats them room temp, like a normal person. The thought sends a pang of nostalgia through me. I don't know him best of anyone, not anymore.

"You really don't want to know?" Zuri's question echoes my thoughts. Of course I do. I've played this guessing game a thousand times with myself. "The No-Adrian Rule is no longer in effect now that you're going to be working with him."

"The No-Adrian Rule is more crucial than ever." I came up with the rule a few months after I quit social media. Zuri wanted to show me one of his posts, but I knew I couldn't see him and not want him. And I needed to stop wanting him. So I enacted the No-Adrian Rule.

I don't discuss Adrian, google him, or ever, under any circumstances, check up on his social media. No creeping on his Instagram. No lurking on his Twitter—not like I ever had a Twitter account. Adrian does, though. Or used to. Whereas I only ever used social media to keep in touch with friends and family, he used it to network and stay connected to colleagues and their work.

But strict adherence to the No-Adrian Rule hasn't stopped me from wanting him. Which is why this job is the best choice, not just for my career, but for myself. After years of shutting Adrian out, I need to come face-to-face with the reality that there's nothing left between us. To accept that he's no longer mine.

This trip is the best way to achieve all my goals in a single swoop: Get back in the water with sharks. Get over Adrian. Get my career back on track and leave love in the rearview.

Zuri grabs a bowl off the open shelving and spoons oatmeal into it. "So if I told you he's internet famous, loves taking selfies with his mega-yacht, and is best friends with that actor we love, you would be cool with it?" she asks, nonchalant, but I can sense she's gauging my reaction.

Adrian, internet famous? When we were dating his profile picture was a shark tooth. That's it. Not him holding up a shark tooth. Just a tooth, laying in the sand. And Adrian's idea of a pleasure cruise is a shark tagging expedition, not lounging in a hot tub aboard a yacht. Zuri could at least come up with a plausible story if she wants me to break my years-long streak of not checking up on him.

"In that case, I hope he has a DJ on staff to spin tunes while we set lines." I mime holding headphones to my ear, one hand on an imaginary turntable.

This earns an eye roll from Zuri, but a smile dislodges her frown. "All right, have it your way."

Have it my way? "My way is not a summer job with my ex-boyfriend," I tell her. "But I'm willing to do whatever it takes to get my life back." And shark research is my life. My passion, ever since I watched my first shark documentary as a kid from a lake town who made it her goal to get to the ocean.

I spent the past couple years on a different path, and while I'm glad I saw it through, and the Great Lakes will always have my heart, they don't have a hold on me like the ocean does. Now, more than ever, I know where I'm meant to be.

Whatever Zuri's found out about Adrian isn't enough to keep me here or she would've told me. I'm not naïve enough to think he's been drifting through life, aimless and pining. The fact that he needs a research assistant is evidence my departure didn't affect his career. What good would it do to check in on him now? The situation is bound to be awkward enough without me accidentally clicking "like" on a post from two years ago.

I'm about to tell her this when a loud thud wallops my eardrums, followed by thundering footsteps. Thank goodness for three small miracles. The kids' presence will forestall any further talk of Adrian's mythical exploits.

A whirlwind of bodies enters the room with as much force as a winter storm blowing in off the lake. Chloe dives for her mom, who sets down her coffee just in time. The boys barrel around the corner, shoulders bumping as they dart into the room. Seth's foot slips on the tile and he crashes down in a tumble of limbs.

"Momma, Leo p-p-pushed me!"

I slide my hands under Zuri's youngest son's armpits and hoist the little three-year-old into my arms. I tip my forehead against his. "He did not, little man. You slipped, is all." Reaching down, I tug at the toe of Seth's fleece pajamas. "These don't mix well with clean tile. Your mom needs to lay off with the overzealous mopping. A little gunk gives traction."

Zuri groans. "That's disgusting, Hope."

I ignore my friend, settling Seth onto my hip. "Wanna help me pack?"

He sniffs, rubbing his sleeve under his nose. "What about breakfast?"

"You can eat in my room. As long as that's okay with your mom?" I look to Zuri for confirmation.

But before she can answer, her phone dings. She digs around in her robe pockets and tugs out her cell, peering at it. "Oh gosh. Trevor's here already."

A Shoreline Dunes local who graduated in our class, Trevor has become good friends with Zuri over the past year. He's here to fix a leaky faucet, and while it's thoughtful of him to text instead of ringing the bell and risk waking the kids, I don't voice this vote of confidence. Zuri's wedding ring is testament to where her heart lies. Far be it from me to encourage her to move on when my own feelings for Adrian are embarrassingly complicated, even after all the time and distance.

Zuri frowns, but a quiet knock cuts short whatever she planned to say, and Seth lets go of my neck and scrambles out of my arms to beat his mom to the door. Faced with the alternative of subjecting my choices to Trevor's well-meaning questions, packing doesn't sound so bad, and I escape to my room.

I take my suitcase out of the closet and unzip it on my bed. The *buzz* of the zipper hits me with a rush of endorphins— adventure awaits. I toss in sports bras and underwear, a few shirts. Shorts and pants. In goes the black cotton dress I wear for every special occasion from interviews to date nights.

Not that there will be any of those. I've only been on a handful of dates since Adrian, each one a disappointment, the lack of connection a reminder of why I thought true love was a myth.

On impulse, I grab the only item hanging in the closet—a chambray sundress flecked with thumbnail-sized white seagulls that caught my eye the last time Zuri and I played tourist in Shoreline Dunes. She encouraged me to buy it, calling it a step up from my usual wardrobe of "afterthought casual." The tags are still on, and I use my teeth to rip them off before laying it atop the rest of the clothes. A new dress for a new start.

"Aunt Hope?"

Startled, I look over to see Chloe at the open door, clutching a bag of hair products. Even though Zuri and I aren't related, her kids grew up calling me aunt, and as an only child, I adore doting on them.

I take the hair supplies from her and wedge them in among my clothes. "Thanks, kiddo. Wanna help me zip the suitcase?"

She nods and clambers up on the bed. I reach to close the bag, but she grabs my wrist. "Wait. Don't you want to pack your favorite hoodie?"

I look down at the hoodie I'd forgotten I'm wearing. Adrian's hoodie.

"This isn't…" I stop myself. Why lie? I wear it almost every day, even on cool summer evenings. Maybe I should've chucked the hoodie years ago with tear-stricken drama, but our relationship didn't end with a big fight. It would've been more fitting to mail it back to him, laundered and neatly packaged, like an unwanted garment bought online. Impersonal. Detached.

"What about this?" I hold up the utility jacket I plan to wear on windy days like I'm pleading my case to a jury, not explaining my fashion choices to a six-year-old.

"That doesn't look cozy." Chloe's dubious tone makes me chuckle, despite the lurch of pain in my chest. But I don't need cozy. Don't need to get comfortable.

The rumble of Trevor's voice from the kitchen pulls her attention and she's off in a flash. Maybe without my presence as a third wheel, Zuri will open up to the man carrying a literal torch for her—the other day he showed up with a battery-powered lantern when a felled branch knocked the power out—and give love another chance.

Not me, though. I'm out to conquer love. Life since I moved back has been deceptively stagnant; all the ups and downs of a wave pool, but at the end of the day, I've been treading water. Today all that changes. I'm headed for the ocean. Adrian is my past, but sharks are my future. I'm not passing up this opportunity, even if it means confronting what—who—I've spent the past three years avoiding.

Tomorrow, the No-Adrian Rule will have a whole new meaning. Shutting him out won't be an option, but neither will getting to know him again. I've got to find a way to work with my ex without letting him in. To spend a summer with the man I once loved with my whole heart, and then let him go.

four

adrian

"Think you've might've gone overboard with all that data?" Gabe is lounging next to me, his feet kicked up on an overturned bucket, chin tucked to his chest as he taps on his phone. Without looking up, he says, "I thought you wanted your sister's opinion, not a full-on consult."

Though we're sitting on the boat—*my* boat, though it still feels weird to call it that, even though the monthly slip rental fee just left my bank account—the spreadsheet doesn't contain tag records or shark profiles. It's an amalgamation of digital data. Views, subscribe rates, watch time. A tally of how effective our channel is at reaching our audience.

I never expected to be dealing with this sort of data. When it became clear to my parents—both professors—that my interest in sharks was more than just a phase, my career path became just as clear: study, research, publish, teach. And the clarity of those parameters fit the stability I craved.

We moved around more often than I was comfortable with during my childhood. Just when I'd settle into a new place, our life would get uprooted by my dad's department losing funding or my mom accepting an offer at a college out of state. Vital for their careers, good for supporting our family, but tough for a kid who thrived on routine. When my sister left for college just as I started junior high in a new city, I felt adrift. By the time we moved again halfway through high school, I'd put all my focus into a planned-out, predictable future. Bachelor's degree, master's, doctorate, postdoc, tenure.

But my tidy career path took an unconventional turn, one I would've been too scared to embrace before Hope, a purpose for all the pieces of my personality that never quite found a home in the work I was doing before. My ability to connect with people, a skill I learned from many first days at new schools in new towns, makes social media surprisingly intuitive.

But peer review is important in life as well as science, and my big sister has always been a person I could count on to give me, if not impartial, then honest feedback. Bringing someone else onto the team for an entire summer is a big step, so today I'm hoping for my sister's long-overdue feedback on the channel and how we're using our platform. She's been surprisingly quiet on the subject, and honestly, I crave her opinion, even if she tells me I'm making a mistake.

I want confirmation that we're not setting ourselves up for disaster, that this is a worthwhile pursuit, and Iris won't hold back when it comes to data analysis. She's a mathematics professor at the University of North Carolina Wilmington, and despite living less than an hour away, still hasn't come to see the boat I've owned for the better part of a year. I should've realized sooner that the promise of a morning spent poring over numbers would be the best enticement to finally get her aboard.

"You haven't met my sister. She's going to want to download a copy to examine in her spare time so she can point out the fallacies in my projections." And that's if she approves. If she doesn't, she won't waste time digging into the data.

Hope would be all-in for a big career shift like this, no questions asked. She would've listened to all my worst-case scenarios, and then found a way to minimize them. She never let doubt hold her back, not in her career, at least.

"Ever considered bringing her along on a tagging trip?" Gabe's question scatters my thoughts like windblown sand.

"Hope?" I realize my mistake in an instant, but it's too late.

He looks up from his phone, thick brows drawn together over the top of his wraparound sunglasses. "I was thinking of your sister. But clearly, you weren't." He smirks. "I would ask who Hope is—"

"No one." But the keyboard is slick with sweat under my fingertips. She'll never be no one to me. She'll always be my first true love, the woman I could never be around without wanting, the woman I can't bear to see again, and yet can't help wishing for our paths to cross, just once more.

"Except—" he draws out the word, and my shoulders knot with tension "—it's obvious from your awkwardness that she's the ex-girlfriend Marissa told me about."

"Why was Marissa talking to you about Hope?" We broke up long before I met Gabe, and it's my story to tell.

"She's a shark researcher, right?" He turns the question on me instead of answering, unusually evasive.

"Was," I say, without thinking. Though the truth is, I don't know. Marissa keeps in touch with her, but I've made a point not to ask her anything that would make her feel in the middle of things, and Hope's life isn't my business. She made that clear when she cut me out of it.

None of which I intend to get into with Gabe. "I mean, yes. She's a marine biologist."

Last time we talked, she was working in Michigan on an invasive zebra mussel study. But for all I know she could've taken a job overseas or enrolled in a PhD program. Though I likely would've heard about it, and the fact that I haven't makes me ache for her. As much as I hate the idea of our paths crossing through work, the possibility she's abandoned the career she was so passionate about is far worse.

Not for the first time, I wish I could go back and be more understanding of her decision to take time away to help Zuri. More supportive. More optimistic that her months away wouldn't turn into years. More confident that her uncertainty about her next step wasn't uncertainty about me. Then again, given the way our relationship fizzled out, I was right to doubt.

I venture a glance at Gabe and discover he's put down his phone and treated me to a rare moment of his full attention. He's obviously not buying my line about Hope. Time to steer the conversation back to neutral waters. "As for my sister, no tagging trips for her. She'll never set foot on this boat unless we stay at the dock. Iris gets seasick on causeways."

"Don't hyperbolize." An unmistakable voice forceful enough to awaken the back row of a lecture hall carries through the muggy air, and I cringe with thirty years of younger-brother reflex.

Iris is making her way toward us, dressed for a day in the classroom, not a research boat. Her block-heeled boots are a slip hazard and the cream linen blazer draped over her shoulders is an invitation for stains. My sister is tall and broad-shouldered like me, with deep brown skin, though her face is round like Dad's, while I inherited our mom's angular cheekbones and high forehead. Her curls are shorter than last time I saw her, a contrast to my shoulder-length locs.

"Water has nothing to do with my queasiness on bridges. That's car sickness." She continues to lecture me with no apparent irony despite sidestepping cautiously with both arms outstretched, like the dock is a swaying rope bridge and not solid wood. Her nose is wrinkled; probably caught a whiff of the pervasive fishy odor I barely register anymore.

No point questioning how she overheard our conversation. Iris honed her eavesdropping skills by listening in on my calls back when our dad still clung to the notion of a cordless phone and landline.

"Motion-sick, then," I say, the habit of arguing with her superseding my goal to seek her advice. "Call it what you will, it's the same thing."

She ignores me, though. Having reached the point where she ought to board the boat, she plants her feet wide instead, hands on her hips, and assesses Gabe through octagonal wire-framed glasses. "You look familiar."

"Gabriel Ortiz." He sits up straighter as if summoned by roll call. "Do you watch our channel?" His tone is so eager that I cringe for what's coming next.

"No," she replies. Feigning interest is against her principles, though sometimes I wish she'd mastered the art of an encouraging half-truth.

She glances toward me, and her face softens. I resent how she can read me so easily—a holdover from our childhood, when she used to talk me through the anxieties I was scared to say aloud. "Heard great things, though. Our parents brag about it enough that Adrian ought to pay them for their marketing work."

There's an edge to her tone, one I've always detected toward the channel, and exactly what I want to address today. Does she not think starting the channel was a wise move, or am I just projecting my own doubts?

Gabe leans over the side of the boat, hand extended. "That must make you the other Dr. Hollis-Parker I've heard so much about."

"The original." Iris stretches to shake his fingertips, not budging from the center of the dock. I'm beginning to wonder whether she'll actually make it aboard. "You work with my brother and cousin?"

He nods. "I'm the photographer and social media manager. Occasional mediator when family drama ensues." When he drops her hand, she bobbles, knees bending to compensate. "Not a fan of boats?"

She shakes her head, the rest of her body stiff. "That's my brother's wheelhouse."

"Pun intended?"

"Never," she says with a visible shudder. The distraction worked, though. At Gabe's prompting, she takes off her high heels and climbs onto the boat with only a brief hesitation.

Desperate to get the morning back on track, I turn toward where I left my laptop. "I want to show you around, but first, let's go over some num—"

That's when I hear the splash.

I spin around, horrified. My sister will never speak to me again if she's gone overboard. But Iris is safe on deck, Gabe at her side. They're gaping at the water with matching looks of dismay. I spring into action, setting down my laptop and grabbing a personal flotation device from under the seat.

More splashing, then someone surfaces near the dock. I hurl the throwable cushion in their direction and leap overboard. Chilly water envelops me, bubbles brushing my chin as I breathe out to keep my nose clear. I kick my way to the surface.

"I can swim!" the person yells, and swivels toward me, arms churning the water into a brownish-green froth.

I recognized her voice in an instant, but that doesn't lessen the shock when I swipe the brackish water out of my face and my gaze collides with indignant, copper-brown eyes.

"Hope?" The second time I've said her name today, twice more than the past two years combined, and for a fleeting moment I wonder if I've conjured her out of saltwater and memories.

five

hope

My last thought before plunging into the murky water is that if I owed Marissa for offering me a job, we're officially even, because knocking me into the marina? Not what I'd call Southern hospitality. I'm pretty sure she was trying to spin me around to go back the way we came, but why? Doesn't matter anyway—good intentions are no consolation, considering I ended up in the water, fully dressed.

Today was supposed to be all about me getting my bearings before meeting Adrian. Groggy from the cross-country drive, I arrived at Marissa's condo well after midnight and crashed on the air mattress, but nerves woke me up early. She told me Adrian had an appointment so we'd have the day to catch up and go over the project in more depth.

At least he's not here to see this disaster. Embarrassing enough to fall off a dock without my ex-boyfriend around to witness. I kick my way to the surface, feet heavy in my sandals, and come up for air, doing my best not to swallow disgusting marina water. A situation not helped when a PFD smacks one of my flailing arms.

Pumping my legs to spin myself around, I catch sight of a

huge guy leaping off a nearby boat. The surface explodes in a splash that sends a wave of water up my nose and down my throat. I gag against the influx of salt and silt. Stinging, my eyes pinch shut.

The would-be rescuer surfaces just in front of me, and I'm still coughing, but annoyed enough to shout, "I can swim!"

My eyes are burning, but I force them open to get my bearings, blinking against the glint of sunlight on the water. The man's face is blurry and unexpectedly close. I rub the back of my hand across my face, and the stunningly handsome face of my long-lost boyfriend comes into focus. Here, in the water, so close I can hear the rasp of his inhale, is the man I lost my heart to.

Adrian's midnight-dark eyes meet mine, emotions churning in their depths. Surprise, concern, and…tenderness? A burst of visceral longing shoots through me, so raw it sucks the breath from my lungs.

To compensate, I drag in a gulp of air, but my mouth is so close to the surface that I inhale water instead. I gag and splutter and something bumps my arm. I recoil at the unexpected touch, but it's only the floatation cushion.

Coughing, I swat it away. Not the most mature move, but the reality of seeing Adrian again has me discombobulated. "Get that thing out of my face!" Flail, splutter.

He shoves it back toward me. "Just take it!"

"You know I'm an excellent—" flail "—swimmer." Splutter, cough.

My chin dips under the murky water again. Turns out it's tough to stay afloat when you're in shock and gagging on seawater. His arm comes around my waist and tugs me upward. I gasp and find his face inches from mine.

"Take," he says, panting, "the cushion."

I take it.

He releases me but stays close, treading water with steady

pumps that send pulses of water against my shins. His knee bumps mine and he pulls back, eyes wide. Droplets glisten in his long, black lashes and hang suspended like crystals in the trimmed beard that adorns his once-clean-shaven jaw. Locs frame his face, the ends dipping into the water. His new look doesn't align with the Adrian of my memories, and I blame the incongruity for the uneven tempo of my heart.

His lips are parted, breath coming fast. Which is weird, because Adrian's as good a swimmer as I am, if not better, and the water is calm.

"Are you okay?" The question slips out in a rasp, my throat hoarse from coughing.

His thick brows pull together, lips pursed, and there he is, the sweet, serious man I remember. "Me? You're the one swimming in a marina." Eyes narrowed, he asks, "Don't you know there's a risk of electrical shock?"

"Because I woke up and chose this," I deadpan.

Irritated, I let go of the cushion and swim for the dock. My baggy tee creates a lot of drag, and each stroke threatens to dislodge my shoes, but I kick hard to put distance between us. When I reach the ladder, I grab hold and haul myself out with zero grace. Worth noting: if this entry back into shark research doesn't work out, I absolutely don't have a future modeling for sexy poolside music videos.

I've turned around to see if Adrian needs a hand up—I don't resent him enough to ignore common decency—but he's already hooked his elbows over the edge. His shoulders bunch with definition, broad lats straining against his soaking wet tee. He's always been big—whenever he wrapped me in his strong, solid arms, it felt like coming home to a safe harbor—but now his drenched shirt clings to sculpted muscles that hint at hours spent in a weight room he used to scorn as a waste of time.

With no apparent effort, he hoists his entire torso out of the water, shirt clinging to pecs and abs that have me swallowing, hard. He swings his leg over with ease and climbs onto the dock in front of me. Adrian in board shorts has always been my undoing, and I can testify some things never change. His muscled thighs are quite frankly indecent. Water slips down his quadriceps in rivulets, tracing a glistening path around his knees, and I look down at my feet to stop myself from cataloging every muscle in his familiar frame that's changed so much.

He's grown impossibly more handsome in our years apart, and I'm standing here with my ponytail hanging lopsided and bedraggled, bike shorts bunched in an awkward wedgie, with the Velcro on one of my sandals undone. I don't usually spare much thought for my appearance beyond looking presentable, but it would've been nice for our first meeting not to happen when I just experienced the real-life version of a dunk tank.

In fact, I've dreamed up a lot of scenarios of what might happen when I saw Adrian again, and none of them included an involuntary swim and attempted rescue. Sometimes I pictured presenting my latest paper at a conference and running into him in the hallway afterward, where he would shower my groundbreaking findings with praise.

Other times, I imagined our paths crossing in a chance meeting at a café—he'd pick up my Earl Grey tea by mistake, see my name scribbled on the cup, and search for me across the room. Our eyes would meet, and I wave a hand as if to say, "All yours" and walk away with my head high, cool and collected… The exact opposite of my current soggy state.

Worth noting that in all my daydreams about a chance meeting with Adrian, I'm never flaunting a sexy new boyfriend. But that's not something I care to explore, especially not with my very real, very sexy *ex*-boyfriend standing right in front of me.

I'm at a loss as to the proper social etiquette for this reunion. A handshake? A firm nod of professional amicability? A hello kiss?

My eyes rise to his lips at the thought. How would it feel

to kiss him now? My lips tingle in anticipation of the gentle scrape of his beard, the decadent pleasure of his mouth claiming mine... Yeah, that would not set the tone for the rest of the summer.

But I never planned to be alone with him. My brain can't handle the discombobulation. Five minutes in and my plan is falling to pieces. Here we are, alone together, and Marissa is—I glance around—there, at the end of the dock, arguing with someone. Wait, I know that person.

Shading my eyes, I squint to be sure. "Why is your sister here?" My heart sinks even further. Adrian's sister and I used to be close, but who knows what he's told her about me since the breakup.

The last time we saw each other was the Thanksgiving meal I shared with their family before I left. I expected to see her again in the New Year, and instead it's been more than three. My stomach turns more sour than the time I drank a pint of expired chocolate milk on a dare in middle school. Clearly, I underestimated the myriad complications that could arise from accepting this job.

Adrian follows my gaze, then his attention snaps back to me. "Why are *you* here?"

"You weren't expecting me?" I ask, though it seems obvious he wasn't.

Sure enough, he shakes his head, which sends his hair into his eyes. He swipes it back over his head, revealing a flash of rounded biceps I do my best not to notice. If only he hadn't gone and made his muscles even more obvious, this would've been easier.

Not true—he's always been irresistible—but lying to myself is the best way to keep functioning at this point.

I open my mouth to explain, but nothing comes out. I can't confess aloud, to my ex, that I'm so desperate to find a way back into shark research that I was willing to work with him. Especially since it turns out that willingness may not be mutual.

My teeth start chattering with the retreat of adrenaline, and Adrian's look of confusion morphs into something mortifyingly close to pity. "You're soaked. Let's get you a towel and then we can sort this out."

He turns and walks down the dock in the opposite direction of the women, leaving a trail of wet footprints on the weathered gray wood. Marissa hasn't looked my way, and I'm hesitant to confront her with Iris around. I could wind up looking like a fool, which is pretty likely, given the morning's events.

Against my better judgment, I follow Adrian. Heck, this whole trip is against my better judgment. Why start listening to common sense now?

The boards echo hollowly under my feet, like I'm walking to my doom, but the familiar scent of briny air is welcoming. My curls are half-dry already, skin sticky and tight, though my clothes cling to me, still sopping.

We pass several runabouts tied up at the cleats, and a few cabin cruisers. I check the boat names as we pass—Adrian and I used to try to one-up one another with finding the most outrageous ones.

I spot a sleek center console tied up near the end of the dock with the word *Praespero* inscribed on the bow in sloping cursive. A dark-haired man is sitting onboard, his back to us.

Forgetting for a moment what we are to one another now, I point it out to Adrian. "Look. That guy's boat is named *Praespero*." I picked up enough Latin from taxonomy to figure out the meaning immediately. *To Hope.*

Joking, I say, "Do you think he named it after me?"

"What?" He glances around and must spot it, because he says, "That's not his, it's mine."

I stop. Dead in my tracks. My head feels…woozy. The way he said it was so matter-of-fact, but Adrian doesn't even own a skiff, let alone a gorgeous boat like that. At thirty, unless he's had a massive career shift, I can't see how he'd afford it. And the name—

"I'm going to grab you a towel, okay?" His soft words interrupt my racing thoughts. Without waiting for an answer, he heads off. Reaching the boat, he hops aboard and says something to the other man, who turns and waves, as if he expected me.

I did not expect him, and I don't wave. My chattering teeth have given way to goose bumps by the time Adrian makes his way back, a rumpled towel in his hands. Brow knotted in concern, he settles it over my shoulders, rubbing my arms through the fabric. The friction jerks me to alertness and we lock eyes—his are deep and dark and serious, and the way he holds my gaze while he buffs away the chill awakens an answering heat inside me.

My lips part, and he steps away, movements jerky. Fumbling, I clutch the ends of the towel at my chest. The terry cloth is stiff, with the faint musty smell of something left to air dry in the summer heat, but I feel less exposed with it wrapped around my shoulders, like the fabric is a barrier to the emotions threatening to escape.

Adrian scratches at his jaw, and my eyes are drawn once again to his beard. What a difference facial hair makes on a face I know as well as my own. The beard accentuates his strong jaw, the perfect complement to his already handsome face.

"I'm going to talk to the others. Gabe is, too," he adds, and I look up to find the other man approaching. "You could come along, or wait on the boat if you need a minute."

It will take more than a minute to collect myself, but the offer is appealing. "You really didn't know I was coming?"

He shakes his head.

Oof, I do not need to be a part of that conversation. "Then yeah, I'll wait here."

The other guy—Gabe?—comes up and smiles. "Hey, Hope. I'll catch up with you in a bit."

"Uh, okay." I want to ask who he is, and how he knows my name. I want to ask why Iris is here of all places, when she barely sets foot on beaches, let alone boats. I want to ask Marissa why she didn't want him to know about me when we're supposed to be working together all summer. I want to ask Adrian why on earth he named a boat after me.

The questions are piling up, and before I can decide on which to ask first, he's already headed toward the end of the dock where the women are still talking, their conversation inaudible.

Using the towel to wipe a trickle of water behind my ear, I watch Adrian's tall figure, unable to pull my eyes away. His shoulders are hunched under the clinging material of his damp shirt, long stride purposeful, like he can't get away fast enough. But a few steps later, he glances back, eyes dipping in a swoop that catalogs my body, the impression of his gaze lingering like a heated caress on my chilled skin.

Shaking off my body's response to him, I tug off my hair tie and finger-comb my curls into a bun, and turn my attention toward the facts. Coming down here without talking to him was a mistake, that much is clear. Adrian wasn't expecting me. And in a few minutes, I might have to face his sister, who may or may not demand a full explanation of why I broke her brother's heart. Although, he doesn't seem heartbroken. Just confused, like me.

Whatever the reason Marissa kept my arrival a secret, I'm not quitting. I didn't swallow my pride and drive all the way down here to go back home empty-handed.

Three months. Three months of enduring Adrian, yes. But three months of working with sharks again. I can do this. I will do this. If this isn't a practical joke, nothing will stop me from getting what I came for.

six

adrian

Drenched and in desperate need of answers, I hustle toward my sister and cousin, Gabe by my side. Maybe the timing of Hope's arrival explains why Iris finally agreed to come out to the boat, though I can't understand why my sister would want to witness the most awkward reunion of all time.

Hope still hasn't mentioned why she's here, but she asked about Marissa, so I'm guessing my cousin is behind her sudden appearance. Iris certainly isn't the type to interfere. She's always let me own my choices, even if they don't align with hers, which is why I wanted her to weigh in on the channel. But none of that matters right now, not until I figure out why Hope is in town, and on my boat, of all places.

I cast a glance at my shoulder to check whether Hope is staying put, and the sight of her on my boat makes me stumble. I couldn't fault her if she changed her mind and decided to follow us. She has just as much a right to answers as I do, but my hands are shaking, and my stomach is clenched tight; all I want is to hear an explanation without an audience.

We pass an angler carrying tackle boxes and a net, baseball cap tugged low over her brow, whose eyes widen when she sees my face, but I walk past before she can make up her mind to ask the question. *Aren't you that shark guy from the internet?* I get stopped pretty often around town, but right now talking to a stranger is the last thing I want.

I want answers, and I'd rather ask my family than embarrass myself in front of Hope. She wasn't surprised to see me, but she didn't know about the boat… And ugh, why did I have to get sentimental with the name?

But I know exactly why, and it's the same reason my heart is hammering from the effort of walking away from her. What I don't know is why she's here, now, when I've long since given up hope of seeing her again.

Marissa darts a guilty look my way when we walk up, confirming my suspicions that she's behind this. "Why is Hope here?"

Iris tips her chin, adjusting her glasses in the same gesture she likely aims at students who are chronically late to class. "Exactly what I've been trying to figure out."

"I didn't know you'd be here." Marissa cuts my sister a glare, then frowns at me, and adds, "Either of you. I tried to get Hope out of there before she could see you, but well…" She gestures toward me, like my soaked clothes tell the story.

"You pushed her in?" My cousin is tough, but I can't see her shoving anyone, let alone a friend, into the marina like a poolside prank.

"What? No! I was trying to get her to turn around, but she tripped. Once you went in after her, I figured the next best thing was to try to hustle Iris out of there while Hope was distracted."

If she was half as distracted as I was, the sun could've fallen from the sky and she wouldn't have noticed.

"But Iris refused to go." Marissa glares at her again.

"Because this is childish," Iris says. "You're in your thirties and still scheming, setting people up—"

"I am not setting them up, for the last time." Marissa sinks down onto the brick retaining wall and blows out a breath, shaking her head. "This is a disaster, and now Hope's probably going to quit on us."

Realization hits me like a punch in the gut. "*Hope* is the new researcher?"

Shoulders slumped, Marissa shrugs like it's a moot point. "She reached out and it seemed like ideal timing. Who better to bring onto the team than someone we know and trust?"

Trust? Hope and I built a life together, and then she walked away and let it fall to pieces. The woman I spent over half a decade with is now a stranger, and my cousin thought she'd be the ideal person to join our crew? There's no way I can work alongside Hope for a day, let alone a whole summer.

"Not happening."

"Weren't you just saying we could use an extra pair of hands?" Gabe chimes in.

I'd forgotten he was there, and his presence is a fresh embarrassment. "Did you know about this?"

His silence stretches a beat too long. Guess that explains the line of questioning earlier. He was trying to gauge my reaction to Hope's arrival. But why not just tell me? Before I can ask, Iris speaks up again.

"I thought I was here to offer feedback on your channel but seems you two are up to your old antics," she says. "Should've known when you teamed up together drama would ensue." Brows arched above her glasses, she divides a glance between Marissa and me.

Once again, I find myself taking the fall for one of my cousin's wild schemes. Except this time, it's not a mobile vet clinic run out of a Radio Flyer wagon. She's interfering in my personal life and putting our work in jeopardy. Ignoring my sister for the moment, I tell Marissa, "It's *our* channel. You're not supposed to make unilateral decisions."

"We agreed we needed another research assistant. Hope is qualified and available," she says. "You're suggesting I should've wasted time searching for someone else with the season already underway?"

"It's too complicated."

"Why, because you two have a history?"

We don't have a history. We have a present. Hope is with me every day—her dry humor, her copper-bright eyes, her pure, undiluted enthusiasm—I can't escape her when she's a thousand miles away. How will I survive the torture of having her onboard all summer, yet further than ever?

Marissa crosses her arms, tipping her head back to look me in the eye. "You're saying you wouldn't hire someone qualified just because they're not your favorite person?"

I flinch. Hope was my favorite person. Maybe always will be, in spite of how things ended. "Don't relegate this to the hypothetical. Hope is my ex-girlfriend." I've never said that word aloud, and it nearly chokes me. It feels like such an understatement for the bond I thought we had with each other.

I glare down at Marissa. "Why don't you invite one of your exes to work with us?"

"You know I don't date scientists. Too inquisitive. I like to keep some mystery in a relationship." She stands up, facing me down, not looking at all remorseful for colossally screwing with my life. *Our* lives. No way accepting this job was easy on Hope.

"But if I did," she says, "I'd be fine with having them onboard, because I'm over all my exes. Hence why we're no longer together."

"You're saying I still have feelings for Hope?"

Everyone stays silent. That's answer enough, and I grit my teeth, embarrassed. This is why I never bring her up. With the revolving door of friends thanks to switching schools so often, Marissa became the friend I could always count on, and with the difference in our ages, Iris helped raise me, so I've never been able to hide my feelings from either of them. Should've known they'd see my refusal to talk about Hope as proof my feelings for her are a jumbled wreck.

Unable to deal with their scrutiny, I peer back at the boat again. Hope's still there, pacing. Waiting for me. Wondering what's going on.

Just like I was, three years ago, waiting for her to make up her mind about our future. Discovering she might not want a life with me, and being too cowardly to find out for sure, until her silence gave me the answer I dreaded.

"Damn it, Marissa." My skin is itchy under a film of salt and silt, my heart feels bruised, and my head is spinning. I could blame the dizziness on the impromptu plunge, but the truth is Hope knocked my world off its axis the day we met, in the best possible way, then left me reeling.

I close my eyes against the sight of her standing in the bow of my boat, named before I'd given up hope of a future with her in it. "She can't stay."

seven

hope

Adrian has been gone for a really long time. Okay, five minutes, max. But five impatient minutes spent steaming in the Southern heat I'm not reacclimated to feels like an eternity. Especially when I'm trying to push away the memory of Adrian's grip on my water-slick skin as he tugged me to the surface—the way his touch made me gasp, the press of his fingertips the reminder of everything I haven't let myself desire for years.

To distract myself, I move into the shade next to the helm and take stock of my surroundings. Most of the boat slips in this small marina are empty, but a guy in a nearby sailboat is having a one-sided conversation with his labradoodle, and nineties pop music blares from a crowded pontoon boat motoring out toward the Intercoastal Waterway.

I could leave too. Get an Uber back to Marissa's condo, grab my stuff, and hightail it back to Michigan. Find a job with no complications. But when the engine noise fades, I become aware of voices, and glance over to see Adrian and Marissa heading toward me, arguing. I freeze, straining to catch their words.

"No, what? She's already here," Marissa says, walking quickly to keep up with Adrian's long strides.

"Under false pretenses," Adrian snaps.

So they don't need my help, after all. I drove across the country for nothing.

Fuming and ready to demand answers, I slide past the wheel and barrel out onto the deck. The boat shifts as Adrian climbs aboard, and I try to course-correct, but momentum propels me straight into his chest.

Arms flailing, I slip on a puddle. He makes a wild grab for my hand, but all he catches is air. I topple backward and land, butt-first, inside…a cooler? I'm wedged into the plastic container, thighs against my belly, feet jutting sky-high.

I take a cautious sniff to gauge whether I'm sitting in a bunch of fish—if this is a bait cooler then I'm officially calling foul play—and catch sight of Adrian's face above me. His lips are rolled together against the smile threatening to break through. Laughter rises up from my own chest, but with my diaphragm constricted like a panini in a press, it emerges as a gurgle.

Adrian's expression turns serious. "Don't strain yourself." That only makes it worse, and soon my whole body is shaking with painful laughter. He joins in, and maybe that should make me mad, but his chuckle is so buoyant I can't fault him for it.

When I finally catch my breath, I attempt a stern look, straining my neck to glare up at him. "First you accuse me of taking a casual swim in the marina, now you expect me to keep a straight face in this situation?"

His teeth hook into his bottom lip, apologetic, and oh gosh, I used to find that irresistible. His gaze flicks down my body, assessing my position, and my skin prickles with heat. He crouches down, the furrow between his brows making another appearance. "This might be worse than the time you got stuck in Gran's rocking chair."

"You *would* bring that up." I keep my scowl in place, even though it's hard not to smile at the memory. His grandma had an antique cane rocking chair on her porch when he brought me to meet her for the first time. It looked so inviting that I plopped down while he rang the doorbell and found out the hard way the chair was purely ornamental. I broke through the seat like Goldilocks, and after that first impression, I'm pretty sure his grandma isn't sad I never moved back down South.

He lifts his eyes to mine, dark and deep, framed by jet-black lashes. "Okay if I help get you out?" His voice is exactly how I remember it. Warm. Deep. Luscious.

I nod. Adrian tucks his arms around me in an unexpectedly tender hold, and my heart pounds into overdrive. This pseudo-embrace shouldn't leave me breathless. I try to visualize a scuba ascent or something equally focus-intensive as he tightens his grip and hoists me into the air.

The cooler comes with.

Goodbye, all semblance of dignity.

One of his arms is hooked under my knees, forearm rigid with muscles, biceps pressed against my thigh. "Let's try again. Ready?"

Another nod, though the details of what I'm agreeing to are hazy because the irrational portion of my brain is soaking up the close contact with the objectively sexy man—emotional baggage aside—endeavoring, for the second time, to rescue me from a tricky situation.

He shifts, widening his stance, and pushes against the cooler with a rough exhale. I squeeze my eyes shut, though whether to capture the sensation of his breath against the delicate skin of my neck or block it out, I'm not sure. The next moment, my legs tumble free and he tightens his grip, holding me against him as the cooler clatters to the ground.

My cheek is pressed to a firm chest that feels like he's been doing nothing but bench presses since I've been away, and I inhale the familiar scent of cedar and brine. *Adrian.* My eyes drift closed in reflex, savoring his embrace for one heartbeat, then another—the rhythm of his breath calming as the ebb and flow of waves at the shoreline.

Then he lowers me to the deck, the slide of my body against his leaving me breathless all over again. He steps back with a sharp inhale, bending to pick up my fallen towel. He shakes it out and wraps it around me, and the gesture is so caring, so like the man I used to love, that I don't protest. But his next words shatter the illusion that there's anything left between us.

"You can't stay." His sympathetic tone makes things a thousand times worse. I'm the out-of-work ex-girlfriend about to be fired on my first day.

The sound of someone's throat clearing behind me has me whirling around. Marissa, Iris, and the guy who introduced himself earlier are all standing on the dock. I thought it wasn't possible to be more humiliated. The past hour has been far worse than any of my night-before-an-exam nightmares.

"Iris, hi." I do an awkward two-handed wave, like I've entered an in-progress video call. If only I could feign tech problems and log off.

"Just grabbing my purse," she says, leaning across to snag the strap. "Evidently I picked an eventful day to visit my brother's boat for the first time."

Her words sink in, and I glance toward Adrian. His face is pained, forehead bunched, mouth a tense line. "So it really is yours? You just went out and bought a boat?"

Iris glances sidelong at me. "Perks of being an influencer."

This is making less sense by the minute. I'm tempted to tip my head to the side in case I've got water in my ear, messing with my hearing. "Influencer?"

Adrian looks me up and down, but it's an altogether different look from before. No heat, all cool assessment. "What exactly did my cousin tell you about what we do?" He says the word *cousin* as if he's wishing he could disown Marissa.

I shrug, dislodging the towel, and drag it back over my shoulders, wanting the semblance of protection. "Marissa was going to fill me in on the details this morning, but she told me you're conducting a survey of coastal shark populations. Tagging individuals in order to track them in long-term studies."

"Yes, but I guess I'm just surprised you'd want to be a part of this."

Is that a dig at me returning to shark research? But he said it so earnestly, like he's genuinely curious. I force myself not to get defensive. This is work, and I need to keep things professional. "I'm sure you're aware my work over the past few years has been with bony fish, primarily in the lab, but my plan has always been to get back into shark research."

I'm not sure why I phrased it that way, like an accusation. Like I expected him to wait for me. For three years? When I'm the one who got cold feet?

But his brows draw together. "I wasn't talking about your dedication to the research. I meant you're sure you want to be with me—" he tugs at his collar "—us, on camera? You'll be a part of every video we share. You're okay with that?"

"What videos?" I'm missing something key here, desperate for him to fill in the blanks. I'm starting to think Adrian not knowing I was coming is the least of my worries.

Confirming my fears that I'm missing out on key information, he blinks at me, mouth slightly agape. Instead of answering, he turns and glares at Marissa, arms crossed, Poseidon gearing up for a sea storm. "You didn't tell her?"

She mimics his pose, and the effect is equally intimidating, despite her smaller stature. "She's here, she's well-qualified. That's all that matters."

Iris clears her throat. "Y'all clearly have some catching up to do, so I'm going to head out." Disappointment lodges in my chest at the realization I might not see her again, which is absurd, because I didn't come here to rebuild a relationship with Adrian's family, I came to make sure he stays in my past.

"Let me know when you want me to look at those numbers," she tells him.

He shakes his head. "I think I'm good on that." Something akin to hurt tinges his words, but I push aside my concern. Whatever's going on between them is none of my business.

"You sure?" She frowns, concern for her brother obvious, but at his nod, she sighs. "All right. Call me though." She turns to go, clearly not planning to tell me goodbye, but something prompts me to speak up.

"Good to see you, Iris." What happened between Adrian and I doesn't change how I feel about her. It's impossible for us to be friends, but there was a time when I thought of her as a sister.

"Be well," she says, and my heart gives an unexpected lurch.

The moment she walks away, Marissa steps closer. "I'm sorry about all this, Hope. I thought we'd have the boat to ourselves. I wanted to tell you everything in person."

"Like the fact that he didn't know I was coming?" I lift my chin toward a very silent, very close Adrian.

"Among other things." Her dark brown eyes are full of remorse. "I just want you to keep an open mind."

"I drove across the country for this, knowing he'd be here." Humiliating, in retrospect. "I'd say my mind is wide open."

Gabe lets out a surprised chuckle, which he covers with a cough. "Can I just say that I'm really glad you're keeping an open mind?" I ought to feel awkward, knowing what he's witnessed, but his smile is wide and disarming. "If you stay, it means I get to spend less time hands-on with the sharks, and more time behind the camera."

"Less time with the sharks is a good thing?"

"Since I'm a photographer, yeah. Guessing Marissa didn't mention me either?"

Add that to the tally. "Are you with the university?"

"Nope, I'm on staff with *Shark Science Crew*."

"The Shark Science *Who*?"

His mouth falls open. "Wait, you don't know about the show?"

My face must make it clear that I do not, and he rubs the back of his neck, eyes wide. "You don't follow Adrian, like, at all?"

A laugh escapes me, but no one joins in. The queasiness erupts into all-out nausea. "Um, no. That would be weird, right? Because he's my ex." My voice rasps out, throat tight. I've just remembered Zuri's words about celebrities and mega-yachts and wonder suddenly if I shouldn't have been so flippant when she tried to divulge the results of her digital sleuthing.

Marissa watches me with raised brows. "See why I wanted to tell her without an audience?"

"Too late for that." I dig in my pocket for my phone, ready to find out for myself since everyone's talking in circles. No point in avoiding his socials any longer, not with the real Adrian standing right here, his touch fresh in my mind, on my skin. But my screen is blank. Fully waterlogged.

I hold it up. "You owe me a phone," I tell Marissa. "And an explanation."

She opens her mouth. Closes it. Fiddles around on her own phone, head down. "I didn't want you to find out this way. But best-laid plans and all..." She passes it over.

She's pulled up Adrian's Instagram page, and I scan it, searching for answers. The grid is filled with shark close-ups and stills of him in the lab, on the boat, behind a podium. His profile picture is no longer a shark's tooth, but a well-framed selfie. His eyes are crinkled at the corners, one hand holding his locs away from his face, the backdrop a blue sky and navy sea. Well, that's an improvement.

What's also improved since we were together is his follower count. It no longer numbers in the hundreds.

Or the thousands.

Or the tens of thousands.

Holy crap. Adrian has over a *million* followers.

This is far worse than a prank. My ex-boyfriend is an actual celebrity.

eight

adrian

Hope didn't know. Her fingers are tight around the phone, knuckles showing through her skin. The towel around her shoulders reminds me of the time we went camping in South Haven, with Lake Michigan a short hike from our campsite. Beach towels tucked over our shoulders as defense against mosquitos, we'd snuggled together by the fire, making wishes for the future on sparks like shooting stars.

If she's got a wish now, it's probably to be anywhere but here with me. She's silent, and her shocked expression guts me. Looks like she really did stop thinking about me after we broke up, just like I feared. Out of sight, out of mind. Free to live her life without the burden of a relationship.

The only good news is I won't have to convince her to leave. Hope deleted her social media accounts years ago, and I can't imagine her being comfortable with this, and Marissa must agree since she kept the details hidden.

Hope passes Marissa's phone back, hands trembling, and I ball my fists against the urge to gather her close and kiss her cheek. Hold her steady against my side. Not my place. Not anymore.

A truth confirmed when she says, "Okay, so Adrian is famous. What does that have to do with me?"

Pushing aside the hurt from her words, I jump in before Marissa can reply. "Nothing, if you don't want it to." Now is my chance to convince Hope to leave. For her sake, as well as mine. "We use our platform for public outreach. This isn't typical fieldwork. I'm sure you could find something more suited to your preferences."

She turns toward me, but focuses on a spot over my shoulder, refusing to connect. "Are you conducting shark studies?" she asks.

"Yes, but—"

"Then this matches my interests." She dodges her eyes toward mine, a flash of copper, daring, but wary. "I don't mind you sharing photos of me on social media."

This is so much bigger than that, and I'm mad at Marissa all over again for not being up front with her. "We have a YouTube channel, Hope. We film all our work, and a lot of people watch our videos."

"Millions," Gabe adds, unhelpfully.

"Millions of people." Hope nods slowly, taking that in. She keeps nodding for a solid five seconds, and I can tell she's completely thrown. Then she stops abruptly and raises her chin to face me. "You're worried I'll make you look bad."

Actually, that never crossed my mind. Hope isn't attention-seeking, nor is she vindictive, and our relationship didn't even end in an emotional confrontation. But now I'm imagining yet another complication from her joining the crew. "Is that why you came?"

Her eyes narrow, copper glinting in a warning flash. "I came here to work. To do a job, to get experience, and to help a friend." Her voice wobbles on the last word, and a flash of regret crosses Marissa's face. "But I was also under the assumption that you were okay with my presence, and clearly, you're not."

There's an accusation in her tone that I don't appreciate. "I haven't had time to process. There are a lot of variables to consider." Calculating the potential fallout doesn't make me a worrier. Risk-averse isn't the insult she makes it out to be. "And being in YouTube videos doesn't seem like your thing."

"Would've said the same about you."

She's got me there. I never would've chosen this for myself, yet despite the exposure, this work fulfills me in a way I never would've expected. "Maybe you don't know anything more about me than I did about you," she says.

I'm not sure whether that's a dig on present me or past me, but either way, it rankles. We always talked about spending our lives together. She told me she was excited to start the next chapter. Then she expected me to not be upset when she hesitated, and ended up making a one-eighty that left us further apart than ever.

"You're right, I don't know you." We haven't spoken in years. Years that have stretched and frayed our bond like a worn anchor line. "You left social media and quit replying to my texts. The Hope I knew would've been brave enough to at least break up with me over the phone." I never meant to say this, but all the effort I've put in to move past the hurt was demolished the moment I saw her again.

She steps closer, into my space, heat and steam radiating off her like a kettle about to go off. "The Adrian I knew would've called me every night instead of sending texts so generic they'd pass for appointment reminders from a doctor's office."

"I was giving you space."

The word echoes in the scant inches between us, and her eyes narrow. "I didn't come here to fight. Or to talk about the past. I wanted a fresh start."

It's on the tip of my tongue to ask why she stayed away from shark research for so long, but I glance over to find Marissa and

Gabe watching us so closely they may as well have popcorn, like our argument is the latest blockbuster.

This is why she can't stay. I won't let us—her—be exposed like this.

A featherlight touch on my knuckles draws my attention. Hope. She jerks her hand away, like I burned her, but the remnant heat on my own hand feels more like a glow, warm and tender.

"I know Marissa wanted to be the one to tell me but honestly, I think it's better I hear about..." She twists her lips, as if searching for the right words. "Whatever this is, from you."

For once, my cousin doesn't argue. She stoops to grab her bag, looping it across her chest. "I know my tactics weren't forthright, but this could be a really good thing, and I didn't think either of you would've given it the chance if I told you everything up front."

She locks eyes with Hope. "I know it might seem overwhelming. But we do important work and have a lot of fun in the process."

Gabe nods, grabbing his laptop. "Heck yeah we do. And don't let this guy convince you otherwise." His black hair is tousled from running his hands through it, but he smiles at Hope like this is a typical day, and I'm grateful to him for making the effort to put her at ease.

"Whatever you decide, it was good to meet you, Hope..." he rolls the word into the next sentence "...we didn't scare you away." He waits, expectant, and she smiles.

"If you didn't before, the bad puns will," I say, grumpy in the face of his good-natured ease.

She shakes her head. "No such thing."

Grinning, he says, "Knew we'd get along." He climbs off the boat, and Marissa makes a move to follow.

"Where are you going?" I ask, with the feeling of being

swept out to sea by the undertow. This is all happening so fast, and I can't seem to find my footing.

"Not far, I'm her ride." Marissa gives my shoulder a squeeze on her way past—perhaps a show of support or a warning not to mess things up. Ironic, coming from the person who got us into this mess. "Be good to each other."

Hope and I used to be good to each other. Good *for* each other. Now, aside from sharks and our dating history, there's far more that separates than unites us. I heave a deep breath to steady myself, and when I exhale, we're alone.

nine

adrian

We moved to the shade under the boat's canopy, meager defense against the midday temps, but better than roasting out on deck without the ocean breeze to cool us off. Unfortunately, it's a close fit for two in here, which means we're now nearly chest-to-chest, and while I may be tied up in knots over the situation, I'll never be too far gone not to be overcome by Hope's beauty.

She doesn't give any signs of suffering a similar distraction. "You want me to leave," she says. Not true. All I ever wanted was for her to stay, but it's too late for that. She crosses her arms. "I heard you arguing with Marissa earlier. You want me off the team."

"That would imply you're on it," I say, and hurt flashes in her eyes. "I know it's not your fault, but Marissa should've checked with me."

"If it's my qualifications you're opposed to, you're welcome to call my previous supervisor for a reference."

"Hope, c'mon. You know I'm well aware you're more than qualified." I studied with her for countless exams, celebrated with her after she defended her thesis. We know each other's résumés as well as our own, and hers would qualify her for many competitive jobs. Which is why I can't understand why she'd want to be here.

"Under other circumstances…" My throat is dry, and I break off. If she was a stranger, it would be amazing to work with someone so knowledgeable and passionate about sharks. But I wouldn't change our dating history, not for all the heartache in the world.

We were bound to run into one another again, but not like this. I can't handle an entire summer of watching every possible *what-if* float through my mind. A summer of irrational hope that things might work out, only to be left behind again.

"You mean, like if we hadn't dated?" she asks, giving voice to my thoughts, and her defiant tone makes my hackles rise.

How is she able to move past it so easily? I rake a hand over my head, forgetting the locs, her nearness transporting me back to when we were dating, and I wore my hair short. The brush of hair against my shoulders is a tangible reminder that things between us have changed, and this isn't someone I can be open with, not someone who I can bare my soul to anymore.

Hope's forehead glistens with a sheen of sweat, and I seize on the best way to keep my emotions in check: polite distance. Manners. Southern hospitality can be a two-edged sword.

"It's hot out here." I wave a hand toward a small cooler—not the one she tripped into earlier. "Would you like something to drink?"

She blinks at me. "Uh, yeah, actually."

Gran always said common courtesy is a good place to start in tough times, and this is certainly one of those. I walk to the cooler I stocked with ice and sparkling water for Iris's visit. Grab two cans and step back into the cockpit with Hope, handing her the blackberry one.

"You remembered."

I look down at the can, confused. Then it hits me, I didn't

even think to ask which flavor she'd prefer. "Well, yeah. I…" No use covering up, so I shrug. "Yeah."

The barest smile dents her cheek, but the sight lifts my heart, like the first glimpse of shoreline after a long day at sea. A bone-deep feeling of relief. Joy, even.

"Why'd you come?" The words sound harsher than I meant. An accusation instead of a question, and I try again. "You knew about me, and you came anyway."

"Besides a job, you mean?" The chuckle she forces out is self-effacing, and I want to reach out for her hand, wrap my fingers around hers in reassurance.

She pops the lid on her water, a cool breath of vapor rising from the can. "I've been staying out of shark science," she says. "Avoiding it, to be honest. Ever since we…" She presses her thumb against the can, denting the tin, but doesn't say anything else.

She doesn't have to. The way our relationship dwindled to an end is seared in my mind. After years of long-distance while she earned her master's degree then worked with a nonprofit in Maryland, I was finishing up my PhD. We'd discussed what life would look like once I was out of school. About how we could finally be together, in the same city. But after years of dreaming and months of planning, when it came time to take action, she told me she wasn't sure where she wanted to be long-term, and I shouldn't base my next move on her.

All the breath left my lungs when she told me. Part of me had sensed a hesitancy during our recent calls, but I chalked that up to her aversion to make concrete plans in any area of her life. She'd schedule flights at the last minute, apply for jobs right before the window closed. So I didn't think it meant anything that she'd always talked about our future in vague terms, because she always told me that she wanted to be with me, however that looked like, and we'd make it work.

And for years, we did. Even though the planner in me wanted

specifics, I knew we had plenty of time to figure things out. But I never imagined we'd be apart indefinitely. That we wouldn't try, at least, to find work near each other. That our relationship might be a series of near misses, getting close enough to touch until life flung us in opposite directions. I wasn't sure I could live with a lifetime of that, even if the alternative was a lifetime without Hope.

We argued, over the phone, which is the worst. Didn't hang up on each other, but ended with goodbyes, not *I love yous*. The hard thing about long-distance—what became the *impossible* thing—is you don't see the person the next morning. There's no breakfast table to make up at, no bed to wind up in at the end of the day, tangled up together until words flow freely and differences are resolved. We had no planned visit on the horizon, and I was too caught up in my head to broach the gap.

The silence stretched for days, until the phone finally rang. But when it did, Hope's quavering voice was on the other end, telling me she was on her way to the airport, bound not for North Carolina, but Michigan, because her best friend's husband had died.

Our fight became an afterthought, a complication. And eventually we became that, to each other.

The bark of a dog on a nearby boat shatters my musing, and I blink away the memory to find Hope biting her lip, the can clenched in her fist.

"I've been ready to come back for a while," she says, running her thumb up to catch a drip of condensation on the can. My fingers curl against the memory of the same touch against my own skin. "But I was putting it off. Hadn't searched job postings. I figured telling Marissa would be a good first step. Accountability. Motivation to quit worrying about how to pick up where I left off and get on with it." She meets my eyes. "I never expected she'd invite me down here. But I couldn't turn down such a great opportunity. And when she mentioned you—"

"I was the fine print you were willing to sign off on?"

Her mouth parts, but then she nods, never one to back away from the truth. "Pretty much. Gosh, that sounds terrible."

I shrug. "I can relate, except I never got the chance."

"To come to terms with seeing me again?"

Icy condensation from my own drink trickles down my palm, the droplets tepid as sweat by the time they reach my wrist. It's baking out here, and I wish we could have this conversation while cruising the bay with a brisk wind to wick the sweat that's settling into my skin, and the task of navigating to keep my hands busy, instead of here at the dock with nothing but heavy air between us. "A heads-up would've helped. But that's not on you."

"I thought about calling. Or texting. But it had been so long." She raises the water to her lips, takes a long drink, throat working in a swallow. I shouldn't stare, but after three years I'm greedy for the sight of her. She lowers the can and I look away, picking at the tab on my own drink. "Would've been nice to know I was walking into a movie set."

It's nothing like that, but in the end, it adds up to being in the public eye, which isn't something she expected. "You really had no idea?"

She shakes her head, and it shouldn't bother me that she never watched. Never saw how my life changed. But hearing Hope say how little I factored into her decision to join the project burns afresh. I should be happy that our breakup didn't rock her world like it did mine. Should be glad to hear she's unaffected, but I'm not. I'm shook.

For three years all I've thought of is Hope, and she didn't even so much as spare me a Google search. She could be lying, but I know her tells. She was shocked as hell to see my page.

"I thought you blocked me at first," I say. "When I stopped seeing your posts."

"Blocked you?" Hope looks confused. "I didn't—" Her eyes

drop to her mug, fingers spinning the cup. "I don't follow any-one anymore. I'm not on social media."

"I know." I asked Marissa to check when Hope disappeared, horrified by the idea that she'd been upset enough to block me. But finding out she'd deleted her accounts altogether made no sense. She was never a big fan of social media, but it seemed like such a drastic step. "Why though?"

"Is it so hard to think someone might want a break from all that?" she asks. "Surface-level connections? The urge to keep up, put on a good show?"

Her quick reply doesn't ring true, but I'm on the defensive after Iris's comment earlier. "So you think this is all a waste of time? Just an ego trip?"

"What? No." She looks surprised that I took her comment that way, and I'm instantly embarrassed. "It just wasn't for me."

There's more to it. I can hear it in the way she bites off the last words, like she's pruning a branch before it bears fruit. I don't want to push, but if she's got a problem with social media, this job isn't a good fit, regardless of our history. "What we do involves a lot of visibility. You sure that won't be a prob-lem for you?"

"Are you asking if I'm ready for my ten seconds of internet fame?" Her eyes shoot to mine in an instant, hesitancy replaced by a fire that kindles an answering one in my own chest, the spark that once united us eager for a match.

I lick my lips, afraid to ask, but desperate for the answer. "I'm asking if you left social media because of me."

"You think I gave up social media for you?"

The incredulous *for you* is a scalpel, excising what meager hope I carried that she might still have feelings for me. Maybe she means to assuage my fears, tell me I'm not to blame, but all I hear is that I'm not worth the trouble.

She tucks a stray curl behind her ear, but it immediately springs free. "Despite the timing, I can assure you my departure from social media had nothing to do with us." Formality is Hope's tell. She's no-nonsense, straight to the point. Maybe it's the truth, but there's more to the story.

Her face clouds over, mouth tightening. "Marissa may have been circumspect about the scope of your online presence, but she did let me know filming the shark work-ups was a component of the work y'all do. I figured it was for a blog or campus initiative. Not something of this scope." She leans back and kicks out a leg, her knee brushing mine and I go still. "But regardless, I'm cool with it."

Part of me is worried about what she's left unsaid, but a bigger part is panicking now that there's no way out. I'm going to be trapped on this boat, all summer, with her.

Silence stretches between us, a longline threaded with countless hooks. Diving into the waters between us seems foolhardy, but for this to work, we have to get comfortable with one another, and fast. She's fidgeting, tapping her nail against the can, foot bouncing in a rhythm I feel under my soles.

I touch her wrist to pull her attention, a small brush of my fingertips, meaningless with anyone else, but Hope goes still, pupils flared, a visible manifestation of the thrum of my own telltale pulse.

"Why are you really here?" I ask. "Of all the places to start over. Why here?"

She frowns. "Isn't it obvious? The sharks."

I laugh at how quickly the reply came. "You haven't changed." Discovering she's the same Hope I fell in love with is bittersweet.

"You have." Her reply knocks me off-balance. "Here, at least." She draws a finger along her cheek, and my thumb finds its way to my own jaw, mirroring her movement. "And here." She crosses her arms to palm her own shoulders, and though she's not touching me, my skin prickles with heat. "How do you find the time to lift weights?"

"Haven't slept well the past few years." I swallow, barely breathing at the sense of imagined contact. At how much I want her to touch me for real.

"Since we…" She breaks off, eyes meeting mine. "Since I left?"

My throat is dry with the effort of forcing down the urge to reach out and draw her close, but I manage a nod. "Yeah, since then."

"And you got a boat?"

I shift, uneasy, thinking of the name on the bow. A wish that came true in the most unexpected way. "It helps to have guaranteed access to a boat. I tried to convince Marissa to be part owner but she said since I had to sacrifice my dignity, I may as well enjoy the spoils."

"Your dignity?" Hope's confused tone throws me before I realize just because she saw a glimpse of our socials doesn't mean she knows how it all began.

"All this came about after a video of me went viral."

She tilts her head. "A video you didn't create? One you had no control over?"

Looks like time apart didn't affect Hope's ability to infer exactly how something so far outside my comfort zone would affect me. "Yeah. Some bystanders recorded footage of me and uploaded it on the internet. It trended for a while." Even now, when I'm used to the scrutiny, the sheer number of humans who've witnessed a random moment of my life makes me queasy. "But it's not the video that bothered me so much as people's reactions."

Hope nods, expression grim. "People. They're the worst."

I clear my throat to cover a laugh. "People," I say in somber agreement, though Hope shoots me a side-eye that has my lips twitching.

"Can I see it?"

Why not? Seems like everyone else has. Last I checked,

months ago, the views were over thirty million. The popularity of the video is half the reason we're standing here on this boat. But if she sees it, she might view me in a different light, and I kind of like that to her, I'm still the Adrian from Before. "I won't, if you don't want me to." She means it. I know in my bones that she would respect my wishes and not search for it later.

I take a seat on the bench and rub the back of my neck. "The video's not the problem." I sigh and backtrack. "None of it's a problem. I love what I do—what we do. I love educating people about sharks."

"But…" she says, settling onto the bench opposite me.

"But it's weird that I got recognition in the field over my pecs, not my research."

Her gaze drops to my chest and a flush heats my cheeks. "Gotta admit, I'm really curious about the video now," she says with a wry grin, and I let out a surprised laugh. "But you know full well you get recognition for your research. None of our peers would collaborate with you if it weren't for your outstanding qualifications."

She's right. Our colleagues don't mess around when it comes to credentials. "Are you saying I should suck it up and get over it in the name of science?"

"Absolutely not. You have every right to not like that piece of it." She crosses her arms, her T-shirt sliding off one shoulder, exposing a peek of collarbone that my Hope-starved eyes latch onto. "But from the sound of it, you've found a way to turn that initial wave of fame into something far beyond your looks. And I'm not surprised in the slightest."

My heart soars at her frank praise. Even though there's no future for us, if she's going to stay, we need to rebuild our trust on a professional level. This would be a start. I grab my phone and search for the video, then pass it over.

Her brow furrows as she holds the phone close to her face,

shaded by one hand, and reads the title aloud. "Sexy scientist saves beachgoers from monster shark?"

I blow out an irritated breath. "The standard sensationalized language that does sharks no favors."

"As if the shark grew legs and is running amuck on a crowded beach." She gives an indignant shake of her head, the curls in her loose bun bobbing with the movement.

A small chuckle escapes me, despite the embarrassment. "Best not give Hollywood any ideas."

Then her thumb hits the play button and nerves quell my laughter. I shift my focus to a nearby cabin cruiser on its third attempt at docking. The passengers in life jackets are calling out conflicting instructions to the frustrated man at the wheel, his face flushed red, and I feel my own cheeks burning as Hope watches the clip.

I know what she's seeing. Me on the beach in red swim trunks, instructing the crowd to step back and give the animal space. Me checking in with the young angler, caught up in fishing line and fear. Me bending over the blacktip shark to pull it into the waves, off the hot sand.

Hope sucks her teeth. "Why didn't he release it right away?"

"They wanted a photo-op." I point to the screen, the sting of watching the video receding. "See the rest of the group there?" Hope nods. "Things got out of hand."

The video ends and she passes back my phone. "You did good."

I shrug. "I work with sharks for a living."

"But you were chilling at the beach. You weren't expecting to have to defuse a situation with a wild animal and a crowd of onlookers." Her words are an encouragement I didn't know I needed. "I don't see anything to be ashamed of."

My lips twist in a rueful smile. "Guess you didn't read the comments."

"About you being the world's most eligible shark scientist?"

Her smile is the slightest tease. At least she didn't mention the ones about the red swimsuit. "That part at least seems to be true, judging by your Instagram."

"I don't want to be—" I bite off the rest of the sentence. I never wanted to be the world's most eligible anything. I wanted to be taken, claimed by Hope. Now all I want is to forget about that side of me. The part that yearns for love, a relationship. Love is unpredictable and I have enough instability in my life.

I lift my hips and shove my phone in my pocket, rethinking that when I remember my shorts are still damp. "Anyway, I decided I could either wait for it to go away or make something better of it, like Marissa suggested. So I started uploading sharky content to YouTube. Shared informative videos about shark research and conservation. Grew our platform with worthy content that I could control."

"And now this." Hope casts an assessing glance around the boat, and I try not to squirm when her appraisal lands on me. "I can see why you're protective of what you've created." Her eyes are soft, and all I can think of in that moment is how much better it would be with her here. How much I've missed her. How I'm not worried about protecting my work, it's my heart on the line. "Do you still want me to leave?"

With her here, there's no hope of moving on. But can I put aside my feelings for her sake? We fell in love the first summer we met. Maybe this will be the summer I finally get over her.

ten

hope

Adrian hasn't answered. He sits across from me, silent, taking time to consider what I've asked of him, eyes downcast and face shuttered, unreadable. Something jealousy-adjacent flares in my chest at the thought of all the fans and followers who've had access to him while to me he's become a stranger.

So much has happened since I left. The internet fame. The career pivot. The how and why is shocking, but his success is no surprise. And even though he left a Mariana Trench–sized gouge in my heart, I am so proud of him. What hurts is that losing him knocked me off-course, yet he kept going without missing a beat.

Until I fell in love with him, I assumed I needed to be single to have the career of my dreams, that planning life around someone else would hold me back, and that belief never quite left, despite how different our relationship felt than what I'd imagined about love.

Ever since I learned a career in science was a possibility, I've been focused on getting there. I was a curious kid, especially when it came to the natural world. Always fascinated by seaweed on the beach or minnows in the shallows. Always asking why. My parents seemed content to accept rather than ask questions. Rather than careers, they both had jobs they neither loved nor loathed. Work was a way to pay the bills, to take care of me and each other.

In my mind, they settled into a boring life, one I never wanted. I equated love with stagnation, or worse, with putting dreams on hold until life intervened and took away the desire. But meeting Adrian changed all that. Our relationship didn't interfere with my dreams or take away my desires. Not until I was ready to apply for a doctoral program.

Adrian was looking for a postdoc position, and it was the perfect time to at least try to be in the same city, or at least the same state. I was as excited to be close to him, to maybe even wake up next to him every morning. But the more time we spent planning and arranging and shifting and worrying over how to mesh our lives, the more I missed the simplicity of our relationship before we tried to arrange our lives around one another. Missed how easy it felt to love him when practicality didn't factor in.

All my worst fears about love being a hindrance seemed to be coming true. So I started looking at universities further away, ones not previously on my radar. I even considered applying to colleges out of the country, anything to put off merging our lives like a shared calendar. I loved Adrian with all my heart, but I worried I'd be settling to work my dreams around his. I wanted to stay together, I just wasn't sure about the next step. Except Adrian didn't see it that way. He thought I was looking for a way out.

"You can stay." The rumble of his voice brings me back to the present. "But if we'll be working together, there are things we need to discuss. Because our relationship—"

I raise a hand to halt this detour into personal territory. "Is in the past. We don't have to talk about it."

He frowns. "We kind of do. I want to make sure this is a comfortable work environment."

Comfortable was how we used to cuddle on the sofa after a day at sea, reveling in the miracle of air-conditioning and crushed ice, my head pillowed on his chest. Comfortable is not arm's length, watchful and wary. But I need to adjust and accept the change. That's why I'm here.

"I appreciate that. What can I do to put you at ease?"

"Put *me* at ease?" The furrow between his brows deepens. "I was worried about you."

That makes two of us, but not for the reason he thinks. "No worries on my account."

His teeth sink into his lower lip, uncertain. "But the fact remains that we used to date. You don't think that might affect our interactions?"

Ugh, I hate this. Hate that this is a million times harder than I expected. Hate that there's no way I can ever trust him with my heart again, even though part of me wants to fling myself into his arms and never let go. "You're right. It happened. *We* happened."

His eyes meet mine, but resolve has solidified in my chest. I'm here to get my life back on track. Our paths diverged three years ago. He stayed on course, and I'm here to find my way back. "We have a history, Adrian. But that's all it is. History." Saying it aloud is as much for my benefit as his. My heart needs to be onboard.

He gives a small shake of his head. "I can't just erase more than five years of memories." Over half a decade. But we've been apart almost as long. "I don't know how to pretend we're strangers."

I didn't come here to pretend, but I'm also not here to open old wounds. "I'm not denying our history." Though it's hard to think of it in the past tense with his presence so immediate—

sitting mere feet away, legs splayed, arms crossed, so near I can see the rise of his chest with each inhale.

"But I just want to move on." Like he so clearly has. "To treat this like a job."

He meets my eyes, expression serious. "It is a job."

I huff out a breath. "One where there's no underlying tension between me and my boss."

"I'm not your boss," he says.

"Supervisor."

His scratches his beard. "I never thought of it that way." I can see the wheels churning in his mind. He's prone to finding worst-case scenarios, and there are a million ways this could go wrong.

But after a moment, he says, "We don't have an HR department, but I'll have our lawyer draft some paperwork to protect your employment. Make it clear you report to Marissa, not me."

"That's a good call." Part of me can't help but notice as much as his life's changed, he's still the man I fell in love with. Considerate. Thoughtful. Careful in all things, except in his handling of my heart.

He holds my gaze, eyes searching my face. Emotions drift across his dark brown eyes like the play of ripples on the seafloor, then his expression smooths into resolve. "Then let's move forward as colleagues, and let the past stay gone."

Exactly what I wanted, though the word feels hollow. But Adrian-as-Colleague is a step beyond the No-Adrian Rule. A way to coexist without the burden of holding on to old hurts. The next step in letting go.

The boat bobs sharply on the placid surface, and I glance up to see Marissa climbing aboard. She sends a tentative smile my way. "Since everyone's here, I thought maybe we could salvage the day with a trip out to Winyah Bay."

"To tag sharks?" I smile for what feels like the first time in

SECOND TIDE'S THE CHARM 79

years, but I temper my expectations. "Or just to get me acquainted with the area?"

"You came to work, right?" Marissa's words are a dare, and I freaking love a challenge, bruised heart or not.

I crack my knuckles. "Heck yes I did."

"Then let's go find some sharks," she says.

Go time.

Wait time, more like. Setting lines is methodical and we have to adhere to the time allotted by the research permits. Once the lines are in the water, we might hook a shark in five minutes or half an hour or not at all. In the meantime, Marissa outlines the data she's hoping to collect this summer to study shark immune response to stress, and Adrian's current focus on migratory patterns of sharks off the Carolina coast.

He leaves us to it, moving off into the stern to work on his laptop. Gabe plops down next to me and opens up his camera case. A rush of queasiness lurches up my throat at the sight. I take a deep inhale through my nose and focus on my breaths until the sensation abates, like I've done countless times on rough seas. But this time what's making my stomach unsettled is the thought of a camera following my every move.

When Gabe hoists a camcorder onto his shoulder, I inadvertently pull back, tense. He must notice my stiff posture, because he leans away from the viewfinder with a reassuring smile. "Don't worry, this will all be edited before we share it, and you'll always get a chance to sign off before we do. No live filming in the field. Boss's orders."

"He's worried I'll do something to embarrass y'all?" I'm worried enough for both of us. I tanked my first and only on-camera interview, but this time I'll be doing familiar work. As long as I can forget about being filmed, I should be fine.

"Not at all." Cooler in hand, Adrian appears, startling me. His physical presence—very physical, with the way his lightweight tee clings to his torso—is going to take getting used to, since for years he's been confined only to my thoughts. "It's our standard practice. For one thing, we don't want to bore viewers with hours of nonaction. For another, it allows us to control the content, to ensure—"

"Shark on the line," Marissa calls out, and I'm on my feet in an instant, worries forgotten. We all rush to the stern, where she hauls in the line carefully, hand over hand, until a fluttering dorsal fin appears alongside the boat. "Little guy." She smiles over her shoulder. "Want to help with the work-up or watch this first time around?"

"Help, obviously." But my hands are shaky as I step in between them. After the tumultuous morning, I feel like this is a performance eval, and considering I just got fired and my new colleague is my ex, my confidence isn't so hot. Once I lean over the side of the boat and reach over to help secure the shark, though, my nerves flee. Marissa's right, it's a small shark, and I instantly recognize the characteristic elongated caudal fin and pointed snout of an Atlantic sharpnose shark.

Catching one is a normal occurrence here, but there's no containing the leap of joy I have at seeing the animal just below the surface, the distinctive shape one I haven't seen in years, yet familiar as ever. I half turn to ask Adrian for a tape measure and catch sight of Gabe. Nerves surge, but he's lowered the camera off his shoulder, holding it casually at his side as his knees flex with the rhythm of the waves.

He smiles. "Figure you deserve a warm-up round, especially given the gauntlet you went through earlier. We've filmed enough tags that missing one won't matter."

Nice of him, but before I can reply, Adrian hands me the thin tape measure, and muscle memory takes over, guided by my years of study. I put the tape on the shark's snout and stretch it carefully along the length of its body and relay the number to

Adrian, who scribbles it in a notebook, hand clamped to keep the pages from blowing in the breeze.

Marissa's frown of concentration hasn't downgraded to a scowl, which is a good sign. We've never worked together but she's got a no-nonsense reputation, and I don't expect her to cut me any slack just because we're friends. I work around her to wrap the tape measure around the shark's trunk and call out the measurement.

"Got it," Adrian says. On paper, this first trip out with him should be weird, but in practice it's anything but. No time to worry about awkwardness when you're dealing with a live animal and every minute counts. I step back at Marissa's direction and switch tasks with Adrian—me taking notes, him stepping in for blood draw.

After taking a tissue sample, he beckons me forward to demonstrate the procedure for implanting the dart tag used for this species. It's a quick procedure that doesn't harm the animal and allows for monitoring on the abundance of this species in the area and will be used for a variety of studies if the shark is recaptured. Then it's time to release the shark.

Simple. Straightforward. Fantastic.

My smile is so broad my cheeks hurt. Just a routine workup, but I'm elated. Energy buzzes through my veins, and the salty ocean air is electric. My limbs are abuzz with adrenaline, but my head feels clear in a way I haven't experienced in years. Adrian steps up next to me, and when he sees my face, a wide grin spreads across his cheeks. Even with his eyes hidden behind reflective blue sunglasses, I can feel the warmth of his gaze.

"Like you never left." Adrian holds out his palm for a high five and I slap it without thinking. The casual contact has my blood buzzing for an entirely different reason than a moment ago, and I yank my hand away, but his touch tingles on my skin, like tiny aftershocks.

His smile fades, replaced by a neutral expression. "Ready for the camera?"

I take another step back, queasy all over again. What if the camera had captured my reaction to that brief moment of connection? What if everything I feel for him will be visible on the screens of the thousands of people who watch the video, and worse, what if holding back while working together leaves me craving him more than ever?

eleven

adrian

Three times today I've touched Hope. Once to steady her when she was flustered in the water—an instinctive grab to pull her to safety, which I barely had time to process. Once when she had that close encounter with a cooler—and awkward as the moment was, the way she clung to me afterward nearly undid me, all soft curves and wary trust.

And just now, a high five, the most platonic of all touches, and yet when our palms met and my fingertips grazed the delicate skin at the inside of her wrist, it was enough to ignite a hunger that's lain dormant for years. A forbidden attraction I absolutely cannot indulge.

Instead, I kept to the boundaries of our arrangement, remaining solidly in colleague territory by tossing out the first thing that came to mind…an offhand, rhetorical question. Given her performance with the first shark, I assumed the camera would be a nonissue. Turns out I was wrong.

The moment Gabe started filming, Hope's confidence evaporated. We had the good fortune to catch another shark shortly after the first—a juvenile dusky. Small enough to handle with ease, but when I glance over to see if Hope's ready to lend a hand, she's frozen, eyes locked on the camera like it's about to leap from his hands and pounce.

"Hope," Marissa says, her voice tight with tension, "time to get started."

With a shaky nod, she steps forward, but her movements are unsteady, like she's in a daze.

"Tape measure," I prompt.

"She knows," Marissa snaps, and I wince. I was trying to help, not undermine Hope, but I get it. I need to chill. My own nerves kick into high gear with a new awareness of being filmed. How will my interactions with Hope translate without context? Our first day of field research together and already the cracks in this arrangement are showing like a leaky fiberglass hull.

"Maybe you should do this one," I hear Hope say, and turn to find her holding out the tape measure toward Marissa. This is a woman who I've seen do a work-up on a five-hundred-pound tiger shark without batting an eyelash, and yet when she holds out her hand, it's trembling.

"Sure." Marissa gestures toward me. "You assist Adrian then."

Great. This is a small shark, less than a meter, which means she's going to have to get close to me. Not a problem with anyone else, but I don't want Hope on this boat, let alone in my space. "I've got it," I tell them, but Marissa frowns.

"Stop being weird."

"I'm not being weird." During our quick exchange, Hope's come over to crouch next to me, and my whole body is tense. I will myself to calm down, not wanting to startle the animal with my nerves. "Really, I'm good here. You'll need to take notes." Preferably from the other side of the boat, practical or not.

She nods, looking more composed, and rises to her feet, then takes a seat and sets the open laptop on her bare knees. I swallow and look away.

My cousin leans around me to measure the shark. Under her breath, she asks, "You cool?"

"Fine," I say through gritted teeth. Not only do I need to keep my composure around Hope, I need to do it convincingly. If there's a whiff of something off between me and the newest addition to the team, we could lose credibility. I need to make sure no one speculates about our history, or who we are to each other. I worked too hard to build this platform to screw things up, and much as I don't want her here, I couldn't bear to have Hope's reputation called into question. The line between who we were to each other and our working relationship needs to be clear as the south Florida waters where we met.

"Uh, Marissa, what's your password?" Hope holds up the laptop. "Lock screen."

"Are you serious right now?" Marissa asks. Her voice is tight with tension, but I can't fault her intensity. The shark is top priority and right now, we're not working as a team. "Just use the notebook."

Marissa wraps the tape measure around the shark's body and calls out a girth measurement to Hope, who mutters, "Shit."

I snap my head up, but she dodges her eyes away. "Pencil snapped."

Gabe digs in his pocket and holds out a pen, keeping the camera aimed steadfastly toward the shark—and away from Hope. He's been silent, which isn't normal for him. Usually, he likes to chime in with funny comments to coax explanations out of us when we forget that what's just another day of fieldwork for us is new territory for viewers. Seems like he's trying to remain unobtrusive for Hope's benefit, but his lack of chatter only adds to my nerves.

Marissa glances over her shoulder and frowns at Hope. "You got those measurements down?"

"Yup, 98 centimeters." She sits back, cross-legged, and makes a notation.

"Eighty-eight." Marissa turns her focus back to the shark. "Pay attention."

It's a reminder for me as well. Hope doesn't need my eyes on her, and normally I'm so focused I tune everything else out. But I don't understand how the camera's got her so off her game. These are basic steps we mastered years ago, and not only did she say her prior job involved fieldwork, she also did all this ten minutes ago with the first shark.

Is it me? I hate to think she's that bothered by my presence. Then again, a few hours ago I did try to send her home.

Gabe steps forward to get a better angle of Marissa, and Hope sits up straight, like I used to when my piano teacher called out my poor posture.

"Just pretend I'm not here," he says, eyes on the viewfinder.

"Yeah. Of course." Hope nods so vigorously I'm worried for her vertebrae. "I'll just stand out of the way and—"

"We need to wrap this up," Marissa interrupts, saving Hope from rambling. "Can you pass me the case of syringes?"

Hope steps forward, freezing when Gabe swings the camera her way. She lifts one hand in what might be either a wave or gesture of surrender and sidesteps her way toward us.

She hesitates, not close enough to step in if need be. I gesture her nearer with a jerk of my chin, and she squats down. She doesn't look at me, but I can't help but catalog her profile in the flat light of an oncoming storm. Upturned nose, rounded cheeks, full lips parted with rapid breaths, like a landed fish trying to draw in oxygen.

Voice low, I say, "He's not going to bite."

"It's a female," Hope hisses, "and I'm not worried about that."

"I meant Gabe."

Her warm brown skin has turned ashen, a match for the overcast sky. She grips the side of the boat like she's about to lose the contents of her stomach, but her next words make it clear that seasickness isn't the culprit. "What about the people watching?"

Before I can formulate an answer, Marissa barks my name, calling my attention back to the task at hand. Good thing my back is to Gabe, or else the lens would probably capture a wide-eyed look of panic not at all suitable for a scientist handling a shark.

The wind is picking up, clouds lowering, and a chill drips down my nape with the first drop of rain. She has every right to worry. I do, every time we upload new content. The potential for a positive impact was enough for me to risk my professional reputation and privacy to launch this channel, but despite our complicated past, I'd never choose to risk Hope.

But she's made her choice. Sink or swim, we're in this boat together. And right now, we're pulling each other under.

twelve

hope

"I low-key wish we hadn't caught any more sharks after the first one," I tell Marissa. I never in my life thought I'd say this, let alone think it. A day without sharks is normally a big disappointment. Typical, yes, but with months or years of preparation and the constraint of narrow windows in which to complete field studies, every day counts. But coming up empty would've been preferable to my nightmare performance.

A few steps ahead of me on Adrian's driveway, Marissa spins around, canvas bag of supplies twirling in an arc with the force of her movement. "You did not just say that to me."

I dodge my eyes away from her incredulous look under pretense of checking out the property. We drove over to Adrian's house to stow gear, and my first impulse was to rush and be out of here before he arrives. But I can't help lingering in the dappled sunlight at the foot of the stairs leading up to his raised cottage.

The house sits on stilts, a porch swing tucked invitingly underneath, along with more practical items like a boat trailer and storage locker. Overhead, a live oak with trailing Spanish moss sways in a breeze tinged with the loamy scent of the

Waccamaw River, just visible through cypress trees. There's a screened-in front porch at the top of the steps, and if things between us were different, I'd already be up the steps to see if the deck offers a clear view of the water.

No surprise that Adrian's a homeowner—our last few months together were spent browsing condo listings—but this place is the stuff of dreams. Idyllic, perched on a waterfront lot with neighbors close enough for comfort but far enough for privacy. The sort of home we used to dream about when the lights were off, and practicality faded away. When our future together could stretch as wide as imagining.

Seeing the manifestation of those dreams, being here, I begin to grasp what my hesitancy must've cost Adrian. How putting the first step on hold poked holes in our watertight trust. How the leak of my doubts worked against his trust to erode our relationship.

But whatever state our breakup left him in, it's clear he's moved past it, and the insecurities that plagued me on the boat come roaring back. All this time I've been tied up in knots over him, while he was building a home. A future. I pass the inviting steps, into the shade underneath the house, ready to ditch the supplies and get out of here.

Glancing around the open space, intersected by sturdy support beams, I catch sight of a pair of kayaks, and next to them, a set of weights and a jump rope. An image of Adrian in a sweat-soaked tank top, rope spinning, lips pursed in concentration, drills into my mind, and I slash my eyes away from the gym setup to find Marissa watching me.

"Did you forget the part where I bungled the units of measurement?" Cringe overtakes me. "I haven't made a mistake like that since middle school. I was basically useless once Gabe started filming."

She takes off her sunglasses, leaving me feeling exposed under her assessing gaze. I know we're going to have to discuss strategies to work successfully with Adrian, but not here, not in the space where his personality—the familiar and the new—is everywhere around us.

"Tell me you're not going to let one bad day get in your head," she says, and lifts her chin to indicate where I should set down my cargo.

I haul the bucket over to an open rack of shelving and set it down, feeling grimy and out of sorts. All I want is to shower off the remnants of this day, but erasing the effects of my performance won't be so simple.

"My first day back and I fell off a dock, Marissa." Not to mention the cooler incident, which haunts me with a slurry of awkwardness and desire, underlaid by my body's inexplicable reaction to Adrian, despite my desire to remain unaffected. "Do you know how many docks I've successfully walked on without falling in? Hundreds, if not a thousand."

She laughs. "That's not the flex you think it is."

"Tell me about it." I let out a frustrated sigh. "That's what makes losing it on camera even worse. So much for a comeback." Adrian's no longer just my ex-boyfriend, he's a colleague I let down.

But the moment I saw the camera, I was transported to the last and only time I was on TV, a city council meeting that went from routine to disastrous. The memory of that colossal screwup kept me frazzled today, terrified of making a mistake that would live on forever on the internet.

"It's day one," Marissa says. She opens a plastic cupboard and stashes the bag inside. "And a lot of today was my fault." A smirk slants across her face. "Well, aside from whatever happened with that cooler. That was all you and Adrian." Her small nose wrinkles, like she regrets the mental image.

Despite my embarrassment, I chuckle. "Can't imagine how that looked from the outside."

"It was tough to watch," she says. "And I didn't tell you the whole truth, but I didn't want to overwhelm you."

"With facts you should've disclosed before I drove down here?"

She grimaces. "My plan was to ease you into it. I fully admit I may have got overexcited when you reached out. At first, I thought you were asking because you knew about the channel, but once it became clear you had no idea…" She shrugs, her slender shoulders lifting under her loose T-shirt. "I should've told you before you came all the way here, but I was worried you'd change your mind."

"That was my decision to make." I raise my brows meaningfully. "With all the relevant information."

"Google exists," she counters.

"You knew Adrian was an off-limits topic for me."

She leans against one of the support pillars, arms crossed. "I didn't realize how far you took it. I've been careful not to bring up my cousin, but I didn't know you'd cut yourself off from the community completely."

"Only in the past couple years." The concrete floor is gritty, and I scuff at the sand with my foot, giving myself a moment to find the words. Sharing my feelings is hard, especially when they feel like shortcomings. "Once I committed to staying for the duration of the Lake Michigan study, it was too hard to watch from the sidelines. Everyone was doing big things." And I was busy trying to get over my boyfriend and figure out the next step in my career. "Which is why I reached out to you."

"Because I wasn't?" Her mouth tilts with an ironic smile, calling out my inconsistency. Even though she never brought up the channel, we talked often about her research and conservation work. Though it wasn't easy to not be a part of things, seeing her succeed never made me feel left out.

"Because you never judged my choices." Not even the decision to leave Adrian behind. "I felt safe coming to you for help."

"And I breached that trust." Her smile falls. "I should've made sure you knew what you were getting into. But I'm glad you stayed."

She turns to latch the cupboard, then walks past me, back out into the driveway. I give one last lingering look toward the kayaks before following her. What I wouldn't give for a relaxing trip down the river to ease the day's stress.

Catching up to her, I ask, "Even though I panicked on camera?"

She tugs open the driver's side door, and I follow suit, climbing inside. "We can work on that. How about you start with watching our recent videos so you can get an idea of how things usually go?"

Exactly what I would've done had I known the full scale of what this summer would entail. Studying, and research is what makes me feel prepared to tackle any challenge. "Trying to butter me up with homework so I forgive you?"

She chuckles and turns the key in the ignition and rolls down the windows. "Is it working?"

"I know you had my best interests at heart, but I'm capable of managing my own life." A few years ago, I might have chosen to let my hurt fester rather than doing the hard work of articulating my feelings, like I did with Adrian. But I've learned not to stay quiet. To work on relationships, even when it's easier to let grievances build up to the breaking point. "From here on out, you need to trust me with the truth."

"I'm sorry, Hope." Letting go of the steering wheel, she shifts to face me, her brown eyes serious. "Jokes aside, I know I screwed up."

If only I'd been able to talk through things earlier with Adrian, maybe things would be different now. But while we lost each other because of a hesitancy to speak our minds, our relationship wasn't destined for forever. My propensity to push boundaries, to leap into new opportunities will always leave him unsettled, and me on edge, worried I'll let him down. He may have taken a chance on starting a channel, but he's still the same cautious man I fell in love with, the one who needs a steady partner.

Friendships are easier. Less messy. Once I leave the team, my choices won't directly affect her, and I won't have to worry about letting her down. "Forgiven."

Day one was an unqualified disaster, but I'm back on a shark study with a good friend. The angst with Adrian will sort itself out if I focus on what I came for, starting with a marathon watchfest so I'm prepared to crush the assignment on our next trip out.

Unfortunately, I have to wait for my shot at redemption. Everyone else has plans for the next day, so no fieldwork was scheduled. I'm all too familiar with the unavoidable reality of weather delays that halt projects in their tracks, sometimes for weeks on end. You'd think a few more days after years of time away from sharks wouldn't matter, but being this close and not being able to get back on the water is like an ice cream shop flipping the sign to closed in a toddler's face.

Part of me is grateful for a breather from Adrian. But a bigger part of me knows that out of sight doesn't equal out of mind when it comes to him. Never has, and if I don't find a way to break his hold on me, I'll be eighty and looking over my shoulder for a glimpse of his smile. His dang hoodie will be moth-eaten and still at the back of my closet—or in this case, crammed under the rest of the clothes in my suitcase, since I forgot to change out of it the morning I left.

Tossing it in the trash at a gas station on the way felt creepily akin to evidence disposal, so I stashed it away from prying eyes. Not like Marissa will be going through my stuff, but with my "room" being an air mattress in the corner of her living room, I don't exactly have a lot of privacy. I took advantage of her being out of the house to check out their channel, since watching videos of Adrian is not something I want an audience for.

In a shocking turn of events, it's hard to remain objective and pick up tips for how to act comfortable on camera while your ex-boyfriend is on-screen. When I find myself staring dreamily at his smile for the third time, I switch to a more productive form of research: seeking out the research Adrian's published in the past few years.

I spend an hour or so on a deep dive of his studies, and don't come up for air until my phone—brought back from its watery demise after hours spent trying out hacks we found online—buzzes with a text. I slam the laptop screen closed like whoever texted me has access to my search history.

Zuri: Scale of 1 to 10: how much do you hate me for not spilling the beans about your influencer ex?

Hope: You tried. I just chose not to listen.

Zuri: Ostrich-syndrome at its finest.

Hope: That's a myth. Ostriches don't actually stick their heads in the sand.

Zuri: Seeing him again can't be all that bad if your ability to bore me with biology factoids is intact.

I press the call button and lift the phone to my ear.

"Hello?" Zuri answers right away.

"It absolutely is that bad." I slump back against the chair. "Also, 'factoid' is a buzzword. Facts is perfectly adequate."

Her groan of annoyance makes me smile but also sends a pang of homesickness through me. I've missed her even in the short time we spent apart. Our friendship has always been of the pick-up-right-where-we-left-off variety, and I'll never stop being grateful for that.

"You could've tried harder to warn me that Adrian is famous."

"Mega famous," she says, and then we're both laughing at the ridiculousness of the situation. "Last time I checked he only had a few thousand followers."

Now that I've had time to come to grips with it, his social media success doesn't surprise me. Adrian's parents had to move around a lot for work and that meant he had to learn how to make friends fast. Between his enigmatic personality and his expertise, it's no wonder people flock to his content.

"Still can't believe I've been sucked into all this."

"In a way, I think it was good to go in with no expectations. No time to talk yourself out of what's a really cool opportunity."

"You sound like Marissa."

"I always knew I liked that woman," she says, and I can't help but laugh. One of my friends tried to warn me, another hid the full truth, but they both thought I could do this. That counts for something.

Still, Zuri knows how badly I botched things the last time I had a big audience; she was there. I tell her about what happened when Gabe turned on the camera. "It was just like what happened at the town hearing, Zuri. Stakes were high, and I lost my cool."

"You should tell them about what happened," she says.

"And lose what's left of my dignity?" Not to mention the shame of letting down my colleagues and friends.

The whiz of a blender comes on in the background. Probably making one of her signature smoothie bowls. My stomach rumbles in response and I pull the phone away to check the time. Well past lunch.

The noise cuts off and she says, "At least explain you're not a fan of going on record. Maybe they have some strategies."

I stand, stiff from sitting in the chair for hours, and grab my purse and the spare key Marissa made for me. "They already offered, but it's not just the camera, it's—"

"Your sexy ex?" Zuri sighs. "I'd be flustered around that man, too."

"Watch yourself, woman."

"Why?" Her voice is deceptively innocent. "He's single, right? Or did I miss that in my snooping?"

Blood thuds in my temples, obscuring rational thought. Zuri would never flirt with someone I dated, no matter how attractive. "Yes." The word leaks past my clenched teeth. "But—"

"But he's Adrian," she says. "And you're not over him."

My mouth falls open, face ablaze. She was baiting me, and I totally swallowed the hook. "You say that like it's reasonable." My lack of denial stings my own eardrums.

"Love is never reasonable."

Love is not a word in my current vocabulary. Regard. Esteem. Civility. Those apply. "Who said anything about love? What I feel for him is an attachment I need to break."

"Sometimes I think you forget that you are not your parents." They met in high school. Went to colleges on opposite sides of the state, but after a year apart, missed each other so much that they sacrificed hefty scholarships and switched to a more affordable two-year school where they could be together. If you hear them tell it, it's the love story of the century, but I never saw it that way.

"And for the record," Zuri continues, "what they have together isn't so bad." There's an edge to her voice, and I bite my lip. She married her high school sweetheart and settled in our hometown, but that's where the similarity ends. She started her own business and chased her dreams alongside her husband.

My parents never seemed to have any ambition beyond marriage and raising me. I'm grateful for their love, and I know putting their all into each other and our family fulfills them, but I could never be content to subsist on love alone. Sooner or later, I'd have to compromise like they did, settle for a diluted version of my dreams.

"I know. But somewhere along the way they convinced themselves they'd be happier with a different life than what they wanted at first."

"They fell in love," Zuri says, proving my point.

But while I never wanted that path for myself, I'd never disparage what Zuri had with Eric, or my parents for the love they share. "If we had moved in together during my doctoral studies, what would happen when I finished? He'd be established in the area, but I'd be looking for a postdoc position. He'd have to leave his job, or I'd have to settle for whatever I could find nearby."

The bitter memory of our last argument comes to mind, him telling me I was focused on the problems, not a solution, and me unable to see why he thought ahead in all things, but wasn't worried about how we'd manage our relationship and careers once I finished school. I push the memory aside and head for my car with the intent of stress-devouring some real Southern barbecue after this conversation.

"You were willing to move across the country to help me," Zuri says.

"But I knew that wouldn't be forever. You'd find your feet, and wouldn't need me."

"So you're scared of forever?"

Another resident is approaching, and I wait for them to pass, smile pasted on my face, though inside I'm reeling from being called out. I hold the phone closer, not wanting to admit this aloud. "I was never one of those people who wanted to find a person and build my life around them. And then I met Adrian and despite all my best efforts, I was starting to."

"And that's bad?"

"It's not what I envisioned."

"Envisioned when? When you were eighteen?" Her skepticism feels unwarranted. Some people know what they want from the start. "You can always revisit your hypothesis. Relationships are fluid. They change over time, just like people do. Love is the constant."

Except, it wasn't. Adrian's love is gone. All that's left between us is the sticky complication of residual familiarity and one-sided lust. "I liked it better when we didn't talk about this." I detour past the parking lot to the pine grove to the side of the complex and plop down on a shady bench.

"You kind of took away that option when you decided to work with him." Murmuring comes from her end of the line, and her next words are muffled, spoken to someone else. "Just a minute, sweetie. Grab your books and I'll be right in." There's a rustle, then she says, "If you're committed to seeing this through, I know you'll find a way to make it work, regardless of your feelings."

Adrian and I fell in love while working on a summer shark study. This time, I need to devise a formula to reverse the process.

thirteen

adrian

One day. I went one day without Hope after years, and yet I'm already craving her like oxygen. The wise thing to do would be to stay away, see her only in the context of the field study. Unfortunately, she's staying at my cousin's all summer, and tonight Marissa is hosting pizza night, a monthly tradition that often includes brainstorming sessions.

It would've been wise to stay away this time, but my excuse for not skipping was the giant pile of dirty clothes by my closet. My washer gave out last week, and I haven't gotten around to getting it fixed. May as well do laundry here and save a trip to the laundromat. Besides, I promised Hope I would treat her like any other colleague. If she was any other scientist stepping in for the summer, I'd be eager to make her feel welcome in our tight-knit crew, and pizza night is the perfect icebreaker.

I transfer the load of towels to the dryer and leave my hide-out before the others start to wonder what's up. The moment I arrived, Marissa informed me tonight we're making homemade pizza rather than ordering in—team building, she called it. Really just a way to get Hope and I used to each other through forced proximity, like building up an immunity.

Marissa stationed me on dough duty at the opposite end of the counter from Hope, who's perched on a barstool, her hair freed from its usual ponytail and floating around her shoulders in juicy curls. She's smiling wide at Gabe's favorite story—how diving with a whale shark led him to a career shift from land to sea—and the rapt look on her face, lush lips parted, eyes sparkling with interest, has me transfixed.

Next to me, Marissa's rinsing cherry tomatoes in a colander. She bumps my shoulder and mutters, "Quit staring, creep."

I narrow my eyes but return my attention to the pizza dough under my flour-dusted fingers, pressing it into a lopsided disk. "Wasn't staring."

"Were too." Trust Marissa to call me out. "Thought you two agreed to keep things strictly business."

"We did." I clear my throat and lower my voice. "We are."

"Mm-hm." She packs far too much doubt into those two syllables. "You're going to have to do a more convincing job of acting like it next time we're on the boat."

"I don't need the reminder." I haven't been able to think of anything else, but that doesn't mean I'm closer to solving it. "Hope was the one who panicked," I add, right as Marissa shuts off the faucet.

My words hang in the sudden stillness. The only noise is the splatter of droplets pinging into the sink from the colander. Gabe cuts his eyes toward Hope, then back to me, silently saying, *Fix this!*

Knuckle-deep in pizza dough, escape is impossible. "Uh, sorry. I didn't…" I find the courage to meet Hope's eyes and am devastated to see no traces of her calm happiness from a moment ago. My fault. "We should've prepped you better. Plenty of the scientists we work with get stage fright." But I've never seen Hope shy away from public speaking, which is what makes her obvious nerves so baffling.

"Happens to the best of us," Gabe says. "Why do you think I'm the one holding the camera?"

Hope huffs out a chuckle. "Nervous as I was, I'd much rather be the one working with the sharks." The laugh seems forced, but I know the sentiment isn't. The work wasn't what threw her off. Was it me?

Marissa dumps the tomatoes onto a kitchen towel. "The problem is, if people watching notice your nerves, they might attribute it to you being nervous to handle the sharks."

Hope's eyebrows go up, like she never considered the possibility. "The sharks were the only thing keeping me halfway chill." She picks up a basil stem and plucks the leaves off, piling them on the cutting board. Her fingers are long and capable, the nails clipped short and bare.

Those same fingers have locked with mine countless times, massaged knotted muscles in my shoulders after long days in the lab—skin against heated skin—slipped around my waist during sunset walks on the beach, and molded against my body later, on the couch, the bed...

Memories like these, even the innocent ones, make it dangerously hard to maintain a façade of professionalism.

"I did some research," she says, and I pull my attention back to the conversation. "Watched some of your recent videos so I have a better idea of what to expect."

My hands go still on the dough, and I keep my head down, but my pulse is racing. She watched our content? That's what I always dreamed of, catching her attention again, showing her that losing her didn't wreck me. But she only watched because she's committed to doing her best, not out of interest in me. She's sticking to the plan, and I need to get onboard.

"Practice might help too." I keep my tone casual to let her know I'm trying to find a solution, not find fault. "Filming something that's not for the channel. Just to take the edge off your nerves."

She shakes her head. "It's the idea of permanence, that peo-ple will be able to watch and rewatch the video, that makes me tense." Her shoulders hitch up toward her ears, like even talking about it is stressful. She scoops up the chopped basil and dumps it into a bowl, the golden-brown skin of her arms pebbled with goose bumps that I suspect have nothing to do with the air-conditioning.

"If I know the video won't be shared," she says, "I don't think I'll feel the same pressure."

The oven beeps, signaling it's preheated, and Gabe sets a sheet pan on the stovetop. "Easy solution. We film a shark-free segment to introduce you. Take the boat out to the bay and let you talk a bit about your background, what got you into shark research, that sort of thing. That way you won't have to worry about doing any actual science while you get your jitters out."

Hope brightens at this, sitting up higher on the barstool, and her eager look is back. So cute I have to bite down on my lip. "I'm game for that. Could I write myself a script?"

Gabe pauses, clearly giving it thought. "I'm not going to stop you, but it might be a better preparation for the rest of the summer if you don't. All our content is unscripted, hence why Adrian never wants to livestream. We can edit whatever doesn't work, but it keeps the consistency."

"Problem is," Marissa chimes in, "we're assisting a team from Charleston next week. They're performing ultrasounds on pregnant sharks."

"You're doing ultrasounds?" The glee in Hope's voice should be contagious, but it just amps up my anxiety over everything going well.

Marissa nods. "We've been hoping to showcase a variety of field research techniques, so this has been in the works for a while."

"Which means there's a lot at stake." All eyes shift to me, but this is the element that unnerves me the most. "Bringing in other researchers means they're putting their trust in us to show their work in a positive light. We've got to make sure everyone is at their best."

The excitement in Hope's bright brown eyes hasn't dimmed, but a new determination shows in the set of her shoulders. "Then if it's not too much trouble, maybe we could film the practice segment tomorrow."

But Gabe's already shaking his head. "Sorry, I'm headed to Bimini. Filming with a buddy of mine. Though of course you could do it without me."

He dumps the tomatoes Marissa washed onto the sheet pan and drizzles olive oil on them, then turns to us with a slight frown. "I could leave my old camera behind—"

"Won't work," Marissa says. "I've got the meeting with Roger tomorrow, and weather looks rough the rest of the week. No good filming an intro in rough seas with the boat pitching around." Roger Bauer is the head of a local ocean conservation nonprofit, and we've been trying to partner with them for a series of videos about the work they do. Roger's got a great reputation, but he's old-school enough that our first few attempts to set up a meeting were met with polite rebuttals.

"Oh yeah." Gabe jostles the sheet pan on the stove to distribute the oil, the metal grating against the burner plates. "You've been angling for that opportunity for months."

I groan but Hope chuckles. "Double points for the fishy pun."

"Don't encourage him," I warn her. "He only does it to get under my skin."

"A noble endeavor." Hope plucks an olive from the bowl in front of her. "Adrian cultivates pet peeves like houseplants," she says.

"Sure does," Gabe says. "Got any insider tips on how best to pester him?"

Her eyes dart to mine, like she's realized we overstepped a

boundary. Instead of answering, she shoves an olive into her mouth and shrugs. One of her cheeks is bulging, and she looks so innocent that I lick my lips, fighting a smile.

Marissa steps up next to me and leans on the counter, watching us. I don't like the gleam in her eyes. "Come to think of it," she says, "you two could film it by yourselves."

"You two as in—" Hope gestures between herself and me "—us?" She sounds like she'd rather undergo a root canal. "Just Adrian and me?" she repeats, sounding even more forlorn, if that were possible.

Would it be so terrible to be alone together? My mind flashes to our tumultuous reunion—her soaked skin and tumbling curls, the inadvertent embrace on deck. Not terrible, tortuous.

"Yeah," Marissa says. "It would be a great way to tease the ultrasound series. Talk about the importance of estuaries and how brackish waters serve an important role as shark nurseries. You two should be fine on your own, unless that's an issue?" She's calling our commitment into question. No choice but to agree or else appear unprofessional.

"Not an issue for me." Hope raises her brows, passing the challenge to me.

I swallow. Hope and I alone on a boat. With a video camera to record the drama. "I think we could handle it." My throat is dry, but I paste on a smile. Teamwork. I can do this, in theory.

Marissa tosses the dish towel over one shoulder. "Good, then that's settled."

Settled. Since I met Hope, nothing about my life has ever felt settled. Her infectious ability to dive headfirst into her interests is part of what drew me to her, but also what pushed us apart.

I scoop up a handful of cornmeal and dust the wooden pizza peel, then slide the dough onto it. With that all set and awaiting sauce, I step over to scope out the toppings. Hope's cutting cherry tomatoes, an array of bowls laid out on the counter in front of her—far more toppings than we usually get. Pepperoni and basil, fresh mozzarella, Kalamata and Spanish olives, sausage draining on a paper towel, and slices of prosciutto.

The sheer variety is another sign of Hope's influence, of how she's always up for trying new things, testing assumptions. An excellent quality in a scientist, but on paper, not a good match for someone like me who craves steadiness in their personal life. But we brought out the best in each other, complemented one another. With her gone, I became more cautious. I never would've sought out a shift in my career if Marissa hadn't convinced me the viral moment was a chance to make a huge difference for shark conservation. Hope would've seized the opportunity, just like she rose to the challenge of filming with us.

Reaching for a can of artichokes, I pitch my voice low. "About what Marissa said..."

She glances up. "You think it's a bad idea?"

"I just want to make sure you're okay with it. I don't want you to feel pressured to work one-on-one with me." Translation: please change your mind so I don't have to go through with it. "This can't be what you signed on for."

She sets down the paring knife, juicy seeds clinging to the blade. "Being alone with you? On camera?" She makes a face. "Not so much. But she might be onto something."

"Marissa?" I ask, and Hope coughs out a laugh.

"Don't sound so surprised. It's happened once or twice."

I let out a grunt of grudging affirmation just to wheedle a smile out of her, gratified when it works.

"But yeah, I actually think it's a solid idea," she says. "We haven't worked together in a while, but we know each other well. It's lower stakes than in front of a boatful of scientists." She rubs her hands down her thighs in a tense motion, fingers splayed on the bare skin below her cotton shorts. The hem is rolled up, and I swallow against the urge to smooth it down. My fingers curl at the remembered sensation of her skin beneath my fingertips, pliant and soft...

Yeah, we know each other well. But I don't think it will make me any more at ease tomorrow.

"Besides, who better to talk about brackish waters than your resident freshwater biologist?"

"Can you imagine what twenty-two-year-old Hope would have to say about that title?"

Hope waves that off. "What did she know?" That she loved me, for one thing. "I'd tell her that life is full of surprises. And I'd show her where I am now. Back where I belong." She's talking about work, but part of me can't help but think she's right in more ways than one.

Every time I stop overthinking and let instinct take over, it feels natural to be around her. But twenty-two-year-old me thought he knew a lot that proved to be wrong as well. He didn't have the experience of losing her. He still had hope, if only for that summer.

"It would be a cool segue though, right?" Hope asks, and I nod, trying to catch up. "I could talk about coming from the freshwater of my home state to the salinity of the ocean?"

"It would, yeah." I hadn't considered that perspective, but trust Hope to see a new angle. To see the value in all her experiences, when I tend to discount any that don't lead directly to a goal.

"Then I'm down for it." She taps the top of the can of artichokes. "Mind handing me the can opener?"

"I've got it." I slide it toward myself, but she places her hand on mine, stopping me.

When I look up, her eyes are alight. "Sure you can handle it? We all know your track record with can openers."

I cannot believe she's bringing this up, but I'm ready to defend my honor. "That was not my fault." One rainy night, we decided to make soup, but I'd recently moved, and my can opener got lost along the way. The only place open that late was a dollar store, so we bought one, but I couldn't get it to work. "That can opener was faulty."

"Worked fine for me," she says, eyes sparkling, and her words bring me back in time. I was standing at the counter, exhausted and grumbling. Hope took it from me and opened the can on the first try. I'd slipped my arms around her waist and bent to kiss her neck. *Where would I be without you?*

Now I know where I'd be, and I'd wish away the knowledge if I could. Take us back to the beginning and start over. But I don't see what I'd do differently. We were long-distance for half a decade, and Hope wanted to prolong that, indefinitely. Our breakup was inevitable from the moment we met. Different relationship goals, even though our life goals align.

I blink away the memory, embarrassed I can't seem to forget these small moments, and open the can with quick turns, then drain the artichokes over the sink and return them to her in a bowl. Step back, away from her tantalizing nearness. We're better off sticking to the boundaries of work. Her joining the crew was just what I needed to finally get over her.

fourteen

hope

No outline. No notes. Just myself and the camera. And Adrian.

I rub my clammy hands down my shorts, wishing for the comforting weight of a stack of note cards in my pocket, or a remote ready to click through a rehearsed presentation. We're anchored in a secluded cove, with no onlookers except for passing boaters and shore birds, and yet my fight-or-flight instinct is in full effect.

Filming a video that will be viewed by thousands of people—bare minimum, Gabe cheerily assured me last night—is my personal nightmare. I conquered my fear of public speaking through preparation and practice, none of which will help me on the spot.

Add to that the very near presence of my ex—the rich shea scent of his moisturizer envelops me any time he brushes past me on deck, a performance tee draped on his muscles like a sheet thrown over a chiseled marble statue, highlighting dips and ridges that are no longer mine to explore—and I can barely remember my name, let alone the bio I attempted to memorize last night.

"Brickish water—shit." The word *brackish* comes out jumbled again. I scratch my clavicle, hot and itchy under the afternoon sun. A faint breeze sends ripples lapping against the hull and stirs the marsh grasses on shore but isn't strong enough to budge the sweat-drenched curls that cling to my temples and nape.

We're on our third take of this straightforward intro segment, but with Adrian behind the camera and the looming reality of thousands of strangers watching in the future, it might take another twenty tries for me to relax enough to get it right.

I would've loved to have memorized this whole talk, but like Gabe said, that would've defeated the purpose. The crew films in real time. This is my chance to get comfortable with the camera so I can focus on the sharks.

After my lackluster—read: embarrassingly inept—performance the first day, I need to prove I'm up for this job. Marissa took a chance offering me this position and even though I didn't know about Adrian's celebrity status, I did sign up to work alongside him.

One ex-boyfriend in the role of cameraman is nothing to be scared of. I just need to relegate the potential viewers to a hypothetical and our relationship to the past where it belongs. Here, we're just two researchers, ones who used to work well together.

Really well, a smarmy voice pipes up, but I shut her down. Those kinds of thoughts won't help me any more than simmering resentment.

A deep breath, and I try again, sweeping my hand in a stiff imitation of Vanna White. "Marsh grasses and brackish water probably don't make you think of sharks." We're anchored near the shore, the waves lapping against thick mud etched with bird tracks. The grasses at the water's edge are bleached to a pale yellow by the briny water.

The ecosystem is reminiscent of freshwater marshes back home, but the pervasive odor of pluff mud exposed by low tide reminds me I'm back where I belong, even if things between me and Adrian are murky as the nutrient-rich water flowing in from the rivers.

"In fact, the toothy creature you most likely have in mind is an alligator, but we're—" I freeze. Should I put it that way? I'm the only one who will be in the video. "*I'm* here today to talk about how estuaries play a vital role in the life cycle of many shark species."

Adrian nods encouragement despite my halting delivery. His eyes are fixed on the screen, fingers holding it tight but gently. I know that grip. I've felt his fingers circling my ankles, thumbs pressed to the joint, felt it on the pulse in my wrist with his lips on mine… And now I can't remember the rest of my speech.

The drone of a passing boat fills the silence, too loud to film over, but when it recedes and I don't start talking again, Adrian lowers the camera to his knee, a slight frown tugging his dark brows together. "This is hard for you."

His matter-of-fact statement makes me bristle. I hate this feeling of incompetence.

"You noticed?"

A smile dents his cheek. "But I've seen you corner fellow shoppers in the canned goods aisle and lecture them on the dubious credibility of some online petitions to save sharks and what they can do to make a real difference in ocean conservation."

I pull my lips to the side. "Am I that bad?"

He chuckles. "It's not bad. It's you, and I—" He clears his throat. "It's wonderful. You're passionate about sharing your knowledge about sharks."

"But this isn't a conversation. It's going to be recorded and shared."

"Most of our videos won't even involve talking to the camera. Today will be the worst of it. I know it's a cliché, but people respond to real. Let your inner nerd out. Share your passion. That's what will appeal to our followers."

"Pretty sure my inner nerd has been my whole personality since I was six."

Adrian grins at that, and I remember how much he loved my nerdy side. Never told me to tone it down or cool off with the trivia.

"But it's not my personality I'm worried about," I explain. "It's that I'll say or do something to make y'all look bad, and the result will be shared a thousand times over."

He frowns in apparent confusion, as if me failing isn't a very real possibility, and the lines in his brow are adorably distracting. "But you've crushed every presentation and speech I've seen you give. You taught seminars in grad school. None of this is new for you."

"But this is different."

"Because of the camera?"

"Because of everything." I peel my collar to the side, trying to get some air on my neck, and his eyes track the movement, sharp and intense. Momentarily distracted, I run my fingertip through the slick of sweat. His lips part and desire flares, low in my belly, forceful enough to keep me still, letting him look, feeling seen.

The loud hum of an engine breaks the stillness and beyond Adrian's shoulder, I spot the plume of a Jet Ski. When my eyes return to his face, his features are blank, like nothing happened. Because nothing did. Nothing will. Nothing but a day's work.

Returning to the subject at hand, he says, "Does it have something to do with why you deleted your social media accounts?"

A nod would suffice. I could leave it at that, and he'd let me, like he let me dodge the question last time. But I didn't accept this job to evade things. I came to face my past so I can run headlong into the future.

I blow out my breath and shift forward, elbows on my knees, rooted in place under his scrutiny. "You've been to my hometown, so you know how it is. Everyone knows everyone, supports each other."

"Yeah, it was cool to see," he says. "I always imagined living somewhere like that."

I know all about the many times his family moved, about the lack of community, and I wonder for the first time if he's found that in social media, if it's more reciprocal than I first thought.

"Well, the research project I was part of had been ongoing for several years. They'd come up with an action plan to combat invasive species, but the town needed to vote on whether to fund the project."

He leans back, settling in to give me his full attention. "Sounds promising."

"It was. The lead scientist had worked for weeks on a presentation for the town hearing. A lot of locals supported the idea, but there were others who thought the money could be better allocated toward other needs." Small-town politics that never change.

"But right as the meeting started, my supervisor got a phone call. His son had gotten a concussion during a soccer game and was on the way to the hospital. He asked who wanted to speak, and no one stepped up, so I did." Worst decision ever.

Adrian smiles, likely remembering the all-nighters I pulled for group projects, not wanting to let my group members down.

"I'd only been on the study for a few months, but I thought I could speak to the opposition of some people I knew personally. The presentation went okay, but afterward, they opened up for questions, and I was...not prepared." The words are inadequate for how poorly I delivered, fumbling my way through questions brought up by those opposed.

He winces, and it's clear he understands how that must've felt.

"While I was busy trying to address all the questions thrown at me, a news crew came in to cover the meeting. Apparently, it was part of a 'spotlight on conservation' series they were doing."

"No warning?"

I shake my head. "Not that I know of. But I wasn't supposed to present, so I wouldn't have been notified anyway. Between the camera and my lack of preparation, I tanked the Q&A. Didn't support our claims with evidence, stumbled over the numbers. The measure ended up getting voted down, and I lost a chance to protect the water that I love." I heave a deep breath. "Not only that, but my rambling failure will live forever on the internet."

"They aired it?" he asks, incredulous, and I shake my head.

"Not on TV, but it's on the city council website."

He looks relieved. "No one watches those."

"Not many," I admit. "But I let down the town and did a disservice to my colleagues. My supervisor was understanding, but I know he was disappointed. It would've been a huge win for them. I'd been planning to leave at the start of the new year. Come back to shark research. But after that, I felt like I needed to stay the course. At least I could make a contribution with my research, since I failed when it came to using my voice."

"Hope." Adrian reaches for my hand, stopping short, and clasps his fingers together instead. "You don't hold the blame for the vote. I'm sure the council members had access to the study."

"But we both know the power of communicating the data clearly. I did the opposite. Spread doubt and made the whole department look incompetent."

"You tried. You stepped up when no one else would—"

"And I botched it." I look away, toward the horizon, indistinct with vapor. "I'd never failed that badly. And it was so public." And personal. Science and math have always been my strength. The knowledge I acquired, a badge of honor. "I let down my colleagues and my hometown."

"Then did them proud by sticking around when you wanted to leave."

His words resonate with deeper meaning. I stuck around

when it came to my career but took the easy out on our relationship. But doesn't that prove I was right? We're better off apart, with him finding a woman who's all in, not harboring doubts.

"I wish you'd reached out," he says quietly.

"And told my estranged boyfriend I'd screwed up so he could give me some version of 'I told you so'?" I know he worried that I'd lose my momentum by moving in with Zuri. That I should find a way to help her without uprooting my whole life. And he was right.

"We'll never know, since you didn't give me the chance."

I didn't expect him to challenge my assumption. To act like my version of our breakup is somehow lacking. "Maybe you could've checked in. Maybe you would've known, if you hadn't left me to figure it out on my own."

"I'm not," he says through his teeth, "the one who left."

My hands are fisted, face flushed, and I want nothing more than to stare him down until he sees things my way. But we set a boundary. I close my eyes, inhale. "No more rehashing the past, right?" His jaw pops, beard a glossy shadow, then he nods. "I only told you this because it's relevant to my employment."

Not true. I told him because sharing is easier than withholding when it comes to him. Because the ache of holding back was a physical pain. But it's a pain I need to endure to keep my heart intact.

"Then as your co-worker," he says, emphasizing the term, "I feel compelled to remind you that you don't have to do this. Given what happened, I don't even think it's wise—"

"Are you questioning my abilities?" Exactly why I didn't want to tell him. Now he knows my weakness, the portion of my life I'd prefer to omit from any job application.

"No. I'm worried that this will negatively affect you. You're right about how public it is, about the possibility for notoriety." He looks me straight in the eye. "You don't have anything to prove."

"I've given it a lot of thought. And while this is hard for me, I want to be a part of what you're doing. I want to show my face, to share my passion."

"If you're certain—"

"I'm certain. I can't go back in time and change what I did then, but I can make a difference here and now. If even one little girl sees this and decides that her dream of being a scientist is attainable, then it's worth it."

He sits back, the worry lines in his brow easing away. "Just know that you can always change your mind. If you start to feel uncomfortable, let me know."

A ball of fizzing emotion burns in my chest. "Thank you. But I want to do this." A thought occurs to me. "And unlike my talk at town hall, I've been preparing half my life for this."

He laughs, the first one all day, and the tension between my shoulder blades slips away. I thought telling him would make me feel exposed, but it's the opposite. More like I've stepped under an oak tree in a rainstorm and can finally catch my breath. Sheltered. Safe.

"In that case, let's try this a different way." He picks up the tripod and hops over the side of the boat and makes his way to shore. With nimble movements, he sets up the tripod in the sticky mud and mounts the camera. He must sense my eyes on him because he raises a finger to his lips. "Shh, don't tell Gabe. He told me not to let this leave my hands, under any circumstances."

That pulls a laugh out of me, and he looks gratified. He comes back over to the boat and climbs aboard, muddy water streaking down his calves. "We'll just be filming from the waist up," he says, when he catches me looking.

He plops down on the seat right next to me. I inhale sharply, muscles tight. "Gotta stay in frame," he explains, and I nod like it's totally normal for us to be touching. If I was hot before, now I'm sweltering. His body is sinfully sexy.

I tug my gaze up from where our half-bare thighs are pressed together. "Now what?"

Unexpectedly, Adrian leans sideways, his arm pressed against my shoulder. For a fleeting moment I relax against him, his solid presence a reassurance. Only a moment, then logic takes over. He didn't sit by me to cuddle. We're at work.

He raises his phone. "Selfie?" And there it is. The reasonable answer. "We can share it before the next video, generate some buzz about the new researcher on our team."

I nod in agreement, words impossible with him so close, and lock eyes with on-screen Adrian, glad the camera can't pick up infrared heat like night vision because I would be a blaze of flustered orange-red next to his cool purple.

He tips his head so close that his beard brushes my cheek. "Say 'spreadsheets are overrated'!"

"Hey!" The shutter noise clicks and I hitch my shoulder into his. "That was uncalled-for."

"Oh yeah?" He shields the phone with his palm and shows me the photo. Our smiles are wide, and unlike most posed pictures, mine looks genuine, not forced. "Perfect shot," he says. "I've learned some photography tricks while you were gone."

While you were gone. A causal reference to a period of our lives that feels both astronomical and insignificant now that I'm back. Insignificant in that his presence is familiar as breathing. Astronomical in how different our relationship is now—from sharing our hearts, our bodies, to each touch being a risk.

"Shady tricks," I say, but when he answers with a laugh, it's impossible not to join in. "Dissing the hallowed glory of well-calibrated data?" Mock-censure tinges my words. "My, how the years have changed you, Hollis-Parker."

He chuckles again, and I love that sound. No point in denying it, when my own cheeks are aching. I haven't smiled this much in years; I'm out of practice.

"Not my fault you're easy to tease." He bends down, riffling through a bag at his feet.

"Says the man with a list of pet peeves a mile long."

"Hyperbole is on that list." Adrian sends a grin over his shoulder, and my instinct is to swat him playfully, but physical touch is a definite no-go. Banter, however… That's acceptable within the confines of a work relationship, right? I ignore the voice that tells me we're veering toward flirting, because right now I'm having too much fun.

Instead, I make a check mark in the air. "Noted. Make that a mile-and-a-half-long list."

He shakes his head, then straightens up, a small remote in his hand. "I know this is counterintuitive, but I think things might go more smoothly if we do this together. You good with that?"

Without giving myself time to overthink it, I nod, and he scootches in a little closer. His hip is snug against mine, and the urge to lean into him is so strong, I overcompensate by tilting away.

He licks his lips, which yes, please. But I mentally scold myself to quit staring. "Are you…" he begins, but I cut off the question with a brusque nod. This will be fine. I'm fine, he's fine as hell, we're all fine. Just two co-workers. Working.

"Ready," I say, cutting off my internal monologue.

"Remember, no one's here but us." He clicks a button and a red light by the lens flicks on. "I'm here on the beautiful Winyah Bay with the newest addition to our team." He smiles at me, and I wave at the camera—should I be waving? Too late. "Marine biologist Hope Evans will be joining our crew for the summer."

The summer. That's it. Three months to pay my dues and put all of this—the messy emotions, the stagnant career—behind me.

"She's new to our team," Adrian continues, "but an experienced researcher, and we're lucky to have her."

His words shouldn't be sentimental, but I can't help but remember how lucky I used to feel with him in my life. Like I won the relationship lottery.

"The feeling is mutual," I say. "Spending an entire season doing fieldwork with sharks is a lifelong dream come true." Before I get all sappy, I launch into the meat of our talk. "Today we're going to chat a little bit about the life cycle of sharks."

I maintain eye contact with the camera, looser than the first few takes. "Hear the word *shark* and you might think of coral reefs or the vast blue of the open ocean." I can't help the smile that always rises at the thought of the stunning diversity of sharks. "But you might not hear the word *sharks* and think of estuaries, the brackish water that forms from freshwater mingling with saltwater."

I pause to keep myself from talking too quickly, and Adrian presses his leg against mine in silent support. Instead of getting tongue-tied at the unexpected contact, I relax against him. We might be strangers now, but we weren't always, and my body remembers.

"I guess my new crewmates thought it would be fitting for me to be eased back into the ocean since I'm from the Midwest. A small town in southwest Michigan, right on the lake."

"And yes, she does mean The Lake, capitalized," Adrian chimes in. "I learned pretty quickly when I visited that if locals are talking about the lake, they mean Lake Michigan."

I frown, turning to him. "Do we want people to know you've visited my hometown?"

His mouth falls open. "Shit, no. You're right. Gabe can edit that out." He cracks a smile. "Second day and you're already nailing this. I'd better step up my game." On another guy, it might be a line, but this is Adrian. Sweet, encouraging, earnest.

It's nice to be on good terms again. To see him at his best, not his worst. Maybe if I remember why I fell for him, I'll be able to forgive myself for staying hung up on him long past when it was good for me.

He starts recording, and I share the part about my hometown again. Out of habit, I hold up my left hand, fingers pressed together and thumb out. Using my other hand, I point to the approximate location of my hometown. "This is where I'm from, right by Lake Michigan, but I'm no stranger to saltwater. It feels good to be back to studying elasmobranchs. That's the class of cartilaginous fish that includes sharks, skates, and rays," I add, unsure how technical they get in these videos. "But after a few years working up north, returning to the salty waters of the Atlantic was a big transition."

"Don't let her fool you," Adrian says. "She was out with us earlier this week and did a shark work-up like she never left."

My cheeks get warm at the unprompted compliment and how he kindly omitted failures that came after. "Even though I didn't need to be eased into the vast ocean, some young sharks do. The brackish, sheltered waters of the estuaries are a pupping ground for many species."

"Though ground might not sound like the correct term for a watery environment—" Adrian leans over and drags his fingertips through the silty water "—pupping ground is the term used to refer to areas where juvenile sharks spend their formative years."

"A shark nursery, pretty much."

Adrian points a dripping finger at me. "You promised."

"But it fits so well."

He turns back to the camera. "If she starts singing 'Baby Shark' I think it's fair that I instigate a mutiny, right?"

"Oh, so I'm the captain in this scenario? I like the sound of that."

Adrian shakes his head, still grinning, and we go on, talking about the various kinds of sharks that begin their lives in the protected waters of estuaries around the globe. It's easy. Simple. Comfortable.

Yes, the camera's rolling, but I'm on the water, teaching people about my favorite subject. The camera isn't my enemy, or a representation of people looking to find fault, it's a teaching tool. That I found my footing thanks to opening up to Adrian is a topic to investigate later. For now, I inhale the happiness of a breeze tinged with salt, and exhale all the baggage I brought with me, even though I traveled light.

Maybe I can do this. Let go of the past. Make a fresh start. Work with Adrian as a colleague, nothing more. One day at a time.

fifteen

adrian

We wrapped up filming by late afternoon. The trip back was quiet, both of us sweaty and worn out from hours on the water. Hope left to get cleaned up at Marissa's and I congratulated myself on resisting the very unprofessional urge to ask if she wanted to grab dinner afterward, alarmed to realize I crave more time with her even after a whole day together.

Since my head is clearly not running the show, I decide to get out my pent-up physical tension with a quick workout. My home gym setup has become a haven, a place to decompress and work my body so my mind can rest. Up until a couple years ago, walks around campus and the rare days spent working with sharks in the ocean were the sum total of my physical activity.

After Hope left, I accepted a friend's invitation to the gym and discovered lifting heavy things is excellent stress relief. My workout routine helped me cope with the pressure of starting the channel, something miles outside my comfort zone.

I push myself today, working out muscles tense from adhering to the new boundaries of our relationship. Breathing through a heavy set of bicep curls, I exhale and feel the tightness leave my chest for the first time all day, weary with the strain of holding my emotions in a vise grip. The weights are slick with sweat by the time I feel ready to process what Hope told me about her time in Michigan.

Her revelation about the council meeting disaster pulled me right back into the lonely days after our relationship ended. I was busy feeling hurt, struggling to reorient myself without Hope, but meanwhile, she was dealing with a career setback, making the hard decision to step away from the work she loved for the good of her community.

Finding out what she went through, and her reasons for staying in Michigan, was like balm on the raw ache of our breakup, easing the resentment of separation. My first instinct was to wrap an arm around her shoulders and tell her she's being too hard on herself, but that's not my role anymore. The thought of it being another man's job has me grabbing a heavier set of dumbbells. But I do want her to be happy. To put her in my past, so I can move on too. Funny how a summer together might be the thing that breaks her hold on my heart.

We managed to maintain a good working relationship today, aside from a couple slip-ups on my part. Easier to move past the awkwardness when we have so much to talk about within the realm of research we're both passionate about.

In between exercises, I watch the footage of us. It looks good. *We* look good. Comfortable, but not in an overly-familiar way. Knowledgeable, and yes, nerdy. What viewers expect and keep coming back for. Hope is going to fit in just fine.

Reaching that conclusion comes easy, but it takes an entire full-body circuit before I feel up to testing that theory by sending the footage to Gabe, requesting him to edit it sometime this weekend. The moment the *SENT* confirmation appears, I freak out all over again.

How will Gabe interpret what he sees on-screen? No doubt

he'll read into our banter, but it's imperative that our followers don't. The idea of exposing Hope to speculation turns my stomach. But it's not just Hope I'm worried about. It's us. Together.

I'm worried about the subtext picked up by the viewfinder. That people will be able to tell who we were to each other—two people who studied together on countless all-nighters, and binged sci-fi movies on long weekends, who knew each other's takeout orders by heart and the things that made them lose their breath.

Two people who knew each other's bodies as well as their own, who kissed and laughed and held and loved their way through five years together. Two people who were months away from sharing a home.

Sweat stings my eyes and I rub my arm across my face. I'm not about to cry over Hope. Not now, when she's my colleague, and we're past all this. Chest heaving, I take a swig from my water bottle. My phone vibrates in my pocket, and I yank it out, grateful for the interruption.

Gabe: No problem. How'd it go?

Adrian: Better than expected.

Gabe: I expected her to push you overboard.

Adrian: She probably wanted to after what happened the other day.

Gabe: How many times did she threaten to commandeer the vessel?

Thinking back to Hope teasing me about my docking skills, I grin.

Adrian: Only once, and I'm pretty sure she was joking.

Gabe: Look at you two, putting aside your differences in the name of science.

He's being annoying on purpose, so I don't bother with a reply. But a moment later, nerves get the better of me.

Adrian: Did you watch it?

Gabe: You uploaded it like two minutes ago.

Adrian: Just don't post it without my okay.

Gabe: Do I ever?

I thank him and pocket my phone to combat the restless urge to rewatch the footage again in search of any telltale hints of our past connection. To get my mind off it, I reply to a few comments on a video we recently reshared that's getting a lot of traction. I should catch up on emails and record a quick update for social media, but not in my sweaty, post-workout state.

Every once in a while, commenters ask me to share my gym routine, but they can find that elsewhere. I'm not a personal trainer or fitness coach, and my corner of the internet is meant to be a reliable resource for shark-related content, not unvetted lifestyle advice.

I head inside to the shower and climb in, turning the tap to cool. Once I'm finished, I crank off the water and step out onto the bath mat, dripping, only to realize there's no towel on the hook because I forgot to fetch my laundry from Marissa's dryer on pizza night. I wipe myself down with brusque swipes of a clean shirt, then get dressed. After setting a reminder to schedule a washing machine repair tech, I text my cousin.

Adrian: Ok if I stop by and pick up my laundry?

Marissa: I'm in a meeting, but Hope's there. Just text her.

Just text her? Like it's that simple.

How do I phrase a text to my ex-girlfriend slash current co-worker?

Besides, I'm dry, no need to fetch the towels right now. Easier to wait until Marissa is back and avoid any precarious alone time with Hope. On the other hand, I promised not to act differently around her because of our history. Marissa will probably ask Hope about it, and then it will make it seem like I made a big deal out of nothing.

My hands are fumbling as I search for the contact I scrolled past for years but never deleted from my phone. Will she still have my number saved? Doesn't matter.

Adrian: Hi, it's Adrian.

Adrian: Maybe you already knew that.

I'm sweating all over again. Nothing says nervous like two consecutive texts. And there's about to be a third.

Adrian: I left some towels there. At Marissa's place, I mean. Are you there? If so, may I stop by and get them? I don't have a key.

Adrian: It's not an emergency or anything.

Make that an even four. I'm the human embodiment of the face-palm emoji. I toss the phone onto my bed before I embarrass myself further. How could it possibly be a towel emergency? Why would she ever assume that?

With a groan, I go out into the kitchen and grab a bag of tortilla chips off the counter and shovel food in my mouth to keep from checking whether she's responded yet. When the bag's half gone and I feel like I have a grip on myself, I check my phone. Nothing.

That's fine. As I so astutely wrote, it's not a towel emergency. Heat flares in my cheeks, and just as I'm about to bury myself in data entry to try to obliterate the memory of the most embarrassing string of texts I've ever sent a woman, a reply pops up on-screen.

Hope: It might not be a towel emergency now, but it's always best to act swiftly to prevent catastrophe.

I couldn't keep the smile off my face if I tried. Another text comes through.

Hope: I'm here, come by whenever.

It's only when my soles hit the splintery porch that I realize I've forgotten shoes. And keys. And any remaining good sense.

sixteen

hope

"Those aren't mine," Adrian says. He's standing outside Marissa's door, and I plan to keep it that way. Inviting him in would be dangerously close to letting him into my life, the opposite of what I came down here to do.

The first text I sent bordered on flirtatious, but I rationalized it by telling myself I had to ease his obvious nerves. I tried to course-correct with the follow-up, and it appears he has the same plan, judging by the way he took a noticeable step backward when I opened the door, keeping a professional distance between us.

"They aren't?" I drop my eyes to the towels in my arms. Right after he texted, I searched for them and found them atop the dryer. I put them on the entryway table so they'd be ready to go the moment he knocked. No need for small talk or lingering in the doorway.

But my plan was thwarted when he shoved his hands into the pockets of his shorts instead of taking the towels. "Mine are striped."

There are only two striped towels in the condo to my knowledge, but I hope I'm wrong. "Gray and blue?"

"Yes." He elongates the word with a wariness that's fully warranted.

"Those are in the washer." Have I been using *his* towels all week? Feels like I invaded his privacy, which is ridiculous. "Prior to that, they were wadded up on the bathroom floor." Sabotaged by the awkward explanation, I put on a cheery smile. "So really, could be worse."

So much for a brief, businesslike interaction to set the tone for the rest of the summer.

"You…" He clears his throat, a guttural rasp that weakens my knees. "You've been using *my* towels?"

The way he says it is faintly accusatory, like I'm some sort of creep. Which, ironically, is how I felt a moment ago, but indignation takes over. "Not like that!"

"Like what?"

"I didn't know they were yours! You make it sound like I'm a towel bandit."

His laugh is a tangible thing, dancing along my skin like a forbidden caress. "Wasn't aware there were specialized designations of bandits." He's teasing me, and I should steer the conversation back to neutral ground, but I can't help playing along.

"You should be grateful," I reply. "You're getting freshly washed towels."

"I know, I'm the one who washed them," he says.

"But you left them in the dryer. If I hadn't used them, the humidity would've seeped in and left them mildewy. If you think about it, I did you a favor." I raise my brows, not minding how dangerously close we are to flirting. "You owe me, if anything."

"So not only did you steal my towels—"

"Borrowed. And not on purpose."

He keeps talking like I hadn't interrupted, an unmistakable twinkle in his onyx eyes. "But you're also holding them hostage in hopes of a token of gratitude?"

"Hostage?"

He shrugs, the motion highlighting his deltoid muscles under the short-sleeve Henley. "If the bandit shoe fits…"

"Oh my gosh, really?" I'm grinning, though.

"Kidding, Hope." He cracks a wide smile. "What's mine is yours." An offhand remark, but his eyes widen.

What's mine is yours. He always said that when we were dating, whether it was his hoodie or his notes from a seminar he thought might interest me. Clearly, he's also venturing into a dangerous place, outside the boundary we've drawn, where the pain of our breakup is fading in light of our time together.

I shouldn't have replied to his text. Should've waited until Marissa was here and—

His phone chimes, and a half second later my pocket vibrates. Weird. I shift the towels to one arm and pull out my phone. An email notification. I tap and discover it's from Gabe.

Subject: Ready for your Shark Science Crew debut?

Adrian is CC'd using the same email he's always had, and it's odd to think he was so reachable, if only I hadn't given up. Pushing the thought aside, I open the email and discover a video link entitled: Freshwater Biologist Talks Sharks?

Nauseated, I clamp my mouth shut tight. I know it's worded as a question to entice clicks, not to call my credentials into question, but the phrasing brings up all the feelings of inadequacy from the council meeting.

"'*Shark Science Crew* debut'? C'mon now." Adrian sounds amused, and I look over and find him looking at his phone, a grudging half smile creasing his bearded cheek. "Hate when he rhymes on purpose," he mutters.

He glances up, takes one look at me, and says, "Hey, nothing's final yet." Stepping forward, he closes the distance between us, dark eyes soft with concern. His solid presence infuses my senses, soaking into me like being submerged in sun-warmed waves. "Why don't we watch it together, then you can tell me how you feel about us sharing it."

"Here?" My voice is breathless, but I don't bother trying again.

He raises his eyes, looking past me into the empty apartment, no doubt noticing my bed set up in the corner, the blankets rumpled in inviting disarray. Above the open collar of his shirt, his throat bobs in a distracting swallow.

When he speaks, his voice is husky. "Have you eaten?"

Wind blows the sandwich wrapper against my face, and I wrinkle my nose against the itch, but the first bite of crispy battered shrimp and toasted roll is euphoria. I ordered on instinct, barely glancing at the menu before deciding what meal would best conquer my seafood cravings, and totally nailed it.

I swallow down the bite and ask, "Why is it that food tastes better by the beach?"

The ocean is visible over the railing behind Adrian, steps away from our table at a restaurant Adrian told me he discovered last year. The sound of rolling waves echoes our past seaside dinners. Shared meals that float at the edges of my memory like the Edison bulbs strung from the pergola above, casting a warm glow.

I tell myself that remembering won't hurt, that I have to acknowledge the good along with the bad if I want to move on. Don't know if it's true, but it feels good to take a break from trying to forget. The drive over was quiet, and we haven't discussed my irrational hesitation to upload the video, given that the purpose of filming content is to share it.

Adrian tears a ketchup packet open with his teeth. The flash of canines does something indecent to me. "Agree to disagree." He's got a napkin squeezed between his arm and torso, and flinches when a gust of wind sends loose sand skittering along the decking underfoot. "Beach picnics are the worst. I'd rather go hungry."

"This from the man who brought a tub of leftover lasagna onto Sinclair's boat for a two-hour trip?"

His shoulders shake in silent laughter, cheeks bulging with food he swallows with a visible gulp, his Adam's apple bobbing above the undone top button of his shirt. I've got to stop paying such close attention to him. He's caught me a few times, but with a perplexed look, like he has no clue how irresistible he is.

"'I said snacks, Adrian,'" he intones in an attempt at a British accent, eyes alight. "'If it requires a fork, it's a meal.' Joke was on him though—" he wipes his mouth with the pad of his thumb "—I ate that shit like a sandwich."

I'm giggling now, the image of Adrian two-fisting the slice of cold lasagna rooted in my memory. "You're a mess, Hollis-Parker." The wind shifts again, bringing the smell of fisherman's bait from the nearby pier to my nostrils, and I swallow, then say, "How is it that you grew up spending summers on the coast, but can't handle a little sand in your sandwich?"

He chuckles. "Ask Marissa how annoying I used to be about it. I would always say I wasn't hungry, but then her mom would make me a meal when we got back." The corners of his eyes crinkle with a smile. "She complained it wasn't fair, but Aunt Kim was on my side. We'd eat a sand-free meal at the table while my cousins grumbled."

I smile, surprised to hear a new story about his childhood, wanting to ask more, but not sure if it's wise. "Zuri's with you on that one," I tell him, deciding to keep things in safe territory. "Says sand belongs at the beach and nowhere else."

"Certainly not in your mouth," he agrees, affronted. "Sand stays in your teeth forever."

"Kind of like the image of you double-fisting that slice of cold lasagna." I press my knuckles to my lips to stop laughing before I accidentally inhale the food I'm chewing.

"You should see the approved snack list he added to the syllabus. Colin forwarded it to me and—"

"Oh my gosh, Colin." I haven't thought of him in years. One downside to not seeing people's life updates pop up online. "It's been so long since we spoke. What's he up to these days?"

Adrian reaches for the saltshaker. "He's with NOAA now. Married, too. Went to his wedding last year." He sets down the shaker and looks at me, eyes inky pools in the sapphire light of dusk. "You went full ghost, huh?"

"Guess I did." I gulp, though I haven't taken another bite. "Hard to watch from the sidelines, so I stopped trying. But I'm here now."

"Where will you go next?" His tone is casual, but I know Adrian. This is the question he's always thinking about, planning for. *What next?*

But we're just working together, and I don't need to bare my soul, so I brush crumbs from my fingers, feigning nonchalance. "Not sure. I didn't expect Marissa to offer me this opportunity, but now I've got all summer to figure it out."

His brows inch up, almost imperceptibly, and if we were dating, he'd make a comment about how three months—two and a half now—is not a lot of time. Ask how anyone is supposed to plan when they don't know where they'll be next season. But we're not, and he doesn't.

"A lot can change in a summer," he says, and though I let my eyes linger a moment too long on his handsome face, I see no condemnation in his expression.

Out of the corner of my eye, I notice the family at the next table over jostling one another. They're huddled over their phones, glancing at the screens, then over at us. The man who appears to be the father, a balding guy with a pink sunburn, pushes back from the table. "I'm not scared to ask," he tells the others.

I glance toward Adrian, who straightens up, like he's bracing himself.

"Hey-o," the stranger says, approaching the table, and it's clear he's had a few drinks. "You the shark dude?"

Adrian smiles, his eyes darting toward the rest of the group, and I follow his gaze to see the kid has his phone out. "Maybe." He stands and holds out his hand. "Adrian Hollis-Parker. I share a lot of videos about shark science."

The man guffaws, loud even amidst the music and dining chatter. "Knew it had to be you, but what are the chances, my man?" He takes Adrian's hand and pumps it. "Your content is the real deal. My boys and I absolutely can't get enough, but my wife says I'm crazy."

I turn and find the woman making a shooing motion. "Harry, you're embarrassing yourself. Get back here and let him eat in peace."

He lets go and steps back. "Sorry, I shouldn't bother you at your meal. Probably wouldn't have if it weren't for that last daiquiri. Vacation. You know how it is." He tugs at the hem of his polo. "I'll leave you to your meal."

"Wait." The boy hurries over, holding out a napkin. "Dad wanted to get your autograph for my little brother. He's sick at the hotel with my grandma."

"You don't need to—" the man starts, but Adrian waves him off.

"Happy to." He stoops to rummage in the bag I noticed him carrying in and comes up with a ballpoint pen, the brand he always liked for notes. "Who should I make it out to?"

"Patrick," the kid says, then adds, "actually, could you make it out to Curt, too? I watch your stuff sometimes."

Hunched over the table, Adrian smiles up at him. "Of course." He hands over the napkin, and the boy holds it flat, careful not to wrinkle it.

"Cool. Thanks."

The woman has been watching with a smile. When Adrian glances over, she tells him, "That's really kind of you." She beckons the others. "Now you two, get back here and let him enjoy his meal before it gets cold."

They thank Adrian, but once they're seated again, I notice them huddled around the kid's phone.

I lean forward and ask Adrian, "Did they take a video?"

He finishes chewing his bite of crab cake, then swallows. "Probably."

"And that's a normal occurrence?"

The food on my plate, so appetizing a moment ago, seems unappealing. Adrian handled the interaction like a pro, but I don't know if I could do the same. What if someone had filmed me talking to the woman on the beach the day Zuri fired me? Instead of autographs, I'd be meme-ified.

"It doesn't happen that often, and it took me a while to get used to," Adrian says, picking up on my mood. "But now I just think of them like students who come up to me after class. Makes it less weird."

"You get a lot of students asking for your autograph?"

He laughs. "Sadly, no. Most of them are immune to my coolness, I think."

"That tracks," I say, grinning. But part of me is still concerned whether this is a smart move for my career. This is a far cry from my usual behind-the-scenes research. On the flip side, three years out of the field is a long hiatus, and appearing on his channel would be tangible proof of my ability to do the job with competence.

"I guess I should be more concerned with our video than theirs." Without giving myself the chance to delay, I pull my phone out of my purse. While I'm scrolling for the email, a loud screech reaches my ears and I look up to find Adrian pushing away from the table. He rises and carries the heavy wrought iron chair around the table.

Transfixed, I watch him—solid and strong as ever, but now his muscles pop in a distracting way I'm not used to—and only jolt out of the daze when he sets the chair next to mine.

I look up—way up, because he's even taller than I remember— and ask, "Are you making room for someone else?"

"What? No." He digs in the bag and sets a tablet next to my plate. "Thought this might make it easier." He pauses, hands clenched around the chair back, so tightly that his knuckles pop, and all I can think is those same hands fisted in the skirt of my dress, dragging me up against him—

"Sorry," he says. "I should've asked before moving over here. I'm trying…"

"It's okay," I hear myself saying, surprisingly calm for some-one whose entire body is aflame. "That's why we came."

I take a sip of my drink, sucking long and hard on the straw while he gets situated next to me, knees bumping mine. The icy liquid sends shivers down my spine but does nothing to cool my desire. I need to stop reacting to him like this, but it's tough when he's being so thoughtful. Not just thoughtful, *professional*.

The waiter walks over and I startle upright. "Can I get you anything else, or are we all good here?"

I can't speak for Adrian, but no, I am not all good. His touch left me muddled and befuddled and all sorts of rhyming words he'd doubtless detest.

"Could we get some tea?" Adrian says. "Unsweet for her."

The waiter turns toward me, hand on his hip. "'Course. Where are you visiting from?"

"Uh, Michigan, originally."

He smirks like I proved his hunch, which of course I did. "Be right back with y'all's tea."

"Not visiting?" Adrian raises his brows.

"Okay, maybe it was a half-truth. But a person should be al-lowed to drink tea however they please."

He grins. "You are allowed to. Just so happens to be that our way is the correct way."

"Oh, please." I push his arm in a friendly, *get-outta-here* nudge that doesn't feel so platonic when my fingertips connect with his solid bicep. My breath catches, and I pull away, remembering I'm supposed to be keeping my distance.

His answer is a throaty laugh and I narrow my eyes, which only seems to encourage him. "Since you brought it up…" He lifts his chin toward my sandwich. "I notice you're getting your fill of real seafood."

"Real seafood, really? We have amazing seafood back home."

"Can it really be called seafood if it's not from the sea?"

"Semantics," I say. "You haven't lived until you've had fresh caught bluegill fried up with some boiled potatoes on the side. And up in northern Michigan they make the most amazing smoked trout."

"Smoked? As in not fresh?" His dark eyes are sparkling with mischief.

"As in delicious." I settle back in the chair. "Now, back to business." After a steadying breath, I gesture toward the tablet. "Let's do this before I get second thoughts."

He glances sharply at me, then must think better of saying what came to mind. Instead, he tilts the screen in my direction.

On-screen, my hair is up in a ponytail that fans out behind my head, face framed against the blue-brown water and cord grass, the green fading to a tawny yellow below the high-tide line. My eyes aren't on the camera but something above it—Adrian's face, I realize as he pushes Play. The clip starts with a few shots of me gesturing, my muted words overplayed by music, then transitions to Adrian's introduction.

It's excruciating to watch myself at first, and I forget to listen for slip-ups I'd like edited out. But next to me, Adrian's presence is calming. Steady but not intrusive. Slowly, I settle in, allowing myself the space to watch objectively. He sips his sweet tea and I munch my sandwich and try to absorb the footage like it's a stranger and not my own self.

The wind shifts, blowing in off the ocean and the strings of lights sway in the gust, causing a glare. He adjusts the tablet and leans closer, bringing our legs into contact below the table.

I do my best to regain my concentration, but it's hard to ignore the enticing contrast of his twill shorts and the hard muscle of his thighs against my freshly-shaved skin. My jean shorts, which I didn't give any thought to before, now feel like only the barest scrap of fabric, rucked tight against my thighs, and I squirm, skin pricked with goose bumps in defiance of the humid warmth.

Adrian glances over. "Cold? I've got a sweatshirt in my SUV."

I shake my head. No way will I risk accidentally keeping another one of his hoodies. We return our attention to the screen. Gabe's edited out the lulls and awkward takes and condensed the video into a concise ten minutes and eighteen seconds.

When it ends, Adrian clicks the screen dark and settles back in the chair. The muffled rush of gentle waves takes over, the sun nearing the horizon. Twilight hovers outside the patio; the server comes to bus a nearby table, and still Adrian keeps quiet, his breathing a comforting rhythm next to me. He's giving me space to evaluate, to think. This is what I wanted from him when I asked to put our plans for the move on hold, and which he gave me in a permanent form when he stopped calling and stepped out of my life for good.

The thought breaks the spell of connection, and I finish the last bite of my sandwich. "It turned out well."

"I think so too." He pulls the tablet into his lap, and his arm brushes mine, all rigid muscle and soft skin. "You did a fantastic job of breaking down the information into palpable pieces," he says.

"Is that a fancy way of saying I dumbed it down?"

"For making science accessible?" He shakes his head, loose

locs slipping over his forehead, and he swipes them back with a reproving grin. "C'mon now, Evans. Don't go Ivory Tower on me. Not everyone has the time or expertise to plow through peer-reviewed articles every day."

"And this is why misinformation abounds."

"Agreed, but we're meeting people where they're at with actual science. Don't tell me you're still on team 'Social Media and Science Don't Belong in the Same Sentence'?"

I smile, remembering our discussions on this topic in the past. I didn't have a strong opinion on it, and Adrian was still forming his, but we liked to play devil's advocate with each other, testing each other's argument for weakness. Debating as foreplay, I realize, looking back.

He straightens up, pivoting toward me, eyes gone bright with passion, and it's impossible not to be captivated by him. "Sharks don't get their fair shake in the media. And with all the bad press and downright unscientific material being shared, we're offering easily digestible, factual information."

When he puts it like that, his decision to share these videos makes a whole lot more sense. Basically, my one-woman paddleboard speeches, but with efficacy and a broad reach. Being a part of this outreach could actually benefit my career in a bigger way than typical field experience.

I hesitate, though. This is the point of no return. Once our video goes live, I'm in it, officially a part of the crew for the summer. Stuck with Adrian and my hurricane of emotions, with no choice but to ride out the storm.

"If you're okay with it, I'll upload it." The screen has gone dark, and he taps in his passcode. My mouth goes dry at the digits he typed. Our anniversary. Maybe it's practical, not sentimental—why change it and risk forgetting?

But I wanted to forget. Tried to forget.

And yet here we are, both of us remembering.

"Unless you'd rather we reshoot?" He looks up, and I realize I haven't answered. "We can try again when everyone is available, now that you've gotten the jitters out."

"You mean now that I've gotten my feet wet, so to speak?"

He shoulder-bumps me. "I should've never reminded you about my aversion to puns."

"You think I'd forget?" I could never forget any facet of him, even if I wanted to, and I'm beginning to wonder if I really want to, after all.

Heart racing, I say, "Upload it."

seventeen

adrian

248k views.

High numbers should make my heart soar, but with every upward tick my mood trends downward. Each view represents another person behind the screen who might spew venom at Hope. Something that she's strong enough to endure, but I'm not sure I am.

The idea of bringing another scientist onto the team made me wary, and that was before I knew it was Hope. With her here, there's more at stake than ever. She's brave to seize this opportunity, and I'd never stand in her way, but just because she's onboard for this doesn't make it easy to stand by and watch.

Jaw clenched, I minimize the browser window. Around 4:00 a.m. I gave up on sleep and brought my laptop out to the sofa, where I've sat navigating between work and the video. Dinner was a success, but what's kept me up is the memory of our legs pressed together underneath the table, her bare skin against mine. How I held my breath, waiting for her to shift away, and instead she pressed just the slightest bit closer, uncoiling the rope of professional distance between us, until I had to bite my cheek to keep composure.

Such small touches, compared to the passion we used to share, yet enough to have my fists bunched in the sheets, wishing she were here in my bed and not on a damn air mattress across town. Seems like a waste, but the whole thing is really. What we threw away. What we lost. But I didn't trust her enough to come looking for her. I'm still not certain she wanted me to, and it's too late now to make a difference.

All I can do is work hard to ensure this summer is a success for both of us. For a while after I went viral, I was sucked into social media in an unhealthy way, mindset tied to the comments and how I'd be perceived. Being the new kid countless times taught me the importance of making a good first impression. I didn't have the luxury of years to build friendships.

But my followers aren't friends, and their esteem isn't tied to my self-worth. To keep the distinction clear, I had to set clear limits. Treat social media like a job and not an extension of my personality, but launching Hope into the cyber ether has yanked me right back into the toxic cycle of worrying over comments and likes.

She's strong, but I know firsthand how trolls worm their way into your mindset, screwing with your self-esteem even when you try to brush them off. The urge to scour the comments to delete any negative replies has my fingers itching, but so far the reaction's been positive, and I force myself to close the tab.

My phone chimes from the side table and I stretch over to check it, knocking a stack of books to the floor in the process. A calendar notification covers the top of the screen. TURTLE SHIFT. I dig the heels of my hands into my eyes. How is it time to head to the beach already?

Still, it's a welcome interruption. Fresh air and a task will help me stop worrying. Hope is committed to seeing this through, and I need to focus on supporting her, not protecting her.

I grab two protein bars from the kitchen cupboard and click off the lights. The seafood platter from dinner is a distant memory and breakfast is a long way off. The porch light flicks on when I step outside. Crickets chirp in the long grass and the low thrum of a bullfrog comes from down by the river. I take a moment to breathe in the serenity, letting my stress seep away.

Twenty minutes later, I pull into the beach lot. I arrived ahead of schedule and am surprised see another vehicle parked in the darkness, though soon enough, the parking lot will fill up with beachgoers and other volunteers. The sea turtle patrol is led by scientists with the aid of trained volunteers who work to protect and monitor sea turtle nesting sites. We also help raise awareness about the importance of protecting the marine reptiles.

Hope got me involved in volunteering down in Florida during the internship where we met, and I connected with a local group the spring after I moved here. Filling my free time helped keep my mind off her in the early days after our relationship ended.

I convinced Marissa to volunteer with me this summer, and we filmed a series highlighting the work of the sea turtle conservation group. But I'm not sure if she's signed up for this shift, since I swapped last-minute with Helena, a chatty retiree who's out of town for the birth of her first grandchild.

The tang of salty air hits me the moment I step out of my SUV. A low dune stretches in either direction, the hiss of waves audible in the darkness beyond. I blink to let my eyes adjust, but my cell phone stays in my pocket. Artificial light disturbs the nesting turtles and can disorient hatchlings.

The light breeze stirring the sea oats is cool on my cheeks as I make my way toward squared-off wooden posts marking the access point for beachgoers. My intent is to sit on the steps for few minutes in silence before the others arrive and let the ocean settle me.

But once I reach the landing, my shins bump into something large and solid. I stumble backward and my heel slips on the top step.

A hand shoots out and grabs my wrist, steadying me. "Adrian?"

Recognizing her voice in an instant, I find myself staring into the face of the woman with a knack for knocking me off my feet. Once again, Hope's turned up where I didn't expect her. But this time, instead of chaos, her presence brings a profound sense of equilibrium. Like my life has shifted into balance. Or maybe realignment.

Her hand is still around my arm, her fingers cool and slender, damp with the mist rolling in off the waves. My forearm flexes involuntarily and she lets go in an instant. Takes a step back. The sense of rightness fades but doesn't disappear.

A hood is pulled up over her head, curls framing her face, the strands stirring in the breeze. She eyes me up and down and I feel exposed, bare underneath her gaze. "You're not a five-foot-one elderly woman," she says. "And where are the promised treats?"

"Treats?" Even though I've been up all night, I'm fairly certain Hope is talking nonsense.

"Last night Marissa got home late and was complaining about having to wake up to volunteer at dawn. I offered to take her shift because who would turn down a chance to see baby sea turtles?" She sounds affronted at the notion, and I chuckle, the sound carried away by the wind.

"The organizers okayed it since I've done this before," she says. "But Marissa told me I'd be paired up with someone named Helena who always brings along a giant tub of homemade baked goods."

"Ah." That explains the question about treats. Grateful I'm not losing it, I empty my pockets and hold out the contents. "I traded shifts with Helena, sorry to disappoint. Will protein bars do?"

Hope boos, jabbing both thumbs down, her hoodie slipping

over her knuckles. "Why'd you swap shifts?" She narrows her eyes. "Please tell me this isn't Marissa trying to set us up. I told her I'm capable of handling my own life."

Interesting to know Hope shares my suspicions about Marissa's misguided matchmaking, but my cousin is in the clear on this one.

"Not unless she can induce labor. I ran into Helena yesterday in Publix. She mentioned she was about to ask for a trade in our volunteer text thread, but I offered to take her shift so she wouldn't need to bother."

"I guess Marissa's off the hook, then." Hope sounds faintly disappointed, and knowing she puts no stock in fate, I'm guessing she doesn't like that there's no logical explanation why we ended up here together. "Can't very well blame her for my insomnia."

A thought occurs to me, and I duck to get a better look at her face. Even in the darkness, the worry in her eyes is impossible to miss. "You read the comments, didn't you?"

Last I checked, the response was wholly positive, but it only takes one nasty comment... My hand automatically goes to my pocket before remembering we need to preserve the darkness.

She shakes her head. "I didn't. Won't."

Won't? I never advised her not to, though that's a good idea.

"But I saw the views count and now I'm pretty sure I'll never sleep again." She pushes both palms back over her head, dislodging the hood, and grips the roots of her hair. "Hundreds of thousands of people have seen us joking about baby sharks. That's almost a quarter of a million humans, Adrian."

I let out a laugh, then turn it into a cough at her side-eye.

She glares at me, eyes glinting, and it's hard not to smile again at her ferocious expression. "Why is this funny to you?"

"It's not, it's just that—" I gulp down my words in a hiccup. I was about to say that she's adorable when she's indignant, but that's not a workplace appropriate comment. Even if we aren't at work, we're supposed to be functioning as colleagues. Not people who used to make love—

"I know posting a video is just another day's work to you," Hope says, pulling my mind back on track. "But this is a big deal for me." Her voice is trembling, and on impulse, I pull her into a hug.

It only takes a moment to realize my mistake, but before I can let go, she burrows into the embrace, arms tucked around me, holding tight. My eyes pinch closed at how amazing it feels to hold her again.

Her cheek is pressed against my chest, and I tip my head down toward her ear, her shea-scented curls tickling my nose. "Do you want me to take it down?" There's absolutely nothing wrong with the video, and removing it will raise questions, but I'd do it in a heartbeat to protect Hope, to hell with the consequences.

"Mm-mm." She makes a small sound of negation, then turns her head, tipping her forehead into my chest, and groans. The vibration cuts through the thin fabric of my shirt and ignites something dormant in me.

She pulls away to look up at me, arms still around my waist. "Why do you always smell good?" Dodging her eyes down, she frowns. "This is the same shirt from last night."

Embarrassed, I pull away. "Figured today might get messy, so I just threw it on when I got up. Since I sleep pretty much—" I break off, horrified.

"Pretty much naked, I know." Her eyes fly wide, outlined in white. "Wow. This has become wildly inappropriate in a heartbeat."

"My fault." The magnitude of my mistake begins to sink in like loose sand at the shoreline, dragging me down into remorse. "I shouldn't have hugged you."

She wraps her arms around herself, drawing my attention to

the logo on her hoodie. I squint… Is that *my* hoodie? The one I thought got lost in a move?

"I didn't mind," she confesses. "But I shouldn't have mentioned how amazing you smell. Or what you wear to bed. God." Burying her face in her hands, she groans, then reappears with a loud exhale. "Can we chalk it up to muscle memory?"

"Something like that." My voice is hoarse, and I clear my throat. "We should probably…" I gesture vaguely toward the deserted beach.

The sun's still below the horizon, but I need to get moving, to put distance between us. I step down into the sand and start walking as fast as the darkness and caution will allow.

Hope is a few steps behind, and after a moment, she asks, "Any new policies I should be aware of?" Her voice is even, with no vestiges of our encounter, and I exhale in relief. This is neutral ground.

"Not really, but I could send you the handbook to look over if you want."

Hope chuckles. "I'll take your word for it, since I'm sure you read it cover-to-cover."

"When they sent the revised PDF at the start of the season, you better believe it."

She laughs again, a warm, throaty sound against the hiss of the waves. I follow her down onto the sand and fall into step alongside her. I'm so used to threading my arm around her waist on walks like these that I have to shove my hands into my pockets to quell the urge.

Our steps take me away from the dune. White-frothed waves sweep toward us out of the gloom, then retreat. We keep our eyes down, searching for tracks that will indicate a turtle's journey from water to a nesting sight. Our goal is to find any nests, then alert Evan and Myra, the biologists who lead the group, and they'll mark them.

Permits allow the scientists to approach turtle nests for conservation and research purposes, and the group's efforts often draw crowds, which gives us the chance to explain the ins and outs of sea turtle conservation, as well as the importance of not disturbing the animals.

"Found any nests this year?" Hope asks casually.

"Yeah, lots. I'd have to ask what the official tally is."

"Not the group, I meant you personally." Her tone gives nothing away, but I recognize the challenge in her words.

I shake my head, then realize she didn't notice with her focus on the sand. "Not yet. But I don't volunteer that often."

"Mm."

"What's that supposed to mean?"

She stops and looks up. "Nothing. Just was thinking of that summer we volunteered together in Florida. I found way more nests than you. Wasn't even close."

I narrow my eyes at her. "You make it sound like a competition."

"If it was, I would've won." She starts walking again, head tipped down, but I see the grin lifting her cheeks, and with the memory of her earlier vulnerability fresh in my mind, I suddenly want nothing more than to keep her smiling.

"Let's make a bet then."

"I haven't done this in years," she says.

"Sounds like you started something you can't finish."

"There's no way to predict who will find the most nests. It's totally up to luck."

Walking with my eyes downcast, I ask, "How do you know I haven't done observation on this particular stretch of beach and noted the most common nesting areas?"

She glances over at me sharply. I haven't, nor have I asked the biologists running this program, but her shoulders are more relaxed, and if this is getting her mind off the video, I count it as a win. Besides, we're not crossing any lines here. Just two scientists making a friendly, professional wager.

"You're bluffing," she says.

"Is that a no to the bet?"

She crosses her arms, the bulky hoodie swallowing her frame, and while I wasn't sure it was mine before, I am now. This whole situation is wreaking havoc with my emotions, bringing me back to a time and place when we were together.

"Okay, we'll test your theory." Hope lifts her chin and looks up at me. "Give me a number."

I shove my locs back, out of my face. She's calling my bluff. "It's not *that* precise."

"Every hypothesis needs to be tested." Tingles dance along my spine at her teasing tone. We might be joking, but the connection simmering between us is very real. To acknowledge it would be crossing a line, but I can't ignore the feeling.

"Think of the science," she says.

"That's all I think of." Lies. I can recall many times when I haven't thought of science, like when she was underneath me, lip caught between her teeth, or on top of me, fingertips trailing down my chest...

I squeeze my eyes shut. This is veering into dangerous territory. "You know what? Never mind." I suck in a deep breath and start walking again.

She keeps pace with me, abuzz with energy in the purple predawn light. "So you're not willing to test your hypothesis?"

"It's not a—"

"Knew you were bluffing," she says, and I stop in my tracks.

Planting my feet, I face off with her. "Winner buys breakfast."

"Aren't the protein bars breakfast?"

The stare I give her is rendered ineffectual by the darkness, so I settle for a heavy sigh. "Granola bars aren't even a snack."

"Then why'd you bring them?"

"Survival."

She laughs, a loud burst of sound that she smothers with

her palm, and I want to pull her against me, to feel her vibrating with suppressed giggles, to dip my nose and breathe in the dewy tickle of her curls. Laughter is not supposed to be this sexy, but everything about Hope is an aphrodisiac, from her luscious curves to her gorgeous mind.

Lowering her hand, she says, "Breakfast is a boring bet."

"What do you have in mind?" It's a challenge, but we don't need a bet for what I have in mind.

"I want to drive the boat if I win." Her answer is a one-eighty from my thoughts, saving me from myself.

Most days I'd prefer to be a passenger, so I never considered that she might want to be captain. Bet or no bet, I have no problem with it, but now that she's brought it up, the wicked side of me is having too much fun goading her to stop now.

"No bet." I start walking again, but she jogs to catch up, outpacing me and planting herself in my path.

"Why not?" She's walking backward, and I have to fight the urge to take her elbow to keep her from tripping over the uneven sand. "It's low stakes. No money is changing hands."

"Not going to happen."

"But you know I learned how to navigate years ago."

Playfully, I dodge around her and catch a whiff of coconut and vanilla underscored by the tang of ocean air. My steps wobble and she's beside me in an instant, keeping pace.

"It's selfish not to share," she huffs.

That brings me to a halt. "I am not selfish." In my mind, I can almost hear her rapid breaths, the ragged brush of her exhales against my ear as I lay beside her, one hand between us…

I halt that train of thought before it goes off the rails, and look over my shoulder at her, gaze dropping down her tall frame. "I gave you that hoodie, didn't I?"

"This—" She looks down, then her hands fly to her cheeks. "Why didn't you mention it earlier? When you didn't say anything, I figured you didn't notice."

I notice everything about her, but that's definitely not an approved topic. Instead, I say, "That thing comes down to your knees. It's pretty conspicuous."

"Mid-thigh at most." She tugs at the hoodie, and the hem slips over her shorts, making it look like she's not wearing any bottoms.

I ball my fists. "Can we not talk about your thighs?" The words come out in a growl, and I check myself. "Sorry, it's just…" I'm worn down from keeping up the façade. "We did so good yesterday. But every time I'm with you, there's a flood of memories. And the pressure keeps building—"

"What kind of memories?" she interrupts, eager, like my answer is the cipher to a puzzle.

"Right now, the kind that makes things…difficult." My voice slips on the last word, and her breath catches.

"Technically," she says, voice low, and I tip forward to listen, lean in, because I'm helpless to stay away, "this is outside working hours."

I keep still as stone, worried if I move, I'll do something reckless that obliterates our carefully-drawn boundary. "Technically." The word scrapes past my bone-dry throat.

"We could call it an experiment," she says, louder now, more certain, or perhaps trying to convince herself. "Maybe this would even make things easier. Not wondering about what it would feel like to kiss each other again."

"You think about that?" It's reckless to invite this moment in the dark, knowing dawn will come, and with it, a reckoning. But I'm losing the battle against years of want. Grateful to surrender, if she wants to fall along with me.

"Sometimes." Sunrise isn't far off, and I catch sight of the flash of white as her teeth sink into her lower lip.

"Right now?"

She dips her chin in a nod, looks up at me. "I don't know how to stop."

That's it. The last sandbag rips and the dam breaks, destroying good intentions and washing caution out to sea. Her lips are on mine and mine are on hers and we're kissing again after three long years of heartache.

Her mouth is sweet and soft, exactly how I remember her, but better, because this isn't a memory. Lips pressed to mine, she steps closer, and I tug my hands out of my pockets and grab her waist to steady her, or maybe myself. She lets out a soft moan against my mouth, and I tug her against me in earnest, swallowing the sound. Her hips rocket up against me and a groan rips from my own throat, stoked by Hope's hungry kisses.

My brain short-circuits and senses take over—warmth, heat, pulsing need—and then she parts her lips and slides her tongue against mine and I'm a man consumed. My free hand skims under her top, sliding along her ribs, my touch firm, the way she loves, and I'm rewarded by a quick suck of my tongue that sends a bolt of desire rocketing through me. She pulls back for a breath, and I heave in a desperate inhale at the disheveled sight of her, windblown and gorgeous in the pink light of dawn.

How have I lived without this? Without her? I slip my fingers into the tumble of curls above her nape and take charge, my lips not ready to be parted from hers, not now, not ever. Inconvenient to want this much, but the fulfillment is sweeter than anything imaginable.

Touching her, holding her...the wet surrender of her hot mouth under mine is a rush of pleasure I never thought I'd feel again, and all the sweeter for it. Her desire seems to match mine, lips parted as she lets me in, our tongues sweeping against each other, coaxing another breathless moan from her that makes my knees almost give way.

She breaks away to press a kiss to the underside of my jaw, mouth warm against the sensitive skin at the edge of my beard, and my throat bobs in a hard swallow. I skim my hands down her hips and pull her against me. She rocks up on her toes, threading her arms around my shoulders, meeting me halfway, and our lips connect again in a deep kiss.

Nearby voices startle us apart. Hope's eyes are wide. A dart of panic shoots through me, more at the implications of the line we've crossed than worries over being seen. My senses are buzzing, and it takes a moment to orient myself. The conversation is coming from the parking lot behind the dune.

Hope's hands are shaky as she swipes at her lips, like she's trying to erase the sensation. "I'm gonna go check in with whoever's in charge." She motions to the first of the volunteers making their way onto the beach, and I nod, dazed.

"I'll uh, make sure to email you that handbook." My pulse hammers, reality dawning like the sun. Whether the experiment was a success or not remains to be seen, but one conclusion is certain: we just went and made our working relationship a whole lot more complicated.

eighteen

hope

Phone in hand, I walk to the end of the pier, debating whether to call or text. I need advice, but how do I tell Zuri I kissed the man I'm supposed to be on my way to getting over?

Days later, and I'm still reeling from the effects of that earth-shattering kiss. I've dreamt about our kisses often enough in the past few years, but I discovered immediately that memories can't touch reality. Adrian's mouth on mine was a reminder of every ounce of tenderness, every ounce of support, of unexpected wonder, that I found in our relationship before.

Everything I'm supposed to be figuring out how to live without.

At first, I tried to rationalize that it was just a test. Kiss him, feel nothing, be free to move on.

But I can't lie to myself. The kiss wasn't a test. It was me giving in to the longing I've bottled up for three years. Rather than slaking my desire, it made me crave him more than ever. And now that I know he wants me—on some level, at least— I'm further than ever from overcoming my feelings. Trouble is, nothing's truly changed. We wanted each other before and the wanting wasn't enough to keep us together.

Tomorrow we're headed out with the scientists from Charleston, and I haven't seen or spoken to Adrian since our kiss. I can't very well talk to Marissa about it—just the idea of her finding out has had me on edge since the turtle patrol shift.

But Zuri will help me find a way to move forward and work with Adrian. Feet planted on the wooden decking, looking out over the endless waves from the height of hovering seagulls, I gather my courage and press the call button.

Instead of hello, Zuri answers with, "I saw the video and you two did so good! You had that cheesy science show banter down. No one would know you're exes."

"Thanks, I think?" She's never been a big fan of documentaries but has humored me by watching untold hours of them and, in return, I've sat through all the superhero movies she loves.

"But I'm not calling about that." If I get sidetracked, I'll lose my nerve. "I did something reckless."

"You kissed that man," Zuri says without missing a beat.

My free hand grips the pier railing so hard that splinters bite into my palm. "How did you know?"

"Because you've been sending me updates since you arrived, and the past few days, nothing. I knew you were guilty about something."

"I'm not guilty." I am tied up in knots, though. "We didn't do anything wrong."

"I agree, but I know you, Hope. You're feeling guilty because you didn't live up to your own expectations."

I hear chatter in the background and ask, "Sorry, are you at work?"

"Stockroom," she confirms. "Your call is a good distraction."

"Glad someone's happy about my situation."

"You're not?"

It's complicated, that's why I reached out. "I was, when I was kissing him. It was good, like an unbelievably good kiss, Zuri."

"Why unbelievable?"

"Because we haven't kissed for three years. Because I can't stand him."

"You can't stand him," she deadpans.

"Okay, I can't stand the fact that I can still stand him after everything."

"Better." The crinkle of crumpled plastic comes across the line. "Is there a reason you can't explore it instead of shutting it down?"

"At the end of the summer, I'll be starting work elsewhere and next year, maybe a PhD. We'd be at the same point we were three years ago, needing to merge our lives, and I'm not willing to base my career options around a person who I haven't even spoken to for years."

"Fair."

I lean over the railing, watching the water churn against the piers below. "But tomorrow I have to work with him again, and we'll have an audience. Like, a live one." I explain about the group from Charleston. "How do I work with someone I just kissed against my better judgment?"

"By questioning your judgment," she says.

"I thought I just established I did that."

"You said yet you keep finding yourself drawn to him, *despite* your better judgment. What if your judgment is skewed in this case? What if, instead of trying to stay away from him, you should try being his friend?"

"Adrian? The man who I dated for five years?"

"It happens."

"Pretty sure the people who make that work aren't fighting this physical attraction."

"Maybe not, but you've already tried keeping him at arm's length and it didn't work. If you like him enough to kiss him, maybe there's something there and the best thing to do is explore it."

The thought is tantalizing. To be able to talk to Adrian again, like we used to, without worrying I've crossed a line. But it's also scary how much I want that.

I must hesitate for too long, because Zuri speaks up again. "Or get what you came for and be done with him. It's your choice. But if your heart wants to be open to him, I say don't deny yourself."

She's got it backward. It would be denying myself to go back on my commitment to get over him, wouldn't it? "How would being his friend solve anything?"

"Let me ask you this. Have you missed him the past three years?"

"Yes. But—"

"Maybe the kiss was you trying to get closer. But intimacy isn't always physical. I get that you weren't sure of building a life with him, but what about a life with him in it?"

Put that way, I begin to see her point. But I'm still afraid that I won't be able to accept anything less than everything with Adrian. Regardless, it's not a decision I could make alone, and not one that I can make today.

"That sounds terrifying and also risky, so I'm going to go with my original plan of ignoring him."

"Ignoring the person you're doing a highly collaborative job with?" Zuri sounds skeptical in the extreme.

"Ignoring my attraction, my feelings."

"Ignoring left you two kissing," she fires back.

Did it? Am I really going about this the wrong way? I can't fathom being Adrian's friend, not after everything, so I dig in my heels. "Admitting we were both interested in kissing each other led to the kiss. From here on out, it's denial until that becomes our reality."

"Don't say I didn't warn you."

"I don't need a warning," I assure her. "We got the urge out of our system. Now we just have to figure out how to work together like it never happened."

★ ★ ★

Field research is a blend of focus, communication, teamwork, and physical exertion. Add in unpredictable weather, wild animals (or not, depending on whether we manage to catch any), and the need to document scientific data, and each day on the boat calls for concentration and teamwork.

Concentration, after a weekend of restless nights caught between reliving a kiss and telling myself to forget it. Teamwork, with the man who I ran away from because I was too scared to admit how much he means to me.

If I had to grade my progress toward my goals on the whole, it would be a solid F.

Get back into shark research? I tagged one shark and then proceeded to choke on the second go-round like a rookie. I did deliver a lecture on estuary habitats with relative competence. I guess that's a Meets Expectations, planting me solidly in the average zone for my career goals. However, and this is a big however, kissing Adrian bulldozed any progress I've made toward getting over him.

Not to mention the beach make-out session totally undermined my first goal, undoing all the effort of getting comfortable with each other the other day on the boat. Now I'll have to survive what should've been the first normal workday of the summer with the taste of him lingering on my lips.

Classic avoidance might work fine in an office setting, with desks and the chance to take solo lunch breaks and escape to the bathroom if the tension becomes unbearable. Not so effective on a small research boat where cooperation is key and communication is a must and close quarters prevent any semblance of privacy.

The other flaw in my plan is that Adrian told me he can't pretend, can't forget. I haven't seen him since the day we kissed and have no way to gauge his feelings. He never even showed up at Marissa's to pick up the towels we forgot about the other night. I have no clue what he's been drying himself with; for all I know he air-dries after showers by walking around his house nude.

I look up to find him walking down the dock—not naked, but still the embodiment of my lustful musings. His hair is held back with a thick fabric headband and he's wearing a form-fitting T-shirt and teal board shorts that hit mid-thigh. When he reaches me, I'm still frozen in place at the enormity of our slip-up.

He hesitates, as if unsure whether to pass by or acknowledge me. "Would've been here earlier, but I missed my alarm." His voice is gruff from sleep, the rasp of it a reminder of the morning on the beach, and the handles of the cooler turn slick in my suddenly-slippery grip.

He moves to step past me, but I make the same choice, accidentally blocking his way. "Ope, sorry." My Midwestern upbringing has me apologizing for nothing, and my embarrassment grows.

"All good."

We both sidestep again, making the same choice, and wind up in another stalemate.

"You go ahead," he says, and before we wind up trapped in another standoff, I hustle toward the boat.

Marissa's waiting, head cocked, eyebrows up, and it's clear she witnessed the entire interaction. "That was fun," she says. "Are you two planning to make this a habit?"

"Working?"

"Being awkward as sin."

"You're the awkward one." I pass her the cooler. "We're just trying to load up."

"Trying is right. Failing is righter." She points back and forth between us. "I thought we solved this. Y'all were so relaxed in the video. What happened?"

He meets my eyes above her head.

"Saw that!" Setting down the cooler, she gives us her full attention. "You two need a minute to talk things out?"

"No," we both say at the same time. Not suspicious at all.

Marissa's eyes are impossible to see behind her wraparound sunglasses, but I can feel the calculation in her stare nonetheless.

"Uh-oh." Gabe walks up, a coil of line over his shoulder. "What'd I miss?"

I shoot Marissa a pleading look, willing her not to make this a thing. "Nothing, apparently." She climbs aboard and carries her gear toward the stern.

Gabe doesn't look convinced, but unlike Marissa, he lets it lie. Somehow, I don't feel like we're off the hook, though. "Awesome job with the video by the way." He leans across the gap between the dock and boat to retrieve his camera from the open compartment near him. "Can't wait to see more of that energy today."

Adrian lets out a strangled cough, and I can't help but picture the energetic activities we got up to on the beach. Why did we dig ourselves that hole?

Gabe shoulders the camera. "Saw the scientists from Charleston unloading gear in the parking lot and I want to get some shots of them walking the gangplank like the rock-star scientists they are."

"Not a gangplank," Adrian calls, though Gabe knows full well what a gangplank is. Marissa told me he grew up in Fort Lauderdale and learned to scuba dive as a teenager. He's probably got more experience on boats than I do, not having set foot on anything larger than a canoe until college. When people find out I grew up in a lake town, they're often surprised to discover I didn't go boating. But that was for tourists; I spent my days on the beach or *in* the waves, not on them. Sounds like Gabe had a different experience. I'd love to hear his story about being raised near the ocean.

"Argh, didn't catch that, cap'n." He hops nimbly onto the dock with a cheeky grin.

Adrian's brows dip in a glower so ferocious that I have to duck my head to keep him from spotting my smitten grin. Why do I find everything about him so irresistible? His rough edges ought to smooth away my yearning, not act like friction to kindling. All I know is I have to avoid him if I have a chance of making it through today.

Avoiding Adrian on deck turns out to be pretty impossible. Which is why I find myself making my way to the helm for a breather. Gabe is at the wheel, beaming like a pirate with treasure in sight as we cut through the moderate swells. I step up next to him, one hand grasping the frame for support, and he turns his wide smile toward me. "Never gets old," he says, voice raised above the wind.

"How'd you get put on captain duty?" I'm grouchy from trying to pretend this is all normal. I'm beginning to think Adrian was right; it's impossible.

Gabe's brows dip together above his blue polarized sunglasses. "We take turns, just depends on the day." He clocks my expression, then lets out a laugh. "Wait, did Adrian tell you there was some rule about it?"

"Yes!" A wave lifts the hull and I flex my knees. "He said no bet."

"Bet?"

My cheeks flush at the wording. "I meant, he told me no."

His smile disappears. "That's weird." Glancing over his shoulder, he asks, "Is he giving you a hard time?"

I blush at his unwitting word choice. "Not at all." More like the other way around. A smirk tilts my lips at the thought, but I'm not supposed to be remembering the kiss. And thinking back, did he actually tell me I couldn't drive the boat, or just that he wouldn't make a bet on it? No way to call him out now, so I settle for glaring toward where he's sitting in the bow with Sylvia and Liam, the doctoral students we're taking out to perform ultrasounds today.

I remember when it used to feel effortless to sit with him. How our friendship blossomed into something more, natural as breathing. The texts that made the distance collapse to insignificance. The beginning of a love story that ended years ago. Now I'm keeping my distance, trying to erase it all.

"I meant what I said about the video," Gabe says, getting me out of my head. "You did an awesome job on camera." He returned two days ago from the Bahamas, but this is the first we've spoken. "Today should be no problem since you'll have the sharks to focus on."

I blow out a breath. "Not so sure."

"I am." He looks over at me. "You seem like the kind of person who doesn't give up."

"Yeah, but there's always the possibility to fail in new and disastrous ways." The thing is, I never used to mind failing. Or at least, didn't let it stop me. Failure leads to new ways of thinking, but I'd never failed in such a major way, and it affected me more than I thought possible.

Gabe shoots me a wry look. "That's a possibility too." He looks down at the GPS, then back at the open water ahead. "I guess what it comes down to, is whether it's worth it."

One of the hardest parts of working in the field for me is the need to make small talk for the long hours of inaction, but it turns out Sylvia and Liam are easy to talk to.

"I've had more than my fair share of experience being on the receiving end of ultrasounds," Sylvia says. "Had enough of them to last a lifetime with my high-risk pregnancy." Flipping her braid over one shoulder, she rises up on one hip to pull out her phone and passes it to me. Her lock screen is a toddler with a precious gap-toothed grin.

"How old is she?"

"Three. Light of my life. She's one of the reasons I'm so interested in conservation. Want to make sure she has an ocean full of biodiversity to explore when she's older. Or y'know, she might spend her days in a studio making clay pottery. Whatever makes her happy," she says with a proud smile, pocketing her phone.

"What's our game plan for today?"

She blows out a breath and settles back against the railing, arms spread. "We're hoping to do work-ups on pregnant sharks, and if so, we'll looking at the species distribution of pregnant sharks, number of pups, what point in gestation the sharks have reached, and whether the animal has been tagged before to see if they're returning to the same pupping grounds."

"However, to do that, we actually need to *catch some sharks.*" Liam, the other researcher, raises his voice for the last phrase, hollering over his shoulder at the water like it might make a difference, and we all laugh.

We've been anchored for nearly half the time allotted for drum lines, a type of fishing we're permitted to use for research purposes only. The weighted drum rests on the seabed, with the line stretching to the surface, a conical buoy attached.

A buoy that hasn't moved aside from the rhythmic bob of waves since we set the line. No movement means no bites. No bites means no sharks to examine.

All part of the job, but after the three years, these extra few minutes are surprisingly hard to bear. It also brings everything I've questioned to the forefront. Today the camera is the least of my worries; working closely with Adrian after our mind-melting kiss has pushed fear of the camera to the back burner. But the familiar setting soon eases my nerves.

Marissa and Adrian are working on their laptops across from me, and I've been chatting with Sylvia about her research while we cut bait. "Do you see a potential policy correlation for your findings?"

"That's Liam's interest," she says. She lifts a scale-coated finger, then grimaces and lifts her chin instead, indicating her colleague. "He's pursuing a PhD in marine science and conservation. He wants to work in policy. Prefers boardrooms to boat decks."

"Heard that," he calls from the stern, "and you're absolutely correct."

He makes his way over and settles on the seat across from us. "Two words: iced coffee."

Sylvia shakes her head, reaching into the bucket for another fish. "Last week it was access to vending machines."

"My love of creature comforts knows no bounds," he informs her.

I chuckle and he makes eye contact, a wide smile stretching across his tanned face. "What's your poison?"

"From vending machines?"

He nods, and I don't have to think. "Snack mix," I say at the same time as Adrian, who's been quiet since I joined the others on deck.

Liam shifts his gaze between Adrian and I, blue eyes appraising beneath the brim of his cap.

"I prefer M&M's," Sylvia says, rescuing us from the awkward silence after our inadvertent jinx. "Sweet tooth."

"Regular or peanut?" Apparently, Liam doesn't play when it comes to vending machine fare.

"Easy," Sylvia says. "Regular, no contest."

"Mm-mm." Adrian shakes his head. "Peanut," he says, at the same time as I do, and I cringe inwardly.

"You two work together a lot?" Liam lifts his cap and rakes his hands through his sun-streaked brown hair in an overly casual way that lets me know he's already formed an opinion.

"Used to." Adrian's voice is neutral. "Small field." He doesn't so much as look my way, and I send him a silent thank-you.

"Have you published lately?" Liam directs this question my way and I'm starting to wish I hadn't left the safety of the helm.

I lick my lips. Questions like these are commonplace, but this is my first time being asked since I've been back. "I co-authored a study on the efficacy of various techniques to stop the spread of zebra mussels in Lake Michigan."

"Michigan?" He frowns slightly. "Long way from the ocean. How'd you end up there?"

My eyes dart toward Marissa and Adrian. They both know my story, but only Adrian was personally affected. Having to explain myself in front of him is uncomfortable, but I knew this might happen when I signed on. "I grew up there. After I earned my master's degree in marine science, I worked in elasmobranch research for a couple years, but a friend of mine lost her husband, and I wound up moving in with her to help her with her kids. Worked in freshwater biology for the past few years."

"Sorry to hear about your friend," Liam says, and Sylvia nods. "I bet you have some cool insight, working in the Great Lakes. What was your focus?"

His easy acceptance of my story, like everything is actually okay, has my heart full. The first stranger that I've had to explain my work history to, and it was no big deal. Granted, he's not a prospective employer or potential doctoral advisor, but a weight I've been carrying for a long time lifts as I delve into my research in Michigan.

At one point, I catch Adrian's eye, and he smiles. No awkwardness, no trace of a barrier, just the support of someone who cared—and maybe still cares—about me. For a moment, the world feels pretty close to perfect.

"I love how you were able to come back to this after your time away," Sylvia says. "I was in a similar situation after I had my daughter. I planned on jumping right back in, but I ended up taking a year. Coming back, I was scared of getting labeled a typical mom, or a cliché. But screw that," she says. "We do what we need to, for ourselves, our friends, our family. And we keep going. That's all that matters."

Her words are an echo of Gabe's... Keep going. Don't give up. Could that be true for Adrian and I, or just wishful thinking? If I'd been willing to try to share a home with him, even at the risk of failure, might things have been different now?

"Don't look now, but I think we're being watched," Liam says in a false whisper.

I glance up so fast my neck spasms and sure enough, Gabe's recording us.

"Just getting B-roll," he assures us.

"Which means?"

Marissa glances up from her laptop. "That he'll have that on all day, and you should ignore it," she says. "Trust me, you do not want to hear him go into the history of filmmaking right now." She drops her chin to her chest and fakes a snore.

"Big talk from someone who once spent over an hour explaining the etymology of the term 'mermaid's purse' for shark egg cases and the unique embryonic development of shark fetuses, complete with illustrative specimen photos from your phone's camera roll."

"When you have access to source material, you use it. Academia 101."

"We were in a karaoke bar."

Liam lets out a laugh. "I've got to confess that I've watched every one of your episodes, but you guys are even more fun in person."

"Right?" Sylvia is grinning. "So cool to be a part of this." She turns to me. "You said you've got an interest in white shark migration, right?" At my nod, she says, "Because Gwen—Dr. Gwen Oswald—are you familiar with her work?"

"Of course." Her research center in Santa Barbara is one of the most prestigious white shark research programs in the United States.

Sylvia looks pleased. "She was my advisor during my master's program. Anyway, the lab offers seasonal research internship opportunities to give scientists experience with technology and techniques to use in their own research."

"I actually looked into applying this spring," I tell her. "But by the time I was ready to apply, the window had closed."

She grabs a towel and wipes off her hands. "Yep, but Gwen was telling me the other day that one of their candidates for the fall term had to drop out and they reopened to applications. I think the deadline is Friday. If you're still interested, might be worth a shot."

Before I can thank her, Gabe raises his arm, pointing toward the buoy.

"Hey guys, I'm still fairly new to this," he says, eyes on the viewfinder, "but I'm pretty sure the buoy rocking like a used car lot inflatable means we're in business?"

nineteen

hope

I'm bent double, hanging over the side of the boat, gripping a rope that's secured around a lemon shark's tail, doing my best not to screw up this shot at redemption. Adrian's at the other end of the shark, with Sylvia between us, LED goggles on as she conducts the ultrasound.

The lemon shark is named because of the yellowish tint of the scales on their dorsal side, a part of the animal that isn't visible at the moment because we carefully maneuvered the shark onto her back to allow us to conduct the ultrasound. The inverted position induces a trancelike state called tonic immobility which helps keep the animal calm throughout the procedure.

"We've got a pregnant shark!" Sylvia says, elation in her voice. "I'm going to go ahead and measure these babies." Water sloshes into my face, but Sylvia is stoic, calling out numbers to Liam, who's taking notes.

Once she's finished, she pulls the goggles off and holds them out. "Want to take a look?"

"Me?"

"Here, I'll take the tail rope," Marissa says. She steps up beside me and I wait for her go-ahead to let go. I've only done this once, five years ago, and the thrill is just the same when I slip the goggles over my face and a grainy image comes into view.

Live pups. Active ones, with tiny rows of teeth, churning around in the uterus. A sight to behold, and I'm captivated.

I slip off the goggles and move out of the way for Liam to place the tag.

"I'll watch this first go-round." I haven't tagged a shark since my disastrous first day, and though my nerves are settled, fear of failure lingers.

Now that Marissa's got the rope, I'm at loose ends, left to play spectator. I haven't screwed anything up, but I haven't been an asset, either.

"Let's get this shark swimming again," Adrian says, and I'm by his side in an instant, ready to assist in undoing the ropes securing the shark. On Marissa's signal and a nod from him, I loosen the knot, slipping it off. The shark swims away, kicking up a spray of water as a farewell, and I sputter out a laugh. Wiping the salty water from my face, I blink through bleary eyes to find Adrian grinning at me.

I did it. A small thing, to release a shark, but I didn't fumble the knot, or fall overboard. Little victories.

After the first shark, we hit a string of good luck. I pitch in during all the shark work-ups, assisting where needed, stepping back when I'm not. The work feels seamless, exciting, exactly how it did years ago before I left. On our last shark of the day, Sylvia holds out the tag to Adrian. "Want to do this one?"

But instead of taking it, he turns toward me. "Hope?"

No tremor in my fingertips when I reach for the tag this time. I don't hesitate, don't waste a second waiting for fears to overwhelm. A thousand people could be watching, and it wouldn't matter. I know how to do this, audience or not.

Adrian releases the tag into my grip, and I raise my eyes to find his inky-dark ones on me, steady. Reassuring. Present.

My hands go still, grip firm, and he lets go. Steps back. He's giving me space. Trust.

I lean over the boat and feel the shark's rough skin under my gloves, working by muscle memory to insert the tag just below the dorsal fin. Simple. Easy.

Exhilarating.

I step away to let Liam and Sylvia finish up and find Adrian grinning from ear to ear. He grabs me around the waist and swings me up into a hug. My arms go around his shoulders, and I'm laughing, joyous, carried away by the feeling of being back where I was always meant to be.

The years fall away and leave us here together in this moment. At the beginning. Full of promise. *What if* no longer a barbed memory but a joyful hope.

He sets me down a moment later, eyes locked with mine in a sure, certain way that makes the world fade away as he comes into sharp focus. The sun appears from behind a cloud, light dancing in the depths of his eyes like sunbeams filtering through the shallows, a depth of emotion in his expression that matches the pounding in my chest.

When my feet hit the deck, I wake from the trance, realizing in a heartbeat where we are. The others are still bent over the side of the boat, working to release the shark, and Gabe has the camera pointed their way, but he's looking at us, his usual grin replaced by a look of concern that has the euphoria of a moment ago evaporating in a heartbeat.

Laden with gear, I trail the rest of the group down the dock at the end of a long, exhausting, productive day. The marina is mostly deserted, with the other boaters at dinner or out on an evening cruise. Sylvia and Liam are chatting excitedly about the outcome of our day with Marissa and Gabe. We wound up examining and tagging eight sharks, three of whom were pregnant. A successful day, and I didn't freeze in front of the camera once, not even after Gabe caught Adrian and I in a spontaneous hug.

The quick embrace seems inconsequential now that several hours have passed. I was probably blowing it out of proportion in my mind. It was just a hug. A joyous, ecstatic hug, born of adrenaline. Nothing intimate, even though it felt that way.

We load the gear into the vehicles, and Sylvia asks for my number to keep in touch about the program in Santa Barbara. When she says she'll send me a text to confirm her contact, I pat my pocket to check my phone and realize I must've left it on the boat.

Not wanting to interrupt the flow of the others' conversation, I catch Marissa's eye. "Gotta find my phone. I'll be right back."

"Okay, but hurry. We want to grab a table before it gets busy."

She invited the others out to dinner before they make the long drive home. The thought of a crowded restaurant makes my shoulders sag, but it would be rude to skip. I want nothing more than to head home and eat reheated leftovers on the couch while the TV drones in the background.

Nights in with Adrian were my favorite. When he was in town, I never felt the need to entertain him or dress up my life for his visits. We'd walk for hours on the beach or sit entwined on the couch and just talk. Just be. Just love one another. And when I went to his place and discovered nothing but peanut butter and sliced bread in his cupboards, I never felt compelled to drag him to the grocery store for a pantry makeover. We'd eat toast for dinner and vent about work, or gush about a breakthrough, or complain about family, and it was perfect.

But now he's making pizza dough from scratch and spending his free time lifting weights. He's changed, in so many ways, and yet the man I kissed is the same Adrian I loved. The man who kissed me on the beach and wrapped me in his arms on the boat for that brief moment today is the same person I lost my heart to years ago.

But I promised myself I wouldn't fall for that man again. Promised myself I'd get over him. And I will not think of how amazing it felt to have him hold me again. Head down, I clamber aboard, pushing thoughts of Adrian aside.

I will not think of his lips, or his talented tongue, or his—

Naked chest, right in front of me.

His head pops through the T-shirt he's in the act of putting on, glorious abs on full display. He wobbles, unsteady and dangerously close to tripping. I act on reflex and throw both arms around his waist—no one else is falling overboard on my watch. His skin is warm but erupts with goose bumps under my fingertips. Shifting my weight, I haul him upright, no easy task given his size.

As soon as he's steady I let go and all but leap backward.

"What are you doing here?" He wrestles his shirt down, which is a pity.

"Looking for my phone." I go from flustered to indignant in a heartbeat, his proximity wreaking havoc on my emotions. "Maybe you should make sure no one's around if you're going to run around naked." Naked is a stretch, considering he's wearing shorts and shoes, but he keeps catching me off guard.

"I thought I was alone." He gestures around the deserted marina. "Maybe you should announce your presence when you go prowling around someone's boat."

"Call me a bandit again, I dare you."

We're toe-to-toe, and I'm staring him down like the self-righteous pain in the neck he is. The kind of pain in the neck I want to wrap my legs around and kiss senseless.

My chest is heaving, and his eyes are fever-bright, the color of polished onyx in fading light. "What would you prefer I call you?"

Mine. I want him to call me his. To stake his claim and not give up on me. On us.

Our lips are a whisper apart and he closes the distance with a kiss that's fevered in an instant, no hesitancy this time. He walks me backward two quick steps until my shoulders hit something solid and I let out a muffled, "Oof."

"Sorry," he murmurs, but I pull him back down for another kiss, because I don't want his sorry—I don't want apologies or looking back. I want his mouth on mine and for his kisses to never end. He rocks against me, and I gasp, his lips curving into a smile I can feel. Then I match the pressure of his hips, take satisfaction when his grin dissolves into a guttural groan that has him sliding his calloused, tender hands down my curves, over my waist, his thumbs slipping under my shirt to expose my skin to the dewy evening heat.

He tilts his head, deepening the kiss, and I ignite under his touch. Until the other day, I hadn't felt this good in ages—years—and from his ragged, wanton breathing, he's as far gone as I am, kissing me with reckless abandon for what's only a moment but feels like eternity.

A loud *snap* sounds from the water below, and Adrian springs away. I whip my head around just as an enormous bird flaps up out of the water and lands on the dock. It waddles in an ungainly half turn, shaking water out of its brown-gray wings.

"Pelican." Adrian's face is grim, like he's meeting an old nemesis, and I press my lips together to keep from smiling. He gets creeped out by large birds—big birds, I said once, which he did not appreciate, though I was thoroughly pleased with myself—and I'm sure the pelican's ill-timed arrival is going to be added to his already extensive list of reasons why he prefers scaled creatures to feathered ones.

The weight of desire is shattered, but it's for the best. We can't keep doing this. Kissing. Wanting. Trying to resurrect what's lost.

I do a quick scan for my phone and spy it on one of the benches. Bending to retrieve it, I say, "I need to go before anyone comes looking."

Adrian's posture is stiff, nothing like the pliable way he fit against me only a moment ago. "I don't think this is working," he says, and I straighten up, on guard.

"What?"

"The kissing, it's not..." He looks away. "I can't keep things separated."

"Because we're just colleagues?" I hate that it comes out as a question.

"What else would we be?" His words are flat, a double-edged blade, and the idea of answering, *Friends* is so ludicrous, I don't know how I ever considered Zuri's suggestion.

"Nothing." We can't be anything to each other, not if I want to keep my heart intact.

With a swiftness that rocks the boat, he passes by, leaving me alone in the fading dusk, the word a hollow echo in my chest. *Nothing.* But he used to mean everything to me.

twenty

adrian

Gabe offered to pick me up for dinner, but I took my time getting ready, partly because kissing Hope is replaying on a loop in my mind—the gentle yielding of her mouth, the needy pressure of her hips against mine, and how the pleasure is destined to end with the pain of separation—but also because I was hoping he'd get impatient and head to the restaurant without me.

No luck. I emerged from my room to find he'd let himself in and was waiting in my kitchen, dressed for a night out in a short-sleeved chambray button-down and jeans, with his laptop, tablet, and phone spread out across the table. He must've sensed my mood, because he kept quiet the entire drive, unusual for him. As we pull into the restaurant parking lot, I suppress the urge to open the passenger door and tuck and roll, making a break for it.

The moment I step out of the car, though, I'm grateful I didn't stay home. The tantalizing aroma of barbecued meat and fresh-baked rolls wafts from the tin-roofed restaurant. Horizon Line Grill is tucked under live oaks and loblolly pines, flanked by a porch lined with wooden benches for nights when the dinner rush line spills outside. Sunset comes early to this pocket of town, and shadows stretch long across the ground, our feet crunching on the gravel walkway.

Gabe halts at the bottom of the porch steps and blocks my way. The hum of laughter and conversation from inside is muted out here. Not too late to go back home, except he's my ride. Plus, tonight's about celebrating a great day at work, and I promised Hope I'd keep things professional. *And then you went and kissed each other.* Twice.

A topic I can't broach with Gabe, not without exposing Hope in the process.

"Are you going to tell me what's going on or do I need to guess?" He holds up a hand. "Disclaimer: I'd go with the former. It's healthy to talk things out, and it'll satisfy my craving for juicy gossip."

Despite my tumultuous emotions, I grin. I really am lucky to have him. Friends have come and gone my whole life, but I hope this friendship lasts beyond *Shark Science Crew,* wherever life takes us. Still, I can't level with him. Hope deserves discretion. Besides, what happened between us is nothing more than chemistry that keeps getting the better of us.

"Nothing's going on." It's the same line we fed Marissa earlier, and without waiting to see if he accepts it, I move to step past him, but he's nimble despite his flip-flops, and cuts me off.

"Okay, a guessing game it is." He taps his clean-shaven chin. "We just spent a lovely day taking pictures of actual baby sharks, so your sour mood can't be work-related."

"Sonograms," I say, even though I know he's baiting me. "And they're fetal sharks."

He merely raises his brows. "People are already watching the heck out of the teaser video—"

"You got that up already?"

"What do you think I was doing while I was waiting for you to finish getting presentable?" He ticks off his fingers. "You helped out some fellow scientists, broadened the public's perception of shark research, and managed to do it all with a minimal awkwardness with your ex-girlfriend."

My smile evaporates.

"Oh." His eyebrows bounce above his frames. "It's the girlfriend part, isn't it?"

"Ex." My jaw clacks shut, biting out the word.

"Just to clarify, we're talking about the ex-girlfriend you hugged today?"

My mouth twists. "Habit."

"Right, right." He leans against the banister, and I calculate my odds of getting around him and making a break for it. He must notice, because he straightens up, arms crossed. "So you got swept up in the moment?"

"Exactly."

His eyes narrow. "But you full-on airport-reunion hugged your ex-girlfriend. You picked her up by the waist and swung her around like you'd just made it home after an unplanned sixteen-hour layover and she didn't freak out about it."

"Would you quit calling her that?"

"What, your ex-girlfriend?"

The term is accurate, but feels so detached, not at all like my messy, deep feelings for Hope. "She's our colleague."

The crickets start up, and I can hear the hum of engines from the nearby highway. "No disrespect," he says. "What I'm wondering, is who she is to you."

"Our summer research assistant," I tell him, sticking to the line we agreed upon, even though my lips tingle at the memory of her mouth on mine, the rush of desire it's prudent we deny. "And I know the hug was a mistake."

"A mutual mistake?" His tone is mild, but his shoulders are set. It occurs to me that this conversation isn't entirely for my benefit, and I'm as pleased by his concern for her as I am chagrined at my behavior. Without all the details, I can see how it might look fishy. Even with all the details, it still feels complicated as hell.

I have to give him something, though, or else he might bring it up with Hope, and that's the last thing she'd want. "We hung out the other day, after we shot the video. Talked." A few diners make their way down the path, and we step aside to let them by. "Reminisced, I guess. I think the nostalgia bled into today, and we got carried away."

He nods, accepting this. "Gottta be honest, I worry about the two of you. This has to be tough. Five years together and you never mentioned her to me." I never told him how long we dated either, so I'm guessing Marissa filled him in. "There's got to be a story there."

"We had plans to move in together, she changed her mind." I shrug, hoping he'll be satisfied with that.

"After five years?"

"Plans change. People change."

"But she's single, after all this time—"

"Gabe." I cut him a look. "Can we eat? I'm starving."

Arms crossed, he regards me for a long moment before letting me by. I waste no time moving past him, up the steps and into the restaurant, the spring-hinged screen door banging shut behind us. The place is packed. I'm in no mood for crowds, but this is our usual spot. Good food, great service, and the owner is a family friend.

Sure enough, I spot Rhonda by the bar, her gray hair cut in a short bob. She locks eyes with me, smiling, and is already halfway around the bar by the time I thread my way through the maze of tables.

"Give me a hug, mister!"

She wraps me in a tight embrace, and the weight on my shoulders eases. Rhonda's basically family. She and Mom were roommates in college and remained close friends. We even vacationed a couple times with her family back when I was a kid. After her divorce, Rhonda decided to quit her job in law to buy this place.

She pulls away and throws a stained towel over her shoulder, rosy cheeks flushed. "Why didn't your mother tell me Hope was back?" I glance toward the table where Marissa's seated with the other scientists, but Hope's nowhere to be seen.

Rhonda follows my gaze. "She went to the bathroom, but ah—" she reaches out a hand, beckoning someone behind me "—here she comes now."

Hope appears by my side, wearing a flowy printed sundress with buttons down the front, jostling against me as someone steps up to the bar in the crowded space. Rhonda gets pulled away to help clean up a spill at a high-top table behind us, but in the chaos, another group wedges us in, trying to get the bartender's attention. We're stuck together for the moment, crushed between the other patrons.

"You're late," Hope says, rising on tiptoe so I can hear her. The buttons on the front of her dress press into my arm, and I don't dare look down. "The others are about to leave. They've got a long drive."

Guilty, I glance toward the table again and see she's right. Liam is shaking Marissa's hand, and Sylvia rises, her jacket over one arm. Never should've let my personal life interfere with a work dinner. "My bad. Gabe and I got caught up talking."

Her eyes flash to my face. She's so close that I can make out the tiny flecks of amber in her eyes, her usually-bare lashes darkened with mascara. "About what?" Concern knits her wide brow.

"He was worried about, well—"

"Us?" Hope's mouth turns downward in a frown. "He saw?"

I shake my head, but before I can explain, Rhonda appears from behind the bar.

"I sure saw," she says with a wink, and my heartbeat accelerates to a dangerous pace. "I watch every one of Adrian's videos." My pulse returns to normal as I realize what she meant. She points at us with the bar towel in her hand. "You better not disappoint with the baby shark content you promised."

I open my mouth, but Rhonda's not done. She turns toward Hope, leaning in to speak over the noise. "Now, before I get pulled away again, what do you think of the transformation?"

"Transformation?" Hope gives the room a puzzled once-over and I can tell what she's thinking. This place looks the same as always. Cane-backed chairs flank circular tables of knotty pine. The bar is held up by glossy white tongue-and-groove boards and the barstools could use a reupholstering. The overall feel is more homey than trendy, but unfortunately, Rhonda's not talking about the décor.

"I have your ex-boyfriend to thank for the inspiration. Or is it boyfriend now?" Rhonda asks, a gleam in her blue eyes.

"Ex," I say, saving Hope the trouble. "She's just here to work with us for the summer."

Rhonda tilts her head, appraising us. "So it's strictly business between you two?"

"All business," Hope says. "Nothing but science."

I venture a glance and see she's got what I call her yearbook smile on: too many teeth and frozen eyes. We're screwed.

Once again, I wish I would've stayed home. Not only did I miss the chance to network, making the evening pointless, but Rhonda knows Hope and I too well. She'll see right through us.

Surprised Gabe hasn't chimed in to rescue me, I glance around and find him at the table where Marissa's saying goodbye to the others. A moment later, my pocket buzzes and I pull out my phone.

Gabe: I told them we had car trouble. You can follow up over email.

Adrian: Thanks, I owe you one.

Gabe: I saw you clock Hope in that dress. Co-workers, re- member?

My face flushes, and I scratch at my beard. Once again, my body not catching on that the attraction to Hope is a dead-end road.

"Everything okay?" Hope asks.

"What? Yeah." I tuck the phone against my chest, worried she saw. "Did you want to go say goodbye to the others?"

"I already did before I went to the bathroom. It would be weird to go back over there now."

"Gotcha." I blow out my cheeks, at a loss what to do. I did not expect to be alone again with her so soon, but I'm starving, and I doubt Gabe plans to leave without eating. Sure enough, I turn and see the other biologists are gone, but their seats have been taken by a couple of Marissa's friends. My cousin's an extrovert, while I'm somewhere in the middle. I love to be around people if I know them well, but I'm okay with long stretches of solitude.

Hope's a straight up introvert though, and I turn back to find her shoulders drooping. I lean down and say, "I didn't drive, but I can order you an Uber." Her eyes swing toward mine. "If you wanted to get out of here, I mean. It was a long day."

The rattle of shaken ice interrupts us, and I glance over to see Angie on the other side of the bar with a cocktail shaker. "Hope Evans," she says. "About time you stopped in." Angie pours a lurid green cocktail, and a server takes it away. The surly general manager at the previous establishment, she stayed on when Rhonda took over and ended up buying into the restaurant as co-owner a few years back.

"How'd you know I was in town?" Hope asks.

"This guy's Insta." Angie hitches a thumb toward me, and I distract myself from all this embarrassment by imagining all the ways I'll make Marissa's life miserable for suggesting we come here tonight. "Rhonda is fully addicted to the shark content."

"You bet I am." She reappears and places a menu in front of us, for Hope's benefit, since I've got it memorized. "Not every day a kid I've known since he needed swim floaties makes it big. And the sharks are way cool."

Angie grimaces. "To each their own. Leave the ocean to the fishes, I say. I prefer a cabana in the shade any day."

"Ooh, cabanas. Now there's an idea." Rhonda's eyes take on a dreamy look and Hope turns to see what she's looking at.

"Stop with that nonsense," Angie says, tsking. "We don't need to do any remodeling. Bad enough you're experimenting with drinks and plastering our logo on everything."

"It's called branding," Rhonda retorts. "Adrian knows all about it, right?"

Fighting to keep a straight face, I hold up a neon logoed cocktail napkin that would look more at home at a Myrtle Beach boardwalk bar than this cozy spot in Murrell's Inlet. "These are new."

A tiny snort comes from Hope, and I catch her eye, giving a small shake of my head. If she loses it, I will too. Angie grunts in apparent disgust and stalks off, muttering to herself.

Rhonda leans across the bar to whisper, "To be honest, I could care less about innovating. But Angie's reactions are priceless, and our customers don't care about this stuff one way or the other, so what've I got to lose?"

Hope lets out a laugh and Angie pops back through the swinging door to the kitchen, eyes narrowed in suspicion at the merriment. Whistling, Rhonda bobs her gray brows with a conspiratorial smile and moves off to take someone's order.

"Glad to see Angie's scowls aren't reserved for me," Hope says.

"Nah, she distributes those as a sign of her esteem, like Marissa." The bar area has cleared out, but rather than head back to the table, Hope lingers, and I take the chance to say, "She's happier with you here. Marissa, I mean." I don't know if my cousin would love me saying this, but it's true. "She has a bunch of work friends, but not all that many close friends. She's missed you."

"It's good to spend time with her again." Hope puts her finger on the napkin I set down, spinning it. "And it's nice to talk to a friend about sharks without their eyes glazing over."

I know she's making light of it, but while many of my friends are in marine science, I get the same feeling at family reunions or the rare times I run into someone from high school, like my career is a novelty. A lot of people don't care about sharks beyond the headlines they see on the news.

Hope's gone quiet, analyzing the water-stained menu in her hands. "I know it's easier if I go, but leaving without Marissa would make a scene and—"

"Why do you think I want you to go?"

"You offered to get me a rideshare. And earlier, you stormed off—"

"I did not storm off. I walked away to preserve my dignity."

"Okay, we'll go with that," she says, smiling. Her lips are glossy and I catch a fruity scent whenever she leans close. Mango, I think. "But we've got to figure out how to act normal around each other."

I'm not even sure what normal is in this situation. "We did today."

She meets my eyes. "Until we didn't." Something in the bold way she meets my gaze, like she's not shying away from the memory of my mouth on hers, has me hot in a second. Which is exactly what we're trying to avoid.

Her tongue darts out, moistening her lips. "And now being at Horizon Line with you… Gosh, I can't even remember the last time—"

"Dad's birthday," I say, then wish I could take back the words. It was a surprise party for his sixtieth, and Hope flew in for the weekend and helped decorate the restaurant. She climbed on my shoulders to hang streamers from the rafters. Kept trying to use my head for balance and I told her I was going to go bald if she kept yanking on my hair.

I swipe a hand over my head, locs gathered half-up. Guess it's good I was wrong about some things.

"How is he? And your mom, is she—"

"Good. Both good. Trying to talk them into retiring, but according to them, they'll quit when they're done, and not before."

She chuckles. "Sounds like them. And Marissa said they're all about *Shark Science Crew*, which of course, they love you," she says. "Not that it isn't amazing in its own right."

I brush that off. "I upload videos of my day job. Nothing revolutionary."

"It is, actually. Can you imagine if we'd had access to something like this as kids?"

"That's exactly what keeps me going on days I want to give it up and go back to the way things were. The realization that some kid might see a guy who looks like him doing shark research and realize he can too."

I've told this to a lot people—in interviews, meetings, conferences—but confessing it to Hope feels different. Despite all the good that came before, I worry that all she'll ever see is the man who gave up on a relationship with her.

She tilts her head, expression thoughtful. "Do you ever take out anyone who's not a researcher?"

"No. We only work with scientists or groups from colleges. Why?"

"What if we did? Give kids a chance to go out on the boat. Experience fieldwork for a day."

"Kids?" I lean back with a half-grimace. "I took Marissa's eight-year-old nephew mini golfing once and it was rough. I can't imagine taking kids out on the boat."

"Teenagers," she clarifies. "High schoolers. Give them a taste of a career with sharks, not the sensationalized stuff that's often portrayed on TV."

That sounds like a huge undertaking. But I don't want to

discourage her from voicing her ideas, and it's a good one, just not sure one I'm sure we'll be able to manage right now.

"You should bring it up to Marissa. She has more experience with outreach programs than I do." Her day job is with an ocean nonprofit, and they might be able to partner with us for something like that in the future.

Hope glances over her shoulder. "I will, thanks. Though maybe not right now."

I look toward my cousin and see she's pulling out more chairs, and Gabe's waving people over. Hope doesn't make a move to join them, and I'm guessing her extrovert batteries are used up.

More time together might not be the best idea, but I can't flip off caring about her comfort like a light switch. "Looks pretty packed over there. You want to chill here?" I nudge out the barstool next to me, quirking an eyebrow at Hope.

She mock-groans. "Am I that obvious?"

"Not at all, but I know you."

Her lips press tight, but then a half smile appears. "Guess that's not always necessarily a bad thing." Oh, but it is. Bad for my heart. But this is my chance to prove we're stronger than the attraction.

She climbs onto the stool, and I take a seat at the other one. Picking up the menu again, she points to a drink. "What's a Paradise Tea?" The noise level in the restaurant has picked up, and she tips toward me, the glint of a gold necklace drawing my eyes down to the glossy skin exposed by her low neckline.

Co-workers, I remind myself. No. More. Kissing.

"It's a—" I blink, trying to find my equilibrium "—it's just a Long Island. Rhonda got inspired to fancy up the place and thinks they need signature cocktails. Angie is fighting her every step of the way."

"What did she mean about having you to thank?"

"She thinks I'm some sort of branding genius. I've told her

a lot of that is due to Marissa, and now Gabe. I'm just the talent," I joke.

She shakes her head. "You're more than that."

"I know. But sometimes I don't feel like the right guy for the job." I rest my elbow on the bar, turning to face her. "I'm not spontaneous. I don't up and start YouTube channels."

"But you did."

"I did, yeah."

"And it worked out. Millions of followers." She grins. "Everywhere we go, you've got fans."

Glancing around, I ask, "Who?"

"Uh, the two women who own this place?"

"Now you're just messing with me."

She shakes her head, expression serious again. "Before, I hadn't given it much thought. But I wouldn't have stayed if I didn't believe in what you're doing. And as for your platform—" her eyes meet mine, and my breath catches "—it's mind-blowing, what you've accomplished. You don't need to hear me say it, but I hope you're proud of yourself."

I shake my head, throat tight with emotion. "It was really great to hear, actually."

She shrugs. "Like you care what I think."

"What does that mean?"

Dodging her eyes away, she says, "Nothing. Just that I'm sure you hear it plenty from people you care about."

She's who I care about. If it weren't for the rules we put in place, I'd be tempted to tuck a finger under her jaw and tilt up her chin until she looked at me with those gorgeous eyes. I'd tell her how horribly I missed her. How I could have all the success in the world, and without her, it feels empty. How I would trade it all for a chance to go back in time and be there for her.

Yearning floods me so strongly that I clench my fists tight against the sensation, or maybe to hold it tight. I want to believe things would be different. That I could trust us not to let go. But the hurt of rejection is too strong to ignore.

Hope's still watching me, and I swallow, running my thumb down the condensation on my glass. "Honestly, I'm afraid of letting everyone down. What if I feel differently about all this in five years and want out? I'm just not sure it's a forever thing, if it's sustainable long-term."

"Is that so scary? It not being permanent?"

"Not for you, I guess." I realize that sounds like a jab, and rush to explain. "You've never been concerned about worst-case scenarios. Or maybe you have, but you don't let that stop you." I smile at her. "Your parents chose your name right."

Hope. She always told me it felt like a verb, not a noun. Not a name. An action, or worse, a concept, undefinable. But I know that's not the case. It's her—she's the definition of Hope.

"They chose it because they always knew I'd come along. Just like they knew they were destined for each other." She makes a skeptical face. "Or so they say. I sure never thought *I* was destined for anyone."

I've had a lot of time to think about this topic since she left. "I don't think we are." She looks up, curious, and I feel compelled to elaborate. "I think we choose who we love. How we love." Good lord, I just said *love*, out loud, two times in a row. Not five minutes since we sat down, and I've already gone way off-script. Straightening up, I raise my hand to catch the bartender's attention.

Without meeting her eyes, I tell Hope, "One thing that hasn't changed here is the hush puppies. Rhonda's still got a knack with the fryer. Want some?"

If my mouth is full of food, no chance for me to put my foot in it.

twenty-one

hope

Adrian is at my elbow, sipping a beer and keeping quiet. We haven't spoken since the hush puppies arrived, eating the deep-fried corn fritters in blissful silence. Well, not silence, because the restaurant is packed, but peace. Not as good as being home alone on the sofa, but substantially better than having to force a conversation with strangers.

Networking with Sylvia and Liam was important—talking with them helped me sort out my goals, and Sylvia offered to send me the information about the white shark research program—but it left me drained. Hiding out here with Adrian ought to be just as stressful, especially with how we left things after our kiss, but like he said, he knows me. I don't have to put up a front or fill the space between us with empty words.

Just as well, since when we talk, things wind up murkier. Kissing him is pure bliss. The sweep of his tongue along mine, the needy way his hands gipped my hips, lifting me up and onto him, is enough to have me reaching for a glass of water to slake my thirst.

I wish I could separate the physical from my feelings. Agree to be co-workers with benefits, or whatever, but I can't, and from his confession, neither can he. I can't kiss him and not want it all—the connection, the friendship, the love.

I've kissed other men in the years since we were together but felt nothing. No desire to bring them into my life, to open myself up to them. Without the emotional connection, the physical stuff has never been worth wasting time on, which is why my intense desire for Adrian is so alarming. What I feel with him is unique, all-encompassing, specific to him, and that's what has me coming back for more, incapable of sticking to our strictly-work relationship.

We've been dodging each other's glances all night, in only the way two people altogether too aware of each other can. More than once I've caught his gaze dip along my body, drinking in the curves accentuated by the seams of my dress. It's been a long time since a man looked at me with such open longing, or maybe I just recognize the hunger in his eyes because it's the same hunger eating away at me despite the half-dozen hush puppies I've put away.

He's in the process of finishing the last bite. He licks his thumb, and a blush blooms against the pores of my cheeks. Adrian goes still, and that's when I realize it's not that he's watching me, he's *sensing* me. With his eyes, yes, sometimes. But other times it's like there's a pulse of energy between us, a wavelength we're both on, and when my emotions ripple to the surface, there's a brush against the piers of his subconscious, or somewhere deeper, maybe.

I deal in what can be measured and tested—in chemicals combining to form DNA expressed in biodiversity. In temperature ranges and food scarcity and predator and prey. But what's between Adrian and me isn't quantifiable. How I felt for him was too close to the love my parents always talk about—the life-altering, heart-over-head kind of love that had them tossing away scholarships and reshaping their dreams. And though that was never the case for us, I worried that the shift in priorities was inevitable, and that's why I pushed him away, before he let me go.

I duck my head, nervous my thoughts are written on my face, even though people have never been able to read me, not unless I spell things out for them. But Adrian is different. He sees into my heart—what I don't express or can't find the words for. He's always seen me, known me.

And he let me go, in spite of it. That, more than anything, is why I'm scared to let him in again.

The last bite goes sandy on my tongue, and I force it down, dry-throated, and take another gulp of water. Gabe, who's quickly becoming a friend in the effortless way I wish I could've managed with Adrian all those years ago to save myself a lot of heartache, squeezes past the crowd and leans between us to grab me a napkin from the garnish station.

"Serrano peppers get ya?" he asks, and I nod, though the fritters have the perfect amount of heat. He gives Adrian's shoulder a squeeze, but something's tense between them. "Came over to check on you. Ready to get out of here?"

Adrian's eyes flick to mine. "Uh, is Marissa heading out too?" The same concern from earlier creases his brow, and while I'm grateful for it, I also wonder what it's costing him to show me this kindness.

"I'd say she's pretty settled in." Gabe hooks an elbow on the bar, turning toward me. "But she's asking about you. Says you've been hiding out long enough." He delivers the message with a complicit grin. "I get it, though. I'm all for socializing, but after twelve hours on the water, I'm ready to tap out too."

I shake my head. "Nah, she's right. I should go be sociable."

The thought of going over to the crowded table and mustering up the effort to smile and act interested in strangers' life stories sounds exhausting. But Adrian's done enough by giving me an excuse to stay over here, and Gabe's clearly ready to go. "Let me just settle my bill and I'll be over there."

"I got it," Adrian says. "But you don't have to—"

Angie plunks a cocktail in front of him, interrupting whatever he was about to say. "Got an admirer." She nods at the neon-blue drink. "The woman at the end of the bar ordered this for you." Using tongs, she plops a maraschino cherry into the glass, with a look of consternation. "People using our establishment as a pickup joint? This is what Rhonda's brought us to. I hope she's happy." Without waiting for a response, she moves off, barking out an order to the bartender.

Brows up, I peer at the drink. "That is…a choice." Inspecting it, I ask, "Are those gummy dolphins?"

"Sharks," Gabe says. "It's their newest signature drink. Inspired by our man Adrian."

"Shut up." I roll my lips tight against a smile, but it's no good holding it back. Rising off my stool to peer at the menu, I scan the drink section. Gabe helpfully points to a cocktail midway down the page.

"The 'Shark Hero'?" I read aloud, delighted, and glance toward Adrian.

His face is a mix of amusement and chagrin, like the year we spent Christmas with his parents, and inside his stocking was a tie with sharks wearing sunglasses, which his mom insisted he try on. She texted me the photo she took, and I kept it as my lock screen for a long time afterward, smiling every time I saw his face.

I'll have to settle for a mental picture of his cute expression this time, since I'm pretty sure snapping candid photos of your co-worker is frowned upon.

"Kind of on the nose, don't you think?" Gabe leans around Adrian to peer at the group of women Angie pointed to. Hard to tell who sent it since they all keep looking our way, expressions ranging from eager to embarrassed to starstruck. "Hitting on you with a drink invented in your honor?"

Adrian ventures a look at the women, who elbow each other

until one of them steps out from the group. He whips his head back around.

"Interested?" Gabe asks, and I find myself holding my breath, waiting on Adrian's response.

"Heck no," he says, and I exhale. "The last thing I need is for Rhonda to take credit for setting me up with my future wife."

Future wife. We never talked about marriage specifically, but we did dream of a future together. I didn't want to get too technical, not until planning became critical, and by then, all the logistics overwhelmed me, made me worry our relationship would change. That taking the next step would make me resentful, chip away at the magic that always existed between us.

But there was a time when I thought I'd marry this man, and now he's talking about meeting his future wife over cocktails. The food I just consumed suddenly isn't sitting so well.

Gabe picks up the drink and holds it high. "Thanks ladies." He salutes them with the glass before taking a giant glug. They might not have heard him over the chatter, but his meaning was clear enough. The woman looks at her companions, hesitating, then lets them tug her back into the group.

Setting it down, he wipes his mouth with the back of his hand. "Bleck, that was awful. Photogenic, though." He eyes the drink speculatively, then pulls out his phone and snaps a photo, glancing toward me with a shrug. "Content."

"If you say so."

He sniffs. "You don't like social media, or is it just a lack of interest?"

I shrug, not wanting to get into it, now or ever, and Gabe pockets his phone. "Sorry, you don't have to explain if you don't want to, but it's such an interesting topic for me, and I'm pretty sure you're the first person under forty who I've met without it."

"That can't be true."

"I mean, people favor one platform over others, and most

don't have public pages, but yeah. You're kind of an outlier."
He pillows his chin on his knuckles. "And that fascinates me."

Adrian shoves him good-naturedly. "Lay off, man. She
doesn't have to appease your curiosity."

But I get it. Not only is it his line of work, but it directly
relates to me being here this summer. I'm surprised no one
pushed further until now. "Probably better y'all know since it
kind of relates to the channel."

Adrian sits up straighter, frowning.

"Remember what I told you the other day, about the town
meeting?" I ask him, then turn to Gabe, and give him a quick
rundown, leaving out the touchy-feely parts and sticking to
the facts.

When I finish, he turns to Adrian. "You knew all this?"

"She just told me the other day." He sounds hurt at the omis-
sion, but we weren't a couple when it all went down, not really. Would sharing what happened and my reason for staying
have had an impact?

"Anyway," I say, not needing to go down that road, "like
I said, the news didn't air my portion of the meeting. But our
town posts all the meeting recordings on their site. Nothing
fancy, just a camcorder set up in the back. My former chemistry teacher heard I'd spoken at the meeting and shared it on
my high school's alumni page."

I muster a grin for Adrian, hoping to keep things light. "Not
a lot of exciting news posted there, so you'd be an instant hit."

He waves this off, urging me to go on.

"Pretty sure my teacher didn't watch the video, and neither
did anyone else who hit 'like.' No one mentioned my melt-
down, just a few generic comments along the lines of 'Cool' or
'Way to go Hope!' The recording was close to two hours, and
my speech only a small part of that." I heave a breath, because
this is the humiliating part, details or no.

"Remember Owen?" I ask Adrian.

"The salutatorian who contested your GPA?" Adrian asks. "Pretty hard to forget a guy who couldn't handle losing to the point he got the school board involved."

My valedictorian status remained intact, but Owen's inquiries sparked rumors about whether I deserved the honor and the hefty scholarship that came along with it that are still circulating in Shoreline Dunes. Gossip is a prime hobby in wintertime when the town's population dwindles along with the temps, but I'd forgotten the longevity and virulence of it until I moved back.

"Tell me you peaked in high school without telling me you peaked in high school," Gabe says, and I snort.

"Yeah, well, I think he was the only one who actually watched the entire video."

"Because what else does he have to do with his time?" Adrian's leg is bouncing on the stool, the vibrations a manifestation of his growing agitation.

I want to press a calming hand to his knee but return to the story instead. "Not only did he watch it, he helpfully added a comment of his own, telling people exactly what minutes contained my 'performance.'"

"Are you kidding me?" Gabe seems almost as upset as Adrian, and I'm guessing he has his own experience with comment sections getting out of hand. "He pointed out your portion of the meeting just so people would watch you scrambling?"

"Yeah, and then took it a step further and made the post public on our town's page. A few people opposed to funding the project made snarky comments like, 'Thanks Hope,' or 'Our hero.'"

The Shark Hero drink on the bar in front of us suddenly seems less funny. Even strangers look up to Adrian, while I let down people I care about.

"Mr. Platt, my teacher, reached out and apologized. Said he had no idea, but of course, it wasn't his fault. And it's silly, really.

Just small-town drama. But I deactivated my accounts because I was tired of seeing the tags." Embarrassed at how much it hurt to see. "After a few weeks, I realized I didn't miss it, so I just stayed off." Didn't hurt that it cut off my chances to check in on Adrian and my old colleagues. It made me less reachable— out-of-sight-out-of-mind, and for awhile, that's what I wanted.

"Screw that dude," Gabe says. "Everyone who commented probably acted nice to your face, right?" I nod and he says, "It's a phenomenon where people feel more uninhibited online."

"Pretty sure she knows firsthand," Adrian says. He's been listening intently, letting me tell the story, but I take a moment to look at him now and see his shoulders are rigid, fists bunched. "And it must be even worse coming from people you know."

He searches my face, and whatever he sees there has his jaw set, eyes steely. "What's Owen's last name again?" There's something dangerous in his tone. I can fight my own battles—have, and will—but him wanting to defend my honor? That makes me feel cared for in a way I didn't know I was missing.

Summoning my courage, I tell him, "If he's petty and vicious enough to spout nonsense in the future, we'll deal with it then. But I'm ready to reconnect with friends and the shark community. I missed out on things—" I dart my eyes away when my lips want to form the words *I missed out on you* "—by disengaging."

"I'll drink to that." Gabe sets Adrian's drink to the side. "Just not this." He flags down the bartender, orders club soda and lime, then turns to me. "Want anything?"

I tap the blue cocktail. "Seems a shame to let this go to waste."

"It's not, trust me." Adrian's chagrin combined with his burly exterior is the sweetest.

"Oh, I'm drinking it," I assure him. This is familiar territory. The joking, the banter. And maybe a small and very petty part of me wants to drink the cocktail intended to woo my former boyfriend. His *future wife*, indeed.

"But first, I think we need to commemorate the occasion. Gabe, mind getting a photo?" I tuck an arm around Adrian's side without thinking, then tense, but his arm slips around me.

Gabe raises his phone. "Absolutely."

A thought occurs to me, and I hold up a finger. "Hang on a sec." I lean over the bar and nab a paper straw. Adrian's hand slips down to my hip to steady me. I straighten and hold it up. "Just in case you want to share."

"You're the personification of evil," he says, but he's biting back a big grin.

"I think the word you're looking for is supportive." Maybe teasing him is skirting the line between friend and colleague, but it's infinitely better than blurring the line with kisses. I plunk the straw into the drink, droplets splashing the bridge of my nose.

Adrian grabs a napkin and dabs them away. My eyelashes flutter closed in an instinctual urge to capture the feeling. When I open my eyes, he's biting his lip. "You really don't have to drink that."

"How bad can it be?" Putting the straw in my mouth, I flash Gabe a thumbs-up to take the photo. He raises his phone and at the last moment, Adrian ducks down and captures the second straw in his lips. His beard is rough against my jaw, his lips near mine, intimate.

Ex, he said. *Colleagues*, I told him. I gulp, and the moment the sugary concoction hits my tongue I splutter and flail, sloshing the drink. The cup, slippery with condensation, drops from my hand. It falls in horrifying quickness to the wood floor. When I dare to look, candy sharks are scattered amidst the wreckage of ice chips, the cherry perched atop the mess.

Adrian stares down at the mess. "Thank God," he mutters.

A laugh escapes through my fingers, then I'm cracking up.

He joins in, belly laughs shaking his shoulders. I'd forgotten how much I missed that sound. Over the years I missed his touch, missed his words of comfort, missed his steadying words in a crisis.

But his laugh... I hadn't known how much my ears craved the sound. How much my heart needed his joy.

Doubled over, he nudges me. "Was that not heinous?"

"So heinous," I agree, when I get my breath back from laughing. "For a drink so blue, it sure had a heck of a lot of grenadine."

"Warned you not to try it." Grinning, Gabe passes back my phone. "I'm going to say goodbye to Marissa. Meet you outside in five?" he asks Adrian, then turns to me. "Pretty cool that you're not letting that loser have the last word. If you ever want help getting set up with social media again, let me know."

"I will, thanks." It's really nice to start rebuilding my network. I'm ending the night with new connections, and Adrian and I managed to find steady ground. My plan to get my career on track is moving along.

"Heard there was an accident." Summoned by the commotion, Angie walks up and peers over the bar. "What happened here?" Adrian and I eyeball each other like guilty students when the principal arrives.

"Sorry, slipped out of my hands." I pick up the glass and hand it to her, thankful it didn't break.

"No need to apologize." She looks at Adrian meaningfully. "You got lucky, young man." Brows raised, she holds his gaze for another moment, then steps away.

Whatever that was about, Adrian's not sharing, because he turns to me the moment she's out of earshot. "Lucky would be if that monstrosity never existed."

"You're going to complain about a drink being commemorated in your honor?" I pull my neck back, blowing out my cheeks. "Fame has changed you, Dr. Hollis-Parker."

A group of tipsy people walks by and he takes my arm, tucking me against him. "Complaining, am I?" His breath a whisper against my ear.

"Sounded like it to me." I lean into him, unsteady, and his hand settles at the small of my back. I drag my gaze away from his mouth, up to his eyes, the lights reflected in them like stars. His hand is still curled around my waist and my fingers contract, bunching the fabric of his shirt. Every nerve in my body is alive, centered on him. "A handful of fans and suddenly you're turning your nose up at perfectly good beverages."

He chuckles, the vibration reverberating through my body. "That's got to be the most shade thrown at a man in years."

I turn, back flush against the bar, the front of my hip pressed to Adrian's. He doesn't back away. "I didn't mean a word of it. Especially the part about the drink being good."

People jostle him, pressing us even closer together, and his laughter stills. His hand is still wrapped around my arm; I drop my gaze to his fingers. Remember how those same fingers used to weave through my hair, helping take down my braids. How those work-roughened knuckles tipped my chin up to meet his lips, how his mouth on mine was a decadent ache and sweet relief all at once.

The crowd parts, and with a shake of his head, he lets go, cool air seeping into the heated space between us. "See you on the boat, Evans."

Professional, distant. No one but me would know he said the same thing in the moonlight outside a restaurant eight years ago, right after our first kiss. Keeping things professional is supposed to help me fall out of love, but he keeps pulling me right back in, without even trying.

twenty-two

adrian

I shouldn't have said it.

The moment the words left my mouth, I should've wished them back, but I can't bring myself to regret it. Hope and I used to laugh when we'd reminisce about our first kiss, about how her roommate almost caught us making out by my car outside the restaurant where we were having dinner with the group. Our first kiss is a hazy memory, but I still can feel the heat and urgency and overwhelming rightness of the way our bodies fit together.

The instant we heard voices, we'd broken apart, and I loudly announced that I'd see her on the boat, in a voice about three octaves deeper than normal, overcompensating out of surprise. She told me later, giggling, how serious I'd looked when I'd used her last name. She called me Hollis-Parker the rest of the summer.

Going out last night brought back the memory of team dinners after long workdays the summer we met, and when I startled away, realizing I was dangerously close to kissing her in public, the same words spilled out. *See you on the boat, Evans.*

Except things aren't the same as that summer almost a decade ago. We're drifting apart, not tumbling together. I wasn't able to take her in my arms and comfort her after discovering she got trolled by that jerk of a classmate, but my protective hackles are up, even though she's not mine to protect.

Physically, I've kept my distance, but I've also kept an eye on the comment section. She didn't tell me Owen's last name, but I remembered a few nights later. McHugh. The urge to find and report his account had my fingers itching, but that wouldn't help Hope in the long run. Neither would overstepping bounds again, risking where we are for the sake of who we were to each other.

Three weeks since I last kissed Hope, and we haven't touched since the night at Horizon Line. No casual high fives, no ecstatic hugs, no catching her by the waist on rough seas. We haven't slipped, haven't stumbled, haven't crossed a single line. We've tagged sharks and filmed with my mentor in North Carolina. Everything is textbook. Routine. Uneventful.

Agonizing. Exactly how things need to stay until the end of the summer and Hope heads off for her future.

We're about a mile offshore today, doing a live question and answer session. No luck catching sharks, so we decided to switch gears before a forecasted storm blows in. Marissa's got the selfie stick at the moment, and Hope's standing in the bow on my other side.

Gabe catches me frowning at the gathering clouds, and says quietly, "Atmospheric."

Ominous, more like. But he's been bugging me about the importance of going live, engaging viewers, and he convinced me this is an opportune time to try. No animals involved, and we get to pick which questions we answer. We're in control, or as much as we can be on the boat in the ocean, talking to strangers. Which is to say, not at all.

"Okay, here's another question," Marissa says. "Amarie wants to know: 'What's an acoustic receiver?' Hope, want to take this one?" She passes over the selfie stick and I watch Hope closely.

So far, no signs that she's stressed about this. Gabe checked in with everyone beforehand and she seemed fine, but I remember the pain in her eyes when she spoke about the last time she had to answer questions from a live audience, on camera.

A few weeks ago, I would've found a quiet moment to check in with her and make sure she's feeling okay with the change, but we've been avoiding any time alone, and breaking that cycle might amp up her nerves.

She holds the phone at the angle Gabe demonstrated, her body language relaxed. July has been hot, and today she's wearing a thin white long-sleeve tee-shirt for sun protection, but it does nothing to hide her generous curves, and I look away before the camera catches my longing.

"Acoustic receivers are one way we track sharks," she says. "Whenever a tagged shark swims near the beacon, its tag pings. We pull the data from the receivers periodically to record it, and it's a great way to discover which sharks are frequenting the area, when, and for how long. However, since the shark has to be in close proximity with the receiver, we don't have the ability to track where a shark is once they swim out of range."

She goes on, explaining the different types of tags used in studies, and I tell myself to relax. We're almost done and so far, smooth sailing. Hope reads the next question aloud. "Jasper99 wants to know what sharks eat."

"That depends on the shark," I say. "Bottom-dwelling sharks like angel sharks eat a variety of things, from fish and skates to crustaceans and mollusks. Whale sharks and basking sharks filter plankton and small fish out of the water." I name a few others, before Gabe leans into the shot.

"TLDR version," he says. "Shark diet is super varied." He's been great in the role of moderator, chiming in when we get bogged down in technical details and moving the session along.

We answer a few more questions, like whether sharks need to swim to breathe, and whether marine biology was our first choice of careers—yes for all of us besides Gabe, who explains how he made the transition into working with sharks along with a plug for his website and social media.

"All right," Gabe says, taking the selfie stick. "We're about done here, but let's end with a lightning round. Rapid-fire." He looks toward us. "Ready?"

My mind is already racing through potential questions and formulating answers, but then I remember... Hope. We didn't prep for this. Her mouth is ajar, and her eyes dart to mine. Her knees are locked, despite the heavy pitch, and it looks like she might keel over.

Before I can say anything, Gabe announces the first question. "Favorite shark? Mine's no secret. Whale sharks. What about you, Marissa?"

"Easy. Carolina hammerhead. Gotta go with a shark from my home state."

I'm watching Hope, wondering how to cut this short, when Gabe elbows me. "Your go, man."

"Uh, tiger sharks."

He hesitates, like he's waiting for me to elaborate, then swings the camera toward Hope.

"Give us something more than Adrian over there," he jokes. "What's your favorite shark, and why?"

Hope licks her lips but seems steadier than a moment ago. "Great white sharks. They're the species that first fascinated me, and I've been lucky to study them here in the Atlantic. A dream of mine is to study white sharks in the Pacific as well and learn more about their migratory patterns."

"Best part of the job?"

Hope raises her hand. "Ooh, me, pick me! Can I answer twice in a row?" The others laugh, and the worry in my chest eases at seeing her relax. "The sharks. That might sound obvious, but they are just such cool animals." She pauses and looks at Gabe. "Are we allowed to say something as trite as 'cool' on air?"

He laughs, and I lean into her, a small show of support, and she squeezes my thigh in response. Not a grope, or a tease. The kind of small gesture of acknowledgment couples do.

Except we're not a couple, and it's been three years since anyone's squeezed my thigh, and weeks since we last touched, and my body's response is anything but innocent.

My nerve endings light up, and Hope jerks her hand away with a muttered, "Sorry."

If the look on her face is any indication, she's as affected as I am. But Marissa is talking about studying nurse sharks on a recent trip to Florida and I try to pull my mind back to the task at hand.

"Next question, and Adrian gets to go first this time," Gabe says. "'My son loves sharks and is headed into high school. What should he do if he'd like to have a career in marine biology?'"

Me and Marissa give our answers, covering all basics, and when it's Hope's turn, I can see her scrambling for something to add.

She palms the back of her neck. "Uh, well one option might be join us on the boat next summer." She stops, staring wide-eyed at the camera like she's realized her mistake. The pleasant smile I've kept plastered on my face slides off as she rushes to explain. "Uh, we're… Well, there's a possibility the team will be launching a program aimed at giving high schoolers the chance to experience field research."

Did she just really announce that out loud, on a live session? I've got to fix this. "Um, actually—" I clear my throat, unsure how to play it off without making things worse.

Fortunately, Gabe jumps in, "That's our allotted hour for questions, but this has been fun. Follow along across social media for a chance to get your question answered next time!"

He lowers the phone and the second he ends the livestream, I turn to Hope.

"What was that?"

"What we discussed." She grasps the hem of her shirt, twisting it between her fingers. "About maybe starting a program for youth."

"Have you run it by Marissa?" My cousin shakes her head. That's what I thought. I whirl toward Hope. "I haven't even heard you mention it since the other night at the bar."

"We've been really busy, and it slipped my mind." Hope lets go of her shirt and crosses her arms, swiveling to face me on the bench. Her bare knees brush mine, but I barely notice. "I get that my timing was bad. But you make it sound like some drunken idea. We were at a work dinner. I offered another way you could accomplish your goals."

"And then announced it to a live audience."

"Live, exactly." Wind whips her hair across her face, but she doesn't bother to push the strands away. "What you said we'd never do."

I feel bad about putting her in an awkward position, but a larger part of me is concerned about scrambling to course-correct thanks to her mistake. "Plans change, right? Isn't that what you told me?" The second the words leave my mouth, I clamp it shut, but it's too late.

All the light leaves Hope's eyes, like someone blew out the flame inside her. Unfair of me to equate our personal issues with her performance at work. We asked her to perform outside the job expectations, with almost no warning. "Hope—"

"We'd better get back to shore before the storm moves in." She stands and moves off toward the wheel, navigating the rolling deck with practiced ease. "I'll drive."

Back to us, she makes her way to the helm. Against the backdrop of white-capped waves and steely clouds, she looks determined, but exposed. She opened up about the lowest moment of her career, trusted me to do my best to ensure she wouldn't be in that position again, and I failed her.

These past three weeks were the calm before the storm. With one careless moment, I let our history bleed into work and tore down all the progress we'd made, only this time, it wasn't for a stolen kiss, it was out of selfishness. I proved she was right to doubt us, and we're better off apart.

twenty-three

hope

We don't film live. You won't have to talk to the camera. No unexpected questions.

Not promises, maybe, but clear expectations, certainly. When Adrian and I shot the intro video together, he assured me I'd just be doing shark work-ups on camera, that anything could be fixed in edits. Lies. Today was the city council meeting all over again, but with an audience of thousands, not a hundred. And while I got the facts right, I let down my colleagues just the same.

I stayed at the wheel the entire way back to the marina, ensuring no one would try to talk to me, and the drive home with Marissa was quiet, both of us gathering our thoughts. We dashed into the condo just ahead of the first lightning crack.

At the kitchen island, Marissa knocks back a glass of water like a shot, then refills it with the filtered pitcher, pouring more into my cup as well. We both chug, thirsty in the way only a day on the water can leave you.

Dabbing her mouth with her sleeve, she says, "That was a mess."

"Which part? Me telling the public about an imaginary program or Adrian and I fighting at work?" I tip up my glass and let the ice fall into my mouth, nervous energy needing an outlet.

She leans her hip against the counter. "Please. That was not a fight." Good to know it didn't look as terrible as it felt to hear him basically accuse me of breaking us up. "I think the worst part was us leaving you out to dry like that. I should've known it would be tough for you after what happened."

I shift the ice to my cheek and suck in a chilled breath. "I thought I could handle it. And it was fine, but then, all of a sudden, my mind went blank, and I was talking on autopilot." I drop my head to the cool granite countertop. "How many people were watching?"

She pats my back. "You don't want to know." I hear the ice rattle in her cup as she takes another drink. "Fortunately, I think it's an awesome idea, so there's that."

I twist my head sideways to peek up at her. "Of course it is. But Adrian's not sure it's feasible."

She rolls her eyes, tugging off her stretchy headband with an audible sigh of relief. She recently took down her braids, and is wearing her hair loose today, the thick coils held away from her face with the headbands she often wears on days at sea.

"He's the worrier in the family. And I get it. My parents moved once when I was like seven—" she squints in thought, spinning the headband on her finger "—maybe eight. Anyway, I was so thrown I wouldn't even go to school for two weeks that fall. I can't imagine doing it as often as Adrian did. My aunt and uncle are great parents, and they did their best balancing career and family, but I think Adrian coped with all that change by thinking three steps ahead."

"Not always a bad thing," I feel compelled to say.

"Who said it was?" She frowns at me, the expression so like Adrian that I grin. "But I have experience with outreach programs—"

"He said that too." Right before he told me it might not be

a good plan. "He also said you have another full-time job, and he'll be busy with lab work and a full course load in the fall."

"I think I know how to manage my own time," she says. "It might not work out, sure. But worst-case scenario, you disappointed a few people. It happens."

I roll my face back into my crossed arms, wanting to block out the memory of my failure. Failures, plural.

"Hey, *it happens*," she says. "You did your best out there, and I bet you inspired at least one person to go look up goblin sharks. They'll wish they hadn't, but…"

I straighten up, chuckling. "I think they're kind of cute."

"They're a lot of things, but cute isn't one of them. Cool enough to get someone interested in shark science, though. That's for sure."

I smile, grateful for her support. "But Adrian started the channel to be an inspiration, and getting people excited about an opportunity and then not delivering is the opposite of that."

"You think social media is the only way he gets involved?"

"I mean, I know he's devoted to teaching." Even back in undergrad, he helped out as a TA.

Marissa sets down her glass. "Should've known he'd be too shy to tell you."

Shy? A man with over a million followers? A man who kisses me with a boldness that makes me blush just thinking of it?

She marches to the coatrack and grabs her purse. "Come with me. You need to see something." With a twinkle in her brown eyes, she opens the door with a dramatic flourish. "I'll drive."

I am never living that down.

In a flashback to middle school weekends, I find myself left standing on the curb of a public library with Marissa's instructions to head to the children's section. The rain let up and now the warm air hangs heavy on my skin, like a blanket left out on the line, thick with moisture.

Palmettos line the sidewalk, and though I've lived in the southeastern United States for most of my adult life, I'll never get over the difference in the flora here. Even the evergreens flanking the building are different from up north—towering longleaf pines, instead of the sturdy white pines back home—though stepping into the library wraps me in a familiar feeling of belonging.

The sliding doors whoosh shut behind me and mute the birdsong, air-conditioning embracing me like I've entered a hermetically sealed chamber, cool and quiet. A librarian seated at the front desk turns from her computer with a smile.

"May I help you with something?"

I hesitate, glancing around the open space. "My…" I stutter to a halt. Co-worker? Ex-boyfriend? Recent make-out buddy? Yeah, won't be going with either of the latter options. "A colleague of mine—" our agreed-upon status resounds with a discordant twang against my heartstrings "—is doing story time here. I don't want to interrupt…"

"A friend of Adrian's?" She breaks into a big smile. "Wait a minute. You're the new scientist with *Shark Science Crew*. Hope, right?"

I appraise her with fresh eyes. Around sixty, I'd say, with the bearing of someone I'd expect to lecture youngsters on how screen time rots their brains. Obviously, I need to check my judgments. "You watch their channel?"

"Darling, we all do." I glance around to see who the "we" is, expecting a legion of librarians to materialize, but none do. "Adrian has been incredibly generous with his time," she says. "He does a program at least once a month at one of our branches, and it's a huge draw for the community. Gets folks in the door and utilizing the library system."

She adjusts her purple reading glasses. "I grew up in Charleston and never much liked the idea of sharks swimming around. But now that I've learned what an important role they play in the ocean—" She stops herself with a small smile. "What am I saying? You're the expert. Don't need me to tell you anything."

Tipping forward in her chair, she uses a pen to point off to the side. "Children's Services area is toward the back. Won't be able to miss it."

I thank her and make my way through low bookshelves toward the rear portion of the library. Sure enough, I hear him before I see him, his always-deep voice tuned to the rich, scholarly tone I remember from sneaking into the seminars he led in grad school, a lush timbre that invites you to hunker down and absorb.

I step past a glossy green shelf, and a semicircle of children seated on a rug comes into view, a smattering of adults on plastic chairs behind them. Adrian is perched on the edge of a low dais in front of the group, forgoing the armchair behind him, no doubt to get on their level. He's swapped out his work clothes from earlier for an aqua blue polo and gray chinos, the first I've seen him dressed up since our night out, and I sweep my eyes away, lest he catch me staring.

Each child is holding a plush shark in their lap—or on their head, in the case of one boy near the front—and listening with rapt attention to Adrian reading from a picture book about Dr. Eugenie Clark, a pioneering marine biologist. I recognize it as the same one I bought as a present for Zuri's kids last Christmas.

Adrian must have it memorized. He barely glances at the pages, instead making eye contact with the crowd, not rushing through, but pausing to let the text sink in, and I find myself mouthing the words along with him, throat suddenly tight.

To see a whole roomful of kids eager to hear about my personal hero, a leader in the field at a time when women were expected to stay out of science, is a huge pick-me-up after this emotional day. Adrian turns the book around to flip to the next page and glances up for the first time.

His eyes land on me and a broad smile lights up his whole

face. His unguarded happiness in seeing me, despite our argument makes my eyes sting. Smile fading, his brows tug together and he mouths, *I'm sorry.*

A whole room full of people in front of him, and his first thought is to apologize. The smile I muster is watery but genuine. A few adults turn my way to see who Adrian's looking at and he clears his throat, hastily returning to the book to pull attention back to him, and just like that he melts my heart all over again. Looking out for me. Shielding me from the crowd.

His next smile is for me, though he's looking at the page. Awareness settles as I watch him, taking in the steady set of his shoulders, how he puts his all into the reading, voice clear and resonant. There's an intangible bond between this man and I, and in this moment, I don't want to deny it. Don't want to reason it away or dissect it. Some things are deeper than flesh and bone. Deeper even than cells and neurons.

Love isn't quantifiable. Hope isn't quantifiable. And suddenly that doesn't seem like a bad thing.

I watch the rest of his performance in a haze, caught up in the story of promise. At the end, one girl with blond curls raises her hand but doesn't wait to speak. "Our family took a trip to the Mote Aquarium. Did you know Eugenie Clark used to train sharks?"

Adrian sets the book on his lap. "Pretty interesting, huh? Her research showed that sharks have intelligence far beyond what people thought back then."

The girl nods, curls bouncing. "I can't even train my puppy."

The grown-ups chuckle and I join in, tears dry and heart full.

"Y'all want to meet another real-life shark scientist? My friend Hope just showed up, and she's a marine biologist like me."

Friend. First the librarian, now him. Maybe Zuri was right, and we could stay in each other's lives. I have a feeling no platonic title will ever feel right—not friend, and certainly not colleague. But maybe I could get used to this new normal. The next moment, twenty-some pairs of eyes swivel in my direction and banish any thoughts about our relationship status.

"Do you train sharks?" a boy asks.

I shake my head. "No. The bulk of my research was based on shark migration along the Atlantic coast. I used a combination of acoustic tags, satellite imagery, and ocean monitoring to ascertain whether there's a correlation between shifting migration patterns and extreme weather." Eyes start to glaze over so I add, "I wanted to know if sharks are affected by changes in the weather."

"You mean storms? I love thunder," a girl says.

"I hate it." Another chimes in. "Gives me the creeps."

I smile at them, not picking sides, though I love the energy of storms. One reason I was drawn to study this behavior in sharks was my own fascination with watching blizzards blow in off the lake, the juxtaposition of angry clouds and swirling, powdery snow. The literal electricity in the air during summer thunderstorms.

"Sharks have senses that we don't," I explain. "Those give them a special heads-up about changes in the weather that humans wouldn't notice without the help of technology."

"Like spidey senses?" The question comes from a kid in a Spiderman costume, complete with a mask. I do my best not to laugh.

"In a way, yes. They can seem like superpowers to us, but in sharks they're biological features. I bet there are a lot more books here you can check out to learn more if you ask one of the librarians."

Adrian stands up, drawing the kids' attention back to him. "Ms. Lucinda has free books for you to take home as well, so be sure to stop by the front desk on your way out." He pulls a basket out from under his chair and makes his way around the room, passing out tickets to the local aquarium. A few people linger to ask questions, and he gives each of them his focus, head inclined, listening intently.

I hang back, watching him interact with the parents and caregivers. He's effusive and kind and it's plain to see he didn't get over a million followers for his pecs. He got them because he cares. And he has an exceptional knack for making other people care too.

I'm on my way over to him when a boy with short brown hair zips past me and grabs Adrian's sleeve. "My grandpa says I'm supposed to say thank you for the shark." He pronounces it *sark*, and I can't help but grin at the cuteness.

Adrian squats down to get eye-level. "You're very welcome." He points to the array of white spots on the stuffed animal's back. "Know what species this is?"

The boy nods. "A whale shark. They're filter feeders."

"My man." Adrian's smile is huge, and he offers the kid knuckles. They fist bump, then the boy runs off to an elderly man who admonishes him with a gravelly, "Slow down, Cameron." He smiles at us over his shoulder. "Appreciate you taking the time. He's been looking forward to this all week. Storm couldn't keep us away, but I hear there's worse on the way. Y'all stay safe," he says, nodding to me.

When the last of the stragglers clear out, Adrian strides over to me and wraps me in a hug, surprising me. "I'm sorry for earlier," he says against my ear. Warmth shuffles through my body, a zing of heat from my hair follicles to the soles of my feet, so deep it sinks into my soul as well.

Until I squeezed his thigh on the boat—another embarrassing memory from today I never want to revisit—we hadn't touched since the night at the restaurant, and this hug is like falling onto a mattress after a long day on my feet, the sting of our argument fading with the comfort of his embrace.

All too soon, he releases me, and much as I miss his touch, I can't help but admire the sight of him all dressed up, skin glowing rich brown under the warm lights, hair pulled back, show-ing off the angles of his handsome face. "What happened today was my fault," he says. "I was so worried about going live, but I let Gabe convince me. And then, well…"

"It was pretty much your worst fear, me spilling the beans about my idea."

"Yours too," he says. "I let you get put in a bad position, and I'm sorry."

"You said that already." It's counterintuitive to make up without touching him, but I do my best. "And I am too. I got defensive, but I know I let you down."

"You didn't." He shakes his head. "We'll find a way to work. I was just…"

"Scared?" I raise my brows, and he nods. "Me too."

"I still should've handled it better," he says. "I do appreciate you making the suggestion. I just needed time to think on it. Roll things around in my mind. Consider the outcome." His lips quirk. "How do I put this? Changes to the status quo make me anxious. It might be the best idea in the world, but if it's new, I need some time to mull it over, or all I see are worst-case scenarios."

I knew this about him. Heck, his response to my decision to leave was proof. But he'd never communicated it so clearly, or maybe I wasn't in a position to listen. "Probably better than jumping into things without considering what might go wrong."

"Leaping before you look isn't necessarily a bad thing," he says. "You innovate, and you're not scared to try new things. You've become a big asset to the team."

The team. It's a reminder that despite the hug, despite the feelings stirred up by his apology, we're colleagues, and after this summer, won't be anything at all to one another. Not un-less I can find a way to be his friend.

"Was it weird that I showed up here?" I'm self-conscious

now that we've gotten the apologies out of the way. "Marissa brought me, but I didn't mean to intrude."

"If it helps any," he says, "Gabe came along last time, so we're solidly in co-worker territory." Earlier today, it would've been music to my ears to hear we're staying within the lines. But my feelings have shifted, and I'm not content to leave him behind at the end of the summer.

"I gotta admit that once Marissa told me you were doing a children's story time, it would've been impossible not to come see for myself." I let my smile show, not bothering to dim it. "You had those kids hanging on every word. I've read to Zuri's kids enough to know that's no easy feat. Half the time they're asking questions or bouncing on the couch or doing hand-stands." I pause. "Though maybe that's Zuri's genes as much as their age. Hard to say."

He laughs. "I think having something to hold helps them concentrate."

"Yeah, about that—you gave them those plushies?"

He shrugs. "It's one way I use funds from *Shark Science Crew*. I remember begging my parents for stuff like that when we visited aquariums and museums, and they always turned me down." I heard the same refrain from families at the aquarium where I worked. "Which I get, now. Serious sticker shock at gift shops. But I thought it might be a cool thing to offer at programs like this."

"Cool?" I grin. "You're basically a sharky Santa." I expect him to groan at the alliteration, but his face lights up, and sud-denly I'm pulling out my phone, scrolling through my pictures. "Remember this?" I step up next to him, angling the phone his way, trying not to notice the cedar scent of his cologne.

He lets out a laugh at seeing the snapshot of himself in a Santa hat, sporting the shark tie with his T-shirt and plaid pa-jama pants. "You still have that photo?"

"I'm definitely keeping it now." I click off the screen and

tuck my phone away. "You're a celebrity. I have to have something to say, 'I knew him when…'"

"Surely you can do better than that." He pulls out his own phone and taps, though not long, before holding it out. It's us at the beach in my hometown. He's shirtless and I've got my arms around his waist, cheek pressed to his bare chest. "Show-off."

"That's from before I ever touched a weight. Nothing to show off."

"Not from where I'm standing." My eyes linger on the photo for another appreciative moment before I realize what I've just confessed. Mortified, I wonder when I'll stop slipping up like this, letting on how I feel. "I'd better text Marissa. She was running some errands and told me to let her know when I was ready for a ride."

"No need," he says. "I've just got some holds to pick up, then I can take you back. Unless you'd rather wait for her?"

Cheeks still burning, I can't bring myself to meet his eyes. "That would be great, thanks."

We reach the front desk and are greeted by the same cheerful librarian. A stack of hardcover novels sits next to the computer. "I went ahead and pulled your holds from the back room." She beams at Adrian, open adoration he deflects with a lopsided smile.

"Thanks, Lucinda." He slides a library card out of his wallet. "How are Duchess and Gracie?"

"Trouble, as always." She scans his card and swivels toward me. "My goldendoodles," she explains. "I bring them in here for our Read-to-a-Dog events. Great motivation for reluctant readers, and they lap up the attention." She winks at the pun, drawing a laugh from me and a groan from Adrian.

"Keep those coming," I tell her. "Puns are this man's nemesis."

"In that case maybe I ought not. We want to make sure he keeps coming back." She slides the first book under the barcode scanner and peers at me over her bejeweled glasses. "Did you know he spearheaded an entire STEAM story time program in conjunction with the university? Convinced several of the faculty to come in every month and give a talk about their job and read a picture book related to it. Some of them even incorporate crafts and hands-on science experiments."

He shrugs off her praise. "They were happy to do it."

Setting the book aside, she leans her elbow on the checkout counter. "An influencer, that's what he is."

He sighs, but she makes a shooing motion, the gems in her acrylic nails flashing. "Hush now. It's not a bad thing, young man. You influenced your colleagues to do good in the community. Your influence in those kids' lives will help get them reading about science and nature. You're wielding your influence for good, and I for one love to see it."

"You're not the only one." I've seen how conflicted Adrian feels about his status, the unwarranted way he feels like his platform is in some way inferior to the work he does the rest of the year.

But what he's doing is an extension of that. He's sharing his knowledge and experience. The years of study and exams and lab work. The long hours spent hunched over a laptop. The sweaty, physical days of fieldwork with no guarantee of usable data. The professional relationships he worked to cultivate. All of it has given him the ability to do the work he's doing online.

"And, Hope." I'm startled that she remembers my name. "My goddaughter was thrilled to see another 'girl'—" she makes air quotes with an indulgent smile "—join the crew."

An unexpected zing shoots through me. There are plenty of women in shark science. Classmates and professors, the late Dr. Clark herself. But media hasn't always done a good job of portraying that reality.

After my slip-up today, the librarian's words are an unexpected encouragement. "I'll tell Marissa, she'll be thrilled to hear. And if your goddaughter ever comes to one of the story times, we'd be happy to chat with her and answer her questions about sharks."

"She'd love that, thank you." She slides the books across the counter. "Don't be strangers, you two."

We could never be strangers. But the question remains: Who are we to each other?

twenty-four

adrian

I hated how I had to rush off to the library the moment we got back to shore, and planned to find Hope afterward to apologize. Once again, her unexpected arrival disrupted my plans, but this time seeing her made my heart lift. She's here, when I didn't expect a second chance.

The moment we pass through the outer doors, weighty heat blankets my pores. Although the air is sodden with vapor molecules, the hazy aura of the sun is visible through the clouds. The rain must've moved off while I was inside.

The *scuff-slide* of Hope's sandals on the sidewalk comes from a few steps behind, and I slow my pace to match hers.

She smiles up at me. "Still haven't made the switch to ebooks?" She used to tease me for the ever-shifting stacks of books piled on the couch, my bed, and even the edge of the bathtub.

"I'm on screens enough for work, especially lately." I shift the stack of books in my arms as she falls into step next to me. "Reading physical books gives me a break from blue light to wind down before bed." The word *bed* rings loudly in the deserted parking lot. Especially since I can remember all too well Hope's head on my bare shoulder as we leaned against the headboard, sharing snippets of what we were each reading. Her dozing off with the lights on, and me tucking her laptop away before settling in next to her.

Does she remember? Or has she tried to forget?

"Figured maybe these days you hit the gym at night, though I guess lugging those around is workout enough." She lifts her chin to the books.

Amused, I say, "Some nights. Though my workouts aren't as intense as before. At first—" I stop myself, because I was about to say, my workouts were most intense at the beginning, when she went to Michigan, and the weeks stretched into a month, and then a season, and I realized she wasn't coming back. Not for me, at least.

"At first…" she prompts.

"Easier to maintain muscle than gain it." My first instinct is to leave it there, but I realize I want to share this. Want to let her in. "I couldn't sleep much, once I realized—" My throat goes tight and scratchy, but no going back now.

I swallow, eyes on the shiny foil cover of the top novel. "Once I realized we were over, I needed something to take my mind off things. A colleague had been pestering me to join him in the gym. Said he needed a workout buddy to stay accountable. I figured it would last a few weeks, tops. But I got hooked on the science of it. Trial and error, seeing the changes in my routine yield measurable results." I approached strength training like I do most things in life: research before action. Analyze, gather information, then put it into practice.

To anyone else, this might sound impossibly nerdy, but Hope is nodding along.

"Not to mention, there's something satisfying about ending the day with an activity I know will go to plan." Self-consciousness overtakes me at sharing all this. "Who would've thought?" I say, acknowledging my penchant for predictability and routine.

But Hope doesn't laugh. "I'm glad you had that. And it sounds like it was good for you, beyond the obvious." Her sunglasses are tucked in her hair, eyes unshielded, so I notice the quick sweep of her eyes down my body and feel a rush of pleasure.

"So you like the new look?" Dangerous territory, but I've been dying to know what she thinks. Her comment in the library about being into my body back before I started lifting weights has me curious.

"Was that in doubt?" A rosy flush darkens her cheekbones, but she doesn't dodge my gaze.

The open admiration makes me itch to pull away my collar from my neck, and I resume walking toward the car. "Well, I didn't used to be so..." I search for a word that doesn't sound like a humble-brag and come up short. "I look different."

"I like different." She gently bumps me with her shoulder. "You look good, Adrian. You've always looked good, nothing you could do to change that."

"Not even a face tattoo? Because your parents might beg to differ."

"Oh my gosh, you remember that?" She laughs.

"How could I forget the Face Tattoo Saga?" I remember everything about her family, everything about our time together. "Your cousin's botched face tattoo was pretty much all your parents talked about when you brought me home that first time. Made me grateful I've got a mild fear of needles. How are they, by the way?"

The rhythm of Hope's steps falters, and I look over to see her biting her lip.

Stopping, I readjust the books, feeling foolish. "Sorry, is family out of bounds? I'm still figuring this out."

"I'm figuring it out too." Hope lifts the top two books off the stack, lightening my load, and the herbal scent of her shampoo has me closing my eyes for the briefest second, steadying myself.

"Pretty sure acting like we don't have a history isn't working so well, all things considered." Tucking the novels against her chest, she searches my face, though with a shyness I'm not used to seeing in her. "Are you open to trying something new?"

Against my better judgment, I ask, "What do you have in mind?"

Her copper eyes connect with mine. "Friendship."

I honestly didn't know what to expect, and I turn the concept over in my mind. "Why?"

Her nose wrinkles in thought and I tighten my grip on the book to dampen the urge to press a kiss to it. "Because I like you. I've always liked you, even when I tried to stop," she says. "And I'm tired of trying."

Her words echo my feelings. "So tired," I agree.

She deflates, not like a sad balloon, but like when she used to melt into me on the couch after a long day. I could always tell when she let go of whatever problem she'd been working through and settled in. Her shoulders relax, and the small crease between her dark brows disappears.

"So what does friendship look like?" The plastic dust jackets of the books are sticking to my arms in the heat, but I'm in no hurry to get to my SUV.

"Openness. Honesty." She purses her lips, like she's making sure she covered everything. "Not skirting around the past three years or what came before them."

"Like whether your parents hate me for not doing right by their only child?" I've thought a lot about her parents over the years, how awful it felt to begin to think of them as family, and then never hear from them again. Did Hope mourn the loss of my own mom and dad?

"Nah. You know they raised me to be independent, and our family has good boundaries. They wouldn't try to fight my battles for me. Not that it was a battle," she says. "The breakup, I mean."

"Was it a breakup?" Another question that's been simmering at the corners of my mind. "It felt more like... Losing sight of one another." Like kayaking side by side and turning to find her on another branch of the river, carried away by the current.

"We both let go." Hope slides her fingertip along the book's pages, and I feel an answering stir on my skin. "Neither of us reached out. I guess you couldn't call it a breakup. But it hurt like one. And I made the requisite breakup bad decisions."

"Like what?"

She shoots me an odd look. "Staying out of shark research, for one."

That comes as a surprise. "You stayed to help Zuri, and finish what you started at work."

"I did, and I didn't." She sighs. "It's complicated. But looking back, I think I was trying to prove I was right in hesitating to take the leap in the next stage of our relationship. To prove I needed the freedom to move at a moment's notice."

To prove she was better off not tied down to me. Three years of unasked questions begin to weigh on me, thick as the humid air, and I long to go back to the lightness of a moment ago. "Well, I've made a few post-breakup mistakes of my own."

"We've already established the workout routine was a good decision. You're not telling me you regret starting your channel?"

I shake my head. "No, and that came later, anyway."

"Then what bad decisions, Mr. Honesty?" She puts her free hand up. "Wait, don't tell me. There are some things I think better left in the dark."

"What I'm about to tell you is definitely one of them," I admit, watching her. Does she think I'm talking about dating mistakes? Despite our honesty pledge, that's a question I dare not ask her, no matter how much I'm dying to know. "It was after I broke up with the girl I dated before you, in undergrad." Feels weird to acknowledge our relationship aloud, but maybe it will get easier. It can't get harder, that's for sure.

"Maggie Aimsley?" she asks. "With the bangs?"

Her comment pulls me back to the time we helped my parents clean out the garage and discovered the yearbook my mom insisted I buy to commemorate senior year. "Her, yeah. After she dumped me, I taught myself to play acoustic guitar."

We've reached my SUV, and she turns to me. "How is that a mistake?"

"The mistake was deciding to showcase my newfound skill at a campus open mic night, where I introduced myself using a stage name."

"Dare I ask?"

I hang my head and mumble, "Leopold Dogfish."

"Adrian."

"I know."

"Adrian!" She's bent double laughing, and that almost makes the shame worth it. Almost. "Also, since we're confessing, you should know you didn't have to mutiny today. I'm happy to let you drive the boat anytime you want."

"You're just now telling me this?" She readjusts the books in her hands, glaring at me over the stack, eyes sparkling penny-bright in the hazy afternoon sun. "Gabe told me weeks ago, but I was curious if you'd confess to winding me up."

"I've been meaning to tell you, but I didn't know how to without mentioning, y'know…"

"The compromising circumstances?"

Heat rises up my neck, reaching my ears, but it's nothing compared to the flame of desire. "Yeah, that." Now all I can think of is her parted lips and breathy moans, my blood stirring at the thought. Clearing my throat, I ask, "So all this time you knew I was messing with you about captain privileges?"

"Yup." Her lips curve in a sly smile and she pokes my chest, right above my heart. "You're lucky I like you, Hollis-Parker."

Lucky, indeed.

★ ★ ★

Day Nine of the "Friendship Experiment" is going much better than previous trials of Strangers and Strictly Business. Things are easier now that we aren't tiptoeing around each other. The pent-up urge to be with her hasn't gone away, but it is tempered by being near her.

The storms that came through last week gave way to clear weather, and with possible tropical storms predicted for next week, we've gone out to tag every day, filming different stages of the process, and I'm happy with the amount and variety of sharks we've caught. Happy too that the change in weather aligns with a shift between Hope and I, a familiar pull that we've stopped resisting.

It's been over a week, and somehow we're moving closer without crossing any lines, like a clock edging toward noon, the hands coming full circle to meet at the center. Instead of avoiding me onboard, she's been seeking me out—offering me first pick of scones when she brought in a box of treats from a local café, or staying late with me to stow supplies. Now she's joined me on the bench where I'm organizing data while we motor up the ICW to film with a researcher who's using drones to study sharks.

Elbows on her splayed knees, her fingers work to undo a tangle of line, the white rope a contrast to her brown skin, deepened to bronze from hours on the water. She lifts her chin, looking out across the bow, and tendrils of dark curls flutter along her cheeks, the baby hairs at her nape curling charmingly upward.

She catches me looking and instead of a glare, bumps her bare knee into mine and gives me a grin that's an invitation, not an admonition. Tipping closer, she looks at my laptop screen. "How're those notes coming along, Leopold?"

She's taken to calling me Leopold ever since I told her about my embarrassment of a stage name. I try not to have flashbacks to our first few months of dating, when she used my last name as a pet name, but it's hard not to draw comparisons. "I'm never going to live that down, am I?"

She shakes her head, and I catch the coconut scent of her sunscreen. There's a small daub of cream along her temple that I resist the urge to rub in. "Never."

"I performed exactly once, in the college's union building. Must you keep the memory alive?"

With the utmost dignity, she presses a hand to her heart, and my eyes drop to the dip of her collarbones, glowing under a fine sheen of sweat. "It is my solemn duty." She drops the pose and grins. "Also, I may have mentioned it to Marissa."

"How dare you?" I groan but can't keep the smile off my face. "I thought we were friends."

"Marissa and I are friends too," she says. "No secrets among friends."

I have plenty of secrets, like how I agreed to friends because I'll take whatever she's willing to give me. Like how at night, I lay in bed in the waterfront house I never dreamed I could afford, and it feels empty without her.

"Fair's fair, though," she says, returning her attention to the knot. "It's not a secret, but something you didn't know about me is that I finally learned how to ride a bike last year."

"How is that embarrassing? It's an accomplishment." She never wanted me to teach her because she said she didn't have time or money for hospital visits.

She grunts out a laugh. "What's embarrassing is that Zuri's seven-year-old son saw me struggling and recruited his friends to help me. Then a bunch of other neighborhood kids came out and all chimed in with advice. One of the moms saw it and uploaded a video to their moms' group. Word is it made the rounds of social media and won some heartwarming moment of the week award for a webzine."

My mouth falls open. "Wait, you're telling me you're also internet-famous?"

She shakes her head. "I'm 'endearingly uplifting for a select audience' famous."

"You've been holding out on me, Hope Evans. You come in here all wide-eyed and starstruck—"

"Oh, is that how it was?"

I shift in my seat to face her, swept up in flirting with her. "Uh, yeah," I tease. "Yet all along you're a star in your own right. Two internet celebrities? Total soulmate vibes." I freeze. This is what happens when I let my guard down. "Not that… I didn't mean…"

"No, no, you're right," she says, copper eyes sparkling. "Internet notoriety is totally a solid basis for true love."

Relieved, I laugh. "Can't have a soulmate that doesn't know what it's like to go viral. They should add that to dating apps." I sit back on my heels. "Anyway, learning from a bunch of neighborhood kids is cool. Iris is the one who taught me. I actually picked it up pretty quick. She's a great teacher."

"Why are you surprised? She's been at it for like twenty years."

"Yeah, but she's Iris."

She smiles at me. As an only child, she's always seemed amused by my sibling rivalry with Iris. "Would you ever guess that I learned how to lay tile?"

"Lay tile?" I'm momentarily thrown by the change in topic. "What for?"

"Zuri wanted to give the bathroom at the store an upgrade."

I can picture Hope being great at that. Skilled with her hands, attention to detail. "I signed up for a cupcake-making class at the library." Somehow this has become a catch-up session and I don't mind at all.

"You can bake now?" She's abandoned the knot to focus all

her attention on me. "Next time I'll skip the bakery and you can bring breakfast."

I raise my hand in a quelling gesture. "Never said I could bake. I said I signed up for a class. After I burnt the second tray of cupcakes I was kindly asked to leave."

She snorts. "Stop."

"Why do you think I volunteer my time there now? Guilt." Joking around is so easy with her, and I'd forgotten how much I missed these lighthearted moments.

She shakes her head, but her smile is wide. "I participated in a 5k."

"You took up running?" She once claimed running was a gait designed for emergencies only.

"Handed out water," she says, and I chuckle.

Bending to pick up the tangled line, I say, "I entered a wood chopping contest."

"What now?"

I look up to find her eyeing me above the rims of her sunglasses. "For charity," I explain.

"Did you win?"

Chuckling, I say, "Nowhere close."

"Is there footage?" Her pupils darken, intense.

"There is." And this time, I wouldn't mind if she googles it.

She nudges her sunglasses up onto the bridge of her nose. I catch sight of my smiling reflection, and for the first time since she came back, don't feel the need to hide how I'm feeling.

"I see your knot skills haven't improved much." She takes the tangled line from me, fingertips warm and soft against my calloused knuckles. "Look at this mess."

"What would I do without you?"

She answers absently, intent on her task. "You'd manage."

I would, yeah. But I don't want to just manage, or get by. Now that I remember how good it is to be with her, even as only a friend, how will I ever go back to life without her?

twenty-five

hope

The hour-long trip up the Intercoastal Waterway to North Carolina has flown by in a happy haze, joking and reminiscing with Adrian. Ever since I took Zuri's advice and asked him if he'd be open to exploring a friendship, the dynamic between us has totally flipped. It feels so good to not have to weigh every word that comes out of my mouth or pretend I don't enjoy his company.

On the career front, I sent in the application for the white shark research internship, after texting back and forth with Sylvia for more details. She seems to think I have a good shot, but the program is intensely competitive. Updating my résumé and completing an application felt good, though, like another step in the right direction.

By summer's end, I'm counting on the attraction between Adrian and I burning out for lack of fuel, the longing for something deeper replaced by gratitude for a friendship that, if not quite what I want from him, doesn't require me to give more than I know how to offer. Until then, though, I'm enjoying the undercurrent of attraction, letting my eyes linger and feeling a rush of pleasure when he does the same.

Someday, he'll find someone to settle down with, and I'll have to give this up, so maybe it's a good time to start the process now. The thought enters my mind just as the motor changes in pitch.

Marissa has steered the boat into a deserted inlet, lined by a bluff covered in beach grass, and Adrian is leaning over the bow, butt in the air, checking the anchor line. Watching him, I decide to leave the task of learning how not to appreciate what I see for another day.

Gabe plops down next to my seat and I jolt upright guiltily, grateful for the heat of the day to explain my flushed skin.

Rubbing his hands together, he glances over the gunwale toward the man on shore who's unpacking equipment from a case. "Think Jason will let me fly the drone?" Jason Ito is a biologist whose study involves using drones to study shark behavior. We're here as part of Marissa and Adrian's efforts to demonstrate a wide range of research techniques.

"Not a chance." Adrian is still bent double, his voice muffled. Straightening up, he wipes his hands on his swim trunks. "I'm pretty sure he only agreed to film with us because he's waiting on grant funding and needs access to a boat."

Leaning over to unzip his laptop case, Gabe says, "Maybe. Would that be so bad?"

"Nah, I know how frustrating that can be. It's part of why I'm glad we're able to do this. But I hope he didn't feel obligated. I would never want someone to do an interview if they're not comfortable."

"Which you made clear in the initial contact. You basically sounded like you were trying to convince him *not* to collaborate with us."

"Why?" This is the first I'm hearing of Adrian's hesitancy. Then again, we've only been on good terms for a short while. "I assumed most people would be eager to work with you."

"They are," Gabe says. "Many of them seek us out. But by

the time Adrian finishes the disclaimers, he makes a cool opportunity sound like selling their soul. He lets the haters get to him too much."

"I keep a balanced perspective, that's all. There are a lot of upsides, but putting your work out there in the public eye is a risk for negative exposure as well." He looks at me when he says this, and a trickle of unease slides down my spine.

Gabe makes an annoyed face. "Your 'balanced mindset' is why Marissa does most of the initial outreach. Like with Bauer." The name sounds familiar, and I place it after a moment—Marissa met with him around the time I first arrived. They wanted to dive with his team to show how acoustic receivers are set up and monitored.

"Who said no, just like I told her he would." The engine noise cuts, and Adrian's response is loud in the sudden calm.

"Originally, yeah." Gabe pivots toward where Marissa's stepping out from under the canopy. "Didn't you say Bauer just gave us the green light?"

"Yeah, we're set to film the team's next dive." She sits down to take off her water sandals and tucks them inside a backpack. "According to him, the board is making a push to become more visible on social media. He asked if our offer still stood, because he figured this would be easier than learning a TikTok dance."

Adrian smirks. "We should lead with that. Get featured on *Shark Science Crew*, no formal dance training required."

"I don't think you're in need of a better pitch," I assure him. "Sylvia and Liam were thrilled to be a part of this. Liam took like thirty selfies for his nephew. And numbers don't lie; you have one point four *million* followers." Inwardly, I cringe. I wish I could forget the number, but every time he posts a video my mind keeps coming back to how many people might see me mess up, to the damage I could do to the field I love by screwing up.

"Followers aren't a good benchmark of credibility," he protests. "That's just a popularity contest. I want to ensure our peers

in the scientific community trust me to put out reputable content." *Content that includes me. But no pressure or anything.*

"I looked at who you're mutuals with." I glance at Gabe. "Is
mutuals the correct term?"

"Eh," he makes a noncommittal noise. "We know what you
mean. And they're legit, right? *Shark Science Crew* is incredibly
well-respected." He clasps Adrian's shoulder. "There's a reason
I wanted to work with you."

"Be that as it may," he says. "Jason didn't seek us out, we
contacted him. Don't make him regret it by asking to fly the
drone the second we arrive."

Gabe flashes a smile. "Me? Never."

"Ten to one he's asking to fly the drone," Adrian says in an
undertone, and I chuckle. Gabe was the first one to get off the
boat, backpack extended overhead to keep it dry, and splash his
way through the shallows to shore. He's chatting animatedly
with Jason, and the scientist keeps dodging glances at the boat,
a curious grin on his face.

Adrian hops over the edge of the boat, landing in the waist-
deep water, and I pass him his bag. "Did you really think he
wouldn't?"

"No. He wouldn't be where he is if he were shy."

"What about you?"

"What about me?" He clutches the bag to his chest. His
muscled forearms are distracting, and the way he grips the bag
effortlessly has me back to our last kiss, when he lifted me up
and hauled me against him like he was ready to devour me.

Not thoughts a friend should entertain, and I pull my focus
back to the conversation. "You're not shy, but you're not an
attention-seeker. How is this so intuitive for you?"

"Because the spotlight isn't on me," he says. "It's on the research,
and the scientists we work with. People might come to my page
to get a glimpse of me, but the channel is focused on education."

He hoists the bag onto one shoulder and splashes a few steps far-ther away as a wave sends the boat rocking. "When I look at it that way, sharing a little bit of myself online isn't such a hardship."

Marissa comes over and lowers herself to sit on the edge of the open door, her feet dangling off the side of the boat. Just as she hoists herself up to slide into the water, a low hum whizzes past my ear and I duck instinctively. Marissa flails her arms and tumbles forward, landing in a belly flop that Adrian stumbles backward to avoid, narrowly keeping his balance. She splutters to the surface, water streaming down her face, clothes drenched.

"Sorry!" Gabe shouts from the beach, holding up the drone controller. He shrugs, an incorrigible smile visible even at this distance. "Blooper reel?"

"I'll show you a blooper reel," Marissa grumbles under her breath, and I look down to hide my smile. I don't know yet what's ahead, but I'm going to miss this.

We're filming for the first part of the day on the beach so Jason can talk about how drones can be used to track sharks in shallow water. This has far-reaching applications for everything from population monitoring to reducing human/shark inter-actions. The day is hot, but I'm buzzing with energy. If I get the internship in California, I'll be doing this type of research.

The others are conferring over the interview portion, and I hang back a little to give them space—Jason seems a little ner-vous about the interview questions, and I know the feeling. He tugs a folded piece of paper out of his shorts pocket. "I wrote down answers to the list of potential questions you sent over."

"Awesome," Adrian says. "Basically, we'll just do a who, what, when, where, why, and how of your current research."

Gabe steps forward, camera in hand. "How being the fun part."

"Guessing that means the UAV?" Jason smiles, relaxing a little at the mention of the tech. "Gadgets always seem to catch people's attention."

"Between the drone and the sharks, can't go wrong," Marissa says. While they confer about whether to do the interview first or launch the drone, I take the chance to grab a snack from my bag, checking my phone in the process.

There's a new message from Zuri, and it's about twice as long as her normal texts. A knot of dread forms in the pit of my stomach and I scan it quickly, worried something happened to the kids. But it's not about the kids, it's about me.

Zuri: FYI I just found out a lot of people in town know about your videos. I was talking with another mom at Leo's soccer practice who said she follows a bunch of nature accounts and the algorithm recommended one of Adrian's videos (she knew his name, so that whole explanation was highly sus...I think she follows him for more than just the shark content) and she recognized you in it.

While I'm reading, another text comes through, and Marissa glances my way at the interruption.

"Sorry," I mumble, silencing it and reading the next text with a growing sense of dread.

Zuri: Leo's friend's dad overheard us, and he said he saw it too and thought you looked familiar. He'd seen you when he picked up his kid from my house a couple times. Apparently a few of his friends also follow Adrian, and it got me thinking, Owen McHugh is still friends with like half our classmates. What if one of them knows about the channel and mentions it to him?

Granola bar in hand, I type out a quick response.

Hope: What's the worst he could do? I barely talk in the videos. My one screwup was on a livestream, and it wasn't anything damaging.

Zuri: That's true. I guess I just went to worst-case scenario. Sorry if I stressed you out.

Hope: No worries. You're protective. It's part of what makes you a good mom.

Zuri: I think you misspelled friend.

Hope: Did I?

A shadow falls over me and a moment later, Adrian squats down next to me, concern etched in his brow. "Everything okay?"

"Yeah, Zuri just gave me a heads-up that a lot of people in town are fans of yours." I force a smile, though the granola bar no longer looks appetizing. "Including a mom who may or may not be following you for thirst reasons."

He makes an ick face. "Does it bother you?"

"Why? I'm not your girlfriend."

"People knowing about you being on *Shark Science Crew*?" Realizing I was hung up on people fawning over him, embarrassment washes over me. Thankfully, he glosses over it. "I know things didn't go so well last time your hometown got wind of a video of you."

I rock back, settling into the sand. The others must've decided to go with research before interview and are caught up in launching the drone. "It shouldn't, logically." Part of me doesn't want to be vulnerable, but if we're doing the friend thing, clamming up will be counterproductive. "But yeah, a little. Tell me I shouldn't worry." The request surprises me. I hadn't realized how much I wanted his comfort.

His lips press into a tight line, his beard making him look somewhat ferocious, and he shakes his head. "I'm not going to tell you how you should feel, but I will tell you I've been hypervigilant about checking for trolls, Marissa and Gabe too. We didn't want to worry you with it, but we're on the lookout, and so far, other than a few random nasty comments, nothing."

They've all been looking out for me? The pit of worry in my stomach fades, replaced by gratitude for such great people in my life.

"We're getting ready to launch," Marissa calls.

I heft myself up off the sand, and Adrian stands too. "Thank you," I say as we make our way over. He sends a half grin my way, but I can tell he's still thinking about Zuri's news.

The drone is a distraction though, and not long after the drone is airborne, Jason spots a bait ball, with sharks feeding in the midst of the swirling mass of fish.

"Check it out." He holds the tablet screen a bit away from himself, and we cluster around to see the silvery mass of fish ebb and flow in the shallows like iridescent waves. They dart and move as one, trying to evade the three small sharks visible in their midst.

"Spinner sharks, you think?" Marissa asks.

"Maybe," Jason says. "Could be blacktips." He'll analyze the recording later. The sharks dart in and out of the large school of fish, agile and quick.

It's been years since I've seen this in person, and my eyes are glued to the monitor, worries over negative exposure and an ex-boyfriend-turned-friend forgotten in the joy of witnessing this incredible behavior.

twenty-six

hope

A tropical storm is gathering strength offshore. Historically, it's early in the season for a hurricane, but Marissa left town a day early for her family reunion out of state to avoid any potential trouble. She invited me to come along, but the allure of getting out of town was outweighed by the prospect of spending an entire weekend making small talk with strangers—my own family reunions are stressful enough.

Solitude is the silver lining to staying back, and at first having the condo to myself was wonderful. I worked on my résumé, delved into a few recent shark studies, and ate a blissfully conversation-free lunch accompanied only by the hum of the ceiling fan. Then boredom kicked in. Turns out half a day alone in an apartment was enough, but I wasn't about to appease my desire for a change in scenery with a potential hurricane about to make landfall.

Instead, I gather all the couch pillows and settle in, laptop propped on my knees, continuing in my quest to watch all the crew's past videos. I'm working my way through the uploads haphazardly, an episode here, an interview there. It's cool to watch how their rapport has grown more polished and free-flowing, less talking over one another and stammering like a log-jammed creek after a rainstorm. Their early videos make me feel better for my own flubs.

Heavy cloud cover moves in, and the gloom and patter of rain against the windows lulls me into a doze. I'm awoken by a knock that rattles the doorframe. Scrambling out of my nest of pillows, I hurry over and peer through the peephole. Adrian is outside, outlined against a curtain of sheeting rain.

Ozone assaults my nostrils when I swing the door open. "What are you doing here?" Knowing Marissa would be out of town, I purposefully didn't ask about his weekend plans. Despite being on friendly terms, we haven't hung out alone outside work, and a weekend without Marissa around as a buffer seems a risky time to put our new relationship boundaries to the test.

"Weather's getting a little dicey, so I thought I'd check on you." Arms laden with totes, he steps around me, shimmying between me and the door, his body sliding along mine for one excruciatingly delicious moment. "I thought you might need some groceries. Don't need to be venturing out in this."

I press the door closed with my back and lean against it for support against the heady rush of emotions whirling through me at the sight of him. "I didn't plan to. Marissa and I shopped before she left."

Setting down the bags on the counter, he puts a sack of oranges in the empty fruit bowl.

"You didn't have to brave the storm to feed me."

"Just a little rain so far." He shrugs off his rain-specked jacket to reveal a form-fitting T-shirt. "I've been checking the radar all day." Fingertips grasping the hood of his coat, he reaches around me to hang it on one of the hooks by the door. His nose is speckled with raindrops, and I catch the deep, earthy scent of his beard oil.

Skin tingling with awareness, I ask, "Then why come over? I'm fine."

"Are you?" He stoops to unlace his shoes. "You've got goose bumps." His words skitter across my bare forearms, and when he looks up at me, worry pools in his dark eyes.

"You let in a draft," I say, rationalizing. Even at its chilliest, South Carolina in midsummer is no match for my Michigan roots. "Physical response to external stimuli." At least that part's true. Him kneeling, mouth level with my navel, is definitely stimulating.

His gaze runs up my arms, past my throat, until our eyes connect, and the perusal lingers on my skin like the echo of his touch. I narrowly avoid closing my eyes at the burst of longing in my chest.

He rises and places a hand against the door, framing me in. Tipping forward, he toes off one of his shoes. "You're not used to this kind of storm." His mouth is near my cheek, so close his lips almost brush my skin, and I should move away, but I stay put, breathing shallowly.

With a long swallow, he looks down, holding my gaze. "I wanted to make sure you're taking the proper precautions." His voice slips low, and I get the feeling we're not talking about the weather anymore.

"This isn't my first tropical storm." My pulse has picked up, and my eyes drop to the hollow of his neck, then swing back up to his freshly trimmed beard, and further, to his lips.

"But you're out of practice," he insists.

I lift my eyes to his. "Are you implying you could teach me a thing or two?" My chest is heaving like I've just run up a flight of stairs, and Adrian's eyes drop to the bare skin exposed by the low scoop of my tank top.

His own breath is coming fast and loud in the empty room. Just us here, alone.

"If you wanted to learn," he says. "Though I recall you have some relevant experience with snowstorms." A wicked, knowing smile creases his cheeks. My mind flashes to the New Year's

Day blizzard that left us stranded at the airport coming back from winter break, when we had no choice but to weather the storm in a hastily-booked hotel room equipped with a jetted tub and king-size bed.

On a shaky inhale, I force myself to meet his eyes. "Are we talking about the same kind of hands-on instruction as that morning at the beach?"

His eyes darken with desire, but there's something else there too. Restraint. Caution. "It depends. Are you asking as my friend? Or something more?"

Until now, I've attributed our kisses to mutual attraction and proximity, at least on his part. My own feelings are troublingly strong, but he's never given any indication he'd want to try again. To reforge the broken bonds between us. I figured he'd been swept up in the moment, tugged under by a strong pull of nostalgia.

But the way he's waiting on my answer, body rigid with tension, has me wondering if he's fighting the same losing battle I am. After a moment, he steps back, depriving me of his heat. "I'll just put away the groceries and leave you be." He turns away, but I grab his wrist.

His eyes fly to mine, and beneath my fingertips, his pulse hammers. "Even though I've lived without you for so long, my heart can't seem to get the hang of it." The truth leaves my mouth and I don't bother holding back. "I thought friends could work. That this could be enough."

"Friends will never be enough for me, Hope." He moves closer, his wrist still caught in my unsteady grip. "But if that's all you have to give, I'll take it, because I don't want to live without you."

I shake my head. "I don't think it's enough for me either. The wanting hasn't stopped. And I know it's probably ruining our chance to keep the friendship up, but I've kept this bottled up for so long. I'm just worried I can't be what you need."

"You've always been more than enough for me." His confession is an echo of my own inescapable reality. A truth that doesn't scare me anymore, not in this moment, and I let go of his wrist, throw my arms around his neck, and kiss him.

His lips part in an instant and the kiss deepens, his mouth decadent and lush, scattering my thoughts like windblown leaves. His hands are everywhere, his touch all I've needed and been too proud to ask for. Delicious and warm and oh—hot. His tongue is slick against mine, tempting me for more.

He walks me backward until I'm pressed between the door and his body, and he presses another openmouthed kiss to my neck, sucking as he pulls away.

"I've been dying to touch you here," I say, sliding my hands down his muscled back.

"I've been dying to touch you anywhere." He's back to my mouth, my lips already plump and wet, our tongues sliding against each other. Our first two kisses were hesitant, an exploration. But now I want to claim him. I want these kisses to be indelible. Come what may, I want what's between us to last, every part of this, every part of us. He tilts his forehead against mine, filling his lungs, and draws his hands up my waist, to my rib cage, and I arch against the door, chest heaving against his.

"You're so sexy, Hope."

Sexy isn't how I seek to look. My body gets me from here to there, it's an extension of my mind. I know a lot of people, my best friends included, who put time into their appearance, and there's worth in it for them. But for me, sexy isn't a benchmark. It's a feeling, and I feel it now, with Adrian, his hands roving over my body, his eyes heavy with desire, our bodies on the same wavelength.

I lift my chin, deepening the kiss. His hands have found my wrists, thumbs circling the thin skin at the inside of my wrists, pinning me, and our mouths are the only connection I control. I take full advantage, sucking his plump lower lip between mine, reveling in his moan, a sound that drives its way straight to my core.

"Adrian." This time it's me who pulls away, breathless, dizzy, giddy. I tip my forehead against his sternum, pulse racing.

"Regrets?" he asks, and I look up to find his brows tugged together.

"Only for all the time we wasted not doing this," I say, and he grins.

"We have a lot of time to make up for." He bends toward me, but right before our lips meet, the room is plunged into darkness. The hum of appliances cuts out with a noticeable click. Power outage.

We break apart and I pick my way across the dim living room to the sliding glass door and peer out. Wind lashes tree branches and the sky is dark, but it's impossible to tell what caused the outage.

"We should probably get out of here," Adrian says, and I turn to find him frowning at his phone.

"The power might come back on in a few minutes."

"Or it might not," he says. "Radar doesn't look great, and no work crews are going out in this."

I'm guessing he's right; the parking lot looks like a swamp. "You said it wasn't that bad."

Adrian steps up behind me, warm compared to the coolness of the windowpane. "That was before we lost power. We need to move inland. If the roads end up flooding, we don't want to be stranded here."

Goose bumps break out on my arms all over again. I don't want Adrian driving in this. "Let's take my car."

"My SUV has all-wheel drive, and I'm more familiar with the roads. If you're worried about leaving your car—"

"I'm worried about you," I half shout, then bite my lip. "Sorry. It's just..." I gulp to clear my throat from worry, but it doesn't work. "Eric lost his life driving on slick roads. And

I know accidents could happen anytime, but..." Worry over losing him burrows its way into my chest, the fear a palpable ache. I rub my palm against my goose-bump-pebbled arm in a poor imitation of Adrian's soothing touch.

"Shit, Hope," he says. "I should've realized." He gathers me into a tight hug, and I let his strength shore me up. Three years since I held Zuri up during her husband's wake. A long time, but emotion heightens my memories.

After a long embrace, he pulls away, hands sliding down to grasp my own. "We're going to be all right." He gives my fingers a squeeze. "This is part of life here, something I'm prepared for. We'll be okay."

He can't know that, but his surety is catching. I grab the emergency bag Marissa reminded me to pack. Add my toothbrush and zip my phone into my purse, then follow Adrian out into the storm.

Rain pelts down, driven sideways by a fierce wind that kicks up ridges of waves on puddles that stretch like rivers crisscrossing the parking lot. Lots of spaces are empty, and Adrian's SUV is easy to pick out. We jog over and it doesn't escape my notice that he stays on the windward side of me, blocking the worst of the gusts. He pulls my door open and waits for me to get in, then rounds the hood to the driver's side, dumping the grocery bags in the back seat.

I pause, wet hand on the seat belt, as a thought occurs to me. His house is on the river, so we can't be headed there. "Where are we going, a hotel?"

His face is grim for the first time all evening. "To my sister's."

twenty-seven

adrian

Muffled from behind the door, my sister's voice is distinct enough to carry. "...Warned you not to buy a house so close to the water." The door swings open, and her eyes drop to the rainwater pooling on her threshold.

I step to the side, soaked shoes squelching on the hallway carpet. "We're fine, thanks for asking."

Iris's eyes pop wide at the sight of Hope. "You stayed?"

I may have neglected to mention I was bringing her. *Can my ex-girlfriend come along too?* Not a simple topic to broach over text.

Still, I didn't realize Hope's presence would come as a total shock. "You really don't watch our channel, do you? Hope's in all our latest content."

"Is she?" My sister packs a whole lot of subtext into two words, but she pulls the door open wider to let us in, not bothering to conceal her open appraisal of Hope.

Maybe I ought to have rethought coming here, but I'd already set up the plan with my sister, and she'd suspect something if I ditched out on it. Not that I plan to give her any hint of what's happening between me and Hope. Especially since I'm not sure yet what to make of it.

I attempt to keep my dripping contained to the tiled, narrow entryway, and Hope follows suit. It's a lot of dodging elbows and hips as we both endeavor to peel off our outerwear without inadvertent contact, like two live wires primed to ignite at the slightest touch. I manage to shimmy out of my jacket first and step past the vestibule to give her room to maneuver.

Papers clutter every surface of the living room, bringing to mind my parents' house, and admittedly, my own. Abstract prints in bold primary colors frame a pair of floating shelves, and on the lower one, math theory texts threaten to dislodge geometric bookends. The other holds a bedraggled collection of potted plants in varying stages of health, like a science fair project gone awry.

"I see you revived the spider plant." I've only visited a handful of times since I helped her move in, what with our busy schedules and my nagging insecurities over what she might think of my online platform.

Iris eyes the wilting flora skeptically. "At the expense of the others. My course load this semester is intense." She swings her gaze toward me, eyes alight with mischief behind her wire frames. "Maybe I should follow your lead and broaden my horizons in case I need a backup plan."

Our conversation about the wisdom of my career move may have been forestalled by Hope's arrival, but her comments today make her stance clear.

"Backup plan?" Hope peels off a wet sock and jams it into her shoe. "You mean the channel? The one with over a million subscribers that he runs in addition to his faculty position at the university?"

"No one's denying my brother and cousin's success," Iris says, which feels a tad disingenuous. "But how can putting your life on display be more fulfilling than pure science?"

"You're a professor," Hope says. "The core of your work is a blend of your own research and teaching. Adrian's doing the same, both through his work at the university and his channel.

It's an extension of his commitment to science and conservation, not a detriment to it."

My jaw goes slack at Hope jumping to defend me. I know
we're friends now—and after that last kiss, my heart's holding
out for something more—but I didn't expect her to come to
my rescue in such a bold way.

Maintaining eye contact with Iris, she sets her shoes to the
side, wiping off her hands on her shorts. "He's working with
college programs and reputable nonprofits, collaborating with
other scientists, and in doing so, demystifying shark research and
shining a light on science-based conservation efforts. Where's
the harm in that?"

Iris's brows are visible above her glasses. "When you put it
that way, I sound incredibly stuffy." For my sister, that admis-
sion doesn't come lightly. "But you left out the part about blurring the lines between his private life and public persona. That
part is still unpalatable."

"What he shares isn't gimmicky." Hope glances my way. She
knows about my efforts to maintain healthy boundaries, and
my distaste for the blurry lines that come with creating content.
"I'm not suggesting you subscribe or even watch their content,
but maybe give him and your cousin a little more credit."

My sister's mouth drops open. I've never seen her speechless,
and I half wish I could whip out my phone to capture the phenomenon, but I'm not so stupid as to try. A timer beeps in the
kitchen and she blinks out of her momentary silence.

"Adrian, could you give me a hand in the kitchen?" She
meets my eyes with a meaningful look it's impossible for Hope
to miss, then gestures at Hope's soggy jacket in the corner.
"You're welcome to use the dryer for your wet clothes. You
could warm up with a shower, too, if you want. The bathroom
is connected to my room."

On her way past me, I brush Hope's arm with my fingertips
and mouth a silent, *Thank you*. Her lips tilt up in a smile that

warms me to the core despite my damp clothes. The warm bubble bursts, though, when I find Iris in the kitchen, waiting for me.

She passes me an oven mitt the moment I enter the kitchen. "Remind me again why you let Hope go?"

"Shh." I wrench my neck in my hurry to look over my shoulder into the living room, but Hope's gone, thank goodness. Historically my sister has embarrassed me in front of my crushes and girlfriends more times than the average person's entire extended family combined. "I didn't *let* her go. She left, and I know it was stupid not to try to make amends, but why are you asking now?"

"Because she just made a better, more succinct case for the validity of your work than I've ever heard from you."

"Maybe you haven't been listening well."

She's quiet, and I turn to find her watching me, an indecipherable look on her face. "Maybe not." The air fryer beeps, and she opens the cupboard and pulls out a bowl. Back to me, she says, "Then again, you haven't reached out much lately."

I've been nervous to reach out since the day she came to my boat, worried what she'd say about me working with Hope.

"I'll make more of an effort." I open the oven and let the heat dissipate until the air clears between us. "Kind of missed hearing you berate my life choices to my face." I meant to lighten the mood, but it comes out sharper than intended.

"I've done a lot of that, haven't I?" It's not really a question, so I pull the sheet tray out of the oven in lieu of answering. "Part of it is me trying to be the supportive older sister I wasn't for all those years."

She got swept up in college and career while I was still a kid, and that was natural, not her fault. But I still felt like I'd lost my closest friend and confidante, and we never regained the closeness we had before she graduated.

We've never talked about my feelings surrounding her departure from my childhood, but my sister's always been unerringly perceptive. "This is you being supportive?"

"I came out to your boat to help you, did I not?" She pushes her foggy glasses up with a knuckle. "Dramamine wasted."

"You took seasickness medication to sit on a boat in the marina?"

"Better safe than sorry." She was traumatized with brutal seasickness on a snorkeling trip when we were kids and vowed never to set foot on a boat of any kind again. I was offended she'd never even offered to see the boat, but now I realize just how serious her aversion is, and how far she'd go to help me out.

"I've been trying to be there for you, but sometimes it's hard not to be overprotective. I've seen what happens to public figures when they make the smallest mistake, and I didn't want that to happen to my brother."

Her words are a reminder of what Hope risked in joining our channel. I hate the idea that being part of our crew exposes her reputation to harm, but I have to trust her decision to stay with us.

"But you're clearly happy, and doing good work, if your ex-girlfriend is to be believed." She's fishing, and I don't intend to bite. "I shouldn't have let my opinions stilt our time together."

"Is there an apology in there somewhere?"

She dumps the air fryer basket into the bowl. "You're really going to make me say it?"

"Little brothers are supposed to be pests," I inform her. "I'd be slacking if I made things easy on you."

Hand on her hip, she smiles. "Yes, Adrian, I'm sorry. Though not as sorry as you ought to be for letting that phenomenal woman slip through your fingers."

Here we go. "Now who's being a pest?"

"I'm just saying you're lucky she stayed after that catastrophic first day."

That sobers me, fast. "You have no idea. She didn't even know about our channel when she took the job."

"And yet, she's here."

"I am." Hope's voice sends a jolt through me, and I whirl, sending samosas flying. One hits my face, another bounces off my shoulder. A few hit the floor, sliding along the tile like deep-fried hockey pucks.

Hope stops one with her foot. "Now might be a good time to mention we've brought groceries." She caught us talking about her, but she doesn't look worried. In fact, she looks comfortable, her hair loose, sweatshirt sleeves pushed up to her elbows, a giant pink scrunchie on her wrist. Relaxed, like she belongs here. In my life. In my heart.

She's here. She stayed, despite everything. For her career, yes. But also, I'm hoping, for me.

A few snacks survived, and we sat down to eat them in the living room, along with some of the fresh fruit and cheese I brought for Hope, paired with a bottle of sweet muscadine wine. Having Hope here shouldn't feel so easy after everything we've gone through, but it does. She's curled up at the end of the couch in sweatpants, irresistibly cozy, and it's impossible not to think how easy it would be to scoop her into my arms and press a kiss behind her ear.

Maybe it's the mellowing effect of the wine and late hour, but Iris manages to avoid touchy subjects, trading stories with Hope like she's been a part of our lives all along. Wineglass clutched to her chest, Hope dissolves into giggles as Iris regales us with students' most outlandish excuses for turning assignments in late, and the sound of her laughter hits me like a breath of pure oxygen.

Eventually, conversation dies down. My sister puts on a movie we've all seen a dozen times, and heads for bed not long after, leaving a stack of blankets on the armchair. Hope curls against me, head on my shoulder, and dozes off. *She's here. She stayed.*

Tonight, that's more than enough.

twenty-eight

hope

The storm died down when it made landfall, but severe flooding and widespread home damage make me glad we made the trip to stay with Iris. Local news says the roads are clear, so we leave after lunch and are halfway back to the condo, driving past uprooted trees and muddy ditches, when Marissa calls. A neighbor told her the power's still out, so we detour to Walmart to buy a cooler, but it turns out we're too late. The electricity has been off long enough that the contents of the freezer are thawed, the rooms dense with prickly heat.

Working in companionable silence we bag up the trash and haul the spoiled food to the dumpsters. Normally I'd be operating at zero battery after a day without alone time, but it's never been like that with Adrian. By not pushing me into conversation, he gives me room to breathe, to recalibrate.

Back inside, he hovers by the doorway. "I have to head over to check on the boat, but I don't want to leave you here, it's stifling." He gestures to the open sliding balcony door, doing nothing to dislodge the humid warmth. "I could take you to a hotel, or I'm sure Iris won't mind you staying there for another day or two."

"The fact that last night went so well is a miracle. I don't want to chance it, no offense."

"A hotel, then. I'll cover it."

Hurt rises at his choice of words. "Why are you speaking like my employer? I thought we were past that."

His brow furrows. "I... I just didn't want to assume."

He's standing at the vestibule, where our passionate kiss took place less than a day ago, and yet he's acting as if nothing's changed.

"Yesterday, you made it clear you wanted more than friendship." I pause for breath, gripping the countertop and gathering my courage. I feel like I'm at the crest of a towering sand dune, the wind roaring against my face, poised to career over the edge. "I would never have kissed you if I didn't feel the same."

His whole face shifts from stony indifference to joy, like someone lit a flame inside him, and an answering spark awakens in my chest.

I don't often find myself lonely. This clawing want inside me isn't a generalized desire for company, it's an Adrian-specific need and I can't muster the strength to deny it any longer. "Unless you'd rather be alone, I'd like to go with you."

Adrian's been in touch with the marina, and they said while several boats suffered damage, his appears to be fine, but he heaves an audible sigh of relief when the *Praespero* comes into view, floating on the debris-ridden surface of the water, hull apparently intact. "Guess we lucked out."

"Better do a full check, just to be safe."

He grins at me. "I love when you talk redundancies and protocol."

By the time we finish going over the boat to make sure nothing's been damaged in the storm, we're both sweating all over again. Marissa texted earlier with an invite to drive up and stay with her family, but I told her I'm good. A road trip sounds exhausting, though I wish I would've booked a hotel when Adrian suggested it, because now I'll have to go further inland to find a good rate. I'm about to ask him to take me back to the condo to retrieve my car when his phone chimes. He huffs out a laugh and tips the screen toward me.

Marissa: Are you with Hope? She's doing the two-word text thing, and I'm worried about her staying at my condo with the power out.

Chuckling, I pull out my own phone.

Hope: "Two-word text thing"? It's called answering your question.

Marissa: Omg, did Adrian show you my text?

Oops. Now she knows we're together and will jump to all sorts of conclusions.

Hope: Don't worry about me. I'm sure the power will come back on soon, and if not, we'll figure something out.

Marissa: OK, but my offer stands. Aunt Clara will be happy for you to stay with us. Just let me know.

Hope: Will do.

Marissa: Now you're just doing it on purpose.

Hope: Maybe so.

I show Adrian the messages, and he lets out a soft laugh, reading over my shoulder. "I shouldn't aggravate her when she's just looking out for me, but it's so much fun."

"I fully support it," he says. "She did invite you here on false pretenses, after all."

"And hid it from you. A few two-word texts are totally called for."

He bites his lip. "We really ought to be more upset at her for that."

"You're not?"

He shakes his head. "Not anymore."

His words hold the promise of what we started in the condo, and of conversations a long time coming, but for now, I'm ready to find some air-conditioning and a hot shower.

I stretch, muscles aching from sleeping on the couch. My clothes are plastered to my body from the sweaty work of cleaning out the refrigerator and climbing around the boat.

"My next stop is home," Adrian says. "If you're not sick of me yet, you're welcome to come along. I'd offer you a hot shower, but I'm not sure I have power either."

Sick of him, after three years apart? "Guess we'd better check."

Adrian's electricity is on, and from the state of his microwave clock and freezer, he never lost power. Not only that, he has an outdoor shower, which means no waiting to take turns. He points out the bathroom, then pulls open the hall cabinet to show me where the towels are.

"Try not to run off with any of them," he says with a grin, before heading outside.

Despite the relief of hot water on my sore muscles, I shower quickly, feeling surprisingly at home in what is so clearly Adrian's space. His shampoo, his bar soap, the cedar scent enveloping me in the steamy room like his embrace. Wrapped in a familiar striped towel, I stoop to rummage in my overnight bag, pushing aside the hoodie he insisted I keep, no longer embarrassed about holding on to it.

I make my way out to the screened-in deck, halting when I realize the shower is right below. Before I can backtrack, the deck wobbles with footsteps and Adrian comes into view on the stairs, carrying a caddy, a towel tossed over one shoulder. His face breaks into a smile when he sees me. "There's something I've been meaning to give you."

He disappears into the house and reappears a moment later. "Well, not give to you." He squeezes the back of his neck, a sheepish grin on his face. "More like, return to you." He extends his hand, palm down, and a thin strand falls from it, the pendant at the end jerking to a stop and swaying slightly in the breeze, like a spider on a thread.

I step closer to get a good look, then smile wide. "My necklace!"

I reach out and he drops it into my hand, the chain spiraling into my palm, barely a weight. "I thought I'd lost it." The gold manta ray pendant is a memento he gave me to commemorate diving with real manta rays during a research trip in Mexico.

Unhooking the clasp, I slide the necklace around my neck, glowering with mock-accusation. "I can't believe you've had it all this time. Who's the bandit now?"

He laughs out loud. The sound is mellow and husky in the evening stillness. When he notices me fumbling, he steps around behind me, gathering my curls in his hands to leave my neck exposed, and tingles dance up my spine.

Hands trembling, I work to fasten the clip, hyperaware of his presence behind me, his grip on my hair a welcome pressure. Evening is a warm shell around us, the loamy scent of the river drifting upward, punctuated by the sharp scent of cypress leaves.

"I should've returned it to you before now." The words are just above a whisper, stirring the fine hairs at my nape. "I'm sorry."

"You don't have to be. Finders keepers." After all, I left it behind, just like the rest of the life I didn't come back for. My voice is hoarse, and I clear my throat, but the emotion remains lodged in place, clogging my windpipe.

"Not just about the necklace," he says, releasing my hair now that the clasp is fastened. I shake my head to settle the curls, then reach for the ever-present hair tie on my wrist.

"Don't." His eyes fly to mine. "Sorry… It's your hair, so you can do what you like. But it's beautiful like this. So full." I washed my hair in the shower and without my usual products it's expanding in the heat, the curls less defined than I'm used to. "I like it," he says. "I always like it. But I don't always get to see it this way." His voice is almost reverent, and I slide the hair tie back on my wrist, feeling suddenly beautiful.

He pulls his towel off his shoulder and drapes it over the back of one of the Adirondack chairs. "I've been wanting to tell you how sorry I am for not trying harder to fix things. For not calling, or texting, or checking in on you." One of his hands is clenched on the back of the chair, as if for support.

I twist my lips. "Pretty sure we were both in the same boat with that one." The words remind me of a question I've been too nervous to ask, but darkness is falling fast, and with it comes the sensation of anonymity.

Aiming for nonchalance, I take a seat in the other chair. "Speaking of boats…you named yours after me?" He might have bought it with the name already on it, and not known, but the coincidence doesn't seem likely. Neither does him naming a boat after me when we hadn't spoken for over a year.

Adrian lets his head flop down, his hair falling along his cheeks. "Yeah, I was wondering when you were going to ask about that." He peeks up at me, bites his lip. "I kind of showed my cards with that one."

Wanting to fan myself from how effortlessly sexy he is, I shake my head. "Except you didn't. I was super curious, but mostly confused." I look away, into the twilight sky. "I really thought you didn't want me here."

"I didn't." His voice is a soft rumble, but my body tenses at his words. "At least, my head didn't. My heart is a whole different story." I know exactly what he means. The past three years are evidence of my heart's stubborn refusal to give over to my head. "But as for the boat, I named it back when I thought we might still have a chance. I thought maybe you'd see it and…" He breaks off. "I guess it was my way of hoping you'd come back to me without me having to say the words. Cowardly."

"Or a really romantic gesture," I counter.

"You hate romance."

I take a moment to consider this. "Not true. I just don't need it."

"No one needs it. But some of us want it," he says quietly, and my heart breaks at what he's saying. I've never been interested in flowers or chocolate, but Adrian used to love when I'd surprise him by having his favorite takeout ordered when he came to visit, and I remember the joy he'd get shaking the presents on his birthday. Toward the end of our relationship, I was so focused on my own feelings that I stopped considering his.

"I shouldn't have expected you to come when I was the one having second thoughts," I say. "I asked for space. If you would've come, we probably would've argued. Might've made things worse."

"Worse than three years of silence?" He shakes his head at the impossibility. "I should've come. But honestly, I was worried you didn't want to see me, and scared to find out for sure."

"I always want to see you. And I think that's why I didn't ask. I was terrified if you came I'd just throw myself into your arms."

"Why didn't you want that?" He sounds hurt, and no wonder. His arms are the perfect refuge, solid and sure, and I've wasted far too much time not being in them.

I tuck my legs up under myself. "Because I've never wanted anyone the way I want you. I was worried how I felt about you would lead me to do something foolish, like my parents."

"But they're happy, Hope." He walks around and takes a seat on the edge of his chair, legs extended in front of him. "Their careers might not be as out-of-the-ordinary as ours, but they provided for all your needs, gave you a loving home. They're some of the happiest people I've ever met. You think they should've risked their chance at the life they wanted just for a couple degrees they weren't that interested in in the first place?"

Put that way, my fears sound ridiculous. Love didn't impede their dreams, it *was* their dream. "But it was never my dream," I say aloud. "I never dreamed of growing old with someone, not until I met you."

He tips forward, dark eyes glinting in the twilight. "You said 'not until.' Does that mean…"

"You know I wanted that, Adrian." I gulp. "I told you, so many times."

"But when it came time to make that a reality, you left the East Coast. You left your *career*, Hope. To be rid of me?"

"You didn't fit into how I'd always imagined my future." He of all people should know the sanctity of plans. "I wanted to keep my life tidy and compartmentalized so I could keep powering on toward my dreams, but meeting you expanded my definition of happiness."

"How is that a bad thing?"

"It's not. It's what kept us together for five years, despite my fear of ending up like my parents." I don't want to hurt him, but if I can't make him understand, help *myself* understand, we don't have a chance. "Moving in with you felt like our lives would be entwined in a way that would be too hard to untangle if I wanted another path. But the truth is, that was just on the outside. Inside, my heart was already tangled up with yours."

I raise my eyes and find him leaning forward, attentive. Like he wants to hear, to listen. To understand. "I spent the last few years trying to untangle that knot, to get over you, only to come down here and realize I don't want to." Twisting the pendant on the chain, I say, "I don't want to be free of these feelings for you."

He's quiet for a moment, and the weight of what I've confessed settles heavy on my heart, knowing he might not feel the same.

"Someday," he says, and I wait, holding my breath. "Not now, but someday, I want to share a home with my wife." The word doesn't sound possessive from his lips, it sounds cherished. Loved. "And I value my own happiness too much to try this again, if that's not what you want."

His honesty, his ability to name his needs, after all this time, is exactly what I crave. To know that we're both safe in this moment to be honest. To give each other's feelings the consideration they deserve without lessening our own.

And I want to gift him honesty, the truth I've kept bottled up tight. "I would've been so much happier these past few years if I hadn't tried to convince myself I didn't want that same thing. With you."

He looks up, sharply, and I find the courage to stand up and go to him, crouching down so that we're face-to-face in the moonlight. "I punished myself, put my dreams on hold, just to prove I would've let you down. But you never tried to put borders on my dreams, all you've ever asked is to be a part of them. And now I'm not afraid to embrace that."

I want to take his hands in mine, but not yet. Not until I know for sure. "I'm sorry for not owning up to how I felt. For not trying to work through things. But I'm here now, not just for my career, but for us. I want a full life with you, all of it."

The barest of spaces exists between our lips. One movement and we'd be kissing. Every part of me—the scared part, the wounded part, the confident part, the yearning and hungry and needy parts—all of me wants to be with this man, to believe that things will be different this time.

Taking my hands in his, he leans in, and presses his lips to mine. Our mouths move against one another, giving and taking, and I lose myself in his touch. The kiss is pure tenderness and trust. Both of us know the stakes. Past, present, future, we're trusting each other with our hearts, our hopes, our dreams.

He cups my face with his palms, thumbs skating along my skin. His touch is gentle, firm, coaxing...everything I've missed and everything I've wanted. His kisses are a promise. We have time, his pace says. We have each other, my kisses reply. The stars come out, moon rising, and we're still here. Together.

twenty-nine

adrian

I wake up with Hope in my arms, and I never want this moment to end. Without a moment to pinpoint the demise of our relationship, it wasn't until almost a year after she left that I woke up, sweating and breathing hard from a nightmare, and realized I'd never hold her again. Never spend hours talking with her. Laughing and kissing and loving each other.

Something I once took for granted, now all the more precious. With dawn, last night's conversation feels like fantasy, but the gold necklace resting against her heart lets me know it was real. We're giving each other a second chance. I won't have to hold myself back around her or try to dam my feelings.

But daybreak also brings more mundane realities—texts from Gabe, requests to collaborate, and unread emails in my university account. One-handed, I type out replies. Hope stirs and tips up her chin, catching my eye.

"Are you working right now?"

I lay the phone facedown. "Sorry—"

"Don't be." She lays her head against my chest again, burrowing in. "This is the life you've worked for. I'm still in awe of you."

Her shoulders drop, and she shifts with sleepy warmth, sliding against me, and I tuck my arms around her. "I never thought we'd have moments like this again," she says, so quietly I have to duck my head to catch her words. "The thing is, what I feel for you is not quantifiable, but the pull is so strong. Even when I thought I couldn't stand you, I wound up here."

"Did you really think you couldn't stand me?"

She shakes her head, cheek gliding against my bare chest. "I couldn't understand why I loved you so much. That's why I didn't trust it."

"Do you have to? We can't see currents, but that doesn't mean they aren't real."

"No, but their effects are measurable. We can collect data, run experiments."

"I'm up for that." I squeeze her hip. "What sort of experiments did you have in mind?"

She squirms, giggling. "I was being serious."

"So am I. I never joke about science."

Shoulders still shaking with quiet laugher, she relaxes against me. "I don't need a test to know how I feel about you is real. But if I did, the last three years was it. The moment I saw you again I knew all my efforts to forget you were hopeless."

I let out a groan, covering my forehead with my arm. "How long have you been holding out to use that one?"

She presses a kiss to my chest. "It's true."

I wrap my arms around her, molding our bodies close. "*This* is true." I kiss her hairline, right above her temple. "I've wanted to be with you every moment since you left, and my only regret is waiting for you to fall back into my life instead of coming to Michigan to tell you how much you mean to me."

"We're not playing the what-if game, remember?" Her thumb rubs my knuckle, soft and comforting. "We're together now, that's what matters."

Wind stirs the oak trees overhead outside my window,

spreading dappled sunlight on the comforter, but we fall silent. Her breathing steadies and slows, and my eyes drift closed. Then my phone chimes twice in rapid succession. I hasten to silence it, but Hope's blinking at me.

"Just notifications on my socials."

She rakes her fingers backward through her tousled hair. "I know you say you're not famous, though I'm sure your followers would disagree. But how does this go, dating someone with such a public job?" Her tone is light, but underneath I know she's thinking about the lack of privacy in my online life. "Does this mean our life is going to become a reality show?"

I like how she said "our life." "In terms of the channel, nothing needs to change." When her brows shoot up, I hasten to add, "What the public sees, I mean. We don't owe them the details of our private life. That's not what my platform is about. I share my personal life to connect with people, but I don't give anything close to everything."

"You don't plan to tell your fans you're taken?" I can't tell if she's asking because she's worried I will or hurt that I wouldn't.

"It's up to you if and when we share. But I don't see any reason to do it right away."

"Good point. I'm taking the most eligible shark scientist off the market," she teases, though her body is tense. "I don't want the internet to turn on you."

"Internet users," I say automatically.

"What?" Her eyes narrow at the non sequitur.

"The internet. It's the vehicle by which information is shared and communicated, it's incapable of conscious action. What you're referring to are internet users—"

"Adrian."

I bite my lip, embarrassed at getting carried away. "Sorry."

She grins at me. "Don't be. It's adorable when you're literal." To prove it, she rises on an elbow and kisses me, deeply.

Long moments later, Hope's cheek is pressed to my collarbone, my arm around her shoulders, and I return to our conversation. "Workplace-wise, we'll need to tell Marissa and Gabe. Sign some documents. I want to make sure you're protected. That your job is separate from us."

"I'm not worried about that."

"I'm not worried, but it's important to me. You're important." I kiss her again, and when I pull away, she shakes her head.

"Gosh, Marissa is going to be insufferable."

Up until now, Hope and I have barely brushed shoulders at work. So even though we discussed the need to be open about our relationship with Gabe and Marissa, I'm still shocked when she drops her backpack and wraps me in a tight hug the morning we meet to help with cleanup at the marina.

Gabe is already aboard the boat, sorting through camera equipment. He plans to document the community's efforts and help raise money for local charities working to support people whose homes were damaged in the storm.

"Felt good to see this boat in one piece." He claps me on the shoulder. "And you, of course."

Marissa is kneeling by the tap on the dock, filling a bucket with sudsy water. "Gabe's got to get the equipment set up, but what's your excuse for not pitching in yet?" she asks Hope, with a gleam in her eye. Clearly, she knows what's up.

I raise my hand, then drop it, feeling like a fool. "Before we get on with things, there's something we need to tell you."

Marissa's brows hitch up and she cranks off the water. Next to me, Hope is stiff, but when I look her way, she smiles and says, "Adrian and I are in a relationship."

Marissa blinks. I look over and find Gabe tapping at his phone screen.

I clear my throat. "Did you hear Hope? We're dating."

Nothing. No reaction.

The silence thins and Gabe glances up. "Wait, is this supposed to be news?"

"Uh, yes." I meet Hope's gaze and she looks equally perplexed. "We just wanted to be transparent about it, since we're all—"

"In this boat together?" Marissa says, and Gabe offers her a fist bump, which she accepts with a straight face, and he laughs. "Look at you, fully onboard with the puns. One Parker down, one to go."

"In your dreams," I tell him, but he seems unfazed.

"Permission to speak freely?" Gabe asks, then plows on, because it's obviously a given. "It was weird when you two weren't a thing. On paper, I mean. All the latent, unresolved, palpable tension." I bristle at his deliberate pile-up of adjectives. "This is an improvement."

I stiffen. "This has been an uncomfortable work environment for you?"

Gabe shakes his head. "Nah, man. This has been an uncomfortable work environment for *you*." Hope lets out a laugh, and he looks her way with a sly grin. "I'm just glad you're finally making an honest man out of our captain here."

My skin prickles with embarrassed heat, but Gabe's good-natured teasing really isn't unexpected.

"If anything, it's been fun to speculate on when this would happen."

"My money was on the end of the season, but that power outage really swept things along," Marissa says. Great, my ally against puns has been pulled to the evil side.

"You bet on our relationship? With Gabe?"

"What? No." Gabe pulls a face. "Not with actual money. That would be crass."

"Iced lattes," Marissa says with no hint of remorse.

"Frozen ones. The kind with whipped cream on top." Gabe catches sight of my glare and desists, but Marissa elbows me.

"Oh, lighten up." She hoists the sudsy bucket. "We're happy for you. Right, Gabe?"

He nods. "Suffice it to say you two like each other in a touchy-feely, non-platonic way?" He looks to Hope, then myself, for confirmation, and when he gets it, slaps a hand on the bench. "Meeting adjourned?"

Marissa clears her throat, and we both pivot around. Her brows are up. "Just waiting on my thank-you."

"For what?"

"If I hadn't invited you here, you two would've never gotten out of your own heads." She pokes Hope on the shoulder. "And you'd still be sloshing around in a lake somewhere."

"*The* lake," Hope says, with emphasis, and I can't help smiling. Her loyalty to the Great Lakes is as strong as my affinity for sweet tea. "And I'm the one who called *you* asking for a job. Not the other way around."

Marissa waffles her hand back and forth like it's a matter of semantics, but she smiles. "All right, so we'll share credit for the discovery, as long as I get lead author status."

Shaking her head, Hope turns to me. "Was she always this insufferable?"

"Worse. One time, she found a gavel in a thrift store—"

"I know you're not about to bring up the gavel incident." Marissa rolls her eyes.

"Wait, gavel, as in—" Hope mimes pounding her hand with a fist "—'order in the court,' gavel?"

"Yup," I say. "She carried it around for an entire summer and used it to silence us whenever we said something contrary."

Hope laughs. "Did it work?"

"You've met Iris. What do you think?"

Marissa pulls a morose face. "Didn't stop me from trying." She sobers and says, "Speaking of passing judgment, do y'all plan to go public with your relationship, or is this news strictly between us?"

"Just between us." Hope squeezes my hand, and my heart fills like a sponge, soaking up the affection. "No need to expose our private lives that way."

"Well, that's a relief," Gabe says. "I mean, it's your call, but as your social media specialist, I had worries over how we were going to break the news without things getting sticky. From the outside, you're the boss dating the assistant."

I hate hearing that, but it's not a stretch to think people might jump to conclusions. "I already called Vicki at the start of the season," I say, referring to our lawyer. "She made sure Hope officially reports to Marissa, and I hold no authority over her employment."

"And regardless, it's not like that." Hope squats down to sort through a bucket of cleaning rags. "We have a history."

Gabe quirks his brows. "A history you're willing to share with the entire internet?"

"Internet users." Hope glances up with a quick grin in my direction.

Marissa shakes her head, like she's aware of my antics. "Yeah, but he's got a point. We don't want it to look like you're dating the new hire."

"She's not new. We've been at this together since college."

"Sure have." Marissa smirks, and Hope tosses a sponge at her. But her smile turns into a twist of her lips. "And I know that, and you know that, but viewers don't."

None of the insinuations would have any basis. She's not some summer fling. But strangers don't care. They'll jump to conclusions, whether for or against us. "All the more reason to keep things quiet. Our relationship is none of their business."

No way will I let our relationship put her at risk. I'll do whatever I can to make sure she's not in harm's way.

thirty

hope

I'm not a runner. I don't take spin classes or do yoga. But I do love walks on the beach. Salt or fresh—the waters of my life have ebbed and flowed—but the shoreline remains a constant. Dark brown palm fronds are scattered across the sand, the only trace of the recent storm. Beach cleanup was a big endeavor, and last night I fell into bed exhausted.

This morning the wind is clean and fresh, and I'm filled with a sense of renewal that has nothing to do with the waterside and everything to do with Adrian. I wonder if lifting weights has become a way to clear his head, like these beach walks for me, or paddleboarding for Zuri, who's currently awaiting my long-overdue call to catch up.

Reconciling with Adrian felt like the perfect choice at the time, and I don't regret my decision for a moment, but everything is so new and tender—mere days stacked against years of separation, that I'm desperate for Zuri's take—for validation that I'm not losing my mind in losing my heart to Adrian again.

I'm hoping to catch her in the small window after she drops her kids off with her aunt for the day and before she gets caught up in whatever crisis awaits her on a busy summer morning.

The rhythmic roll of gentle waves against my ankles hasn't settled my uncharacteristic nerves about the call, but Zuri's unconventional, "Is he our friend or foe?" greeting has me smiling. She's my best friend. Whatever happens—is happening—with Adrian, she's got my back. And truly, I'm excited to share the news. Tentatively excited. Honestly, I could use reassurance that I'm not malfunctioning with how right this feels.

While I'm working out my reply, she keeps digging. "I mean, last I heard he saved you from a hurricane—"

"Tropical storm. To qualify as a hurricane, wind gusts have to exceed—"

"We're saying the same thing." Her brush-off has me chuckling. "I need to know if your friendship survived the storm." The jangle of keys comes through the phone, and Zuri's voice is muffled for a moment. "Because a few weeks ago you were ranting about a deep yearning to throw him overboard."

"I never said that." Not explicitly.

"It was the general vibe of your texts. That, and 'my ex is too hot for his own good.'"

"*My* own good," I clarify. "Being sexy is not cramping his style whatsoever. And also—" I cast a glance toward the horizon, lip caught between my teeth "—he's not my ex. Currently."

"Not your ex," she repeats. "Currently." Not a question, but delivered with the implicit expectation that I explain myself.

I oblige, letting the gentle pull of the waves lead me a few steps into the water. "We talked, after the storm."

She lets out a breathy laugh. "Talked, huh?"

"Yes, talked." My cheeks are blistering, and the sun's not even up. She's jumped into teasing me with all the gusto of a middle-aged dad cannonballing off a springboard. I'll have to remember this when she decides to venture into the dating pool again.

"Okay." Zuri stretches out the word, humoring me. "And

during this *talk*, what happened?" I don't need to be in the same room as her to detect the air quotes she puts around the word *talk*, but I take the chance to get to the heart of what I called about.

"Things got pretty serious." I recall the heaviness of the moment, before he took my hands in his. The years of uncertainty, on both our parts. "I mean, this is not just any guy. This is Adrian. We dated for almost six years. So starting over feels seriously high-stakes."

Wind cuts through the speaker, like she's walking outside. "That's what you're doing? Starting over?" Her tone gives nothing away.

"Yeah, it is. We both agreed it's what we want. What we've wanted, for a long time." Sand shifts under my feet and I walk backward to firmer ground. "I know it's the opposite of what I came down here for, and maybe it shouldn't feel this way, but, Zuri, it feels right." Putting my trust in feelings is new, but putting my trust in Adrian is not, and I'm holding tight to that.

She's silent for a long moment, and when I can't take it anymore, which is probably about three seconds, I ask, "What are you thinking?"

"I'm wondering what changed. You were adamant you couldn't adjust your life for him, for anyone, and you don't even know where you're headed in the fall."

All of that is true, except one thing. "My heart changed. I realized that the only thing holding me back was my doubts, not Adrian. Three years ago, he was willing to move to be with me near whichever PhD program I chose. He didn't try to steer my choices, or confine me."

"But now he's an assistant professor. He runs that channel with Marissa, and her job is there."

I was nervous to tell Zuri all this, but part of me really thought she'd be happy for me. "Are you trying to talk me out of this?"

"I'm trying to keep you from getting hurt. To make sure you're thinking this through." Fear prickles inside me. Worries that love was muddling my decision-making is what I struggled with last time, and now, when I thought I went in with my eyes wide open, she's accusing me of my worst fear.

"That's in the future," I protest. "We just started dating again."

"But when it comes down to it, what if he doesn't want to come to you? Are you willing to compromise, and go to him? Or will it always be him making the concession, until he starts to resent you?" It's as if she's seen inside my heart and exposed everything that made me doubt.

But this time, I'm choosing to believe that we can make different choices. That we can make a future together. "I don't know yet how it will work," I admit. "All I know is I spent three years without him, and it didn't make me happier. It didn't feel like freedom." Saying this aloud strengthens my resolve that this is the right choice. "I'm at my best when we're together, and I trust us enough to find a way."

"Then I'm happy for you." Zuri's approval comes through crystal clear, though I'm having trouble believing I heard her right until she adds, "Really, truly, incredibly happy for you."

I throw my arm up in the air. "What?"

"What do you mean, 'what'?"

"What was all the getting-inside-my-head questions like you were the psychiatrist from my nightmares?"

She cackles, the fiend. "That was me checking in on you. What else are friends for?"

"Um, to be supportive?"

"I am, now that I know you're making a good decision." Zuri is the best kind of friend, honest enough to trust when she tells me what I want to hear.

I blow out a breath, relaxing as iridescent waves curl against my bare toes. "So you think this is good? It's honestly impossible to be objective in this situation."

"What you had with Adrian was special. I know you two were going through some tough times, but if you hadn't stayed here…" Her voice slips, like she lost her footing on a patch of ice. But she recovers quickly, in the agile way she has, and my heart breaks that she's had to develop that ability. "Let's just say if I thought he was no good, I never would've encouraged you to take the job."

"By encouraged, you mean fired me so my hands were tied?"

She murmurs noncommittally before clearing her throat. "I know I haven't been in a relationship since…since losing Eric, so maybe I'm not the most qualified…" She trails off again, and I want to jump in and reassure her, but I can tell it's important for her to say this. "But he and I did make it through a lot together. And one thing I learned is you can't move forward if you don't accept and acknowledge the past. And it sounds like you've both done that."

We have, but things are shaky and new and not ready for any test. But we have another month of summer. Another month of days spent working together and nights we can spend remembering what we love most about each other. Shoring up the pieces of our relationship with newly-discovered connections. "It's freaking terrifying, Zuri. But I want this. I want to try."

"Trying is good," she says. "In fact, I think it's incredible. You're brave to give each other a second chance." Her voice cracks, and I know she's thinking of Eric, of true love. Real love, the kind I never thought existed until I met Adrian.

The beachgoers around me come to a halt, many of them with phones aloft, and I turn back toward the horizon just in time. The sun dislodges itself from the cocoon of the ocean, begins its bright ascent into the sky.

I inhale, filling my lungs with salt-scented air.

"I always thought that to succeed in my career, I couldn't

be in a relationship. And I never had to confront that fear until we were about to move in together. But I've come to realize I made a lot of false assumptions. Now I want to have both."

"You deserve both," Zuri says. "And from the looks of your recent videos, you're crushing your career goals."

My cheeks flame all over again. "Not you too."

"Oh yes, me too. Me and the kids love watching them. They make me check for new content every morning."

The reminder that people back home are watching pierces through the fog of my happiness. I don't know how Adrian handles the exposure, but I'm glad that so far, I haven't embarrassed myself. "I'll make sure to tell Gabe he'd better pick up the pace on editing so the kids don't have to wait so long for new content."

"Are you kidding me?"

"Well, yeah—"

"Sorry, not you." She lets out an irritated huff. "My cashier for the day just texted that she's sick, but I'm supposed to lead the morning kayak tour. I'm going to have to let you go so I can work on finding someone to cover her shift."

"Maybe I should rethink the move," I say, teasing, though I do often wish I could be in two places at once.

"Don't even joke, Evans. You're right where you need to be. And besides, Seth called dibs on your room."

We end the call with promises to talk soon, but her words stay with me as I pocket my phone and sidestep a terrier who's pulling on its leash in an attempt to get at the sandpipers darting along the waterline. Chats with Zuri always leave me both comforted and challenged. She's like a motivational speaker and fairy godmother rolled into one and I am one hundred percent lucky to have her.

The sky is a lush blend of pink and orange and peach, like sherbet ready to be scooped and I can't resist snapping a photo, even though my phone does the colors no justice. I text it to

Zuri, a small offering of my day, a visual "wish you were here," no words required.

Once it's sent, I realize this is the kind of thing I used to do with Adrian all the time but stopped once I moved to Michigan. At first it was grief, but then it was resentment. It felt disingenuous, and I didn't want to try to push past that feeling or talk through it with him. But now I do. I want to let him know I'm thinking of him, carrying him with me, wherever I go.

Raising the phone again, in selfie mode this time, I pivot until the sun is visible over my shoulder. I shrug a few times, arm flapping in a motion reminiscent of an irate pelican, until the neck of the hoodie falls off my shoulder to reveal the strappy ties of my swimsuit. It feels weird to pose for a solo selfie in public, but that's a me thing. Beach selfies are so ubiquitous, no one spares me a glance.

I turn on the camera and wave, trying to pretend the hair in my face is alluring, not a windblown mess that has me wishing I'd grabbed a hair tie. I consider blowing a kiss, but that's something I've never done in my life and Adrian would probably think I'd been abducted. I end the recording and send the clip to Adrian before embarrassment stops me.

I'm here, thinking of him. And I want him to know that. A moment later, my phone vibrates. Heart pounding irrationally, I read the text.

Adrian: Best. Sunrise Ever.

Affection fills me, steaming chamomile tea poured to the brim. So simple. So easy. And yet I'd stopped trying. I thought it was easier to close myself off, but it didn't stop me from being hurt or from losing him.

He means so much to me, and I want him to know that, beyond a shadow of a doubt. I want to try again. I want us to succeed. I want that life-changing, heart-on-the-line love we once had. It will be a long journey to get there, but this is a start.

Hope: Would be better with you here.

Adrian: Give me ten.

Another notification appears, obscuring his text. I move my thumb to flick it away, then freeze, sunrise forgotten. An email in response to my application to the California white shark research internship.

Subject: Internship Interview
Greetings Hope,
Thank you for your interest in the great white shark research program internship. We would like to continue to the next stage of the process and invite you to participate in an interview next Wednesday, July 31. If you no longer wish to be considered for this program, please let us know as soon as possible.

I continue reading, eyes scanning the email, but my mind goes immediately to Adrian. He doesn't even know I applied. Whether I get this job or not, I don't know where I'll end up next year. My future has always been fluid—water and waves—and I'm worried Adrian needs me to be stone.

thirty-one

adrian

I pause at the top of the dune steps and watch Hope. She's on her knees near the water's edge, scooping wave-wet sand into a crooked tower, her shoulders working under the crisscross straps of her swimsuit. A hoodie lies on the sand next to her. My hoodie. The one I lent her and she held on to. Even when life pulled us apart, she held on.

I was in line at the café when I opened her text. Watching the clip on repeat made me miss hearing my number called, and I lost out on the last cinnamon bun, but it was worth it. We used to send each other photos all the time, and I know things will never be the same, but maybe this is a sign they can be even better.

"Pardon us." A cheerful voice jostles me out of my musings. I step aside to let a group of women in floppy hats and overstuffed straw totes descend the weathered wooden steps. I kick off my canvas slip-ons, then stoop to retrieve them and head toward the water. A gaggle of fleet-footed sandpipers dart away at my approach, and Hope lifts her head and looks around, smiling when our gazes lock.

"You brought breakfast?" Curls whip across her face and she uses a sandy thumb to push them aside.

With a nod, I lift my chin toward the horizon. "How was the sunrise?"

She leans back on her heels and smiles up at me. "I love how that's a standard greeting in beach towns, though it's all about the sunsets where I come from."

My heart trips at the word *love* like a metal detector calibrated to signal the tiniest hunk of iron. "Still jealous that you got to grow up with a beach in your backyard."

"Not my backyard. But yeah, close enough." Holding her hand out, she lets me haul her to her feet. "But you saw your share of summer vacation sunrises out here. No one wants to watch the sun set over a frozen Lake Michigan in January."

"Not even you?"

"I mean, it's still pretty gorgeous," she says, and I don't bother trying to hold my smile at her unabashed love of her home state.

"And cold." Just thinking about the frigid evening she dragged me down to the beach to watch a winter sunset in Shoreline Dunes has me grateful for the hot July sun.

"Freezing," she admits. She's so beautiful in the soft morning light that I can hardly believe how lucky I am that we found our way back to each other. Filled with affection, I lift her hand to my lips and kiss her sandy knuckles.

A smile crinkles her eyes. "I thought you hated sand in your mouth." Clutching my arm to steady herself, she brushes her thumb against my lips, but that just spreads it around. I try to hide my grimace when the sand grains trickle down into my beard, but she clucks her tongue.

"Hang on." She bends over to swipe the hoodie off the ground and pops back up with a coy grin when she catches me looking. Lifting one of the sleeves to my mouth, she wipes at my face. "That's better." Placing her hands on my shoulders, she presses her soft lips to mine.

I keep my eyes open, watching hers flutter shut, vulnerable. On instinct, my free hand drifts to her waist and I gather her against me, wanting to keep her close, but the bag of pastries crinkles between us.

She lets out a groan against my mouth. "Please tell me we didn't just crush a cinnamon bun."

Loath to let her go, I step back and open the bag. Hope peers down into it with a forlorn expression. "Good news and bad news," I say. "They ran out of cinnamon buns, but peach muffins are much more smush-resistant. No frosting to ruin." Digging inside the sack, I procure a muffin with the buttery, ginger crumble topping mostly intact.

She makes a gimme motion and sinks her teeth into the top without bothering to remove the cupcake liner. I use my thumb to swipe a sugar crystal from the corner of her mouth, then lick it off, intrigued when her eyes track the movement.

Drawn by the food, a seagull swoops down and she gives the bird a glare that would make Marissa proud. Its only response is to cock its head.

I pull out a second muffin, making sure to hold it close lest the bird get any ideas.

"Another peach one?" she asks, once she's swallowed.

I nod. "Knew you wouldn't want to share."

"Smart man." She shakes out the hoodie with one hand, letting it catch the breeze, and lays it on the sand. She flops down with another don't-even-think-about-it look at the gull, who cocks its head, beady eye trained on her, but doesn't budge.

I settle in next to her on the wedge of fabric that she left open for me, close enough to feel the warmth radiating off her bare legs, glistening with sweat in the rising heat. I take a bite of muffin to steer my mind toward public-beach-appropriate thoughts.

"Don't want to wait to eat yours later?" Her eyes are playful. "Might get some sand in your teeth."

"I think that ship has sailed."

Her mouth drops open. "Did Adrian Hollis-Parker just utter

a nautical pun?" She puts the back of her wrist to her forehead. "Be still my heart, I may just swoon." And she does, collapsing backward onto the sand, her bare stomach bouncing with laughter.

"A man tries to loosen up and this is what he gets?" I pretend to glare out at the waves, but a smile tugs at my cheeks. Her fingers close around my wrist and she pulls me backward, onto my elbows.

"I like you earnest."

I gaze down at her. "You do?"

Smiling, she traces her fingertip along my forearm. "I like how you're stoic in the face of joviality while inside your soul is smiling."

"You can see into my soul?" I tease, but she nods solemnly.

"I can, and I love what I see." She goes still and so do I. For a moment, I can't breathe. She gulps, her trachea bobbing beneath her delicate skin. Then the shadow of a cloud passes overhead and she sits up, rubbing her hands across her arms.

A moment lost. Or maybe it was never there, the imagined glimmer of a fish underwater, an angler's hope. Was it wishful thinking to believe she was about to say the words I long to hear? She turns to me, lip caught in her teeth, and her eyes have lost their spark. "I have to tell you something."

My mouth goes dry, the crumb topping gritty in my teeth. I don't trust my voice, so I merely raise my brows, hoping I look encouraging and not desperately in need of confirmation she's not having second thoughts.

"I got an interview," she says. "At the lab in Santa Barbara."

"With Dr. Oswald? I didn't even know you'd applied." I shouldn't be surprised she hadn't told me; we only just stopped tiptoeing around each other a few weeks ago.

"I haven't told anyone but Zuri. And at the time, we weren't together..." She's picking at the muffin wrapper, and I hate that she's nervous to tell me this.

"That's awesome news." I reach out to squeeze her knee in reassurance. "When's the interview?"

She looks over. "You're okay with it?"

We're just starting over, and California is far away, but I've never asked her not to consider an opportunity for my sake, and I never will. "Of course. I'm thrilled for you."

She's still tense, squinting out at the water. "If I get it, the job won't start until late August. But now that we're together—" there's a slight hesitation in her words, like she's uncertain of us "—I didn't mean to blindside you with this. Just forgot all about it with all the storm cleanup, and well, you know..." Her smirk tells me I haven't been the only one fighting to keep my thoughts in check. "But I think it will be a good stepping-stone, and it buys me some more time to figure out where I'll end up long-term."

That's a minefield, and I dodge it with a kiss to her cheek. "I bet you'll get it."

"That's just what you have to say as a boyfriend."

My lips curve into a smile. "A boyfriend?" I tap my chin. "Who's the lucky lady?"

"Oh my gosh, stop." She huffs out a laugh, then leans against my shoulder. "She is lucky though."

Sensing she's let her guard down, the seagull hops closer, and Hope sits bolt upright, on alert. For someone who teases me about my dislike of birds too large for physics, she sure has a thing against seagulls.

She pinches off another piece of muffin. "We can make it work, right? California is far."

"Do you still want to make it work?" I hold my breath, wondering if this is too much, too soon, for our new relationship.

"With all my heart," she assures me. "But I'm just worried." She folds the muffin wrapper in on itself once. Twice. "What if I love it there and end up staying?" I know what she's asking. Before, we planned to find a place together after we finished our studies. But now I'm established. And if she settles on the other side of the country...

I take her hands in mine, crumbs, sand and all. "Right now, let's focus on us. Here and now. And when that time comes, we'll give each other the space to work through it together." My cautious side is begging me to tread lightly, but I'm done listening. Risking the present for the sake of the future cost me Hope, and that's not a price I'm willing to pay.

She leans in for a kiss, and I meet her halfway. My eyes fall closed, surrendering to my heart's desire, to this woman I want to spend my life loving. She lets go of my hand to wrap her fingers around my arm, holding tight, anchoring me, and our kiss deepens as we lean into one another. I savor the sweet taste of her lips, knowing we may not have many more moments like this for a while. But I'm more certain than ever I want a future with Hope, a life with her, even if that means letting her go, again.

thirty-two

hope

I shift the plate with the remnants of my lunch to make room for my laptop. Parallel-parked cars line the shady street outside, and there's a constant flow of people in and out of the café, but I'm one of the few patrons dining in, and opt to stay unless it gets crowded.

In between work and spending time with Adrian, I've been prepping for the internship interview and searching for other jobs. Many of the ones I'm interested in require a PhD, but instead of being disheartened, I'm excited at the thought of embarking on the journey I planned to start three years ago. The only question is where, not if.

Adrian's been wholly supportive, and his positive reaction to me potentially leaving validated my decision to trust him with my heart again. I know we'll be fine if I go to California, but the question is, what happens after? The interview is tomorrow, though, so I keep my focus on the task at hand. I angle the screen out of the glare, pop in my earbuds, and get to work on sample interview questions.

After about an hour, I get a text from Marissa, and look up to find her in line at the counter. I give a wave and return to my prep work, but my concentration is broken, and it's all too easy to navigate to the *Shark Science Crew* page, where I discover Gabe's uploaded the latest video.

Nerves rise like clockwork at seeing myself on-screen, but I take a sip of icy green tea to settle my stomach. In the thumbnail, Adrian and I are standing side by side onboard the *Praespero*, green-blue ocean stretching to the horizon behind us, the wind whipping curls across my cheek, which I'm totally ignoring because I'm too busy gazing at him. Good lord, I look smitten. Well, I am, and judging by the way he's smiling down at me, from the way he's put his trust in me—Adrian is too.

The moment of eye contact lasts only a moment, though at the time it felt like a lingering look, one that gave me confidence to continue. Adrian faces the camera and smiles, teeth flashing bright against his beard. "So, we have some exciting news. Next week we'll be diving with a team from a regional nonprofit to retrieve acoustic receivers."

The Hope in the video pulls a face. "You made that sound level zero exciting." My grin is at odds with my words, though. Like I said, smitten.

"What's the alternative?"

On camera, I scrunch my nose in apparent thought. "We'll be diving beneath the waves to bring you sea-worthy content?"

"I think you meant watch-worthy... Oh." His face clouds over, but there's a smirk tugging at the edges of his mouth. Gabe's got steady hands, so you can't tell, but he was totally cracking up at this point.

"I feel like we ought to have a challenge where y'all send us your best ocean puns," I tell viewers. "Anyone up for that?"

Hearing this, Adrian frowns down at me, and watching it, I swoon. He's so freaking handsome, and his presence is magnetic, even through the screen. No wonder people flocked to follow him. "I didn't sign off on this."

On-screen Marissa pops in the frame. "I did. Post them in the comments and we'll pick some of our favorites to share."

"Watching our latest video?" I look up and see real-life Marissa has returned from picking up her order at the counter.

I close the laptop, feeling silly. "Watching these is one of my strategies to feel more confident about being on camera."

"Okay, we'll pretend you weren't just watching it because of my cousin." She pulls a foil-wrapped sandwich out of the bag. "You two are so mushy. I thought you would've mellowed out with some time apart, but it's gotten worse. Being around y'all ruins my appetite." The last sentence is spoken around a mouthful of bacon and lettuce, and I laugh.

"Clearly."

She gestures at her mouth, then swallows. "This? This is fuel to endure all the love vibes floating around." She takes another bite. "The last thing I need is to be caught up in a relationship. I'm happier on my own. But Adrian's my baby cousin. I've known him his whole life, which is how I knew he was happier with you."

For a moment, I think I misheard her, but her mischievous smirk proves I didn't. "Is this you admitting you've been matchmaking all along?"

"I can neither confirm nor deny, but I will say, y'all did not make my job easy." Grinning, she wipes her hands on a napkin and reaches for the mouse, waking up her computer, like she didn't just admit to orchestrating our reunion.

"Maybe I should say thank you, but since you pushed me into the marina—"

"How many times do I need to tell you, tripping you was an accident?" At this point, I truly believe her, but her reactions always make it worth bringing up.

My phone vibrates with a new message, halting our bickering. Figuring it's Adrian replying to my last text, I shield the screen from Marissa—she may be an unlikely cupid, but that doesn't mean she's got a right to be all up in our business now that we're officially back together—but it's not from Adrian, it's from Gabe. My mood plummets as I reread the text.

"Hope?" Marissa questions. "What is it?"

Gabe's message causes my eyes to flick upward to my laptop screen, frantically scrolling. "Have you checked the comment section lately?"

She wipes a smear of mustard from her lips with a napkin. "No, why? Did someone post another cringey pun?"

My phone is buzzing insistently; Adrian calling. But I need to see this for myself. Hands shaky, I click on our most recent upload. The comment has already racked up several replies.

WaveChaser58: Hope Evans, this you?

Below, the user posted a link, but I know better than to click it. Gabe did though, so I know exactly where it leads—to the Shoreline Dunes official page and the post of me ruining the chance for conservation funding.

There are already thirty replies to the commenter, but I don't look at those either. Marissa comes over to stand at my shoulder. "Shit."

My phone rings when I'm on the way to the car, Marissa by my side, and when I see that it's Zuri, I put her on speaker. "Is Owen seriously this upset over high school grades?" I ask.

"I saw your text, and that's why I'm calling," she says. "His brother stopped in the shop this morning, and you know how people love to talk when they're at the checkout." She acts like chitchat is a hardship, when I know it's her favorite part of working the register. "He was saying Owen's wife just had a baby and they've been at the hospital for the past few days while she recovers."

"He's married?"

"News to me, but I can't see someone being up to no good in the delivery room, or having the energy for it, for that matter."

"You would know."

Marissa gives me an inquisitive look and I hold up three fingers. "Three kids?" she asks, eyes wide.

"Who's that?" Zuri asks.

"Sorry, it's Marissa," I say. "You're on speaker."

"As in your cousin-in-law?"

"Don't even start, Zuri."

Her husky laugh comes from the phone, and Marissa joins in. "Anyway, Owen did have a part in it, in a roundabout way, by posting the video originally," Zuri says. "But I felt like you should know he doesn't seem to like, have a vendetta against you." Kids are laughing and yelling in the background, and I'm guessing she's at the park. "Not sure if it being random helps any though. Regardless, this sucks. How are you doing with it?"

"Honestly?" I lean against my car, then regret it when my skin touches the hot metal. "I'm kind of relieved. The fear that people would see that video has been hanging over my head all summer." I never wanted to talk about it, because I figured it made me weak. "But now that they have, nothing happened. A few comments, sure. But those people don't know me, and they don't have a bearing on my real life." The damage to the freshwater conservation effort is already done, and no amount of people watching can make that worse. I've come to terms with the loss, and so have all my old colleagues, who are working on other projects, pushing forward. Just like I am. "I have an interview coming up for what would be an amazing internship, I have Adrian."

Out of the corner of my eye, I notice Marissa start to make a gagging face, but I shake my head. "Don't even start. Not when I know you wanted us back together all along."

"Wait, what?" Zuri's voice is full of eagerness. "You didn't tell me this."

"Another time." She's going to be stewing, waiting to hear the tea, but right now I need to deal with the video situation. "Adrian's calling, so I'm going to let you go."

With a quick promise to call later, I switch to the other line. I'm doing all right, but someone used Adrian's channel to try to hurt me. I have a hunch he's not okay with that.

thirty-three

adrian

"This is exactly what I was worried about, Hope." I'm pacing the dock at my house, and each loose board feels like a personal insult. I can't imagine how Hope's feeling. But she showed up a few minutes ago and seems a lot more chill than I am, so I want to remain calm for her sake. "You sure it wasn't that guy you went to high school with?"

She shakes her head. "It doesn't seem like it. The Shoreline Dunes social media pages are public. It could've been any of your followers."

Any of my followers. The reality one of them dredged up that low moment in Hope's career because of her proximity to me is hard to bear. My hands clench into fists, and Hope makes her way down the dock and wraps me in a tight hug. "You're not responsible, okay? I knew the risks when I agreed to stay on, and realistically speaking, this isn't a big deal."

I hate that she's comforting me, when she's the one who got targeted. "I don't want to say you're wrong. It *will* blow over, and no one with any real pull will be swayed by the comments." I rub her back. "But it's a big deal because people said some really shitty things about you. And I hate that it happened because of me."

"It didn't." Her head is tucked against my chest, and that, more than anything, slows my rapid heartbeat. "It happened because whoever shared it gets their kicks from bringing other people down."

"And I gave them a platform to do it on."

She pulls away, staying in the shelter of my arms, but looking up at me with impossible tenderness. "You gave *me* a platform. To start over, to regain my voice. You gave me a platform to share my passion for shark science with people like that librarian's goddaughter. You're really going to wish that away because someone came after me in a comment section?"

Once again, she has me at a loss. "Have I mentioned how incredible you are?"

"Once or twice, but I think it's better if you show me your appreciation."

"Oh yeah?" My pulse is still racing, but her calm in the face of this storm is beginning to settle me. Except, when her eyes travel in a slow dip along my body, my heart rate picks up again. "What do you have in mind?"

Raising up on tiptoes, she drops her voice to a sultry whisper. "I've been dying to take your kayaks out on the river since day one." She lowers herself back down, rosy lips curved in a teasing smile. "Why, what were you thinking?"

Chuckling, I pull her in for a quick kiss, then she slings an arm around my waist, and I joke with her as we make our way back toward the house. But worry still churns in my gut. As much as I love having her at work, the longer she's with us, the more chances of a repeat of today, and that's not something I can stomach.

Today is our first on-camera dive, and the timing could not be worse. I had to log off social media for a couple days because I was too tempted to reply to the trolls. The only thing keeping me from pulling the plug was our commitment to the group of researchers we're assisting.

We decided deleting the original comment would just stir up more controversy, but Marissa's been keeping up with any ugly comments, and things seem to be dying down, just like Hope thought. She assures me she's fine, but when Gabe started explaining how the GoPros would work for today's dive, she seemed shook.

We're riding along with the crew from the conservation group on a charter boat to the acoustic receiver site. Marissa asked if I'd stay topside to narrate so she could dive with the others. She always claims I'm the face of the operation, but the truth is she hates being left out of the action. I don't relish it either. Hanging back means I have no control over what goes on beneath the waves, and with the mean-spirited comments about Hope and the failed funding, I already feel helpless.

They'll all be wearing cameras, but we won't be livestreaming, even though Gabe's been pushing for it. Too many factors to risk it just for extra views. Working in the ocean, there's so little we can control, like currents and the weather, that it's important to focus on what we can—our equipment, proper dive procedures, and our reason for filming, which is to engage and inform, not rack up followers.

Maybe it's the lack of sleep due to what happened with Hope, but a lingering sense of unease permeates the air, like a storm is brewing, even though the sky is dotted with fleecy cumulus clouds. As we near the coordinates of the acoustic receiver, I take the opportunity to stoop down and check the tank hoses again.

Gabe is chatting with the other scientists, and he angles a questioning look my way. We did all our checks back at the marina, and they'll do another pre-dive, so he must be wondering if something's up. I offer a tight smile and stand, not wanting my nerves to rub off on him.

Making my way to the stern, I take a seat by Hope. Between the trolling incident and her interview, we haven't had much alone time together. She's got her wetsuit zipped. "Too bad you can't dive with us."

"We'll have to schedule a trip out ourselves soon."

"Oh, good idea." She leans in like she's going to kiss me, but at the last minute, bends to adjust her flipper. "Getting too comfortable," she says under her breath. "Forgot it's not just our team today."

I know the feeling. Now we're officially together again, it's easy to forget to keep our distance. "Just make sure you stay alert during the dive."

She gives me an odd look, and I itch the side of my neck, irritated I forgot to put my hair up with the wind today. "Sorry. I'm just on edge after what happened. And this is our first time doing something like this. Not to mention Roger isn't a fan." My leg is bouncing, and Hope presses her knee to mine, quick and light.

"Hey," she says, voice low. "This is exciting. I don't have to talk. I get to do some science, and I might even see a shark down there. I think you're just upset because you have the boring job."

"That too." This time my smile is genuine. "But I'm excited for you. Any word about the internship?" She only had her interview yesterday, but the committee said to expect a response within a few days.

"Not yet. Good thing we don't have service out here. Stops me from refreshing my email." Standing, she makes her way to where the others are finishing their preparations. Everyone shoulders into their tanks, and I'm happy to see the other group in good spirits about being filmed.

"We're looking forward to our fifteen minutes of fame," Dennis, one of the researchers, says. Turns out despite their supervisor's hesitancy, the rest of the team is enthusiastic about appearing on our channel. They did an awesome job during the short interviews we conducted before setting out.

"Or is it fifteen seconds these days?" He laughs. "Whichever it is, I'm looking forward to being able to tell my family I'm on TV."

The other guy, Harry, elbows him. "It's not TV, it's the internet."

"And isn't internet how we get all our streaming these days?"

"Touché." They lower their masks.

Gabe makes his way over to the ladder leading down into the water. He claps a hand on my shoulder and squeezes. "Time to feed the algorithm."

"Yeah, yeah. The algorithm." I picture a little gremlin in a toolshed, plugging wires into an old switchboard. He must've said it on purpose to goad me out of my funk. "Don't take any risks."

"You do know I've logged more dives than you and Marissa combined, right?"

"Don't rub it in." I grin, but my stomach is in knots despite the calm waters. Being the one topside always makes me nervous. The waiting, not having any control over what's going on beneath the surface. But this is a routine dive with experienced divers.

Still, my eyes are trained on the surface where they disappeared as the minutes tick by. Right on time, Gabe and the scientist he was buddy diving with surface and some of the tension leaves my shoulders. "All good?" I call out.

But Gabe shakes his head and pulls out his regulator. "Something's off with Hope. She had to switch to her octopus," he calls, referring to the spare regulator carried in case of emergency. Instantly I'm running through potential scenarios.

I watched all of them perform safety checks, and we're vigilant about maintaining our dive equipment. Tense minutes later, Hope surfaces, then Marissa. They kick their way over to the boat and climb aboard, Hope's face ashen.

I hunch down next to her, taking her hand in mine, not caring who sees. "What happened?"

"I don't know," she says. I check her over as she talks, but her lips aren't blue, and she seems coherent. "All of a sudden, I was sucking nothing. Regulator malfunctioned somehow."

Marissa's eyes are wide. "Scary moments, but she handled it well. Switched to her backup air and we took our time on the ascent."

Twice now, Hope's been at risk—physically, professionally—because of working with me. Last time we were together, worry about losing her career held her back from committing, and now I'm starting to wonder if maybe she was right to have doubts.

thirty-four

hope

My hands are still trembling from the scary moments underwater. I've never experienced an equipment malfunction on any of my many dives, but that's exactly why we take precautions. Though he's doing his best to act calm, it's clear Adrian feels like he must have missed something, but this could've happened on any dive.

We're headed back to shore, and everyone is subdued. The other team of scientists is chatting amongst themselves, but beyond Marissa and Adrian checking in with me every five minutes, none of us has much to say.

As we near land, my phone chimes with a notification. I pull it out of my bag, eager for a distraction from the tense mood. Once I open the email, my pulse kicks up for a completely different reason.

"I got the internship!" The words are out of my mouth before I realize I've spoken, and the others crowd closer, congratulating me.

They ask for details, and I hand over my phone, too overwhelmed to read the email aloud.

Adrian slips his arm around me for a quick side-hug. "Knew

you'd get it." I lean into him for a fleeting moment, absorbing his reassuring presence as much as his words, but my emotions are in a frenzy, and doubts creep in, poking holes in the buoyant rush of excitement.

I'm thrilled to have gotten the internship but leaving early is bittersweet. I never thought I'd wake up excited to do science in such a public way, but can't deny the variety of this work lights me up. Each day is different. I love a challenge, and I'm happy here, despite someone unearthing the video of my screwup.

The toxic comments didn't faze me like I thought they would. Letting my colleagues down will always be something I wish I could undo, but strangers picking apart the moment has no hold on me. I did worry my apparent lack of knowledge in the footage might hinder my prospects, but receiving the internship offer is proof one mistake won't hold back my future, not if I'm brave enough to keep chasing my goals.

But the timing of the internship means I'll also be losing out on precious weeks with Adrian. After years apart, I've been reveling in our reconciliation.

The other day when we were having breakfast on the beach, I almost blurted out that I loved him. Mentioning the interview was a convenient excuse to keep from prematurely confessing my love, but holding back didn't change my feelings. I can't help loving how he's steady where I'm restless, and how being around him never feels old. I love every part of him, even though it's cost me so much. Even though last time, it didn't work.

Palmettos and homes on stilts in bright candy colors flash by as we drive up Route 17 on our way to meet Gabe and Marissa for a late dinner. She invited the other crew but they said they were worn out, and I can sympathize. Noticing my exhaustion as we hauled our tanks off the charter boat, Adrian suggested we eat at his place, but fabulous as that sounded, I didn't want to miss out on what might be my last team dinner.

"You're going to accept the offer?" From the driver's seat, Adrian glances my way.

"Definitely." I smooth the crinkled hem of my shorts. "It's only for a semester, but it's an incredible opportunity." Much as I love it, my job here is temporary. At summer's end, Adrian will go back to the lab and teaching, and getting the internship means I have somewhere to go as well. "I've been looking into their doctoral program, and it could be a good fit." I don't want any limits on my career, and I've shared with him how I think earning a doctorate is the best way forward.

"That's amazing." He reaches over to squeeze my thigh, and I love the casual way he does it as much as how good his skin feels against mine.

"I'm really happy for you," he says. "About the internship, your future—"

"Us." Grinning, I take his hand in mine. His fingers are chilled, but I blame the air-conditioning, until I notice he's not smiling anymore.

"What's wrong?" My own skin goes cold.

"I've just been thinking…" Those words in a context like this never bode well, but I keep hold of his hand, unwilling to assume the worst. "About what you said about not wanting to fit your career to me." His profile is lit by the fading sun, the roadside trees dark silhouettes against a fiery sky. "Not wanting to compromise."

"That was before. It had nothing to do with you and everything to do with my preconceived notions about love." I can't erase how I felt or how it affected our relationship, but I wish I could show him how differently I feel now.

"But when the internship is over, I'd never want you to choose a college on the East Coast on my account."

"I wouldn't." I look down at our interlocked fingers. "I'm not going to turn down the perfect fit just to be close to you, but I'm not scared to admit anymore that I'd rather be near you."

Our relationship brings me joy. He brings me joy, and there's nothing wrong with love factoring into my future.

His jaw ticks, the muscles tense under his beard. "But people found that old footage because of your proximity to me. What if it had cost you this opportunity?"

"Even if it had, that wouldn't have been your fault. Any prospective employer could've found it."

"Not as easily," he says. "And what about today?" His eyes flick to the rearview mirror. "You wouldn't have been diving if it weren't for me. I just don't want to hold you back, or worse, hurt you."

The only way he could hurt me is by giving up on us. "I wasn't upset by the comments, not once I processed it. It's been—" I look out the window into the twilight, searching for the words "—empowering, I guess, to go through that and realize they can't hurt me. And was today tense? Absolutely. But I did exactly what I'd been taught, and I'm okay."

He slows as we near the turnoff for the restaurant, disentangling his hand from mine to switch on the turn signal, and I mourn the loss of contact. "All I want is for you to have the life you deserve, and that doesn't include being picked apart on social media."

I wring the seat belt in my fist. "Is it me you're trying to protect, or yourself?"

He glances at me, sharply, then back toward the road. "My life is so different than three years ago. I just wonder if us being together is worth it for you. I couldn't bear to stand in the way of the life you want." He meets my gaze for a brief moment, his eyes intense and honest in the most heartbreaking way.

"The life I want is with you. But it sounds like you're having second thoughts."

"I just thought we'd have more time to figure things out." He maneuvers into a vacant space, then shifts to face me. "You've got big decisions to make for your future, and I don't want our relationship to be a factor, not if it keeps you from what you want most."

What I want most is to be with him and study sharks. Both. It doesn't have to be either/or, I realize that now.

"This is what I want." I gesture between us, my answer unequivocal. "I want to know that at the end of the day, you'll be on the end of the line, or the other side of the bed. I want to know that wherever life takes us, we'll have each other."

My throat is tight, but this time I'm not going to let pride keep me silent. "You told me you did too."

"I did." He slips his hand around mine, thumb tracing my knuckles. "I do," he says, and my heart starts beating again. "I want that. But it feels like everything is happening so fast." He rubs his jaw, brows adorably furrowed. "I think I need time."

"Time?" What I asked of him three years ago.

His sigh is heavy over the hum of air-conditioning. "Three weeks ago, we'd just gotten on good terms. Three months ago, I never thought I'd see you again. It's a lot to process. And I'm worried about a lot of things. Our future, your future—"

"Is not yours to worry about. If I chose to stay here and turn down the internship, that would be my choice. If you end this, all you're doing is making my choice for me."

"I don't want to lose you." He holds my gaze. "This isn't me breaking up with you. Not unless you want it."

I shake my head, not caring that I'm showing my hand, because he's worth it. "Then what is it?"

"I'm just asking for time for me to sort through my feelings while you're in California. I want to be with you. That hasn't changed. But I need time to figure out how."

The irony of his request is lost on neither of us. I meet his eyes, dark and fathomless despite the golden glow of the setting sun, willing him to see a future with me. If time is what it takes, I've got all the time in the world.

thirty-five

adrian

Hope is gone. Has been gone, for weeks. I'm back on the beach for sea turtle patrol after another sleepless night. I thought having space to think without the rush of emotions I experience when I'm with her would bring clarity, but I feel more lost than ever.

A gull takes flight, wings beating the air as someone approaches, and for a brief moment I imagine it's Hope. Imagine I never told her I needed space to process, and she's here, surprising me by flying in for the weekend like she used to when we were dating. But the person next to me is tiny and smells like supercharged espresso. Definitely not Hope.

Marissa passes a coffee over and I mumble a thank-you. "Have you seen the comments on the latest video?" She falls into step alongside me, eyes downcast, checking for tracks in the sand. "Everyone's asking where Hope went."

"I turned off notifications." I don't need any reminder she's gone, not when I'm so tied up in knots over whether I'll ever have her back in my life again.

"If your phone is in airplane mode, you can skip that step."

She's been nudging me to go fix things with Hope, but my head is still too jumbled.

"I can't go to California until I figure this out. Last time we dated, I didn't want to believe our relationship could have any repercussions on her career, but now I know better." Steam rises out of the coffee lid, but shivers crawl up my spine at the memory of the worst comments. "I can't ignore what sacrifices Hope might have to make to be with me. She's already come under fire."

"Which she handled with complete poise."

"And then immediately got put in harm's way while filming a dive for the channel."

"The regulator was faulty," Marissa says. "They just announced a recall last week. No way to predict a mishap like that."

All true, but my heart doesn't run on logic. I jam my hands in my pockets and look out over the ocean, hoping the waves will work their calming magic. "This is everything I was afraid of when we started."

"Not everything," Marissa says. "You had a far more extensive list." She takes a sip of coffee. "As I recall, you emailed it to me in multiple iterations."

I cut her a look. "I'm serious. I hate how our work might affect Hope in the future. Maybe this is my sign to cut our losses."

"Why are you so focused on the negative amidst all the positive?" The answer is obvious, and she waves a hand. "Never mind. We both know it's because Hope means the world to you, and I get it. But she'd hate to be the reason you abandon all this. Giving up your life to be with her isn't the solution."

She's right. Not to mention I can't think of a single thing anyone in my family has given up on. Not piano lessons, not science fair projects that literally went up in smoke, and certainly not an educational platform.

Marissa turns toward me, expression serious now. "I'm not

trying to negate that it could've been a sticky situation, but you act like we were out there on a pleasure cruise."

"I don't even want to parse that phrase."

"Then don't, because you know exactly what I mean. This is important work."

But sometimes the line between our mission and myself gets blurred. And if Hope got caught in the crossfire because I felt the need to push boundaries... "Is this hubris?"

"Thinking you can control the world? Heck yeah it is."

"I meant the channel. Using my viral moment to create this."

She steps around a jellyfish stranded by the tide. "We didn't start this channel for the likes or accolades. You took what could've been a party anecdote and turned it into an educational tool that reaches millions. I've known you since you were in diapers and even as a kid you let other people hog the limelight. You never once wanted to do any of the plays Iris and I put on."

"That says more about the quality of your scriptwriting than anything," I say with a reluctant grin.

She shakes her head. "Just saying. The fame is something you've had to adjust to, not what you crave."

"But before he went over the edge—" the double meaning isn't lost on me, and I shudder at the thought of what could've happened if Hope hadn't been prepared "—Gabe said he had to feed the algorithm. Which is just shorthand for saying he wanted to create watch-worthy content. Half of the job is to stay relevant."

"Bullshit," Marissa says. "Our job is to spread knowledge and raise awareness. Gabe and I didn't dive for views, and neither did Hope. We dived because we love this work and we know how important it is. And we're not the only ones. I got a call from Roger Bauer."

The non sequitur has me instantly alert, no coffee required. "Did he have second thoughts about working with us?"

"He certainly had thoughts." Brows raised, she takes a sip of coffee, drawing out the suspense. "He was thrilled about the positive response to the first video and asked if we're willing to film a whole series with them."

An errant wave rushes in, dousing my feet up to my ankles, but I barely notice. "Seriously?" I rake a hand over my head. "That's... Wow. Not what I was expecting."

Marissa tilts her head. "Let me guess, you were expecting the worst."

I bristle at her accusation, but before I can answer, the slap of flip-flops comes from behind us, and I look over my shoulder to see Gabe walking up, a donut in one hand and a tote in the other.

"What's in the bag?" Marissa doesn't bother waiting for an answer, just walks over and slides the strap off his shoulder to peer inside.

"Homemade donuts," he says, mouth full. "A nice volunteer gave them to me. Said to pass them along to Adrian as thanks for covering her shift." He takes another bite and lets his head fall back. "Delicious. Now I see why you guys give up your mornings for this."

I cross my arms. "What are you even doing here?"

"Marissa told me she planned to try to talk some sense into you, and I figured it was time I spoke up too." He wipes his sugary hand on his shirt with zero shame. "I think you're making a mistake thinking Hope would be better off without you."

"I shouldn't care that my job makes my girlfriend's life more complicated?"

"Did you hear that?" Speaking in an exaggerated whisper, Gabe nudges Marissa. "He said 'girlfriend.' That's promising."

She pops the lid on the storage container and asks me, "Who said relationships are easy? Hence my desire to stay single."

"Not helpful." Gabe rolls his eyes. "But yeah, relationships take work. Doesn't mean they're not worth it."

I mull this over for a moment. "But love should be simple."

"Love is simple. Relationships aren't."

"Hence why I needed space."

"Maybe," he says. "Or maybe you're not used to being in a relationship and you defaulted to figuring things out on your own. But if you care about making things work, you have to talk to her. You're in this together, or not at all."

Marissa hands me a sugar-dusted donut, like food might help me process this conversation. "Hope wants to be with you, even knowing firsthand what's at stake. Why are you second-guessing things?"

"Because I can't ignore what I'm asking of Hope when I tell her I want a future with her. There are so many variables."

"Not ones that matter," she says. "All it comes down to is the two of you."

I should be annoyed by this ambush, but things are finally becoming clear. I've been trying to think through every scenario, to work out all the odds, but suddenly it hits me; I can't control every outcome. I can only control my choices.

It's time to stop sitting by and waiting for the worst-case scenario. I want to plan on a best-case scenario. I want to go back to being the guy who took a chance on a long-distance relationship with a woman I'd only known for a couple of months, a woman who turned out to be more than I ever could have hoped for. I want to take a risk, even though it might fail spectacularly. I want to believe we have another chance at forever. I want to dream again, with Hope.

thirty-six

hope

Studying great white sharks in California has been fantastic. Being away from Adrian—emotionally, as well as physically—has not. He asked for time and trusted me enough to be honest about what he's experiencing, and I care about him enough to wait. In the meantime, I've been doing my best to keep him out of my mind, but it's impossible to loosen his hold on my heart.

The bulk of our time is spent in the lab, where it's easier to push thoughts of Adrian aside while working to decipher data or running experiments. But today we're out on the water in a dinghy that's only a little longer than the juvenile sharks we're hoping to tag, and I can't help but picture him by my side, waiting with breathless anticipation to see a familiar shape in the shallows below.

But I blink away the desire, determined not to spoil today with fantasies that might not materialize.

Keith, one of the PhD candidates working on the study, has a hand on the outboard motor, piloting the boat through the glassy water. He's wearing a neck gaiter as defense against the sun burning off the last of the morning fog. "Anyone know a good sea shanty?"

"I've got a classic," Marty says. He's sitting in the bow, holding a tagging stick used for placing a tag from the boat. One of the senior scientists on the research team, Dr. Martin Norris has a reputation for being a great mentor, always accessible for questions or advice. "Maybe you know it. It goes like this." He clears his throat, then sings, "Here, fishy, fishy."

Everyone else onboard groans, though I chuckle.

"Too early for that." Gwen's voice is a raspy grumble, but she's grinning, tanned face coated with a chalky sheen of zinc. "You get used to their antics," she assures me. She's balancing a clipboard on her knees, gaze sharp as she scans the water.

"This your first trip out to study white sharks?" Marty asks when the laughter dies down. "I recognize the look. Awe and excitement."

"I still feel that way, and I've been doing this for twenty-five years," Gwen says. "It's a privilege to get to study these animals."

"It is," I say. "Being out on the water always reminds me of the first shark documentary I watched as a kid. They had all these close-up shots of sharks underwater. Cruising. Then they did a scene cut to a group of scientists on a boat, chatting and consulting a chart." I realize the chitchat on the boat has fallen silent, and I pause. I don't know what compelled me to share this memory, but when it becomes clear they're all waiting for me to continue, I find my voice.

"The camera panned away again, but I remember wanting to climb in that boat with them. To look over their shoulders and see what was on the paper. What sort of data? What were their research methods? Of course, I didn't have that sort of language yet, I was eight." There's a murmur of laughter, and my discomfort at being the center of attention eases.

"But I wanted to know every detail. To toss out the buoys and sort through the tackle boxes and find out the purpose for everything. And what about the sharks? What did they do when they went where the camera couldn't follow?"

I spent the summer flipping through books and sounding out the scientific names of all my favorite sharks, stumbling over the Latin words until I got it right. My mind goes instantly to the name on the bow of Adrian's boat, taking heart in the knowledge that he's held on, all this time.

"The more I learned, the more I realized what I had left to learn. And I don't know…" I shrug, shy again. "I just love how I could do this my whole life and still have more to explore."

Marty smiles at me. "And now you're the one in the boat."

"I am, yeah."

"Dang," Keith says. "Wish I would've had you as an undergrad. You make our job sound way cool." Mingled snorts of laughter and mock-indignation rise up from the group, but Keith shakes his head. "I'm serious. Students must love you."

I bark out a laugh louder than the sea lions lounging on the beach. "Not so much. I tend to accidentally bombard people with facts."

"Really? Because we watched you on *Shark Science Crew*," Gwen says, lifting her eyes from the green-blue water around us. "Seemed like a natural in explaining things."

"You watched us?"

They all nod. "Are you kidding me? Adrian and Marissa are legit," Keith says.

"You too," Gwen tells me, and I have to fight to keep my mouth from dropping open at a compliment from her. "I think you're selling yourself short. My mother, who's never once managed to sit through hearing about my research, shared one of your videos with me. Asked why I couldn't have explained things so clearly years ago."

My eyes go wide. "I'm…sorry?"

She smiles. "Don't be. I was thrilled to actually have a two-sided conversation with her about sharks for once." Her expression turns thoughtful. "Is outreach where your interests lie? Because there are some great programs I could recommend getting involved with."

My knee-jerk reaction is to say no, but Marissa mentioned something along the same lines a few weeks ago. I turned her down, certain without her extroversion, it wouldn't be a good fit. But maybe it's time to be open to new paths again.

The boat radio crackles and Brittney, the researcher on shore using the drone says, "We've got a shark about three meters off the bow. Starboard side."

The news has us all swiveling in our seats. No telltale dorsal cutting through the waves, but when I unbend my knees and half stand, I see it—a dark shape cruising just below the surface.

Gwen lets out a whoop and Marty hoists the tagging stick. "Hope, ready to take photos?"

This time my hands are steady. "Born ready."

She grins at me. "I know the feeling."

We come up alongside the shark, swimming in a sinuous motion, deep gray against blue. As we draw alongside, the animal angles away and Keith turns the boat to follow.

My pulse builds, heart thudding in a crescendo as I peer down into the water at the shark's streamlined body. I could do this every day and be happy. But every night, I wish I could go home to Adrian.

The room lights flicker to full brightness as Marissa's talk concludes, and she steps to the side of the podium to answer questions from the cluster of people who've gathered up front. I stay seated, searching the crowd making their way to the exits for the same person whose name I scanned the program for: Dr. Adrian Hollis-Parker.

I haven't heard from him since I left, and as the weeks went by, I stopped checking my phone every moment and settled into life here. The palm trees are taller than the palmettos I'd grown used to, the water colder. But there are sharks, and new friends, and today I drove to Los Angeles to hear Marissa speak at a conference. She didn't mention Adrian, and I didn't ask, scared to hear the answer.

Now I know how he must've felt when I asked for space. Zuri thought maybe he was trying to turn the tables out of spite, but that's not Adrian. He doesn't want to get back at me for how I hurt him, he wants to figure out how not to hurt me. But every day he stays away, he's doing just that.

At any rate, he's not here. Not listed in the program. Not appearing from backstage at the end of Marissa's presentation to profess his love with a podium mic. He didn't fly in to surprise me, and I'll have to accept that he might never come.

Unable to handle the claustrophobic confines of the auditorium any longer, I send Marissa a text.

Hope: I'll be out in the lobby.

Grabbing my purse, I slide past the few people remaining in my aisle, then head out the heavy double doors into the bright atrium. Pockets of people are gathered at tall tables, chatting in a network-y sort of way that reminds me I should make use of this time. But first I could use a drink in my hand to make me feel more at ease.

I glance around and spot a beverage station set up on a long table. Weaving my way through the knots of people, I reach the table and see a carafe of hot water. Perfect. I fill a cup and set it down while I sort through the selection of tea bags in search of something decaf. But when I turn back around, my cup isn't there.

"Who steals a cup of hot water?" I ask aloud, venting my frustration over missing Adrian, and certain no one will hear me above the din.

But a voice responds from over my shoulder, close enough

to tickle the hairs on the back of my neck. "Are you calling me a water bandit?"

I whirl around and there he is. In dark gray slacks and a pullover that does indecent things to his pecs. He's cradling my teacup in his big hands and while this isn't technically a café, nor have I just presented a groundbreaking paper, the situation is so close to my old fantasies of a chance meeting with him that I blurt out a frazzled version of my well-rehearsed speech. "The water's all yours."

He blinks. "Uh, I don't want it. That guy—" he lifts his chin toward a balding man walking away from the table "—was going to toss it, so I saved it for you." The water sloshes slightly; his hands are trembling. "I probably should've called first. But I wanted to talk to you in person. I know it's been a long time, and last time we talked, I was a mess." He bites his lip, and it takes everything in me not to close the distance between us. "What I'm trying to ask is—" he takes a deep breath, vulnerability tugging his brows inward "—can we talk?"

Words I've waited weeks to hear. "You came a long way for the answer to be no."

"The distance doesn't matter. The choice is yours."

As if I would refuse. "Okay." I pluck the cup from his hands, the warmth of his fingers seeping into my chilled skin. "But you'll have to get your own drink." I grin up at him, unable to resist teasing, though my heart is in my throat. "No running off with mine."

We're ensconced in a pair of plush chairs near an escalator, and fronds from the nearby plant keep tickling my arm with blasts from the vents, but I barely notice the irritation, because Adrian is here.

He waits for me to take a sip of tea, then says, "You were right."

I swallow carefully, uncertain how to respond. Does he mean I was right to leave three years ago?

"I wasn't just trying to protect you. I was also trying to protect myself." He leans forward, elbows on his knees. "Uncertainty scares me. Having things out of my control affect people I care about is an awful feeling. I didn't want you to be in harm's way because of me, but I also didn't want to give you a chance to hurt me. I wanted to know what our life together would look like every step of the way."

He glances out the floor-to-ceiling windows, the lines of his profile tight and full of apprehension, his beard not quite as neatly trimmed as when I left. But when he looks back at me, his gaze is soft. "If I couldn't see it all laid out, I didn't know how to believe in it. I was so caught up envisioning the many ways it could go wrong that I failed to see how right things already were between us."

"But I did, and you shut me out."

"Which is exactly why it took me so long to figure this out," he says. "I tried to work through things on my own, but that's not how relationships work. I should've been fully open with you, the way you were with me two months ago."

"Has it really only been that long?" It feels like a lifetime.

"I haven't counted exactly, but yes." He gives me a half smile. "So it's been bad for you too?"

I nod. "Not all bad. I mean, there are sharks—"

He laughs, mouth wide, head tipped back, so loudly that a few people nearby turn their heads, but I don't care. I join in, heart full of joy at the way this man makes me feel.

But there's feeling, and there's knowing, and I need to make sure we're on the same page. "What made you ready to trust me with this now?"

"I realized I wasn't sheltering you from risk, I was hiding. It scared me to be in that vulnerable place again with you, after what happened last time."

My hands go cold and clammy at his words, and I set the cup on the table next to me to avoid spilling it. "Adrian—"

"The risks still scare me," he says. "Sharing videos is a risk, no matter how careful I am. But I do it anyway because I believe we're making a difference." They are. I see it every day in the people who respond to the videos I haven't been able to stop watching, even though it's been painful.

"And if I'm honest, staying with you, when you have a hold on my heart I can't seem to break, that's a risk. Because losing you the first time shattered me. But the things I want take courage. You're worth risking my heart, Hope."

I take a moment to digest his words. None of this is easy, for either of us. But he broke the silence. He came all this way to try.

But he also had a right to hesitate, and I want to know if he's sure. "It's a big thing, to start over. And we're so different; I thrive with uncertainty, but you love a life that's mapped out. I don't want you to feel like you have to change in order to be with me. And I know I can't, or won't, and it's really the same thing."

"We don't have to change in order to be together," he says. "That's partly why I was so scared of committing to this again. I didn't want you to be with me at the expense of your dreams." He scoots to the edge of his seat, so close, I could touch him, but I don't. Waiting.

"But my career has taken a drastic turn, and I've seen the value in pivoting. There's a whole world of possibilities. We just have to be patient with each other. And creative. Because make no mistake, I do want to be with you." He never looks away, his gaze unwavering, voice steady and sure—about me. "Wherever you are. Whatever you're doing, I want us to be together."

Together. My heart latches onto the word and holds tight. "I want that too."

A smile streaks across his face like the sun's rays filtered through a cloud. "I know you need time to decide your next steps, and I want you to have the space you need, but I want you to know my heart is yours, and I'm ready to keep figuring this out, with you, for as long as you'll have me."

With that, he stands up and makes his way through the crowd until he's out of sight.

"He just walked away?" Zuri's incredulity has me picturing a trio of exclamation marks punctuating her words, and I smile in spite of my own bewilderment.

"Right?" My free arm is hooked around my knees as I gaze out over the Pacific surf, phone to my ear. "I was still trying to absorb everything he told me, and by the time I decided to follow, he'd left."

Unsure to what extent Marissa was involved in helping Adrian find me, I wound up texting what was probably an incoherent excuse and drove straight from the conference to the nearest beach.

I spent the next hour dodging beachgoers as I paced the shore, not caring when the hem of my only pair of dress pants got ruined with sand and salt. Too wound up to sit still, I stayed in motion. Walked until the sun was low over the horizon and the sunset reminded me of home. And then I called Zuri.

I told her his whole speech, what I remember of it. The details are fading fast; my senses were so heightened in the moment, and now all I remember is the essence of his words. The care in his eyes. The way his hands knit together when he spoke, the only giveaway of his nervousness. The way he told me he was certain of me.

"All that, and he didn't even give me a chance to answer."

"Sounds like he wanted to give you the same space you offered him," Zuri says. "He let you know how he feels, but maybe he thought you might need time to think things over with the pressure off."

"But all I felt was relief at hearing how much he wants a life with me. The worry I used to feel that falling in love might steal my dreams is gone, because I know it's the opposite with Adrian." I used to only be certain of one thing: I wanted to spend my life studying sharks.

Relationships matter—I don't know where I'd be without Zuri to clown around with and Marissa to debrief with. I love my parents and their support has been a constant in my life. But a romantic relationship never seemed worth the hassle. Before I met Adrian, I didn't see how a boyfriend would fit in my life. Didn't feel a lack that needed to be filled.

But things with him were always different. We were a match, and it wasn't about filling a gap, but about adding joy to my already full life.

Zuri's asking me something, but I miss it. "What did you say?"

"I said, then why are you talking to me and not him?"

Restless again, I get to my feet and walk closer to the foamy waves. The sand is damp from the tide's retreat, but I'm not bothered. I feel grounded near the water's edge, able to focus.

"Because the problem I keep coming back to is logistics. How do we mesh our lives?"

"Logistics?" She lets out a snort of disbelief. "You've been in love with this man for years, and he loves you back, and you're talking to me about logistics?"

My mouth twists at her humbling assessment. I can hear noise in the background. "What are you doing, anyway?"

"Laundry." I picture her sitting on the couch, a show on in the background, working her way through heaps of clean clothes. The same way we used to spend many evenings before I left, rehashing the day's events. "Don't try to change the subject."

She knows me too well. "I just worry we're going to keep having this same struggle. I'm never going to want my next steps set in stone." I curl my toes against the cool sand.

There's a moment of not-quite silence, where the only sound is the rustle of clothing being folded, then she says, "I think you're bound to disappoint one another. Go through struggles. Misunderstand one another. But you can choose to love one another through the difficulties. Apologize and forgive and work to do better, to understand one another better."

"So you're saying it will all work out in the end if we go on loving each other?" Sounds like something my heart would say, except this time my head is in full agreement.

"All you have to ask yourself is if it's worth figuring things out together, one step at a time. Is a life with Adrian better than living without him?"

Yes. Unequivocally yes. I lived without Adrian's love for three years and missed him every moment. I've missed him every moment of these weeks of silence. "If anything, I've always felt like my love for him was overwhelming."

"No such thing as too much love," she says simply.

Her words are permission to meet Adrian where he's at, and trust him to do the same for me.

My hand goes to my heart, aching. He's made mistakes. I have too. But he came looking for me this time. Not pushing, or forcing my hand. He came for me, and now he's giving me the space to come to him.

Sharks and Adrian. Adrian and sharks. Career and love. The solution is to try. The answer is keep on loving him.

No such thing as too much love. How I feel for Adrian, the enormity of it? That's not something to fear, but to revel in. To run toward, not away from. I don't want to turn my back on love. I want to face it head-on, like a sunrise.

thirty-seven

adrian

I got home late last night. Alone. Woke up early and aching from pushing myself through a hard workout. Holed myself up in my office on campus all morning, then spent the afternoon in the lab. Finished for the day, the need to keep busy, keep my mind off Hope and what she might be thinking propels me to the marina instead of home. I take a rare trip out to the bay on my own, returning at sunset.

At first, flying home right away seemed like the most caring thing to do. Show I don't have any expectations, that the next move is hers. But as the day fades with no word from her, I begin to question the wisdom of that choice.

Loath to go home to an empty house, I catch up on maintenance tasks until well past dark, when all the other boaters have left, and the shop has closed. I'm washing down the deck when I feel a tap on my shoulder. I spin and drop the hose immediately, drenching my shoes, but I barely notice because a streak of long limbs and curls and soft curves that I'd know anywhere cannonballs into my arms. *Hope.* Her arms are around my neck, fingertips pressing into my shoulders. I grip her tight, my face burrowed into her neck.

She smells like sunshine and aloe vera. She's warm and solid and *here*.

"I missed you," she says into my shoulder, the brush of her lips a touch I'll never take for granted again. She pulls away and meets my eyes. "I'm so tired of missing you."

Her words reverberate into my chest, the perfect summation of my own feelings, and there's only one thing left to say, something I can't hold back any longer, no matter what comes next. "I love you."

Her eyes crinkle, smile bright. "I was hoping you'd say that." Then her lips are on mine, sure and sweet, and I'm lost. Found again in the promises of her touch. My fingers swipe against the delicate curve of her jaw, thumb brushing her cheek, her body molded against mine.

A moment later, she pulls away with a soft laugh. "My shoes are soaked."

I glance down and see the hose gushing at our feet and hurry to shut it off. When I return, she's standing there, looking shy. My brain can't quite process that she's here, and I grab her hands to reassure myself.

She holds on tight to my fingers, face tipped up, eyes full of tenderness. "I didn't get a chance to tell you this yesterday, but I've missed you every single day since I left. Missed talking about my day with you. Missed hearing you grumble about your pet peeves and roll your eyes at my cheesy humor."

Chuckling, she says, "I thought love was sky writing and roses and all sorts of things I never saw the point of. But then I met you. And I realized love was inside jokes and listening to each other and dreaming together. Love doesn't have to be big and loud. It's quiet and steady and there when you need it. It's rare, maybe once-in-a-lifetime. And it's worth holding on to." She squeezes my hands. "*You're* worth holding on to, and I'm so glad we didn't give up."

She hasn't stepped closer, but I swear I can feel her heart beating in time with my own, and when she gazes up at me, her face is radiant, even in the darkness. "There's no going back to who I was before you, and I've stopped trying. Loving you makes my life better. *You* make my life better, and I believe in us."

Overcome, I wrap my arms around her. "There's no doubt in my mind that you're the person for me."

She pulls away, but it's just to pull me down into a kiss. Slow and hungry, we take our time, rediscovering each other. Her lips part and I slide my tongue against hers, relishing her soft moan. I reach down, thumbs tracing the curve of her shoulders. I want to take my time. I've got three years to make up for.

Her skin is warm but pebbled with goose bumps. At my touch, a shiver runs through her. "Cold?"

She hooks her fingers into my belt loops. "Hot."

The word shatters my restraint and I tip her chin up with my knuckle and claim her mouth. Her hand grips my waist, bunching my shirt. We're not holding back any longer, no doubts between us as our mouths slant against one another. Three years we missed. Three years of not touching her, holding her.

Her fingers clasp my shoulders, holding on like we're at sea and not moored in the marina. Dizziness blurs my vision, a sailor in no want of shore or shelter, content to drown in the swells of her curves. Hopeless. That's what I am. Lost for this woman.

Whatever time we have together, I'm determined to spend it showing this woman how much I love her. My Hope. My shelter from the storm.

thirty-eight

hope

Never ever did I expect to experience a kiss like this again. I wouldn't be surprised to look overboard and find the water steaming. Adrian's lips are fire, leaving a trail of smoky sweetness in their wake. When we leave, he'll have to swing me over his shoulder and carry me, because no way could I stand on my own two feet right now, and I'm not mad about it.

By unspoken agreement, we slowed our pace, living in this moment, unable to stop tasting one another, teasing one another, drawing out the sensation. There's an exquisite sweetness to kissing him. I revel in all the textures of us—the warmth of his hands, the firmness of his hands on my body, even as I tremble beneath his touch like ripples on a tide pool. Moving by touch, I feel fabric give way to skin as I trail my fingers along his waist, emboldened by the hiss as he sucks air between his teeth, eyes pinched tight, when my fingers lock in his belt loops to tug him close against me.

"Hope."

I kiss him, closemouthed, our lips soft.

"Hope—" he pulls the barest inch away, speaking against my lips "—you're killing me."

I'm loving him, is what I'm doing. For three years I held back, and these past weeks apart were torture. Placing a hand on his chest, I splay my fingers, feeling his heartbeat under my palm. My other hand rises to cup his shoulder, sliding down to the swell of his biceps.

"Your body has changed so much, but not here," I say, pressing a thumb to his full bottom lip.

He laughs, his beard brushing my knuckles, and goose bumps spread across my skin. I love the warmth of him. The immediacy of his presence.

"I love how you've stayed the same. Still so soft." He cradles my jaw and kisses me. "Gorgeous as ever." My eyes fall closed, but I can feel all his attention on me. Our kisses are languid, water droplets sliding down a glass bottle on a summer-hot porch.

Our kisses are flames in a fireplace, turning snow drops to steam on a winter evening. Our kisses gain speed, the rushing of a storm-swollen creek in spring, the breath-stealing bite of wind while cruising on the open water. My chest is tight with want and need and something deeper—love. A feeling I'm not scared to name. Not afraid to fight for.

My fingers slide up to his nape and into the twists of his hair, rooting him in place, guiding him, angling our kiss deeper. His tongue is a hot sweep against mine, his hands are on my waist now, holding me tight.

The hum of a motor churns in the darkness, and we pull apart, shielding our eyes from the bright lights entering the marina.

I scrape an unsteady hand over my head, reaching for my hair tie, but my wrist is bare.

"Use mine," Adrian says, handing it to me.

Once I've pulled my curls into a bun, he holds my hand as we climb off the boat, mosquito bites that I hadn't noticed before pricking my legs. I pause to bend down and itch them, and he waits, never letting go of my other hand.

"I talked to my sister."

"Okay." I drag out the word, because after all the revelations of the last few days, this doesn't feel exactly noteworthy. "How is she?"

He wrinkles his nose. "I didn't ask. But good, I assume."

I would comment on this, but she probably didn't ask how he was, either. Pleasantries are inconsequential in the Hollis-Parker household. "What did you talk about?"

"About whether I'll be failing if I decided not to seek tenure. If it would be viable to pursue the channel long-term and work as an adjunct professor." He looks over at me as we walk slowly between the moored boats, their shapes indistinct beyond the darkness of the dock lights. "Basically, I wanted her to sign off on it. Tell me I could open myself up to change, and things wouldn't end badly."

"What did she say?"

"That I always do my homework, and this is no different." He laughs quietly. "She told me to trust my own judgment. That it hasn't steered me wrong yet."

"That must've been good to hear."

"Sort of. It was also intimidating, because now whatever next step I take, I have to own it. I want to stop thinking small, playing it safe because I'm scared to fail. I don't know yet what the changes will look like, but I'm open to whatever comes my way. I've changed my outlook because of you."

"Adrian, I would never want you to change for me."

"I didn't. My perspective did." He bites his lip, clearly searching for the right words. "Your ability to go after what you're passionate about without second-guessing it led me to see it's okay to explore. You've made a huge positive difference in my life, and I'm better for having loved you."

"So you wouldn't go back and change things?"

"I would go back and tell you every day that you're the most phenomenal woman I've ever met. I'd tell you I'd love you to the ends of the earth and be here for you however you need. I'd come to visit you in Michigan, and have you show me around the lab where you worked. I'd tell you how scared I was that you weren't coming back, but that I was determined not to let the fear get in the way of me loving you. But even if I had to endure the loss again, I'd never choose to go back in time and not fall in love with you."

The edges of my vision blur, like saltwater has slipped inside my goggles during a dive. "I love you, Adrian."

"What are the tears for?" he asks, brushing his thumb against the corner of my eye.

"I can't believe I ever tried to live without you. I don't ever want to have to again."

"You won't." He tugs me into his arms. "I intend to be inventing new pet peeves to make you roll your eyes long past when you've stopped thinking it's cute."

I pull away and meet his eyes. "Who said I think it's cute?"

"This did." He dips his thumb into the smile-crease by the edge of my mouth. "And this." He drags his fingertip along my lower lip to the other corner of my lips. "And here." He retraces the path with his thumb and my mouth parts in response to the delicate pressure. I rise on my toes, our kiss another promise.

thirty-nine

adrian

So much has changed in the past few months. Hope and I spoke only three hours ago, not three years, and we've only been apart for three weeks this time. She joined me on my previous trip to film in Hawaii, but this time it's all conferences, and between working with us, researching prospective colleges, and being mentored by Marissa as they work on fundraising for the student outreach program we're hoping to launch next summer, she's been busy.

After finishing the internship, she decided to come back to South Carolina and continue on with *Shark Science Crew* for the time being, narrowing down her area of focus before applying to a doctoral program. She also rejoined social media, and with Gabe's guidance, gained an audience eager for the shark facts she loves to share. With the followers came the trolls, but she has a total lack of interest in haters' hot takes. People appreciate the quirky, no-nonsense way she delivers facts and her single-minded passion for the career she could never leave behind.

I'm still at the university, but with the success of our channel came greater career flexibility, and I've worked to expand my connections so that wherever Hope settles on for her next step, I can join her.

Unlike her fans, I get my daily dose of Hope through a stream of texts and coffee-line calls and late-night hotel chats when I'm traveling, but nothing beats seeing her in person, and I've got big plans for our reunion tonight. She thinks I'm arriving right before an after-hours donor event at an aquarium we partnered with. During our chat earlier, I kept the secret of how I'd reached out to the aquarium director, who remembers Hope from her time here, to get access to the place before the event starts. I had to keep muting my phone so she wouldn't hear the gate check announcements and ended the call quickly with promises to be there before the first speech.

I've never done a grand gesture, so I checked in with friends and family to see what they thought of my plan. When I got their approval in the form of a high five from Gabe, a why-not shrug from my cousin, and a thumbs-up text from my sister, I felt confident to proceed.

Gabe wanted to hide and take photos to commemorate the moment, paparazzi-style, but I told him in no uncertain terms that this is not a proposal. Besides, he's flying in late from a work trip of his own, giving a presentation about the responsible and effective use of social media in marine conservation, though he took time to arrange a livestream for donors who couldn't make the in-person event.

Instead of the board shorts she's used to seeing me in, I bought a deep blue suit for tonight, and the stiff material on my shoulders isn't helping my nerves, but this is a special moment for us, and worth getting dressed up for. Then Hope arrives, and breathing comes easy, though my fingers twist tight, clasped in front of me.

She walks through the aquarium doors with my cousin, laughing at something Marissa said. She's wearing a shimmering halter sheath dress in ombre shades of purple, green, and blue, like the iridescent sheen of mermaid scales. Her curls are loose, floating to her shoulders, one side pulled back with a glittering clip. Another step and the slit of her dress reveals she's wearing sneakers. The sight pulls a chuckle out of me, even as my chest goes tight.

Marissa points down the hallway leading the other direction, like she's making an excuse to step away. Hope glances around, and our eyes connect, her face splitting into the biggest grin. Then she's running toward me, dress bunched in her fists, and she launches herself into my arms. I spin her around and she says, "You're full of surprises, Dr. Hollis-Parker."

"Good surprises?"

She kisses me, soft and sweet. "The best," she says, and slides down until her feet touch the floor, looking me up and down with twinkling eyes. "You look amazing as always."

I make a show of flapping the edges of my jacket. "For real? I could've skipped this whole ensemble?"

"I never said that." She takes my hands, swinging them between us. "I thought you'd be late."

"If you'd rather, I could go home and get comfy. Keep on this jacket and change into sweatpants. Log in from my laptop—"

She cuts me off with another kiss. It feels so good to be able to show her how much I care without holding back, without worrying what tomorrow will bring. Whatever happens, I know we'll weather it together.

I pull away and take another long look at her, drinking in the swells and dips of her curves. "This isn't the dress you sent me a picture of." She'd texted me a picture of herself in a fitting room wearing a cotton, shark-patterned dress that flared out at the waist. The one she's wearing tonight hugs her curves from neck to calves.

"Marissa talked me out of that one. And Zuri." She wrinkles her nose in mock affront. "But don't worry, I found a workaround." She pulls aside the skirt of her dress to reveal her sneakers. Up close, I can see they're covered in tiny blue sharks. "And here." She turns her head to reveal a sparkling hammerhead clip. "Also, never fear. I kept the other dress for future occasions. Marissa won't always be around to keep me in check."

I let out a laugh that echoes through the empty space. I used to meet Hope here on weekends we spent together—her in cargo shorts and a T-shirt, with musty boots I always insisted she toss in the trunk first thing. It feels weird to be in this space all dressed up and grown up, to have come so far and made it back to each other.

"This dress might be more gala-appropriate than the shark dress, but it doesn't hold a candle to your outfit." She smooths her hands down my lapels. "It's ridiculous how sexy you look, Hollis-Parker. Did you come straight from a casting for Bond?"

Can't lie, her admiration fills me up. "I'd gladly be a consultant for the franchise. Debunk some silver screen myths."

"Ooh, yes. Changing the public perception of sharks. First step social media, next up, Hollywood."

With a chuckle, I take her hand. "Want to go shopping?"

A crease appears between her brows, but she lets me lead her toward the aquarium gift shop. My heart is thudding in my chest. At least if this gesture falls flat, there will be no one around to witness it. Hope doesn't like the limelight and wouldn't appreciate me professing my love in front of a crowd, but she deserves to know just how much I treasure her.

The glass doors of the gift shop are propped open, stars projected in a slow kaleidoscope of motion on the ceiling in the dim blue light. A popcorn machine is sitting right inside the door, the scent of hot butter and fresh salt making my stomach rumble, loud in the stillness, and Hope laughs softly.

She hasn't said anything, and I don't dare look at her, not yet. I open the Plexiglas door and scoop popcorn into a bag, handing it to her, and when I do, I see her eyes are shining with happiness.

"No food or drink allowed in the gift shop," she says, pointing to the large sign by the register. "Breaking the rules for me, Adrian?"

"You're worth it." Placing my hand on her waist, I lean in and gently kiss her. Beneath the rough sequins of her dress is the soft, familiar swell of her hip, and I close my eyes, memorizing the feel of her. When I pull away, I add, "Plus the aquarium director said you clocked in early every shift, so she trusted you."

A laugh bubbles out of Hope, fizzy as a soda can cracked open in July and at the sound, my nerves evaporate, leaving me with an effervescent happiness.

"You have some time to shop before they come looking for us." I hand her a basket from the stack just inside the door, then steer her deeper into the store with a hand at the small of her back.

She looks over her shoulder. "I can choose anything?"

"Anything." But her gift should be hard to miss.

She wanders around a few displays, with me a step behind, waiting for her to see it. She stoops down to look at a T-shirt on a low shelf, and the box in the shopping basket slides to the front with a quiet jingle.

Her eyes dart to the basket, and she claps a hand over her mouth. She lifts out the rectangular box and stands up. "Adrian, what is this?"

"Yours," I say simply.

With trembling hands, she pops the lid and lifts out a silver charm bracelet. I'm not sure if they're trendy or not, but I'm hoping she appreciates the nostalgia. Each charm has significance. A great white shark—her favorite. A manta ray—so she'll never have to worry about leaving her necklace behind. A circular pendant of Michigan, surrounded with all five Great Lakes engraved in blue—I made sure of that. And a heart.

Gently, I reach around and flip the heart over, laying it in her palm so she can read the inscription, my mouth forming the words as she reads them aloud. "What's mine is yours."

"And it's a heart so…" I rub my hand against my jaw, suddenly worried this is too cheesy, but when she looks up, her eyes are glistening, smile bright. "What I'm trying to say is that my heart is yours."

"This is too much," she says, bracelet cradled in her palm.

With a glance at her face to see if it's okay, I wrap it around her wrist and fasten the clasp, relieved my hands are no longer trembling. Her skin is warm, pulse rapid under my fingertips, and I squeeze her palm. "It's just a shopping trip."

She shakes her head. "It's not. It's our first date. But better."

"You remembered." I wasn't sure she would, though I did my best to re-create it. We drove up the coast to the boardwalk on Myrtle Beach and did all the touristy things—stopped in at least a dozen souvenir stops, gorged ourselves on fresh seafood, got our hands sticky with cotton candy and shared a giant lemonade to slake our thirst after a bag of popcorn neither of us was hungry enough to finish.

Pressing a kiss to my lips, she pulls back and says, "I never want to forget."

We'd ended the night by catching the end of a concert out in the street. Right on cue, a song starts piping through the speakers. There's a rustle by the door and I turn to see Marissa crouched by the Bluetooth speaker I'd set up, Iris hovering over her. "Nothing to see here. Just mobile tech support," my sister says.

Marissa pushes a button and the volume increases, flooding the room with Nat King Cole's melodious voice. "See y'all at dinner." She grins and they both slink away, my cousin nearly as tall as Iris for once, thanks to the platform sandals she's wearing.

I turn to see Hope's tears are gone but her smile is wider than ever. "You went all out."

"No ma'am," I say, tugging her close. "I'm all in. I know this is a lot."

"Perfect. It's perfect." She tilts her head to look up at me, the soft scent of vanilla on her skin, eyes glistening in the low light. "Amazing. Wonderful." She squeezes my hands. "I love you."

I believe in finding that perfect person, because I have, in Hope. But staying together? Building a future? That takes work. That takes commitment. That takes the persistent, joyous belief that my life is better with her in it. And that's something I'll work to show her every moment of our lives together. For now, I lean down and kiss Hope Evans, my forever. The sunset to my sunrise.

forty

hope

I never thought I could be this happy in sequins and makeup, but sitting in a room surrounded by people eager to fund opportunities to give aspiring young marine biologists a real-world introduction to shark research is hard to beat. Oh, and there's the fact that my favorite scientist, who also happens to be the sexiest man in the room—or any room for that matter—is sitting next to me, sharing the experience, our fingers intertwined on the table.

He looks sickeningly good in his blue suit, his skin radiant, the dip between his collarbones exposed by the open top button of the crisp white shirt underneath. The flickering glow from candles in the centerpiece plays across his face—a face I've seen more often in 2D than real life lately—and I lean into the solid warmth of his shoulder, just for a moment, to remind myself he's here with me, and to hold fast this moment in my memory for the times when he's not.

When I pull away, he glances over at me and nudges his knee against mine. "I missed you." The fresh scent of cedar reaches me as he shifts closer and murmurs, "Think we can skip out early?"

I shush him with a finger to my lips, careful not to smudge the red lipstick Zuri helped me reapply in the bathroom a few minutes ago. Her presence here tonight was another surprise from Adrian. Having my best friend, my rock for the years we've spent together and apart, here to celebrate with me tonight means the world.

She's watching us, intent and serious, but when I make eye contact, she gives me a subtle thumbs-up. Apparently, she put Adrian through the wringer when he called to book her tickets, and he aced the test.

She's bought a new pair of glasses since I last saw her—clear frames that accentuate her broad cheekbones and straight brows—and looks effortlessly gorgeous in a burgundy jumpsuit. I can't remember the last time she had a night out, but you'd never know from her relaxed poise that she's a mom of three running on caffeine and toast crumbs. I plan to stuff her full of Southern cooking before she leaves, and I'm sure Adrian will try to talk her into siding with him on the sweet tea debate.

Marissa and Gabe are on the other side of the table, heads tipped together, arguing over whether the acoustics are doing the slideshow justice. Their whispers are animated enough to draw the attention of the people near us, but they're oblivious or more likely, unconcerned. On Adrian's other side, Iris is posing for a selfie with her turquoise clutch, her hair twisted into sleek Bantu knots. Marissa wrangled her into our shopping trip and she surprised us both by forgoing her usual chic pants ensembles and choosing an off-the-shoulder gown.

She shows the picture to Adrian. "I'll tag you in it," she says with no irony, and it's pretty sweet. I noticed she's recently started commenting on his posts, long-winded questions which he always answers as thoroughly as if she were an inquisitive stranger. Or maybe like a younger brother with something to prove. I smile a little at the thought.

The uplighting along the walls casts a soft focus over everything, like we're underwater, and I have the sweetest feeling of relief. Of finding my place. Of a bright future, even if the next steps are hazy. The bracelet Adrian gifted me glitters with memories, and there's plenty of room for more. I twist the chain, admiring each charm, and holding on to the last one like a promise. *My heart is yours.*

Iris gestures for us to scoot closer. Snaps a picture of Adrian pressing a kiss to my cheek. Then they're announcing me— I'm supposed to give a speech about how my entire journey led me here. A few of Gabe's photographer friends are here to document the evening, but I'm not worried to speak in front of this crowd, because if I stumble, all I need to do is keep going.

There's no limit to what I can do or discover. I want a future with this man by my side, the man I never stopped loving. Our lives and hearts are forever intertwined. Adrian is my person. Maybe not everyone has one, but I do. And my heart is his.

epilogue

hope

Adrian holds his phone up, his other arm around my waist. "Say 'olives are a fruit'!"

"Ew." I laugh, and he clicks the photo button. "Where do you come up with these things?"

"Facts." He turns and enfolds me in his arms. "I think the word you're looking for is facts."

"Trivia," I counter, rising on tiptoes to kiss him. Gulls swoop overhead, and a pelican has been paddling around the boat, receiving glares from Adrian all morning, but other than that, we're alone in the muted light of dawn.

We're gearing up for our third round of "Spend a Day with Shark Scientists" and we always document the entire day to share later. I've come to love the visual memory, the record of how far we've come and how far we've yet to go. Toward each other, and on this journey. Okay, so maybe the voiceovers and sappy music are what make it all feel so weighty, but regardless, the camera is no longer my enemy.

A couple hours later, the teens start arriving, some dropped off with a quick wave, others unable to detach themselves from anxious parents. Local baked goods are a staple at these events, and the orange cinnamon rolls are always the first to go, followed closely by peach-ginger muffins, which is why I stowed a few on the boat earlier. Perks of being in charge of the operation.

One mother breaks free of the group near the refreshment table and makes a beeline for me. My hackles rise. Historically, this won't end well. I square my shoulders, ready to brave the encounter and do my best to not ignite a slew of retaliatory comments on social media.

"Are you Ms. Evans?"

With no escape route evident, I nod.

"You're the shark woman my daughter won't stop talking about."

Biting back a remark about feeling like a fish-human hybrid, I crane my neck, looking for evidence of said offspring, who might be more tactful, though unlikely.

The woman turns and points. "She's there, in the high-tops." She points out a teenager, laughing with a group of girls. "She somehow got three of her friends to sign up, too, though I don't know how they convinced their stick-in-the-mud parents." She swings her gaze back toward me. "Thank you for this."

"Uh, you're welcome," I stammer, realizing that this isn't the tirade I was expecting.

"My daughter's always loved animals, but since she discovered your channel, it's sharks all day. She elected to take high level math courses this year. Enrolled in a biology course at our community college. She's a force. For so long I felt like all she needed was direction." Her eyes are shining now. "What you're doing is about more than just the sharks. I hope you know you're in the right place."

She must notice that I'm having trouble finding the words to thank her, because she keeps right on talking.

"Have you ever thought of doing something like this for

adults? My daughter's made me a convert." She looks down. "Not that it would go anywhere for me but…"

"Are you kidding?" I finally find my voice. "That's an amazing idea. Space camp but for adults."

"With sharks instead of stars."

With a chuckle, I say, "Key difference." Emotion tightens my throat, unexpectedly. "It's definitely something I'd need to bring up with the team. It might not be feasible, but I love that you raised the question. If we ever start up a project like that or find out about another program nearby, you'll be the first to know."

"You bet I will. My daughter signed me up for your emails." She shakes her head at the audacity, but she's smiling. "Take care, and I'll see you at five p.m. sharp," she says, leveling a maternal look that so resembles Zuri I have to bite my tongue not to smile. She walks off and I inhale deeply through my nose, catching the scent of seaweed and gasoline from the nearby pumps. A shadow falls across me and I open my eyes. Adrian.

He leans down to ask, "Are you crying?"

I shake my head. "I'm…" I huff out a laugh and dab a knuckle at my eye, turning away from the inquisitive teens. "Yeah, maybe I'm crying. That woman…" I trail off. "She told me I was in the right place. Even though I already knew that, it was really nice to hear."

"Why are you surprised? You're doing amazing things here, Hope."

"We're doing amazing things, together."

He steps closer, like he's getting ideas, and I narrow my eyes. "I love you, but you do realize the parents are watching."

"Platonic and professional, at least until we get home," he says, and puts his hands in his pockets. "But you know that I couldn't do this without you, right? I absolutely could not handle a boat full of kids without your help."

"They're pretty cool, once you get used to them."

"I think you mean, once they get used to *you*."

I shoulder-bump him.

"Just saying," he says, a twinkle in his gorgeous dark eyes, "it helps our cause that you're way more intimidating than any shark we'll encounter."

"All part of my plan." I tap my temple, then turn to the crowd and cup my hands around my mouth. "Okay, young scientists, circle up. Guardians, you're free to disperse. My co-captain and I will have these youngsters back at the dock by five o'clock. If you need to get in touch, call our office and they'll radio the boat."

"I thought you were *my* co-captain," Adrian grumbles loudly enough for the kids to catch.

"My name's on the boat, so I think that's pretty conclusive," I say, and several of the teens chuckle, but some are scowling. Those are Adrian's people. The ones here for the science and not the corny jokes. And the ones craning for a look at all the equipment lined up, with hands already half-raised to ask a question? That's me as a kid. Thinking life was all or nothing, wanting to skip the nonessentials to get to the good stuff. Little did I know, that *was* the good stuff.

Life is about taking it all in. Making space for the people I love. Changing the world by chasing what I'm passionate about. Am I lucky my soulmate loves sharks? Of course. But we've worked hard every day to build this life. Learned to lean into each other when the storm comes and keep right on loving one another when it passes.

★ ★ ★ ★ ★

acknowledgments

This is the cool moment where I get to reflect on all the incredible people who've had a role in making this book a reality. Deepest thanks to my phenomenal agent, Rachel Brooks, who was unwaveringly enthusiastic in her support of this story. When I told her I wanted to write a romance about two shark researchers, she was onboard from the start (pun fully intended) and encouraged me throughout the whole process of finding the perfect home for Hope and Adrian.

To my editor, Errin Toma—thank you for believing in this story! The book benefited immeasurably from your thoughtful input and commitment to getting to the heart of the characters' journey. I am incredibly grateful to the entire team at Canary Street Press for all their hard work on behalf of this book.

I have been fascinated by sharks my entire life, and writing this novel has been one of those unbelievable full-circle moments. Although *Second Tide's the Charm* is fiction, and the research depicted in it is fictionalized as well, it was important to me to bring as much authenticity to the marine biology element of the book as possible. Besides being the perfect excuse to watch more shark documentaries, I read tons of books (thank you, interlibrary loans), articles, and blogs on the topic, but there is nothing like insight from a professional in the field. Huge thanks to real-life marine biologist Lily Rios-Brady, who gave generously of her time and expertise, answering my questions about sharks and field study. Any mistakes in representing shark research are entirely my own.

To my critique partners, my writing group, and all the friends who have read my pages and given feedback, thank you! Huge thanks also to the booksellers, librarians, and bloggers who continue to connect readers with my novels.

Thank you, always, to my husband, for your encouragement, for your love, and for never failing to help me puzzle out even the most tangled plot questions.

Readers—some people say not to write for anyone else, but I write for you. I write to bring you joy. I write to make you laugh and lift your spirits. I write to create a world where you get swept away. Thank you for choosing this book.